Heirs to an Empire

PATRICK
The hard-drinking patriarch, he fought his way to the top—and left a trail of scandal and destruction in his wake.

MARY MARGARET
Devoted wife, manipulative mother, she will go to any lengths to preserve her place in society . . . and to protect her family's good name.

CAITLIN
The loyal "good daughter," she has sacrificed her life to the family's interests—and must hide her love for another woman's man.

SHEILAGH
Bad, beautiful and love-starved, she ran away from repression and heartache . . . and a shocking secret too painful to share.

MICHAEL
His hatred of his father drove him to a passionless marriage and far from the family enterprise—but crisis and shattering revelations call him back into the fold.

CATHERINE LANIGAN

The Way Of The Wicked

AVON BOOKS ◆ NEW YORK

THE WAY OF THE WICKED is an original publication of Avon Books. This work has never before appeared in book form. This work is a novel. Any similarity to actual persons or events is purely coincidental.

AVON BOOKS
A division of
The Hearst Corporation
1350 Avenue of the Americas
New York, New York 10019

First Avon Books Printing: February 1993

This book is dedicated to my father,
attorney Frank J. Lanigan,
who died on Valentine's Day 1992.

I love you, too, Daddy.

Acknowledgments

Though I grew up in an Irish Catholic family near Chicago, the Killians' story bears little resemblance to my own experiences. In fact, it is only with the love, support, and encouragement of my mother, my brothers, and my sister that I was able to delve as deeply into the darker side of the Killians' psyches without reproach. Therefore, it is to my family that I am most grateful.

Much gratitude to my mother, Dorothy Lanigan, my right-arm researcher, who not only combed the Illinois historical societies and libraries for interesting anecdotes about Chicagoland, but who also answered each of my desperate phone calls when I needed tiny, yet fascinating details about the Depression and war years.

Many thanks to my sister, Nancy Lanigan Porter, owner of Celebrations to Go, who took me to my first, but not last, fancy food and confection convention. Her connections and suppliers in the gourmet chocolate world proved invaluable in my research. I also learned that $37.50 a pound is *not* too much to pay for these little bites of heaven.

Appreciation to my brother, Dr. Ed Lanigan, who not only helped me with the medical aspects of this book, but whose good humor has always helped boost me up when I was down.

A very special thanks to my brother, Bob Lanigan, of Lake Forest, Illinois, who not only arranged for me to see 95 percent of Chicago in less than two days, but who graciously leased his wife, Deborah, also of Irish Catholic descent, to me as my guide through Oak Park, the Irish South Side, Irish North Side, Wilmette, and the Irish West Side.

In particular I would like to thank Deborah Hayes Lanigan's father, Bill Hayes, for his valuable input on the history of Chicago during the thirties and forties.

In addition, I was aided by many friends, both in Chicago and Houston, who gave their love, support, and concern during a very difficult personal year for me.

Scott and Debbie Arthur; John and Gaye Boren; Vicki Bushman; Cherry and David Hickson; Kathryn Kimmons; Connie Kirkham; Craig Longhurst; my uncle, Dick Manning; Judith McNaught; Janet Murphy; Stacy Okrei; Geneva Pampuro; my son, Ryan Pieszchala; David Saperstein; Molly Smyth; Christy Walker; Dr. Ed Zabrek.

To my agent, Mitch Douglas, who believed in me even during the times when I found it nearly impossible to keep the faith.

In addition, I am most grateful to my editor, Ellen Edwards, who not only loved this book from its inception as much as I did, but whose diligent hard work made my vision a reality.

God bless you all.

Special Appreciation

To my ICD representatives Paul Kilber in Chicago and Renee Oldham in Tyler, Texas.

To my Avon Books representatives Ken Trout in Texas and Ron Wilson in Maryland.

To Christine Dunham in Houston, Texas, who has accompanied me to countless book signings over the years and who has always been one of my strongest cheerleaders.

To Denis Farina at Avon Books in New York: a big hug.

To Denise Little at B. Dalton, Jim Duffy at Waldenbooks and Cathy Kadek at Levy Home Entertainment and Maryann Rosalia of Sher Distribution Company, much appreciation.

A special hug to my friend, Nancy Reiner, of Waldenbooks, Houston, Texas.

To Doug Mote, Karen Tank and Kathy Akins of East Texas Distributors in Houston who have always been my biggest boosters.

To Dorothy Jones of Randall's Food Stores in Houston, my staunchest ally.

To Majerek's Hallmark and Reader's World in La Porte, Indiana.

To all my book buyers in Texas: Bender's Square Books, The Book Scene, Musabelles and all the rest, thank you.

You are the ones who help to keep the stars in my eyes. God bless you all.

Prologue ───────────────

Like a spun sugar jewel, the new McCormick Place reflected the early June sun off its Mies van der Rhoe–inspired architecture. The new construction replaced the old McCormick Place, which had been destroyed by fire, and had been opened now for only a year. Its two buildings, separated by a great plaza, had attracted more conventioners than ever before.

Everyone in the industry had been eagerly awaiting the Midwest Fancy Food and Confection Convention. They arrived by car from Duluth and Milwaukee; by plane from Louisville and Indianapolis; and by yachts from other lake shore towns. Some wealthy and noted Chicago confectioners attended the convention for its promotional and marketing advantages; others came to do the real business of settling contracts, ordering supplies, and making sales.

The yachts were anchored in the adjoining Burnham Park Yacht Harbor, and it was here on the first day of the convention that the sound of champagne corks popping was as loud as the chatter and buzzing of human voices.

The Killian yacht, appropriately christened *Emerald,* after the name of the family-owned chocolate company, bobbed up and down in the choppy Lake Michigan waters. Only family members, several trusted employees, and, of course, the much-favored press were invited to the opening-day brunch.

Moet de Chandon splashed over the edges of Waterford crystal flutes. Patrick Killian, president of the company and head of the family, raised his glass in a toast.

"To Emerald! Long may she continue her reign!"

"Hear! Hear!" The cheer bounced across the deck and drew many smiles from those present, but they were thin smiles, a bit forced.

It should have been a happy day for the Killians, but an undercurrent of tension strained the party. The journalists were too busy sampling the free food and champagne to pay attention to the stiffness in matron Mary Margaret Killian's expression, the nervous twitch in her son-in-law Clay Burke's left eye, or the impatient clucking tongue of their secretary, Martha O'Boland.

But Caitlin Killian Burke, Patrick's daughter, noticed it all. Something was not right about this afternoon. Initially she had passed it off as opening-day jitters. It wasn't until later that she knew her instincts were trying to warn her of impending danger.

All the Killians were good at keeping secrets, Caitlin thought. And as she watched her father hold sway over the crowd, she realized that he was their best-kept secret of all.

Patrick was full of himself that day, acting as if he'd invented the new concoctions that were certain to impress the judges. Truth be known, Patrick knew little about chocolate making. It could not even honestly be said that he was a good businessman. What he was, was a hell of a salesman, and he had a knack for selecting wise council.

The secret of Patrick's success was his family. It had taken a family effort to put the sales of the Emerald Chocolate Company ahead of all other gourmet chocolates, both foreign and domestic, and now Emerald was second only to Hershey in domestic sales of the almond chocolate candy bar.

Caitlin, Clay, Mary Margaret, and even Martha O'Boland provided the corporate vision Patrick so desperately lacked. In the old days, he'd been a good salesman, helping his father get the company started, but that's where his talent ended. He needed his family.

Patrick had spent decades convincing the family that *he* was the brains. *He* was the power. And stupidly, Caitlin thought, we all gave him that power.

She saw the sun glint off her father's silvery white hair. She couldn't help admiring him for having pulled off his charade for more than fifty years now. There had to be merit in that, she thought.

Patrick spread his arms out over the crowd. The glaring sun reflecting off the lake caused him to squint as he spoke. "Drink up, everybody. It's time for us to go inside. Clay? Caitlin? You two have first shift at the booth?"

They nodded agreement.

"And everything is prepared for the truffle judging?"

They nodded again.

"All right then. On to another Emerald victory," Patrick announced with a bob of his head to each of them.

Everyone followed Patrick off the boat, down the ramp, and across the plaza to the convention hall. The crowd blended into another group of people who anxiously pushed the Killians into the building. Caitlin was about to reprimand the tall man behind her when she heard him say: "Hurry up! Don't you know there's chocolate just waiting for me inside?"

Caitlin couldn't help but laugh to herself. It made her feel good to know that other people felt precisely as she did about the sweet bites of paradise she invented at Emerald Chocolates.

The Killian party went straight to their booth, which was decorated in gold and green, the colors of Emerald Chocolates, and had been set up for the judging.

Patrick picked up a truffle and held it to the light as if it were a precious jewel. His eyes were possessive as they inspected the gloss of the chocolate, the tiny edges of the delicately made chocolate leaves and flowers that decorated the top. Gently he arranged the marrons glacés on the gold doily. He might not have known how to stir the couverture so that it didn't scorch or separate, or the process of adding heated cream to the couverture that transformed the chocolate into ganache, or how to grind hazelnuts into a fine paste and then blend them with the ganache, but he did respect a winning product when he saw one. The glint in his eye told Caitlin that her father believed he had a winner in this rosette-shaped white chocolate truffle.

"Caitlin!" Patrick called.

"Yes?" Caitlin went to him.

"These look wonderful. Do you think we can top the story *Time* magazine did on me three years ago? And where is that idiot from *Chicago* magazine? You told me he would be here, damn it!"

Caitlin laid her hand on his huge forearm. "Don't worry. I saw him at another booth when we came in."

"Oh, shit. Not Mars? Or that upstart from Joliet . . ."

"No, Father. Just calm down. You'll get plenty of press today."

"Sure," he grumbled.

"You always do." Caitlin smiled. She looked up. Two men in black suits wearing the official judges' ribbons were coming toward her. A bevy of photographers and the food editors of nearly every midwestern newspaper followed them.

The older of the two judges was a pleasant-looking man with European-cut clothes who spoke with a British accent. He had a weak chin and heavy jowls. The second man had smaller features with strong cheekbones, ruddy complexion, and almond-shaped, discerning brown eyes.

Caitlin remembered reading in the convention brochure that he was Monsieur Boileau, from Paris originally and now based in New York. He was one of the top chocolatiers in the country.

She nervously clenched her teeth. This year's winner would have to be more than a cut above, she thought, since Monsieur Boileau demanded perfection.

Caitlin chewed a fingernail as her eyes skimmed the truffles and marrons glacés on the antique silver trays, gold mesh under the truffles that were filled with Courvoisier and cream, and snowy Irish linen squares beneath the mocha almond truffles. Were the details exact enough? Too spare? Too romantic? Maybe they should have used more contemporary colors. Her stomach lurched. She wished she were anyplace but here.

The British judge chose the white chocolate truffle first, which was a surprise to Caitlin.

She watched him. He was a nibbling judge, which she didn't like. How could a person tell if the chocolate burst in the mouth as it should with such a little taste? She watched as he pecked away at the chocolate, looking up at the ceiling, then back at the truffle. She chewed her fingernail again. Lord! She was getting anxious.

She looked to Monsieur Boileau, who bit solidly into the dark-covered chocolate. Instantaneously the man's legs buckled and he dropped to the floor. He grasped his throat as if he were trying to pull out his own windpipe.

Caitlin gasped and screamed, then raced toward the judge. The crowd in the booth surged forward to surround the stricken man.

His eyes bulged. He began writhing on the floor. His legs flopped and smacked the carpet. People cried out and called for help, as others ordered the crowd to push back to give the man room to breathe.

"Somebody call an ambulance! Somebody call the police!" Patrick yelled.

A woman in a pink Villager outfit headed for a security guard, who flipped on his walkie-talkie and summoned the medic.

As Caitlin watched Monsieur Boileau twitch twice more and then lie still, she realized he must have been poisoned. But with what? And why?

Her attention turned back to the British judge. He had only nibbled at the chocolate. Was the poison in all the candies, or just one?

The man's face was filled with panic and he looked as if he was in shock as he stared at his fellow judge. His eyes went to the chocolate in his hand. He clutched his throat and started gasping.

Caitlin wanted to stop his pain, but she didn't know how or why this horror was happening. Who would want to kill these judges? And why had the murderer chosen Emerald Chocolates as the murder weapon? No, this couldn't be happening. It made no sense. No sense at all.

The emergency medical crew shouldered its way through the crowd, followed by more journalists and photographers. Caitlin had never seen so many cameras. The flashlights going off began to blind her.

Patrick grabbed her arm and pulled her away from the crowd. "Come on," he urged. "Let's get out of here."

Mary Margaret and Clay were behind Caitlin as they weaved their way through the amassing crowd and raced out of the main hall. Caitlin tried to turn around and go back, but her father had such a tight grasp of her arm, she couldn't get away. She had always believed her father was a coward, but she had kept the secret to herself. Now the rest of the world would know it, too.

Caitlin placed a dime in the pay phone and dialed the operator, who placed the New York call and billed the charges to Emerald Chocolate.

Her mind was whirling. "God, Sheilagh, where are you when I need you?"

Her hand was trembling. She was scared. Really scared. When she was young and truly frightened, she would turn not to her mother and never to her father, but to her older sister, Sheilagh. It was no different now.

"Sheilagh will know what to do," Caitlin mumbled to herself. Sheilagh would be there. Sheilagh would keep her promises.

Cailtin felt as helpless as a child. Her adult world had gone spinning out of control, and her only anchor was her childhood memory of a pact she had made with Sheilagh and her brother, Michael.

"Swear it," Sheilagh had demanded.

They had placed their hands over one another's as they sat in the Killian kitchen in Oak Park and agreed to stand up for one another, to be there for one another no matter what.

It was a sacred vow that none of them had taken lightly. None had abused it. They had believed in and supported one another over the years . . . even the difficult years . . . the years when their family was being ripped apart. When they were very young, they allied themselves against the enemy, their parents. Later, when life became more complicated and heartbreaking, they found love enough to believe and trust in one another even when they threatened one another.

Caitlin shared a special bond with Sheilagh and Michael. It had been a long time since she'd called upon either of them to come to her aid. But murder had a way of eliciting desperate action.

The receiver was picked up on the other end.

"Sheilagh? Is that you?" Caitlin asked. "I need you, Sheilagh. Please come home."

Chapter 1 ───────────

June 6, 1971
Wilmette, Illinois

CAITLIN STOOD ON the front steps of her Greek Revival house waiting for the paperboy. She had spun through all the network television channels and the local Channel 9 news early morning reports, and there had been nothing. So far, the reprieve they had all prayed for had been granted.

She sipped hot coffee from a mug and glanced up the sidewalk. She could hear the sound of a bicycle approaching and the intermittent plopping noise the newspapers made as they landed on her neighbors' doorsteps. Then she saw the red-haired eleven-year-old who faithfully delivered their *Chicago Tribune* every morning.

Eddie waved as he approached, but his usual toothy smile was wan. It was not a good sign. He tossed the paper and it flew a little too quickly toward her, landing lightly like an angel of death. Caitlin's hand shook as she retrieved it. Not enough pages, she thought, not enough *other* newsworthy events happening in the world. She knew the story would be there. She hoped it wouldn't be on the front page.

Slowly she pulled the rubber band away and unfolded the wings of the dark messenger. EMERALD CHOCOLATE KILLS, read the headline across the bottom of the lower right-hand column. Caitlin's heart banged inside her chest and her eyes burned as she quickly read the story.

> Emerald Chocolate Corporation, headquartered in Chicago, is being investigated by city police for the cyanide poisoning deaths of one Chicago man and one New York man, both judges at the Midwest Fancy Food and Confection Convention held here at McCormick Place. Both men were in the process of judging the Emerald Chocolate entries in the handmade candy division when they fell victim to the poisoning. The Cook County Coroner's Office issued a statement today that the Emerald chocolates had been laced with cyanide. The families of both victims allege that Emerald Chocolate Corporation president Patrick Killian, and the vice president, Clay Burke, are responsible for the deaths. Police are still investigating the homicides. No arrests have been made. None of the Emerald Chocolate representatives was available for comment.

Caitlin felt as if the blood had been instantly siphoned out of her body. She turned back toward the house and quickly sought protection behind the massive locked door. She walked across the black and white marble foyer through the dining room and into the kitchen.

Clay was sitting at the kitchen table, an untouched mug of steaming coffee in front of him. He was staring out the windows into the garden. He did not look up when she entered the room. "It's there, isn't it?" he said.

"Yes." Caitlin waited for a reply, a word, a gesture, but he remained unmoving, as if the will to fight had left him.

For months Clay had seemed to be detaching from Caitlin, but because they were so swamped with work at the factory, she had not paid attention. Now she had seen his depression deepen and settle firmly about him. It wasn't just the crisis over the poisoning that upset Clay, though the incident had exacerbated his feelings of hopelessness. His mood had changed over the past eighteen months, and Caitlin didn't know how to cope with it.

She had tried to talk to him many times, but he would only wave her inquiries aside as if they were nothing. He told her he was overworked, which he was. That he was tired, which he was. After urging, he went to the doctor for a physical, but there was nothing wrong. His disease was of the spirit. Caitlin had begun to fear that Clay, the love of her life since her childhood, was having an affair. The thought sickened and frightened her.

Caitlin tossed the *Tribune* into the trash compactor and went to the table. She sat across from him, reached out her hand to touch his, and forced a smile. Clay picked up his coffee and drank deeply. He still had not looked at her.

Caitlin thought her heart would break. She didn't know what to do or where to turn. What was even more terrifying to her now was Sheilagh's imminent arrival. What if Clay fell in love with Sheilagh all over again? What if Clay's depression was due to some undeniable need for the passion he'd once shared with her sister? Caitlin couldn't stand the thought of losing him, but to lose his love to Sheilagh a second time . . . God! She felt tears bite the edges of her eyes. Her stomach lurched and she tasted bile in her throat.

Caitlin needed Sheilagh, but she wanted Clay, too. What could she do? What was the right thing for him? Should she stand back and let him go? Was that love? How could it be when she felt as if she needed to hang on to him with twice her resolve?

Clay's shoulders slumped lower as he leaned back in the chair and looked at her. He studied her apathetically, as if she were not quite visible and therefore not worth considering. Fear again upended her stomach.

How could this be happening to them? Caitlin thought. She and Clay were the golden couple, the envy of all their friends. Since their marriage, they had had very few arguments. They had both maintained energetic careers in the family corporation. They were not jet-setters by any stretch of the imagination, nor were they famous or saving the world from corruption or invoking social change. They were simply two married people who loved each other and had raised a wonderful daughter together. Clay had turned fifty-two this year, and she was only forty-eight. They had a great deal of living yet to experience, she thought.

But perhaps Clay didn't feel the same way she did. It was obvious that he believed some part of his life was over, because he was not happy.

Caitlin had to admit that she was not happy either. Clay had shouldered the responsibility of her father's company for well over two decades. Patrick was a figurehead president. He took the glory, and Clay did the work. Patrick Killian was an alcoholic. Caitlin had no difficulty in passing judgment on her father, although everyone else in the family turned a deaf ear and a blind eye when Patrick drank.

Because of their problems with Patrick, Clay was forced to spend all his time and energy on the business, which left Caitlin out in the emotional cold. He was perpetually on the phone or in meetings. Even when he came home at night, he still made transcontinental calls until midnight most nights. The pressure was on for Emerald to expand into larger world markets. Clay told her that he had to make these sacrifices for the sake of progress. But Caitlin knew it was *she* who was being sacrificed.

Caitlin had always dreamed of the day when she and Clay would have the house to themselves. She wanted to be newly-weds again. Share romantic midnight suppers by the fireplace, make love in the bathtub and in the gazebo in the backyard. Clay was always too busy, too tired, too preoccupied. Caitlin felt abandoned both by her daughter, who had moved to her own apartment, and by her husband. She had never felt so alone in all her life.

Desperate, angry tears stung her eyes. She fought them back. "Do you think we should telephone Carin? I doubt she will have heard about the poisonings in Galway. Isn't that where she is this week? Maybe she's already back in Dublin by now." She glanced about the kitchen, thinking it was good to consider something besides her marriage and Clay's depression. "Now, where did I put her itinerary?"

Clay shook his head. "Leave her be. She'll be coming home in a couple days. She'll find out about this mess soon enough.

God knows when she'll get another vacation . . . especially now. It's going to take a miracle to work our way out of this pit."

Caitlin knew he was talking about himself as much as he was the business. She wanted to go to him, put her arms around him, comfort him, but the fear of rejection paralyzed her. She tried to be positive. "I'm glad Father called a board meeting. It will be good to have Michael's vote on what we should do."

Clay ran a hand impatiently through his hair. "Jesus, Cat. I know what to do! What does a surgeon like Michael know about the recall on all our chocolate that the FBI has demanded? What does Michael know about the raw cost of shipping and disposing of all that product? Or how it will affect our profit for the year? Does he know how to strategize the public relations nightmare we have ahead of us? We'll be lucky if we don't become the joke of the decade.

"Christ! Cyanide! If somebody wanted us dead, why didn't they just use a fucking gun?

"Poison in the chocolate. It can't get any worse. And it's the half-truths that scare me. Was it deliberate? Or did rat poison just fall into the vat of couverture? I mean, what the hell happened? And why?" Clay paused for a moment and took a deep swallow of his coffee. Caitlin said nothing but gently laid her hand on his shoulder, hoping he would know she supported him.

"What should we do?" she finally asked.

"We have to take the offensive. We should run ads on TV and radio, immediately denying our knowledge of, or participation in, any negligence. We should issue an apology to the families and begin proceedings to make restitution to them. We should take out a whole page of sympathy notices in the *Wall Street Journal* and in the *Tribune*. We should affix blame ourselves before the police do. Beat them to the punch. Call it murder."

"But who would want to kill those judges? And if they weren't the intended victims, who was?"

"One of us. Patrick is my guess."

"Why?"

"Why not?" Clay harrumphed a bit maliciously. "Truth is, he's made plenty of enemies over the years, but I agree. If the intended target was Patrick, a gun would have been more expedient."

"Then the cyanide was meant for the judges?"

Clay nodded. "Somebody really wanted to fuck up Emerald Chocolate."

"They got what they wanted."

Clay rubbed his unshaven face in an angry gesture of frustration. "They did. And they can have it. I'm sick of being possessed by your father's company."

Caitlin peered at him, realizing Clay was revealing more of himself than he had in a long time. She wanted him to continue, to share his pain and misgivings with her, but she knew she needed to be cautious. She wanted desperately for them to be close again, but she didn't want to press too hard. "It's been difficult for you—"

"I'll live," he said, cutting her off.

They had rounded the board and were back to square one. Caitlin felt exhausted. She wanted to try again, but didn't have the emotional stamina for it.

"I'll go check the television again. See if anyone has picked up the story," she said, and left.

Caitlin rushed out of the room before Clay could respond. In the den, she flipped on the television to WBBM, the CBS affiliate, and watched the face of the newscaster as he related the details of the poisoning. Caitlin felt like an automaton, barely conscious as the walls of her world cracked and began to tumble down. She didn't hear Clay when he came into the room and stood behind her.

"What are you thinking?" he asked with only a whisper of real interest. She knew that he did not want to hear the truth. Pretend, he was telling her, pretend for just a little while longer that none of this is happening. Imagine it is only a dream.

"I was thinking about the candy. How I have loved chocolate all my life. It was always such fun. It didn't ask anything of you. Just gave pleasure." She rose and turned off the television. "Now the pleasure has been poisoned. It seems ironic that this should happen now. Not even the candy is fun anymore," she said, and then turned her back to him and went upstairs to dress for work.

Clay marveled at Caitlin's indomitable strength. For months he had pretended not to hear her pleas to communicate with her, yet she had never shown her own fears. He could see them lurking like a hazy cloud behind the sparkle in her eyes. Her faith in him and in their life together had not dimmed over the years until now. How much did she know? Obviously it was enough for her to see the chinks in his armor. He was not as strong as Caitlin, though she thought he was.

Caitlin loved her family, right or wrong. She believed, or needed to believe, that they were just as loving and forgiving as she was. Clay knew differently. He didn't trust a damn one of them. He knew that if for one second Patrick Killian found him negligent in any way that might have precipitated this crisis, Clay would be axed without a grain of regret on Patrick's part.

Clay had been fated to be part of the Killian family since the first day they'd all met in 1934, though he hadn't known it then. Perhaps none of them had.

They'd all been children then, he and Caitlin, Michael, and, of course, Sheilagh. Although he doubted Sheilagh had ever truly been a child. There was nothing childlike about her. She'd always seemed to him a woman in a child's body, and whether Mary Margaret would agree or not, Sheilagh had been perhaps more wise as a child than any of the rest of them were as adults.

Clay knew that Caitlin feared his feelings toward Sheilagh. He supposed that was only natural. He probably would have the same misgivings if the tables were turned. After all, Clay had been married to Sheilagh. He knew he would not have been capable of forgiving and forgetting as easily as Caitlin had. Or had she? Was his wife really so strong, or was she just the consummate actress in the family?

Clay slumped onto the overstuffed sofa. God, he had so many doubts lately. He despised himself for not being in control. He wanted to pull everything back together, had been trying to for weeks. His impotent attempts had created more chaos. Perhaps it was time for the truth.

Clay wondered what Caitlin would say if he told her he'd had enough of her family. He was too old to take orders from a man he didn't respect, had never respected, and he wanted out. How would she feel if he told her that he would go to any lengths to force a resignation from Patrick? That he, Clay, could continue on with Emerald Chocolates only if he were president. It was that, or he would leave. He would start his own chocolate company, give Patrick a real run for his money.

Clay knew he possessed the knowledge and skills to create a premier chocolate company. Without Patrick Killian to deal with, he could implement hundreds of progressive ideas that Patrick refused to consider.

For years Clay had felt he was fighting a multiheaded hydra. To Clay, Emerald Chocolates had become Patrick's veto, Mary Margaret's patronizing and manipulative control, and Michael's apathy. Only Caitlin sided with him, but she was a peacemaker, always mediating between her parents and him. Clay almost always acquiesed, "for the good of the company."

It made him sick when he thought of the hundreds of times he'd given in to please Patrick, please Caitlin. Now he had to please Clay.

The time had come for him to move on. He could only hope that his wife wanted to go with him.

Patrick Killian puffed a thick cigar as he looked out the fourth-story window of his office at the scene below him in the parking lot. News vans, press cars, and police cars swarmed like locusts. Patrick sucked in a cloud of smoke and blew it out slowly.

"Bastards," he said as his secretary, Martha O'Boland, tapped on the door and entered the room. She stood meekly across the desk from him.

"Did you see them, Martha?"

"Yes, sir," she replied, looking down at the stack of phone messages in her hand.

"Parasites. Vultures. They thrive on this kind of misery."

"Yes, sir."

"Came to see me bleed, they did," he said contemptuously as he inhaled the cigar again. He turned and looked at Martha for confirmation. It was an unusual gesture for him, because Patrick Killian believed that he needed no one for anything—ever.

Martha looked past him out the windows. "They won't see you bleed, sir. Not yet."

Patrick snorted. "At least someone is on my side."

"Mr. Killian, Clay and Caitlin are due here any minute, and your wife has arrived."

Patrick jerked the cigar out of his mouth and cut her off. "My family doesn't give a damn about me. Especially now. Let's be clear about that. This press conference is Clay's idea. Not mine. I don't know what good it will do. I say we should avoid the bastards. Let them fill their rags with something else."

"Sir, you've always catered to the press. They like you."

"*Liked*, Martha. Past tense. The press is a necessary evil. Never forget that. Given half the chance, they'll turn on you every time. I don't trust them." Under his breath he muttered, "I don't trust anyone."

Martha lowered her eyes and did not respond. She looked as if she wanted to disappear. She fumbled uncomfortably with the memos in her hands. "These need your attention, sir."

He glanced at the files and memos. "What are they?"

"Bills that need to be paid, but I can take care of those for you if you want to leave it to my discretion."

"That's fine. Or have Clay deal with them."

"There are no less than twenty requests for interviews from newspaper people and free-lance journalists. I assume you won't grant any, but I need to call them back with a reply. It won't take me long. Then you have a luncheon appointment with the local head of the truckers' union—"

"Cancel it," Patrick interrupted.

"I don't think that would be wise."

"Goddamn it, Martha. You act as if Emerald will still be here tomorrow!"

Martha looked at him, aghast. "Of course Emerald will be here. This company must endure. I have always believed that," she said with conviction.

"That three-week vacation you took back in April has done you a lot of good, Martha. At the time I thought you were headed for a breakdown or something. You'd been working too hard. But now you seem far more cool and confident. You are a capable employee. Loyalty like yours is hard to buy, Martha," he said, though as usual when serving up compliments, there was a hollow ring to his words.

"Thank you," she replied. "I'll take care of these details for you. No need to bother Clay with them. He has a lot on his mind, too, I'm sure." Martha headed for the door.

Patrick turned back to the window, thinking this all seemed unreal to him, as if he were watching someone else's life in a movie. Just then he saw Clay's Cadillac pull up to his reserved parking place. The reporters and journalists surrounded the car as Caitlin tried to get out. One of the reporters nearly knocked her down, which clearly made Caitlin angry. She slammed the car door on one of the photographers' camera straps. She was shaking her head and trying to get past the reporters.

Patrick laughed to himself. "I'll bet she'd belt one of them, given half the chance."

Clay was taking a less demonstrative approach, answering questions as he walked toward the building. The reporters liked Clay, and it was evident in their deferential attitude toward him. Patrick could see him shaking his head back and forth, then later, nodding it up and down. Clay took his time with each one, not cutting them off, yet not bending to them either. "Clay shoulda been a politician like his father," Patrick grumbled.

The crowd dispersed as Caitlin and Clay entered the building.

Patrick jammed his cigar into a crystal ashtray just as the door to his office opened. Since there was no knock, he knew it was his wife, Mary Margaret.

Stress had aged Mary Margaret well beyond her sixty-eight years. Although she was tastefully dressed in a navy blue and white suit with matching spectator shoes, the distress in her eyes betrayed the cool composure the world was accustomed to seeing in Mary Margaret Killian. "The police want to talk to you," she said. "An Inspector Gregory, I think, is his name."

"What did you tell him, Mary?" Patrick demanded.

She stuck out her chin defensively. "Nothing," she replied, calmly retrieving her control.

"That's good. Of course, you have nothing to say to them. You aren't involved . . ."

"Of course." She sat in one of the two green leather chairs Caitlin had recently reupholstered. "I'm never involved."

He sensed her overwhelming anger. All those decades of festering wounds she had borne were coming to the surface. If this was to be his bloodletting, he'd always known that Mary Margaret would be around to watch his pain, maybe even wield the scalpel herself.

"I've already talked to a couple of those bozos. Who is this Gregory guy?" Patrick asked.

"I haven't the slightest idea. But he's certainly been busy this morning. He's interviewed over half the factory staff. Did Martha tell you he talked to her?"

"No. But then, she never says more than two words to me."

Mary Margaret nodded in agreement. "I wish they would all leave. They make me nervous."

"What difference does it make now? The damage has been done. Our name has been linked to a poison. Fifty years from now, people will remember this. No one is ever going to buy our chocolate again."

"That's preposterous. People forget all manner of things over time," she said. She jerked her eyes off his, but remained calmly sitting in her chair.

Patrick could almost hear the words she wanted to say but never would. *Except for me, Patrick. I remember everything you've ever said or done. Every indiscretion, every pain, every heartbreak. I remember them all . . . the dates and times of day. I've kept track on a very, very large mental chalkboard.* That's what she wanted to say but didn't, he thought. Instead, she remained as aloof, poised, and mannerly as a statue. A cold, untouchable statue. Like the Madonna in the church to which she prayed every morning at seven-thirty. He had always wondered what it would take to crack her alabaster facade. In over fifty years he'd never seen her falter. She was always right, and he was wrong. And for a man who had made many bad choices in life, it was hell.

Just then Clay and Caitlin came into the room. Caitlin kissed her mother's cheek and sat in the chair next to her, holding her hand. "You shouldn't have come in today. It's not necessary for you to be here, Mother."

"I felt if we showed a united front, perhaps the press would leave us alone."

"Fat chance of that," Patrick growled, and looked over to his son-in-law. "I want those cops outta here. I don't care what you tell them, but get them off my back."

Clay was surprised by the urgency in Patrick's voice. "They're doing a routine investigation. I'm not afraid of that. Our best defense is the truth. Once the culprit is identified, we can join with the public in its outrage. We want to know who the murderer is and why, just like everyone else. And according to Inspector Gregory, the murderer is not just some off-the-wall kook, but most likely one of us here at Emerald."

Patrick eyed Clay intensely. "That is the most preposterous bullshit I've ever heard. No one at Emerald could ever do such a thing." He guffawed nervously. "If they did, that would mean they wanted to destroy . . . me."

"I understand that." Clay's voice was stern, flat, and coldly blunt. There was no refuting his disdain for Patrick. Years of subservience, of cleaning up Patrick's corporate and personal messes, had finally pushed Clay to the limit. "It's *your* company. What do you intend to do?" Clay asked.

"What?"

Clay squared his shoulders. "You heard me. Which way do

you want to go with this? Yours or mine?"

The din of gathering news reporters seeped through the office door, pressing Patrick for a decision.

The pendulum on the grandfather clock in the left corner swung back and forth. It was nearly time for the press conference to begin.

A bead of sweat trickled down Patrick's temple.

Patrick eyed his son-in-law sardonically. "Just what are you saying, Clay?"

"I'm telling you that I'll handle all your shit for you, but I want you to step down."

"And if I don't?"

Clay smiled the first relaxed smile he had in months. "Then you may handle this crisis in any way you see fit. I won't be around to do it for you."

Caitlin gasped. Mary Margaret threw her hands over her mouth and looked to her daughter for confirmation. Caitlin shook her head. "I didn't know . . . anything . . ." she whispered.

Caitlin's eyes flew back to her husband. Clay was standing firm. She knew he would not back down. She also knew he relished this confrontation. As she glanced at her father, she knew that Patrick knew it, too.

Patrick felt as if he were sinking in a quagmire. He was surrounded by Judases. His son, Michael, the wimp, had called earlier and said he had an emergency at the hospital. He was reneging on his promise to Caitlin to come to Chicago. The hell with him, Patrick thought. Michael had abandoned him and the company long ago. His son was a self-centered bastard, and not once had he ever been there for him. Obviously he never would.

Now Clay was turning against him, too. Patrick should have expected something like this. Clay was an outsider. One thing that life had taught Patrick was never to trust anybody. Not friends. Not family.

"You ungrateful son of a bitch. You planned this, didn't you? Did you set up this poisoning scheme to ruin my company?"

Caitlin shot to her feet. "Daddy! How can you say that?"

"Easy," he replied. "Because I just hit the truth, didn't I?" He rounded the desk and stood in front of Clay, nearly eye to eye except that Clay was taller. It was the first time since she was a child that Caitlin had seen her father use his enormous girth as a force for generating energy. Patrick broke out in a sweat, but his eyes were like white-hot coals turning the perspiration to vapor. He was an intimidating sight. Caitlin remembered too easily how she'd once been afraid of him.

Patrick jabbed his square, fat finger into Clay's shoulder. "Pack up and get the fuck outta here. I don't need you. I continued to allow you to work here because you were married to Sheilagh. When that marriage didn't work out, you went after Caitlin. She fell for your lines, but I want you to know this—I never did. I always saw through you. I knew this day would come. It's just as well. Now, get out of here."

Clay was still smiling when he walked toward the door. He'd never felt so free and in control of his life. Just as he reached the door, he stopped. He'd been so immersed in his anger and then relief that he'd forgotten about Caitlin. He turned and found her watching him with tears in her eyes.

"Clay, don't go. Tell him you didn't mean it," she said, and turned to her father. "Stop it now, Daddy, before it goes too far. How can you say these things to each other at a time like this? The whole world is against us. We need to fight them, not each other. Clay . . . please." She held out her hand to him.

Clay's mind was clear for the first time in a long while. He hadn't meant to provoke this fight, but he had. It had all tumbled out, and he felt good now. If he allowed Patrick to accuse him of murdering innocent people and didn't fight back, he would feel as if he'd lost his soul. This was as good a time as any to let the fight begin and end.

But as he stood with his back against the door, he realized how much he needed Caitlin, how lonely it was going to be without her. They had worked together nearly all their adult lives. There had been times when he'd been frightened at how mentally in tune they were. Lately they had drifted apart, and as he looked at her now, he realized just how wide that chasm was. She knew it, too. And for the first time it hit Clay how perilously strained their marriage had become. Suddenly he was afraid of her answer.

"Come with me now, Caitlin. Come home with me."

She rose from the chair and started toward him. She heard her father's breath rush from his throat like a whirlwind.

"You're a Killian," Patrick said. "First, last, and always. This is your family."

Caitlin looked back to her father. "That's true. I am."

"Somebody has to put our family name back right," Patrick said. "We can do this together. You and I."

Caitlin couldn't believe her ears. All her life she'd wanted her father to need her. Ask her to help him, show that he valued her, but he never had. She'd never been the pretty one, the talented one—Sheilagh had been all that and more. Caitlin had never been the center of attention. Now she was.

"Say you will, dearest," Mary Margaret said in a pleading whisper.

In the midst of the greatest Killian family disaster, Caitlin had found her glory. She turned to share her moment of triumph with Clay. But he was gone.

Chapter 2

June 7, 1971
New York City

SHEILAGH KILLIAN VALLENTI paced the living room of her New York apartment with a scotch and soda in her hand. She'd been in a sullen mood for two days, and nothing seemed to drag her out of it. She wore the new Christian Dior silver satin robe she'd bought at Saks Fifth Avenue, and that didn't make her feel one bit lighter. Nor did the fact that her recent face-lift had healed beautifully. She passed the Venetian mirror, noting that the fabric elegantly skimmed the curves of her trim figure. Her perfectly cut and styled shoulder-length auburn hair was untouched by gray. She looked every inch the "femme fatale" the public imagined her to be. The gleam in her green eyes was put there by love. She should be happy, but she wasn't. She was angry.

She kicked the *New York Times* across the room and watched the words EMERALD CHOCOLATE KILLS sail out of sight. "Son of a bitch!" she hissed through teeth that had been clenched ever since her sister, Caitlin, had called a second time the day before. It was the first time in her life that Sheilagh had ever known Caitlin to be hysterical. Caitlin's life was in tatters. Sheilagh herself felt the ground slipping away inch by inch as she listened to her sister's pleas to come back to Chicago.

"I need you for moral support, Sheilagh," Caitlin had said. "Carin sent a wire that she's staying in Ireland for another week. We have no idea where she is. She left no number to call and no address. She has no idea about what has happened."

"What can I do, except set Daddy's teeth on edge?"

"I need you for *me*." And then Caitlin had started crying again.

"Clay hasn't really left you, Caitlin. He'll come around. Obviously you two need to talk. Besides, would it be so bad to leave Emerald? Maybe you both should."

"Sheilagh! What are you saying? We've worked so hard . . . all these years I've put in. I've built something here, and so has Clay."

"Really, Caitlin? It doesn't sound like it to me."

Caitlin's voice had turned angry. "I should have known not to call you. You have your fine life there in New York. Why should you care what happens to any of us . . . to me?"

"Caitlin, please . . . I wasn't deriding you. You're the best thing that ever happened to the company. And to Clay."

There were sniffles on the other end of the phone. "He wanted you first . . . Maybe he still does."

"Judas Priest, Caitlin. That's ancient history. Besides, haven't you read the tabloids? Tony and I are making romantic history. At least we're doing the best we can for two old chickens."

"Are you really happy?"

"Yes, really. It took a long time getting here, and hell to pay along the road. But yes, Caitlin. I'm happier than I've ever been."

"I know it's asking a lot for you to come back. It won't be easy for you."

"How *is* the witch from hell, anyway?" Sheilagh asked derisively, referring to Mary Margaret.

"She's older now, Sheilagh. Time heals . . ."

"Bullshit! She hasn't changed toward me, and we both know it. But all that aside, if you truly need me, I'll be there."

"Oh, God, Sheilagh, I can't thank you enough. I know it's going to be hard, but I feel so alone. I've never felt this way, and it's awful."

"Funny, I've felt that way most of my life, and I liked it." Sheilagh laughed, and after a moment, Caitlin laughed along with her.

"I'll pick you up at O'Hare. Just let me know the time and flight number. Okay?"

"You got it. Anything for my baby sister," Sheilagh had said, and hung up.

Now Sheilagh massaged her temples, hoping to ease the pounding, but the headache would not abate. She took a deep swallow of the scotch. Her stomach was tied in knots. The last thing she wanted to do was go back home. How odd that now, in her fiftieth year, when she had finally found love and peace with herself, she should be called back there. She couldn't help wondering how much Chicago had changed since she'd left thirty years ago. The Blackstone Theater was still there, but what was it like now? Did kids still get a leg up in acting there the way she had in 1938? She tried to remember the names of the producer and director she'd worked with, the kids in the chorus, but no faces came to mind. The kids she had grown up with were scattered all over the map. Was Resurrection Church still there? What about Ascension Church on East and Van Buren? How had her parents' house changed? And the Emerald Chocolate offices—Caitlin had written that they had newly remodeled, and she wondered how they looked.

"They always say never to go back," she mumbled aloud to herself, and took another swallow of her drink. And she hadn't gone back. Not for thirty years . . .

Every time Sheilagh thought of Chicago, she conjured up visions of her father and mother standing over her life like two Colossus of Rhodes, ready to crumble, fall, and crush her to death. That's the way it had always been. Why should she think they would be any different now? The one thing Sheilagh knew about her parents was that the whole world could change, but they would always be the same. Maybe she should have taken comfort in that fact.

She sighed and slumped onto the white raw silk sofa. She looked over to the black lacquered baby grand piano, where she kept photographs of her family in sterling silver frames. Clay, Caitlin, and Carin dominated. There were three of Michael and Bridget. There were none of Patrick or Mary Margaret. Sheilagh didn't want to be reminded of her failures or her sins.

Sheilagh's heart felt like lead. All these years she had kept in touch with her brother and sister when they came to New

York to see her while on business trips. She had made several trips to Houston to visit Michael, and Caitlin was always only a phone call away. To actually return to Chicago was another matter.

Suddenly her nearly perfect world had spun on its axis and tipped the balance scales. She was uncertain if she had the courage to face her demons. Caitlin had always thought Sheilagh was the strong one, to strike out on her own in a strange city, but in actuality, she had been running away all her life. She wanted to keep it that way.

This commitment to her sister could be her undoing. She wanted to tell Caitlin that it was too much to ask. She wanted to stay in New York, in the shelter of her tidy world. Caitlin had never asked anyone to do anything for her. It was Caitlin who was the strong one, the most giving in the family. Caitlin still did the mediating among them all. Caitlin still hoped the family could be mended.

It was hard living up to Saint Caitlin, the moniker Sheilagh had given her when they were children, but now it was Sheilagh's turn to help. This wasn't going to be a fantasy where she altered the landscape of her past and substituted new and loving parents. This trip was for real, and Sheilagh was scared to death.

June 7, 1971
Houston, Texas

Michael Killian jogged his black Lincoln Town Car past the parked ambulance on Fannin Street on his way to Baylor Cardiology Research Center. God, how he loved this work he was doing. Ever since 1969, when Denton Cooley had performed the first artificial heart transplant, Michael had believed that the Texas Heart Institute was making strides more important to mankind than walking on the moon. Houston was where all of it was happening, as if the greatest minds of medicine and science had all converged on this subtropical town. To think that he was a part of it was exhilarating. He could barely conceive of the impact, the explosion of knowledge he was handing down for future generations. In only a few short years, he and his associates were performing heart transplants as easily as dentists filled cavities. It was an exciting realm he wandered here in Houston, and he rejoiced in every blessed moment of it. Yes, he thought. He was one lucky son of a bitch.

The Lincoln careened around a stalled Cutlass Supreme. He hated being late for work . . . again. Bridget had started another argument over his planned trip to Chicago. The crisis over the chocolate poisoning had hit the *Houston Post* and the *Houston Chronicle,* bringing scores of phone calls to the Killians' River Oaks home. The calls were upsetting to them all, but especially to Bridget since she was home all day. Bridget had immediately packed off their children to spend a month in Switzerland—Shea, now seventeen and in her junior year in high school, and Blake, twelve.

Michael had protested vehemently, to no purpose. He did not want the summer disrupted more than it already was. But Bridget did not want the children involved in the crisis. One of her friends from her modeling days in Chicago now lived in Saint Moritz and had insisted Bridget send the children to her. They would go mountain hiking, boating, bicycling, and meet new friends. Michael wanted the children with him. Bridget wanted to protect them.

That morning, Michael had been deep in thought, wondering what Shea and Blake were doing, when Bridget had walked into the room. One look at her tight expression had told him she was about to explode.

"I don't see why you have to go to Chicago. What business is it of yours?"

"My sisters need me," he said simply.

"You can't stand your family. You've told me so a million times. We live here so that you can be away from them. This is their problem. Let them handle it."

Michael glared at Bridget. "Why don't we get down to the real reason, Bridget. You don't give a damn about my family. All you really care about is whether I'll be able to make this charity ball on Saturday."

"I've worked hard on this ball, Michael. And though you never appreciate anything I've done for you—"

"Don't give me that shit. Your charity work is for you . . . to see your name in Maxine's column. You're the one who wants to go to the best luncheons and teas . . . just in case Betty Ewing is there and puts your picture in the *Chronicle.* Nobody cares if I go to that ball . . . least of all you."

"What a heartless bastard you are, Michael. None of that is true, and you know it."

"I know nothing of the sort. You need me there because of the work I'm doing with Denton Cooley. You like the fame."

"So do you!"

"Sometimes I think you don't know anything about me. I love my work. The fame is insignificant. In fact, it gets in the way of what I'm trying to accomplish."

"Don't be so self-righteous, Michael. You sound like your mother."

"I'm nothing like my mother! You hear me? Nothing."

Her eyes narrowed. "Are you trying to convince me or yourself? Take a good look at yourself, Michael. You are a Killian . . . through and through. Self-centered, selfish . . . you exude moral indignation."

"If it's so bad being married to me, Bridget, then why don't you leave?"

"And relieve you of the guilt you'd feel if you had to admit you'd failed? No way. You want a divorce . . . you file."

Michael whirled away from her and slammed his coffee mug on the glass-top table. "I don't believe in divorce."

"Bullshit. You're scared you'd burn in hell, because that's what you've been taught. Grow up, Michael; this is the seventies. You just don't have the balls to divorce me."

His lips had curled into a smirk. "I don't have to have any. You have plenty for the both of us." Then he had walked out.

Bridget's words had cut Michael to the bone. She had sounded too much like his father all those years when he was growing up. Michael made peace. Patrick made war. If by some miracle any measure of harmony came into the Killian household, Patrick found a way to create a crisis.

Patrick demanded control. Control of his business, control of his wife, and most of all, control over his children. From Michael's childhood perspective, because he was the only son, Patrick had manipulated Michael most of all.

Like Sheilagh, Michael had never had any desire to own or run the chocolate company. He was not especially driven to become rich, which his father wanted so desperately. Michael wanted to help people. He was not certain when this desire had come into his life, because to him, it seemed always to have been a part of him. If he could put a date on the birth of his life's passion, it would have been February of 1934. His mentor had been the most unlikely of all the family members— Sheilagh . . .

Sheilagh had abandoned him when she ran off to New York, and for a long, long time he hadn't forgiven her.

Michael pulled into his reserved parking space, locked his car, and rode the elevator to his office, still thinking of Sheilagh. In all these years, she had never gone back to Chicago . . . and with good reason. Yet now she was. She was more courageous than he would have been under the circumstances. If Sheilagh could go back and face her demons, so could he.

No, he thought. Bridget was wrong. He did have balls. Especially when it mattered.

Chapter 3

Late May, 1971
County Clare, Ireland

THE RENTED FIAT 600 buzzed past a donkey-drawn wooden cart filled with hay and grass. The farmer drew his weathered face into a smile and waved at the two women.

"I love this country!" Carin said to her grandmother, Aileen Burke, who was driving the Fiat much too fast down the country lanes of County Clare.

"Aren't you glad to have all that tourist crap out of the way? Everybody kisses the Blarney Stone, but do you know anyone who has gone to Tara to stand where Saint Patrick chanted 'The Deer's Cry' to protect himself from the Druid witches? And I thought the ancient underground tunnels and hieroglyphics at Newgrange and the flat stone dolmens we've seen were more intriguing than Stonehenge," Aileen said, merrily winking a bright green eye at her granddaughter.

Carin shot her grandmother a sidelong glance. "I must admit going on vacation with an archaeologist is a definite departure from the ordinary. But it's not the sights that have made this trip interesting, Grandma, it's you."

"Thank you, my darling. I deserve the accolade, if I do say so myself. Not many women of my age know how to have fun anymore."

"Grandma, the fact that you are seventy years old has nothing to do with it. You've always been weird." Carin laughed uproariously, and her long, auburn curls shimmered in the afternoon sun.

Aileen pressed her foot to the gas pedal and they sped off. As they careened around a sharp curve, Carin could see off to her left the natural limestone wildflower-covered terraces called the Burren. She inhaled the early summer air and let the scent of the land linger in her lungs. Never had she felt quite so welcome by everything she'd seen and everyone she'd met. Long ago, when the Irish were mostly peasants, they believed that should they not offer their last morsel of food and the warmth of their peat fire to a stranger, they would incur heaven's wrath. That sentiment still existed, Carin had found. The Irish were jovial and expansive and couldn't wait to help with travel directions, or better yet, to solve every problem in one's life.

County Clare was an intriguing Eden with its pastoral meadows, its misty bogs with their mysterious light known as "ignis fatuus," and its dangerous coastline. Legends abounded of banshees, witches, fairies, plant divas, forest sprites and nymphs, leprechauns, and brownies. All of which were present in nature to help and hinder mankind. Even today, Carin believed that nature continually waged a battle between good and evil at the cliffs of Kilkee at Moore Bay, where powerful winds were mighty enough to force the cascading water back up a waterfall and sheer off splinters of the cliff and fling them onto the pastureland far beyond the ocean's edge.

Summer had laid golden blankets of ragwort across the meadows. The rape had begun to ripen, and on the limestone hills of Burrin, Carin spied lichen, moss, and emerald grass. They had visited the tiny stone shops in Ennistymon, whose store windows were filled with bog oak souvenirs and models of jaunting cars, those horse-drawn wagons where the passengers sat back to back facing out. Ireland was completely different from life in Chicago, where man was pitted against man, and family members battled one another for slivers of love. Carin thought she could remain in Ireland forever.

Lisdoonvarna was only fifty miles south from where they intended to stay that night, at Butler Castle. Carin reached into the glove compartment and pulled out the travel brochures for a description of the castle, since it was not as well known as Dromoland, Lismore, or Limerick, King John's Castle. In fact, Butler Castle in County Clare was not mentioned at all.

"You won't find anything about it in there," Aileen said, tapping her finger on the brochure yet keeping her eyes on the road. "Butler Castle has only recently been opened to the public. It's a real find. An associate of mine at the university told me about it."

"What makes it so special?"

"Remember when we passed Galway and I told you we had just entered a different kind of Ireland?"

"Yes. You said it was enchanted land. And truly it is. The blue lakes . . . sorry, the loughs, the gray stone lacework we saw in Connemara . . ."

"I'm not talking about natural wonders. I mean real enchantings."

"You mean ghosts," Carin accused. "Grandma, have you booked us into a haunted castle?"

Aileen twittered with delight and her narrow shoulders lifted in triumph. "Haven't you always wanted to stay in one?"

"Can't say that I have." Carin crossed her arms over her chest and wedged herself between the seat and door so that she could look Aileen squarely in the face. "Fess up, Grandma. You don't honestly think we're going to see leprechauns and fairies, do you?"

"Why not? Anything is possible in this world."

"I think you've gone off your gourd, Grandma."

Aileen bit her lower lip, suppressing her frustration. "You are an intelligent child, Carin, but your mind is too narrow."

"God, you're not going to tell me to drop out, turn on, and tune in, are you?"

Aileen shot her a frank look of disgust. "All I'm saying is that there *are* things that happen in other dimensions that we Homo sapiens refuse to acknowledge simply because we don't have 'scientific data.' But I believe someday we will."

"And you are gathering data, correct?"

"I am. If I can't find the magic in Ireland, then I suppose I will have to go to my grave acquiescing to my colleagues that they were right and I was wrong. The most interesting study I've ever undertaken has been the paranormal. My appetite for it is insatiable."

"Oh, Grandma, you said the same thing when you got your Ph.D. in archaeology. Then it was philosophy, then anthropology."

"Don't forget my masters in literature, and I've got enough

hours in metaphysics that equate a Ph.D. What can I say? I'm a good student, that's all."

"Do you intend to teach this paranormal stuff at the University of Chicago?"

Aileen laughed heartily, and a tear of mirth dropped from her eye. "Could you see that? No one would give a second thought to giving me the ax, and then they would claim senility. This trip is for you and me alone. Not even your parents are to know. Especially not Mary Margaret."

"Especially not," Carin replied ruefully.

"She would just love to get something on me. Officially, I mean. She's tried too many times to turn the family against me. It's odd. She and I are contemporaries, yet we are polar opposites. Her thoughts are out of sync with the world, almost as if she were born in the wrong century."

Carin looked out the window as they passed a young girl carrying a creel of peat on her back. "Maybe she was." Carin didn't like thinking about Mary Margaret or wasting her breath discussing the one person in her life who perpetually stomped on her dreams of becoming a writer, who had spent the past five years cajoling, demanding, and intimidating Carin into joining the family business. Carin was good at her job as marketing and advertising director. Excellent, in fact. She could hold her own with the best advertising firms Chicago had to offer. But her heart was not in it.

Alone, Carin puttered with a novel she wrote in secret. Probably no one would ever read the damn thing, but at least she could someday say to herself she'd done it. Truth be known, Carin was more like her grandmother Aileen than anyone else in the family, including her mother, Caitlin.

Caitlin clung too tightly to Mary Margaret's skirts, always looking for approval, which Carin believed her mother would never find. Carin often wondered if Caitlin had always been that way. Hadn't she ever been independent, questioned everything the way Carin did? When Caitlin had been her age with her life before her, what dreams had she had? To hear her mother tell it, chocolate was her world . . . that and Clay. Was that all there was? Was it enough?

Carin found it hard to believe that romance, even with someone as wonderful as her father, could be fulfilling. She couldn't keep from thinking of her aunt Sheilagh—the mysteries, the purported scandals and fame that surrounded her. Sheilagh had left Chicago and gone out into the world and done something with her life. Even her uncle Michael had rejected the family business and gone into medicine. He was famous in Houston, pioneering heart research and exploring new surgical techniques. There were many who couldn't say "M. D. M. Anderson Hospital" without speaking Michael Killian's name, the two were so inexorably linked.

Carin wanted to be like them. She wanted to break away from the family business but not from the family itself, the way Sheilagh and Michael had been forced to do. Unfortunately, the business and the family were like two halves of a whole. She didn't want to lose the solid ground, the security of the Killian family. To do so would be risky. Carin had never been a risk taker. Yet she walked through the days of her twenty-third year feeling as if she were a hundred. She had no one to blame but herself.

"Grandma, perhaps you are right."

"I don't believe this. I am?"

"Uh-huh. You've always stretched your horizons—looked for adventure, mental and physical, no matter what your age."

"Funny, I thought that was what life was all about. I'm only seventy. Definitely not ready to give up any of my dreams," Aileen said emphatically. As if she'd read Carin's mind, she added: "And neither should you."

"I know, but what can I do?"

"That is precisely why I wanted to give you this trip. You, my dear child, are a fuddy-duddy."

"I am not!"

"Are too," Aileen bit back. "I'm hoping you can clear your mind of sales records, marketing graphs, and bottom lines. Look around you. This is the only land on earth where fairy tales persist. Only the Irish are keeping legends and myths alive. True, it is an impoverished country, with half the population moving to America and England to find jobs. But the ones who stay don't concern themselves with hustling the next sale. They are living life the way it was meant to be lived. I'm hoping you take some of that philosophy back with you."

"And you think finding ghosts will improve my outlook?"

"I think you could use a good jolt."

Carin caught the soft gleam of love and concern in Aileen's eyes. "Grandma, you are priceless."

"Precious. I am precious, dear," Aileen taunted amusingly.

The Fiat rolled down a long hill and turned toward the sea. As they drove closer to their destination, Carin could smell the salty air.

They passed thatchless cottages, long abandoned by weavers and farmers who had gone to seek their fortunes elsewhere. Sheep dotted the emerald countryside, but they were unattended, and there were clusters of dairy cows feeding on pasture grass while a lone white horse picked its way around jutting limestone boulders.

"We should see the castle soon now," Aileen said.

Carin leaned forward in the seat, scanning the countryside for a glimpse of castle battlements.

Suddenly a tall limestone tower caught a shaft of sunlight and shot it back to earth like a harbor beacon.

"There it is!" Carin squealed, and pointed to the right.

The Fiat bumped along a jutted mud road. Carin placed the flat of her palms on the roof of the car to keep from being tossed from side to side.

"And I complain about the potholes on the Eden's Expressway!" she exclaimed.

This castle was "new," only two hundred years old, Aileen explained. It was three stories high with twin forty-foot towers, complete with battlements on each end, which were purely for the sake of decor since in the eighteenth century there were no marauding Danes. Between the towers stretched a long stone structure in great disrepair. As they drove closer, Carin noted that only the first-floor windows had glass panes. The upper-floor windows were taped and covered in clear plastic to protect the interior from the elements. The two mammoth arched Gothic wooden doors had been newly sanded and repaired, but not yet refinished. Stones had crumbled along the rooflines and battlements. Two of the six chimneys were virtually unusable. To Carin the castle looked like a hollowed-out skeleton. The driveway was unpaved and probably had not been regraveled in years. An enormous cloud slipped between the sun and the earth, and shrouded the castle in gloom.

"I think you'll get your wish, Grandma. If ever there would be a haunted castle, this one is my choice!" Carin said sarcastically, then shivered as she looked at the gaping windows and black splotches on the stone walls where lichen, ivy, and mosses had once flourished.

"We aren't actually going to stay here, are we?" Carin asked as Aileen stopped the car.

Aileen opened her door and got out. "I think it's charming."

"Charming? This? Bella Lugosi wouldn't stay here."

"Nonsense," Aileen replied, and started up the steps to the front doors.

"Grandma! Come back here!"

"Don't be such a twit." Aileen waved Carin's objections aside. "Does one knock at a castle door? There's no moat, so I can't very well sound a trumpet."

Carin shrugged her shoulders and waited as Aileen lifted an iron door knocker shaped like the Irish Claddagh. Still there was no sign of life anywhere.

"I don't understand it. We *are* expected, after all," Aileen said.

"I'll go around back and see what I can find," Carin offered, and skirted the front of the castle. It was not an overly large edifice, certainly not like the châteaux in France she'd seen in the travelogues on television. This castle was no more than 120 to 140 feet long and only about 65 feet wide. She knew Chicagoans with homes larger than this.

As she rounded the northwest corner, she realized that the pink rhododendrons here and along the front of the castle were newly planted. So, too, were the shaped boxwoods and holly.

"Hello! Hello! Anybody home? Anybody to castle?" she called, smiling to herself.

Just as she came around to the back, Carin stopped dead in her tracks and gaped openmouthed at the garden before her. Never had she seen anything so beautiful, so meticulously kept and well planned. Astonishingly, nearly all of it was new. The sea pinks, yews, wild heather, and evergreens were young. Only the tall pines and broad-leaf trees bore the mark of centuries. In the center of the garden was a nonfunctioning fountain and a half-built gazebo.

Dazed by the beauty of the garden, Carin wandered closer. The stone walkways looked ancient, as if laid by the Romans a thousand years ago. However, some of the stones were new, and many areas were obviously recently installed. It was an odd juxtaposition of past and present.

Still, there were no signs of life . . . no servants, no landlords, and no gardeners.

At the end of the maze, still low enough that Carin could easily see over the top of the hedges, she spied a dilapidated Victorian-style greenhouse. The black cloud that had hung over the castle skittered across the sky. Sunlight struck the beveled-glass panes of the greenhouse, splintering the rays into shards of color. Red, purple, blue, and green lights danced like pirouetting fairies, and for a brief moment, Carin almost believed in magic.

A shadow moved inside the greenhouse.

"Hello! Is anyone there?" she called as she opened the door and entered the steamy interior. Water hung like jewels on the leaves of the newly misted plants. Her eyes were assaulted by all manner of exotic flora and fauna, hardly any of it indigenous to Ireland.

A man was bending over a bird of paradise. He glanced over his shoulder at her and then straightened. He smiled, and Carin thought that the fairy lights from outside had just danced through the door. "I'm sorry. I didn't hear you," he said in husky tones.

Carin couldn't decide which part of him she wanted to look at first, his gleaming dark brown hair, sea blue eyes, or the tight biceps under the rolled-up shirt-sleeves. He was easily six foot two inches, with broad shoulders and a narrow waist. But it was his smile, comfortable yet sensuously appealing, that kept magic in the air. She smiled back, a wan, dim thing born of trepidation. She'd never stood in the presence of an Adonis before.

He wiped his dirty hands on the dark blue apron he wore and moved closer.

"You must be . . . the gardener," Carin finally said.

"Of a sort. And you must be the Burke party. You are our first visitors. We've been expecting you, but you're early."

"I am?" Carin watched how the muscles in his arms contracted and then bulged when he lifted a potted bromeliad.

"We weren't expecting you until this evening."

"Then someone should speak to the house servants. No one answered the door."

He walked closer to her. Carin stopped breathing, fully cognizant that he was responsible for her respiratory problems. Suddenly his powerful body was within touching distance. He smiled again, and Carin was dumbstruck by an invisible force she had never experienced before. She tried to find words, but her mind and tongue failed. *No wonder the Irish believe in myths,* she thought, gazing up at him. *These people live their legends.*

He stood looking down at her for a long, embarrassing moment. She blushed. He coughed and cleared his throat. Then he moved past her to the door. As he did, a pungent scent like a wet sewer assaulted Carin's nostrils.

"Ugh! What's that smell?" she blurted out.

"Shit. Sheep shit, to be exact. Marvelous for the flowering plants. I'm an expert at humus products. How about you? Is horticulture a fancy of yours?"

The aura shattered. Carin found reality less colorful, but a more comfortable and safe terrain. "I can't say that it is. My grandmother is waiting out front. Perhaps you could have one of the staff show us to our rooms?"

"Staff?" he replied quizzically. "I think you had better know now, I am the staff." He stuck out his dirty hand, looked at the clump of sheep manure on his fingers, and withdrew it. Again he wiped his hands on his apron. "I'm Richard. I'm the butler."

Carin didn't understand. "Are you the cook, too?"

"Yes, but I promise to wash before I chop the vegetables for the stew."

"Thank God." Carin smiled at last.

"Shall we?" he asked, and bowed theatrically as he opened the door for her.

After Carin introduced Aileen to Richard, they entered an enormous vestibule floored with intricate parquet wood. Classical moldings detailed in white against pale aqua walls created an eighteenth-century decor. A wide staircase carpeted in a black, red, gold, and cream floral-patterned rug soared majestically to the second floor. In the center of the vestibule hung an Italian bronze and crystal chandelier, still not electrically wired. A crystal vase overflowing with snapdragons, roses, and daisies sat atop an English wood pedestal table.

Carin was unexpectedly delighted by the cheery interior. "What a beautiful room," she said. "When we drove up, I never dreamed it would be anything like this."

"I take that as a compliment," Richard replied. "I repainted this about two years ago, but the colors are an exact match to the original paint."

Carin scrutinized the intricate frescoed moldings and realized that Richard could easily get work at the Chicago Art Institute doing refurbishing. He was a curious man of many talents, she thought as he ushered them down a long, stone-floored hall covered with threadbare Persian runners to their room. It was a surprisingly sunny place on the south side overlooking the garden. While Richard went to gather their luggage, Carin inspected the room and bath.

The four-poster intricately carved mahogany bed was not what Carin had expected. This was a bed truly fit for a lord, and eiderdown-soft. When Carin sat down on the faded gold damask bedspread, she sank half a foot into what felt like a cloud.

Aileen took her reading glasses out of her purse to inspect a silver-backed hand mirror. "Just as I thought. Sheffield Sterling. And very old." She bent and examined the Hepplewhite writing desk, the gold gilt fauteuil chair, and the burled-oak French armoire. "Everything in this room is authentic, Carin," she exclaimed. "I can't believe these people are allowing tourists to use their family heirlooms like this."

Aileen took off her glasses, folded them, and tapped them against her temple as she mused about their surroundings.

Carin touched the delicate Chinese famille verte vase on the rosewood nightstand. "I thought your friend told you all about this place."

"She's never been here. She only heard of it through a relative who lives in Ennistymon."

"So does that mean you want to leave?" Carin asked apprehensively, thinking of Richard again and wondering what he looked like without the sheep shit.

"Heavens no! I'm all the more intrigued. Well, my dear, you asked for an adventure, and I think we found it. I can't wait to learn the history of this castle."

"Oh, me, too." Carin sighed, scrunching a down pillow under her neck and conjuring a vision of Richard naked . . . bathing off the dirt and sweat. She imagined the water droplets running down his shoulders to his chest, then to his abdomen . . . She closed her eyes and let herself drift off to sleep, hoping to perpetuate her fantasy in her dreams.

Half an hour later, Carin, now rested, found their luggage deposited outside their door. There was no sign of Richard. She was surprised at how much she had wanted to see him again. *What is the matter with me?* she thought. She'd never reacted this strongly to a man before, at least not in the first five minutes of meeting him. Her thoughts and emotions had suddenly taken on a life of their own. She'd always prided herself on self-control, but now it was as if she'd taken every bit of it and chucked it out the window.

As she hauled their suitcases into the room and deposited them on the luggage rack, Aileen watched her granddaughter.

"He wasn't there, was he?"

"Who?" Carin replied blithely, glancing up into Aileen's knowing eyes. "Oh, you mean Richard?" She opened her American Tourister train case. "Why would you think I was looking for him?"

Aileen rolled her eyes. "I'm a mind reader," she joked. "Of course, it has nothing to do with the fact that as soon as you heard the thud of our luggage outside the door, you awoke from a sound sleep and sprinted to the door. Too bad you couldn't move that fast for your high school track team, dear." Aileen chuckled as Carin snatched her shampoo, Ban roll-on, and Lady Gillette from the case.

"I'm taking a bath," Carin announced, and strode to the bathroom.

"Make it a cold one, dear," Aileen teased.

Carin took a quick bath in a turn-of-the-century claw-footed porcelain tub. The water heater did not work well, and she was never able to bring the water temperature above lukewarm. She lathered quickly with a lavender-perfumed soap she'd bought in Dublin since the travel agent had suggested they provide their own soap and washcloths, which few of the Irish inns dispensed. She dried off with a thin Irish linen towel monogrammed in gold threads with an ornate *B*. Again, Carin found herself dreaming about Richard. She wondered where he would be sleeping tonight. Were there servants' quarters on the other side of the castle? Or would he be sleeping in a room near hers? Most important, how could she find out without sounding indiscreet?

At three-thirty there was a sharp knock on the door. Carin answered it.

Richard stood there, bathed, shampooed, and smelling of a spicy soap. He was dressed in a pair of jeans. No bell-bottoms, thank God, she thought. He wore a white shirt and a long white cardigan sweater with shawl collar and leather buttons. His smile was twice as bewitching.

"I've come to take you to tea," he announced.

"How lovely," Carin uttered.

His eyes twinkled as they drew her into them. "Indeed."

Carin was lost in that netherland between his sexy Irish brogue and the deeper intent of his words. She found she wasn't breathing again. Lord, how she hated the power he had over her. Keep cool, she told herself. "The tea, I mean . . ."

Carin stammered. "Come, Grandma."

Aileen hadn't missed a single one of the sensual sparks flying between the two. She followed Richard and her granddaughter down the hallway. Richard pointed out a framed tapestry, an eighteenth-century bronze candelabra, a family portrait, a Tudor chest. As he spoke, Aileen noted the calm assurance in his voice and the aplomb with which he described the intricacies of the castle. He moved with a natural grace that told Aileen this was no mere gardener.

"Since the castle is undergoing renovation, the upper floors are off limits," he explained. "In fact, only half the main floor is usable."

He ushered them into a pretty octagonal room lined halfway around with a banquette. Brightly colored cushions were propped along the wall, and when Carin sat down, she realized that the bottom cushions were merely down-filled bed pillows wrapped in linen sheets. The table had an interesting wrought-iron base fashioned in the shape of an angel. The workmanship was excellent and probably commanded a small fortune. The tabletop was only inexpensive glass, however. The windows were green, pink, blue, and yellow stained glass in a Victorian motif. Obviously this alcove had been an addition to the original structure. Huge baskets of ivy hung in the corners of the room. Half the pots were cracked crockery. This was the oddest castle, Carin thought.

Richard had exited the room, and when he returned, he was pushing a wooden tea cart that bore an exquisite Russian samovar, Limoges cups and saucers, and milk, lemon, and honey in Waterford containers. Scones, cookies, and watercress sandwiches were stacked on a sterling silver epergne.

Richard served the tea, handing each of them an Irish linen damask napkin. All of which seemed very proper to Carin until he sat down next to Aileen and filled a plate for himself. Carin had never experienced an occasion when staff and tourists ate together.

"Don't you need to see to your other guests?" Carin inquired with a hint of criticism.

Richard ignored the reproof. "There are no other guests. It's just us."

Carin was confused. "But you are expecting others."

"No."

"How do you expect to run a hostelry with no staff and no guests?"

His lips twitched. "Are you questioning my management skills, Miss Burke?"

"I didn't mean to imply . . . that is, well, it's really none of my business . . ."

"No, it isn't," he retorted. He took a deep breath, leaned back in the banquet, and relaxed a bit. "You Americans are a curious lot, aren't you?"

Carin fidgeted under the well-deserved censure. She *was* curious. She wanted to know everything about him, and now he knew it. That was dangerous.

Suddenly Aileen began laughing. "You will have to forgive my granddaughter's obtuseness, Lord Butler."

Carin's eyes popped wide open. "Lord?" Her eyes darted to Richard. "You're not the gardener?"

"Yes, I told you, and the Butler."

Carin's cheeks flamed scarlet. "I apologize. I must have sounded like a snob."

"You did." He laughed heartily with Aileen. "But you are forgiven. In fact, I quite enjoyed playing the charade with you. Please forgive me."

Carin smiled warmly at him. "We're even, then."

"I hope so." His response rolled sensuously off his lips. His eyes locked onto Carin's face for an inordinately long pause before he began again. "So you want to know all about Butler Castle," he said, glancing briefly at Aileen and then back at Carin.

"The castle was built by my ancestor, Patrick Butler, in the late seventeen hundreds when he won the land and the title for a favor he had performed for King George. I would love to tell you that it was an illustrious deed, but it wasn't. My ancestor was a botanist, as was Lord Bute, who introduced botany to King George. My understanding is that they were fast and hearty friends, though not politically aligned, off and on over the years before King George went completely crackers in the end.

"Anyway, Patrick had produced many hybrid roses and various strains of hay, grasses, and barley that were heartier than those of the time. Patrick lived on this land as a cottager of sorts and refused to leave it and move to England to study at the Royal Observatory. The politics of that time are confusing even to me. However, the Butlers were Catholic, and all lands had been confiscated from the Catholics by the Protestants. Thus by 1776, only five percent of lands remained in the hands of Catholics. George not only let my ancestor remain in Ireland, but gave him the land on which he lived. For a long time it made a bit of bad blood with the neighbors, I can tell you that.

"Time passed, and he must have been a good egg, because he seemed to be well liked. No one tried to overthrow him or oust him off the property. His hybrids brought English trading dollars into the country, and naturally the impoverished Catholics of the area did enjoy that. He built the castle, and when he died, he handed down a tidy sum of money and, of course, the title. The estate was self-supporting for nearly a hundred years, but then the farmers and cottagers began leaving. No one could blame them really."

Still lost in his thoughts, he continued. "My parents never lived in the castle. It was too run-down by then. We lived in the white cottage over to the east. There," he said, pointing out the window. "When I was young I used to wonder what it must have been like to live here then. The parties, the visits from English dignitaries and royalty. It was Patrick Butler who drew up the plans for the garden. It's always been my dream to restore them. I've nearly done it, too. But the castle—well, that is a different matter. It takes a great deal of money for even minimal repairs. That's why I came up with the idea of opening it to tourists."

Carin watched as disappointment settled onto his face. He seemed lost in the past when he spoke of his ancestor, with whom he obviously felt a deep affinity. Both Patrick and Richard were horticulturists, and both seemed tied to this castle.

"It's going to take a lot of tourists to help you rebuild," Carin said kindly.

Richard drained the last of his tea. "I know. But I have to start somewhere."

Aileen refilled their cups this time before regarding Richard thoughtfully. "Tell me, Lord Butler, you don't impress me as being a country squire. You were born and educated in the city."

"How did you guess?"

"Your knowledge of the world is clearly more cosmopolitan than country. Not to mention that what you have accomplished here would be impossible without money from an outside source."

"Good God! A mind reader!" he exclaimed.

"I'm right?"

"Yes. I studied financing and a bit of marketing in London. I worked for an investment house for three years after college, saved my salary, invested it, and then four years ago I moved back here."

Carin was clearly awed. "You didn't give up your dreams, did you?"

"I'd rather die."

Carin envied him . . . admired him. He'd done what she was afraid to do. She wanted to remember this day and all that Richard had said. He had found it necessary to subordinate his dreams for a time, to earn enough money to put them in motion. Maybe that was all she was doing now. Was her own subconscious leading her more than she knew? She prayed she had the kind of courage Richard possessed, so that when the time came for her to take a stand, she would be equal to the challenge.

As the late afternoon sun dimmed, the room became washed in the diffuse colors of the stained-glass windows. A wistful mood settled over the trio as all three imagined what twilight must have been like when the castle was in its glory two hundred years ago.

Carin glanced up from her teacup to find Richard's blue eyes studying her. A sudden jolt like electricity shot through her body. Later, Carin would claim she felt a physical connection being made. It was as if some phantom of fate had pulled the switch that controlled the path of her life. Something had changed, though she didn't know what. She was to journey into a new realm. The old Carin would have been afraid. But this new one was not.

Then, just as suddenly, Carin realized that her grandmother had been right about Ireland. It was a land of magic.

Chapter 4 —————————————

$\mathcal{L}$ORD RICHARD BUTLER slept in a sleeping bag in the castle library. There was a low-burning fire in the grate to keep him warm, since early June nights were notorious for producing chills in drafty castles. He rolled onto his left side and awoke for the fifth time that night. He punched the pillow and rearranged it under his head, hoping to eliminate the crick he'd developed. He closed his eyes and opened them again. He gazed into the tiny flickering flames and once more found himself thinking of Carin.

She was beautiful. Too beautiful. She was the kind of woman who could tie a man in knots. Richard had known her now for less than twelve hours, and already he had to struggle to think of other things. He had already made lists in his head of all the tasks he must accomplish tomorrow before taking his guests on a tour of County Clare. New spark plugs for the Land-Rover, groceries at Collins' Store in Ennistymon, a postal stop to get his mail, then next door to the tobacco shop for a pack of Boston cigarettes and a copy of the *Irish Times*, which kept him well informed of world events.

"And everywhere I go, I will take Carin with me," he said to himself with a smile.

His mind was filled with the soft timbre of Carin's voice, with the intoxicating glow in her eyes and the smooth texture of her skin. When they'd sat to tea—hell, when he first saw her in the greenhouse—he thought he was looking into the face of an angel, and he'd wanted to touch her then. But he'd been afraid she would vanish. His luck must be turning, because she was real. The more he got to know her, the more he liked her. She wasn't coy; she didn't pretend to be brainless the way some London girls did. Nor was she like the country girls, friendly but lacking a broader knowledge of the world. He was a country squire, but he still liked city women. Carin was the first woman in years who reminded him of London, of the city, of what he missed.

Of what he would never miss again.

At twenty-nine, Richard thought he had known every kind of woman during his years at university and then in London. He had dated artists from Chelsea, prim governesses and school-teachers, a topless dancer who liked wearing her hot pants and white "slicker" knee-high boots to bed, two Twiggy look-alikes, an actress, a pediatrician, and a horse trainer. Richard was often accused by his chums of being a Lothario. Women were meant for fun. He'd never thought of them as being anything other than sport. In the back of his mind he'd assumed someday he would marry, when he was close to fifty, but only because he would be going through some kind of middle-age panic and finally feel the need to reproduce. The idea of a woman fulfilling any role other than occasional bed partner and the mother of his child seemed unlikely to Richard.

During his London heyday, when the Beatles reigned and he was frequently mistaken for Sean Connery, Richard had had any woman he wanted. He took them to funky pubs where they would listen to the newest sounds coming out of the marijuana-smoking rock groups. Richard had lived in a swanky flat and decorated it in modern earth tones with the big bonus he earned in 1966. He drove a bottle green Jaguar, purchased with the 1967 bonus. He considered himself a man about town. He was too busy working, cutting deals, and trying to get laid at night to understand that his life was as shallow as a cardboard cutout.

One April afternoon while strolling down King's Road watching miniskirted girls watch him, he bumped into an old Irishman and knocked him down.

"Hey! Open those eyes, will ye?" the old man snarled at him while struggling to get up.

"I'm terribly sorry," Richard apologized, and offered his hand to the old man. "I hope you aren't hurt."

"Would it matter to ye if I was?" the old man grumbled.

"Of course it would. I certainly did not run into you purposefully. It was just that I was . . ."

"Lookin' at the girls, eh?" The old man winked, and his wrinkled face stretched into a smile. "I used ta do a lot of that meself, I did."

"And now?"

The old man brushed off his tweed coat and glanced at the blonde coming toward them. She was wearing a black and white houndstooth-check miniskirt, white blouse, and black man's tie. Her straight hair, which hung nearly to her waist, swung back and forth as she walked. Her eyes were rimmed in black kohl and heavy with false eyelashes. Her narrow lips parted over gleaming white teeth as she bestowed a friendly smile on Richard.

The old man watched her pass, bending around Richard to catch the very last glimpse. "Now? I still watch, but it's a waste of time, since I don't intend to use one anymore."

Richard was curious about the man and his cryptic comment. "Use? What do you use a woman for?"

The old man bent his head around and looked up at Richard. There was a curious, unsteady gleam in his eyes. Richard was mesmerized by those eyes and the man's low, quiet voice. "I use them for nothing. Just as you do. Not for love, not for marriage, not for treasuring as they should be."

"How . . . how . . . do you know what I do?"

"I was young once. Now I've wasted that, too."

Richard was spellbound by the man and suddenly understood exactly what he was implying. It was as if the world, or his world, had stopped spinning on its axis and for a moment out of time something strange and marvelous had happened. Richard stood aside and examined his life. He realized it was empty.

He had no real male friends. The guys at work were conciliatory toward one another, but every last one of them would slit his mother's throat to keep his job. Richard had to admit that half his time was spent watching his back. He was only as good as his last deal. The big coup was the one coming up, and once he landed a big account, the accolades lasted five minutes, he spent the bonus checks in less time than that, and was again faced with the challenge of making an even bigger and better deal for the next client. Filling the coffers of Throckmorton, Kent and Wells was like trying to plug up a cosmic black hole. Impossible. They were never satisfied.

Richard had bought the whole package. He thought he was cosmopolitan. He wanted to be rich, free, and unfettered from the lands and responsibilities that had killed his mother and caused his father to have a heart attack last month. He had fallen for the Hollywood scenario of life. If he were to meet himself on the street, would he stop and think that he, too, had just met James Bond? He dined with American clients at the best restaurants in London, attended the theater, ballet, and opera—none of which he liked—just to keep a client "on line." He played golf and tennis and let his clients win. Nothing about his life was real. He'd been living among cardboard props. That day, he knocked them down and started living.

"I've got to be goin' now," the old man said, and walked away.

Still in a daze, Richard spun around to call after the man, but he'd completely disappeared. He checked in several of the shops, a café, and down to the end of the block and back. He raced in the opposite direction and then crossed the street. He quickly scanned all the taxis and buses. He did not find him. There was no crowd for the old man to lose himself in, since the noon hour was over and the crowd had thinned. The old man had simply vanished into thin air.

For nearly four years, Richard had not thought about the strange old man and how much his own life had changed since that day. Instead, he'd pretended to himself that the old man had never existed and that his life had taken a new turn the following week when his father died. The funeral arrangements, legalities, and wake were exhausting, but more exhausting was the thought that he was alone, truly alone. He had no brothers, no sisters, and his mother had been dead for years. He hadn't expected his father to die so soon—someday but not now. "Someday" was supposed to be in the future, the distant future, a concept that bestowed a false immortality on Richard's world. Suddenly he found himself with a run-down castle that his father had done little to maintain. He knew his father would not care if he simply let the castle deteriorate and lived in London. But Richard cared.

It had been a very long time since Richard had genuinely cared about anything.

Four years of backbreaking work had not deterred him from his dream of returning Butler Castle to its former glory. Each day as he tended his plants and reconstructed the fabulous gardens, he wondered if Patrick Butler was looking down on him in approval.

Richard's dream was a big one, a financial killer. To restore the castle would take four times the original cost. Even in his heyday years in London, Richard had come nowhere near that kind of money. For months he kicked around the idea of moving back to London, back to Throckmorton, Kent and Wells. They would welcome him back. After all, he had been the largest producer in their employ.

Richard was filled with doubts. Could he really do it again? Did he have that killer instinct or had he mellowed over the years? He liked country life with no traffic, no telephones, but his idea of opening the castle to tourists was a bad one. He couldn't afford any staff, except for Lidia, who came in the mornings to prepare meals for the day. He couldn't afford to pay for advertising—he couldn't even afford a telephone. Richard feared that his days as a hostelryman would be short-lived.

The day was approaching when he would have to leave his castle and postpone his dream.

"I have to go back," he told himself. "Nothing is more important than my castle."

He rolled onto his side and looked at the flames one last time before closing his eyes. A vision of Carin's face loomed in front of him. He wondered what it would be like to lie next to her and hold her. His hands ached to touch her cheek, her breasts, her hips, her . . .

"Stop it, old man, or you'll drive yourself crackers," he said with a chuckle. Then his laughter died with the last of the flames. Just as he fell asleep, he thought, Too bad you aren't a rich American heiress, Carin Burke. Then I could marry you, spend your money on my castle, and we'd live happily ever after.

Chapter 5

THE FOLLOWING MORNING Carin entered the breakfast alcove and her heart sank to her stomach. Standing at the table was a lovely Irish girl. It was not her long chestnut hair or porcelain-perfect skin that Carin noticed. It was the fact that the girl was pregnant.

He's married, she thought. *Fool, fool Carin. You're smarter than this.*

The girl was smiling at her as she stopped setting silver on the table.

"You must be Miss Burke," she said sweetly, her rosy cheeks glowing. "I'm Lidia. I do the cooking."

"I'm Carin. My grandmother will be along any minute." Carin held out her hand and shook Lidia's. "I'm very happy to know you." As Carin sat down, a dozen questions assailed her: How long have you been married? When is the baby due? Does your husband often go around making sensual overtures to your guests? Do you know your husband and I cavorted naked in my dreams last night? There were a dozen other questions Carin could have asked. Instead, she returned Lidia's smile and said: "What's for breakfast?"

"I brough' a rasher of bacon. Eggs, cottage pie, marmalade to go with the bread I baked this mornin'. Ye tike yer coffee white or black?"

"Black."

"An' yer granmither?"

"Black, also."

"We eat our meals here the Irish way. Sometimes it's too much fer the Americans at breakfas'. Too much fer lunch, always at two o'clock, and not enough for yer high tea . . . sorry, dinner. No supper, though."

"I'm sure it's all wonderful," Carin replied cordially, hoping Lidia did not suspect her designs on her husband. Carin wanted to sink underneath the banquet and quickly plan an end to their stay at Butler Castle.

"I be gettin' yer coffee. Lord Butler should be in shortly to join ye. He always sees to th' plants in the mornin' and then he helps me fill the larder with the supplies I bring in."

This time she would not be caught off guard, Carin determined. "Will you be joining us also?"

Lidia blushed and giggled. "Thank ye fer askin', but the help never eats with his lordship or guests."

Confused, Carin glanced at the table, set only for three, then to Lidia's stomach. What a brute this guy was . . . letting his pregnant wife do all the work while he made idle conversation. And forcing her to refer to him as her "lordship." Carin had a good mind to educate this girl on the new women's lib movement. "Lidia, may I ask you something?"

"O' coerce."

"Lord Butler told me that he did the cooking. Obviously that's not so."

Lidia laughed, a bright, tinkling sound, and passed her hands over her swollen abdomen. "He's had to help me lately. He doesn't like it none, though, I will tell ye. And wi' guests, he has much to do. We manage, though."

Just then Aileen entered the room dressed in the new wool tweed skirt and jacket she had purchased in Dublin. "Good morning, all," she said brightly. "Good morning, Lidia."

"Mornin', ma'am," Lidia replied gaily.

Carin was stunned. "How did you know about Lidia before I did?"

"Child, you sleep too late. I've already been on a tour of the gardens with Richard and met Lidia as she was coming from the cottage."

"What cottage?"

"The one Richard grew up in, of course." Aileen picked up a piece of wheat bread and buttered it. "That's where they live."

"Who lives?"

Aileen took a bite of the bread and purposefully prolonged Carin's agony. It was all she could do to keep a straight face. "Lidia and her husband. Charming place. Like a doll's house. You should see what Lidia can do with Irish lace. She has these curtains in the—"

Carin thought her nerves would snap. "You mean Richard."

Lidia burst into laughter and held her stomach as peals of mirth echoed down the castle hall. "Ye can't be thinkin' that his lordship and I . . ." She looked down at Carin's grave face. "Oh, no! But you do!" Lidia laughed again.

Carin knew her cheeks must have already gone from scarlet to purple. She glared at her grandmother. "He's not married then."

"No, dear," Aileen admitted. "Lidia is married to Ian. Richard, it seems, is nearly a confirmed bachelor. The worst kind."

"Why do you say that?"

Aileen clucked her tongue and picked up another piece of bread. "Most of them—not all, mind you, but most—think they haven't missed anything. Truth is, that's what life is all about."

Carin groaned. "Grandmother, now you sound like Mary Margaret. Marriage isn't the end all and be all."

"Not for some, that's true. But I believe we come to this earth to love. Relationships with other people are important. A good marriage is a wonderful way to walk through this life. If you were really truthful with yourself, Carin, you would admit that you agree with me. Most of your girlfriends are already married and having their first babies, just like Lidia here."

"I'm a career woman," Carin said, all too aware that she was the only one in her group who had graduated without a huge diamond on her left hand. Within three months of graduation, she'd been a bridesmaid for eleven of her best friends. Now they were all pregnant or trying to get pregnant. Baby-boom babies creating another baby boom. It wasn't that Carin didn't have dates; it was that she was bored by the male friends of her girlfriends' husbands. They were into football; she was into new sales promotions. If they liked Strawberry Alarm Clock, she liked Johnny Mathis. If they hung out at Mr. Kelly's, she wanted to go to the Pump Room. She was always out of sync. Carin never told anyone, not her mother, her grandmother, or her best friend, that she wanted it that way. Carin was scared to death of falling in love. It was her secret.

She looked up at Lidia, whose eyes shone with a disturbing pity.

"I'll be gettin' that coffee fer ye," Lidia said in nearly inaudible tones.

From the back of the house, a door slammed, and the sound of boots against stone echoed down the long hall.

Richard was back, Carin thought, and immediately sat up straighter. A light flashed in her eyes, her lips jumped into a smile. When he walked into the room, he seemed even taller, his shoulders wider and his face more handsome than yesterday. Carin felt light-headed just looking at him.

"Good morning. How rested you both look today," he said cheerily, and plopped down on the banquet. "Today I'm all yours."

I couldn't be that lucky, Carin thought.

"What would you like to do?"

"What *can* we do?" Visions of Richard holding her in his arms filled Carin's mind.

"I have only a few errands, but after that, perhaps you might like to try your luck at some angling. Say, brown trout fishing. The fjords are beautiful this time of year."

"But it's raining," Carin countered.

"Misting," Richard corrected. "It can rain fourteen different times a day in Ireland."

Aileen immediately perked up. "You two go right ahead. Lidia and I have already planned our day. She's going to tell me all about your ghost, Richard."

"Oh, no. You didn't fall for that old tale, did you?"

Aileen was crushed. "The ghost is the reason I came here. Among other things," she added quickly. "Are you saying there is no ghost?"

"Not that I've ever seen." He grinned at her. "But it can make for a delightful time pursuing one, I suppose."

Aileen nodded. "I thought it would be a lovely prelude to our witches' banquet tonight."

Carin gasped. "Our what?"

Richard touched Aileen's hand, signaling he would do the explaining. "It will be a rousing good time. There are no real witches, Miss Burke, just a reenactment of medieval times. Anyway, that's tonight. I have other festivities planned for your stay, things that other tourists wouldn't ordinarily do."

Aileen clapped her hands together in glee. "I do like you, Lord Butler."

"Do you think you could call me Richard? Lord Butler is so formal."

"Absolutely not. I've never known a real lord and I rather enjoy it, if it doesn't bother you too much."

"Anything to please my guest," he said, and bent to kiss her hand before turning to Carin. "Then it's just the two of us off for the trout."

"Fine," Carin said, secretly elated.

They drove southwest along the rocky west cliffs of Ireland to Richard's favorite fishing place. Here, he told her, they would not be interrupted by other fishermen or tourists. She noticed that he kept his conversation on the particulars of the trip, as if she were a tourist and he the guide. For brown trout fishing she needed no fishing license, and no fee was charged. There were so many beautiful and secluded lakes and waterways to choose from, but most of them in the West were not as frequently visited. He had already packed all the fly-fishing gear they would need. Rods, automatic fly reels, hooks, sinkers, floats, wet flies and dry flies, filled the back of the Land-Rover.

A muted rain continued to fall softly around the rocky lake inlet as Richard stopped the car. Carin picked her way across the huge boulders, sliding on wet moss and losing her footing. Richard followed behind her carrying the gear.

"This is good," he said, coming to the edge of the lake.

Carin scanned the bleak landscape and saw only a single thatched, whitewashed cottage in the distance. Dazzling emerald lichen crept over the rocks. Wildflowers dotted the grassier areas in fascinating clumps, as if nature had commissioned its most seasoned designer to the job. Carin stuck her hand in the crystal-clear water and found it icy cold.

"You'll need these," Richard said from behind her as he held up a hideous rubber contraption.

"What is *that*?"

"Waders, love. These are a bit shorter than mine. Here, I'll help you into them."

Richard held them out and bent down for Carin to step into the ugly brown rubber. There were golashes that he placed on her feet and then carefully buckled to stay watertight. Carin nearly lost her balance again on the slippery rocks.

"Hold on to me," he said, taking her hand and putting it on his shoulder while he finished with the buckles.

Carin liked the feel of him. His shoulders were massive beneath the flannel shirt and wool sweater he wore. She let her fingers grip the hard muscle, and when he stood again, she indulged herself by allowing her hand to slide down his arm. She held his hand a bit too long, she knew, but she couldn't help herself. She tried to think of something to say but could only look into his eyes.

Confusion wrinkled his forehead, though his eyes lingered a heartbeat too long on her lips. He squeezed her hand, and Carin felt a jolt of electricity shoot through her body. She was shocked to discover that she wanted to kiss him, needed to kiss him. But how could she actually do it?

Richard did not let go of her hand as he bent down and picked up two hats, placed one on her head and the other on his own. "You look quite fetching," he said huskily, tipping the brim of her hat back and gazing into her eyes once again.

Carin glanced down at the waders and golashes, and began laughing. "I look like a clown!"

"Ah, true, but a dry one," he teased.

Richard grabbed a rod and pulled her into the water. "You've never fly-casted before, have you?"

"How'd you guess?"

"I've a trained eye for this work." He carefully positioned her so that her stance was steady. Then he stood behind her and began her instruction.

Each time he pulled her arm back to demonstrate the proper flick that she must give the rod to produce the exact trajectory for the line and fly, Carin's mind was spinning its own lines. She liked the feel of his hard chest against her back, his arms around her, and the closeness of their faces. She tried to tell herself that she was just lust-crazed. Chemicals, enzymes, hormones. That's all this was. It couldn't possibly be the man himself who was exciting her. She hadn't known him long enough.

A crush. That's all it was. A summer crush. He was humoring her because she was the paying guest. Maybe he did this with all the women who came to Butler Castle. *No, Carin,* she told herself. *You're the first to visit the castle.* Maybe he was just practicing on her. In the months to come there would be lots of tourists, wouldn't there? *Not on this side of Ireland,* her logic echoed loudly. This was the sparsely inhabited side of the country. It was along this western fringe, in the Gaelic-speaking area, that the old Irish folkways were observed. It was precisely for this reason that Aileen had insisted they come here. This was Ireland at its most primitive and most romantic.

As Richard's cheek brushed Carin's again, chills swept across her skin like a winter fog. *This land is bewitched,* she thought, *and I've already been caught in this spell.* His warm breath invaded her ear. She barely remembered what he said, but she could feel his words as if they had a life of their own. She wanted to remember the particular inflections and intonations. Then during the nights when she slept alone, she could call up his words from her memory and pretend that Richard was with her again.

"I love to come here, Carin. Not so much for the fishing as for the thinking." He had not removed his arms. His face was even closer. "Sometimes I think that I can hear my mother's voice talking to me, consoling me. Maybe there are ghosts, as your grandmother thinks. I don't know."

"What does she say to you?" Carin asked, turning her head slightly to glance at him. His gaze was cast out upon the lake. It was almost as if she weren't there. He was talking to himself. Disappointment sat on the edge of her heart.

"She tells me that I'm not alone."

"Do you . . . feel alone, Richard?"

"Most of the time, no. I have friends in the area, and I'm usually so tired from working all day, I don't have much time to think about it. But sometimes I walk around my castle and the only footsteps I hear are mine. I look at all I have done and the gargantuan task that lies before me and I think, What's it all for? Who really cares about this old castle except me? But I swear to you, Carin, I never realized how alone I was until I came here with you."

Slowly he turned his head, and his lips nearly met hers.

"I'm sorry I make you feel bad," Carin whispered over the lump in her throat. Of all the things she had hoped he would say, this was not it. Was he dreaming of some other girl? Was he secretly in love with Lidia? She felt a tear creep into her eye and burn like acid. She didn't want him to know that already he had become important to her. She wanted to play this love game by the rules, but she was a newcomer. She had not studied the program.

"It's not you," he said, and lifted his hand to touch her cheek. "It's *because* of you."

"It is?"

"I want to thank you for coming here, for choosing my castle. I hardly know you, but you've helped me see things clearly that for a very long time were confused."

"Glad to be of assistance," she replied, letting her gaze dwell on his sensual mouth. Her thoughts wrestled inside her brain. Should she make the first move? Should she take a chance? Could she live with the embarrassment and the rejection if he didn't respond the way she wanted?

And then she knew. The risk was much too great.

"How . . . how did you say I should hold my wrist?"

There was no sign of disappointment in his eyes at her change of subject. Carin thought her banging heart would explode with humiliation when he casually continued his instruction.

"Like this," he said, and cast out the rod. Within seconds the line dipped as a fat brown trout met his doom.

Richard reeled in the fish, took it off the hook, and placed it in the rattan basket he wore on his belt.

"Success!" he exclaimed. "I think you've hooked the biggest one in the whole lake."

"Oh, I doubt that, Richard," she replied, hoping he could not hear the baleful sound in her voice.

Richard was so enthusiastic about Carin's fishing abilities that he pressed her to cast again and again. By one o'clock they had not only filled the wicker basket but had also strung another two dozen trout on a line. To Carin's delight, she found she actually liked this sport. The rain mist had continued on through the afternoon, making the open land seem closer and cozier, muffling the sounds of the birds and the lapping lake.

For long periods they fished in silence, lost in private thoughts. For Carin the mindlessness of the perpetual casting and spinning brought a myriad of reflections. She thought mostly about the book she'd started writing over a year ago. Suddenly she knew precisely how she should restructure it, how to infuse it with emotions that heretofore had evaded her. Her creative energies were coming to life for the first time.

The one thing that she had observed about Richard was that he never pried into her life. At first she took his lack of curiosity as an insult. She had wanted to know *everything* about him. Didn't he want to know about her? But then she remembered how tight-lipped her own Irish family was, and surmised that the native Irish were probably more so. This time she decided to take a risk.

"I'm going to be a writer someday," she announced.

"What are you waiting for?" Richard replied as he cast out his line again. The fly floated on the water.

"I haven't had the time," Carin replied. "My job is so demanding . . ."

"Keeps you from accomplishing everything you want." He nodded. "I know that feeling, Carin."

"You do?"

"Yes. I used to be like that. Then I realized I could spend my life cutting deals or fulfilling dreams."

"And you decided to rebuild your castle."

He came to stand beside her. "I'm a dreamer. That means I can think with my brain and my heart." He grabbed her hand and held it over his heart. She could feel heat, rhythm, life. "My heart is thinking. Do you feel it?"

"Y–Yes . . ."

Suddenly he put his hand over her heart, resting it on the upper swell of her breast. "Yours is the same. Only you are young. You haven't used yours as much. I want you to use your heart, Carin. Let it out of its cage. Dream as big as you want. I have."

"I'm afraid."

"I know. You jump like a jackrabbit when I come near you. Why?" He was squeezing her hand very tightly. His heart pounded like a jackhammer.

"I don't know."

"I do . . ."

Suddenly he switched her hand from his chest to hers. She ached for the loss of his touch. "You see? Now your heart is beating like mine. It's nearly the same. It's because you have come here and seen a dream being built, isn't it?" His words were demanding, insistent.

"Yes."

"Tell me why you don't want to find your heart."

"I can't . . . It's impossible."

"Nothing is impossible."

"For me it is. I have obligations . . . responsibilities to my family."

"Like what?"

"My family owns a business, and I have to help."

"What kind of family would force you to live for them?"

Carin hung her head. How was he able to hold up this frightening, glaringly brilliant mirror to her so easily, so quickly? "You just don't know . . . The Killians have a way about them. My grandparents can be very intimidating."

"Killian? I thought your name was Burke."

"It is. My mother's parents own Emerald Chocolates. I work for them."

Richard stood back a step. Surprise widened his eyes. "Not *the* Emerald Chocolates? Why, they're stocked all over London and Paris and Munich."

"And Rome and most of Spain and even Japan now."

"Everywhere except Ireland."

"We'll get here, too. The rest of the British Isles are on this year's agenda. We just haven't found a regional distribution director yet, is all."

"I'm sorry, Carin. I didn't know." He took a step closer, put his hand under her chin, and lifted her face to his. "But it doesn't have to be that way for you. You can still dream. You'll make it someday, just like you said."

"Oh, Richard. Do you really believe that?"

"I do. And so should you." When he smiled she thought the sun had finally broken through the rain. "I'm very glad you came to Ireland, Carin."

"So am I, Richard. So am I."

Chapter 6 ────────────────

*T*HE WITCHES CAME in disguise to weave their spell. They first appeared as an ordinary laundress who had pressed and steamed two velvet gowns for Carin and Aileen to wear to the banquet. The sea blue French court gown was for Carin. Though in excellent condition, it was an antique. It was trimmed in silver and gold braid around the low-cut bodice and the edges of the elbow-length flared sleeves. Underneath the sleeves were three rows of ruffled white alençon lace. The panniers were fashioned of whalebone and bastiste fabric and formed the expansion on either side of her hips, while two slips of intricate white lace peeked out from beneath the hem. Aileen's gown was a similar creation in an autumn bronze color with cream-colored lace petticoats and ruffles.

The second witch appeared as an ordinary postman on a bicycle who delivered a brown-paper-wrapped parcel containing an imitation sapphire and diamond necklace and earrings. Lidia explained that they were borrowed from a friend of hers in Galway.

The third witch appeared as Ian, Lidia's husband, who assembled a jumble of friends to play ancient Celtic "airs" on the bagpipe, flute, harp, and lute.

Carin nearly felt as if she were under a witch's spell that transported her back in time as she dressed in the two-hundred-year-old gown and walked through the castle halls on her way to the banquet room.

The banquet hall of Butler Castle had been locked for nearly thirty years before Richard turned the key in the door and set about cleaning, waxing, and restoring the parquet floors and dark-paneled walls. A banquet table to seat thirty was surrounded with high-backed chairs covered in crimson brocade. The dark wood table gleamed with antique Limoges china arranged on shiny brass charger plates, Waterford crystal, and sterling silver. Obviously they were not the only guests invited for dinner, nor was this to be a simple gathering.

Carin looked overhead and realized that the bronze chandeliers held beeswax candles, as did the wall sconces. A log fire roared in the huge hearth on the far wall. Over the carved mantel strewn with summer flowers hung an enormous tapestry depicting hunters, dogs, deer, and men and women in eighteenth-century attire and illuminated by tall candelabra. A long hunters' table held candle-warmed chafing dishes. There was not an electric light or appliance in the room.

At the far end the musicians were tuning their instruments. She smiled as they continued to play. The music was foreign to ears that had been exposed to little more than the Top 40 on WLS radio and movie musicals all her life, but Carin loved it. Eerily, it sounded familiar to her as she approached them, suddenly beguiled by the tinkling sounds and mournful plucking harp cadences. The music bore Carin's senses back into time as if she were indeed *there*.

Everything around her was of another dimension, the sights, sounds, and smells, so that when she turned around and saw Richard standing in the doorway, she dropped to her knee in a formal curtsy.

He looked every inch the lord of the manor dressed in Patrick Butler's deep blue velvet knickers, white stockings, gold brocade vest, waistcoat, and blue velvet jacket. His shirt was snowy white linen with a lace-edged ascot around the neck, and lace cuffs. But it was the awe in his eyes when he looked at Carin that stunned her. He crossed the floor in long, purposeful strides, as if they had been parted for weeks. He took her hands in his and pulled her to her feet.

"I knew you would be this beautiful," he said, and impulsively kissed her on the cheek.

Carin had never known that a mannerly, formal kiss could be so thrilling. No wonder the people had clung to their traditions so tightly. Perhaps there was something to be said for pomp . . . and romance.

"Thank you for the beautiful gown. I feel like Cinderella. Where did it come from?"

"It belonged to Patrick Butler's wife, Mavreen. I'm afraid you put her to shame." His gaze lingered on her face before he turned to Aileen. He took her hand and kissed it. "And you are ravishing."

Aileen grinned and winked at him. "You needn't waste your Irish charm on me. But I must admit I feel a bit magical myself tonight. You have been overly generous."

"Nonsense. This night will re-create only a fraction of the glory that Butler Castle once enjoyed. Besides, I have an ulterior motive."

"You do?" Carin asked.

He nodded. "Unfortunately, this is a money-making venture. It's the first banquet of many that I intend to serve during the tourist season. I advertised for only a week in the *Dublin Times,* and I'm amazed at the response. This is my maiden voyage, so to speak, an experiment to see if my idea is profitable. Our guests tonight will be mostly Americans, some French, and two German couples. However, as my houseguests, I thought you might enjoy dressing the part, as it were."

"I know I do," Carin gushed, absentmindedly fingering the necklace.

"Come," he said, and offered an arm to each of them and marched them over to the fireplace, where three pewter tankards were set on a tray. "This is mulled wine, although Lidia insists I refer to it as 'witches' brew' in keeping with our theme." He withdrew a red-hot poker from the fire and sank it into each of the tankards. He lifted his tankard in a toast. "To dreams," he said.

Carin could barely take her eyes off Richard, knowing that his toast alluded to their conversation earlier that day. She wondered if he had any idea how much he was becoming a part of her dreams.

The creak of the front doors, a shuffling in the vestibule, and the sound of voices announced that the other guests had arrived. Richard left Carin's side to tend to his duties as host; without him she felt oddly bereft. She didn't understand why his presence should mean so much to her, but it did.

While Carin watched Richard introducing himself to the tourists, serving them the witches' brew and ushering them to their assigned seats, Aileen watched Carin.

"Was your fishing expedition successful, dear?" Aileen inquired playfully.

"Huh?" Suddenly Carin's thoughts were dragged back to the present.

"Richard is not like anyone I've ever met before," Aileen offered. "If this were America, people would laugh at him. He's an idealist and a romantic. He lives alone, which in their parlance must mean he's a hermit, asexual, kinky, or a misfit.

Society would analyze him to death, and not once would ever figure him out. But here, he fits right in. He *is* a throwback to another century. Look at him, Carin. He's having the time of his life."

"Grandmother, what are you saying?"

Aileen turned purposeful but loving eyes on her grand-daughter. "I'm saying I like him, Carin. I like him a lot. And so do you. In fact, I would venture to say you've already fallen in love with him . . ."

"I most certainly have not!"

Aileen did not smile. Her words were earnest. "You've never been in love; that much I do know about you. But *I* have. I know I'm jumping the gun here, because you have to sort out your feelings for yourself. But the one thing you will have to understand about Richard is that he will never leave this land. This castle is more a part of him than Emerald is to the Killians. You remember that. This man's destiny is here, Carin."

"Meaning?"

"If you choose him, you are the one who will have to adapt."

Aileen's gaze shot across the room to Richard, and she smiled. "When I look at him, Carin, I see Ireland . . . all the tradition, magic, ancestry, and romance it has always had and always will have."

Carin wanted to wave her grandmother's concerns aside, but she couldn't. She was afraid that her future had already taken a new path. She couldn't go back. She wanted to go on. She wanted to go the limit.

"I'm afraid," Carin finally confessed.

"I know. And I understand. Clay and Caitlin never would listen to me, but all that aside, something has happened between you and Richard. I'd have to be blind not to see it."

"I'm afraid he doesn't feel the same way."

"Why don't you ask him, dear?"

"Do you think I should?"

"Wouldn't you rather know?"

"But I've known him for only two days."

"Carin, you're talking to the *wrong* woman. I knew your grandfather for only three days when he proposed at the top of the Ferris wheel on Coney Island. It was my graduation trip from high school."

"It can happen that fast?"

"Not always, but it can. I can only speak from experience. I think deep in our hearts we all *know* these things. It's just that young people today scrutinize love to death." She looked over at Richard again. "I'll bet Patrick and Mavreen didn't think twice."

"But that was two hundred years ago."

"Loving is a matter of the heart, Carin, and the need for love has little to do with time or place. It's impossible to force love if it isn't there. You and Richard have found something special, and I hope you are wise enough to recognize it."

Carin grasped Aileen's hand and gave it a gentle squeeze. "I hope we are, too."

Once the guests were all seated, Richard escorted Carin and Aileen to their places, introduced them to everyone, and then called for dinner to be served.

A flurry of women and children all dressed in appropriate peasant costumes rushed from the kitchens bearing soup, bread, salad, the brown trout that Carin and Richard had caught that day, huge bowls of steaming vegetables, and pitchers of mead, a honey and distilled apple drink popular in the Middle Ages.

Richard gave many toasts and kept the conversation lively by explaining the history of his castle to his guests. Then a juggler and a mime entertained them. But the highlight of the evening was when Richard stood and told the witches' tale.

"In the town of Kilkenny, where the Butlers originated, lived a woman, Dame Alice Kyteler, who in the year 1324 managed an inn. She was a beautiful woman who, by the time she was forty, had married four times. Each of her husbands had mysteriously died from one illness or another, and each time, Alice had been left the richer in both cash and property. The townsfolk whispered 'witchcraft' for years. After the death of the fourth husband, another suitor appeared for the hand of the still beautiful Alice. The tales of witchcraft grew amongst the townfolk until the whispers turned to outrage. Finally the lord justiciar of Ireland proclaimed that Alice was truly a witch, and sentenced her to be whipped at the cart's tail and burned at the stake, along with her accomplices, who were innocent employees and friends. The night before the execution, Alice made her own plans.

"She threw a party. While her guests feasted on fare much the same as you are tonight, resourceful, clever Alice made her escape. She slipped into the night, out of Ireland, and was never seen or heard from again. Her accomplices were not so fortunate and went to their deaths cursing her name.

"When the authorities went down into the cellar of Alice's tavern, they found herbs, ointments, red cocks' and peacocks' eyes . . . the proof that Alice had indeed been brewing potions. Whether for love or money, we shall never know."

Generous applause filled the room as Richard finished his tale. Lidia and the waiters appeared with "sweets" and two traditional dishes, sherry trifle and carrageen, which Richard explained was made from a seaweed called carrageen moss and flavored with lemon but still salty in taste. After dinner the musicians played for another half hour for dancing before all the guests were given a tour of the garden and the other castle rooms on the first floor that were open for viewing.

When the last guest left, Aileen thanked Richard and excused herself for the night.

"I suppose I should help her with her gown," Carin said reluctantly.

"I'll ask Lidia to help her. Please stay up and join me for a brandy. Hmm?"

"That would be lovely," Carin replied eagerly, not wanting the evening to end.

While Richard returned to the kitchen to fetch Lidia, Carin sought the warmth of the fire in the banquet room. He returned with two brandy glasses and a bottle. They pulled two chairs closer to the hearth, and he poured the drinks.

"Why didn't you show us this room when we first got here?"

"I didn't want to spoil the surprise. You do like surprises, don't you?"

"Yes." She looked down into the amber liquid. *Take a chance, Carin,* she told herself. "In fact, everything about this part of our trip has been a surprise."

"Good ones, I trust."

"Very good," she said, and sipped the brandy. It warmed her throat and dulled her timidity. "You've been the best surprise of all."

"How is that?" he asked, placing his drink on the hearth and inching to the edge of his chair until their knees nearly touched.

The firelight, now dimmed in its dance, cast a golden haze over Richard's face. His eyes were no longer the bright blue she'd seen on their first encounter in the greenhouse, nor were they deeply pensive as they'd been that morning on their angling trip. Smoky sensuality colored their depths and drew her to them. She felt trapped by him, wanting and needing a union.

He leaned forward and took her drink from her. He downed the remaining brandy in a single swallow and put the glass on the hearth next to his. He took her hands in his and examined them, each finger, each nail, and the tracings of the veins that lay near the surface. He pulled the left hand to his lips and kissed the palm. He placed his thumb over her wrist as he pulled each finger into his mouth and then slid his tongue up and over each finger, one by one.

"Your heart is beating very hard again, Carin," he said, his voice throaty. "Only this time I won't disappoint you."

His head was bent down over her lap as he drew another finger into his mouth and suckled it. Carin felt intoxicated. He placed his left hand on her knee and slid it up her thigh, crushing the precious fabric beneath it. He grasped her hips and pulled her closer to him and then placed his head in her lap.

He took her hands and placed them in his hair as he kissed the velvet gown that covered her abdomen, then her waist, up to her rib cage. When he reached her breasts, he groaned.

"My God, you are beautiful, Carin . . . and I . . ." He raised his head, and before she could say a word, his lips had seized hers.

There was nothing timid about his kiss. His mouth engulfed her and swept her into a whirling voyage. His lips were insistent as they took her, possessed her. It was as if they were coaxing her soul out of her body and now she was his prisoner. He caressed her shoulders, throat, and torso, sending flames of heat roaring through her body. As his tongue ringed her lips and sought the honeyed interior of her mouth, Carin felt she would explode. A soft cry escaped her throat, where he swallowed it and kept it for his own. His hands clenched her hips, his fingers seemingly digging through the velvet into her skin. She felt completely exposed to him, naked, but instead of feeling ashamed, she reveled in the sensation.

She responded to his need with an even greater need of her own. She kissed him back, touching his tongue with hers and dancing around it. She sank her hands into his hair, clutching him and pulling him to her. Again and again she plunged her tongue into his mouth, wanting to be made a prisoner, welcoming his bold insistence.

Her heart hammered wildly in her chest, inciting her emotions to riot. She was hot, breathless. She mentally cut the shackles of restraint that had kept her filled with fear. She reveled in the feel of his lips, hands, and tongue, and she rejoiced as passion obliterated logic. She wanted Richard . . . all of him. She would settle for nothing less.

Carin never felt the shoulder of her gown being lowered, but when he tore his mouth from hers, she felt bereft. Then he sank his lips onto the hot yet tender skin of her throat, and she found the sensation deliciously unbearable.

Like the flutter of falling violets, he rained delicate kisses on her throat, then further down onto her chest before he lowered the gown to expose her breasts. He traced the upper swells with his tongue, coming to the edge of a nipple. He prolonged her agony by evading the sensual area and sliding his tongue to the valley between both breasts. Up and down, up and down he traveled, kissing, sucking, and ravaging until Carin thought she would scream out for capture. Then suddenly his mouth hovered over hers again. His eyes were filled with need when he gazed down at her. "I have to hear it from you, Carin. Tell me you want me."

"Oh, God, I do . . ." she said breathlessly.

A wicked grin fluttered at the edges of his lips. He took her hand and placed it over his swollen erection. "This is how much I want you. Tell me again."

"I . . . I want you . . ." she whispered, though she thought she would swoon from the effort.

He eased up her skirts and caressed her thighs. His hand moved higher. "Your skin is very warm, but is it from me? Or just the dress? Tell me . . ."

"It's you, Richard." She groaned again as his hand moved higher still.

He pushed her thighs apart and then yanked her satin bikini panties away from her skin. "Now I will know if you speak the truth." His tones were insistent, but not as bold as his fingers when they sank into the dewy moistness. This time it was his groan that she heard.

"God, it is me . . ." he said as he pushed his fingers inside her.

He kissed her mouth with more passion, more excruciating desire, than Carin had ever known. His tongue joined with hers as his fingers darted in and out of her. With his thumb he teased and caressed the source of greatest sensation.

Jolts of electricity shocked Carin's nerve endings. She slid her hips toward him, forcing his thrusts deeper inside. She was falling into a long, dark tunnel from which she knew she could never escape. She wanted to feel every touch, every erotic sensation he was creating in her. She wanted to feel his skin against her skin, his heat match her heat. Never had she felt so recklessly alive, and she was joyful that it was Richard who had brought her to this precipice.

Her heart sang odes to the carnal sensations he was creating with his lips and fingers. He could never, ever touch her deep enough or long enough. She was insatiable, and it was Richard who was to blame for her cravings. He pitched her higher and higher onto a plane of wanton erotica. And still she wanted more. She needed more than his body; she wanted his heart, but how would she claim it? Was there some incantation that would make him hers alone?

She placed a kiss on the top of his head, a sign that she wanted him to continue his sorcery. She was lost to him. She clutched his head and pressed him to her breast.

Suddenly his tongue was on her nipple. Nipping, biting, teasing. New shock waves shot through Carin. She groaned and choked on the breath that raced up her throat. It was torture. It was exquisite. Her body was wracked with spasms. His fingers, once darting about her core like hummingbirds, were now fiercely insistent marauders hammering away at the gates to her soul. He was drawing her out of herself, forcing her to experience sensations she never dreamed existed. He was her teacher showing her the far edges of passion, and with each new horizon, she craved more. She leaned further into the strokes, begging for release.

Suddenly she seemed to shoot into the stars like a comet borne on the winds of passion. She sailed into the cosmos where time and space were one. Suspended on the wings of pleasure, she slowly floated back into her body.

Reluctant to leave the pulsating walls around his fingers, Richard continued to caress her long after her climax. He kissed her breast, her throat, her ears, and finally her lips.

"You wanted me to do that, didn't you?"

"Yes . . . oh, yes."

"I wanted it more than you."

"You did?"

He looked down into her eyes, the gleam of passion still flickering in their depths. "I want even more." Again he took her hand and placed it on his penis. "I still do. But I want you to take me. I want you to show me."

"I . . . I . . ."

"You're afraid." He kissed her deeply again.

"I'm afraid of many things. I'm not as modern as you might think."

"I already know," he said. "I find that your being a virgin is highly flattering."

"It is?"

He bent his head and kissed her breast one last time before pulling the gown over it and then readjusting the sleeve. "This isn't just another affair for me, Carin. That's what you've been thinking, isn't it?"

"I wasn't sure."

"Look at me," he said, taking her head between his hands. "I'm not some free love hippie you met on a backpacking trip in Europe. And I'm very well aware that you will have to go back to Chicago in a few days. But somehow we will have to find a way to be together, Carin."

"Together?"

"I don't know how to explain this, because it has never happened to me before. But tonight, seeing you in that gown, the way you mixed so easily with my guests, it was as if . . . well, as if you were meant to be part of me, of this castle."

"Are you sure, Richard? Tonight was fantasy. This is 1971, and I'm not Cinderella."

He laughed lightly and shook his head. "No, Carin. This isn't a fantasy. What I'm feeling is all too real. I have a tendency to rationalize my feelings . . . even block them out. Perhaps it's because the night was fantastic and we dressed like this that I was able to shed my inhibitions. I don't know. It's all crazy. But it is real, Carin. For me it is."

He was looking for assurance now, she knew. He needed to know that she felt everything he did. The reality was that she would only be here two more days. Then she would leave Ireland. But would it be forever? Once she was back in the brash Chicago daylight, how would she feel about Richard? Was being with him just a romantic idyll? Every fiber of her heart and soul told her that she should cling to what they had right now. She should take his love and run to the stars with it. But she was a practical woman. A career woman. She had responsibilities. Aileen was right. He was like a throwback to another century. Few people would ever understand him. But she did. God help her, she did understand him.

"I don't know, Richard. I'm so confused."

"I want to know what you feel, not what you think," he demanded.

"I feel . . ."

"What?"

"That I'm falling in love with you. But I don't want to. Because I have to go back," she uttered with a sob.

"Don't go."

"What?"

"Don't go back now. Stay here with me. At least for another week. Get to know me. Get to love me, Carin. We can figure this out. We'll think of something. Your job can wait. They can manage without you, can't they?"

He dabbed at her tears, and before he could take his hand away, she kissed his palm and pressed her cheek against it.

"I suppose they can. But then what will happen?"

"Why don't we just wait and see?" He smiled. Then he took her in his arms again and kissed her deeply, reverently. "Oh, my love. Don't you see? You were meant for me."

Carin lost herself in his words and then in his embrace. She felt oddly comforted in his strong arms, as if he could shut out the world, alter the course of fate, and change her life. Tomorrow she would wire home and inform them that she would be staying in Ireland for a few more days. After all, what could be so critical that Caitlin or Clay would need her for? They would be just fine without her.

Aileen slept soundly in the down-filled bed until the sound of a falling log in the hearth awakened her. The room was bathed in an amber glow as Aileen pulled up onto her elbows and saw Richard and Carin standing at the end of her bed, still dressed in their costumes.

"Are you two still awake? What time is it?"

Neither of them answered her; they just continued to smile at her. Aileen blinked her eyes, trying to wash the sleep from them. "Carin? What's the matter? Didn't you hear me?"

Again there was no answer. Then, as she watched, Richard turned to Carin, put his arms around her, and kissed her. Then they both looked back to Aileen and smiled again.

"Carin? What is going on?" she asked, becoming perturbed.

The light from the fireplace flickered again, and when it did, Aileen noticed that Carin and Richard did not cast shadows onto the wall.

"Who? What . . ." Aileen was covered with goose bumps.

"Everything is as it should be now," the woman said without moving her lips.

"You aren't Carin," Aileen said with sudden conviction. "You're Mavreen . . ."

Then the apparitions disappeared.

Chapter 7

June 7, 1971
Chicago, Illinois

MARY MARGARET PREPARED another evening meal for Patrick, just as she'd done for over fifty-one years. She snapped off the ends of a half pound of fresh green beans, placed them in a Revere Ware pan in an inch of water with pepper, salt, butter, a tablespoon of sugar, and a dash of nutmeg. Then she placed the pot on the new harvest gold electric stove and turned the heat to low.

When the children had been living at home, she'd had domestic help off and on over the years. A cleaning woman once a month, and later, during her social-climbing days, once a week. She'd even had a cook or two, but she never felt they were as good as she was at food preparation.

There was very little her family had needed her for in the past twenty years. Oftentimes she wondered if they had ever truly needed her as much as she needed them. But that was an old woman's quandary, she thought. Such thoughts had never crossed her mind when she was young.

Mary Margaret whacked off the fat on two thick pork chops and slid the sharp knife sideways into the meat to make an opening for stuffing. She filled the pocket with a combination of Italian bread crumbs, chopped parsley, and grated Swiss cheese. Then she dunked the chops in beaten eggs and rolled them in the Italian bread crumbs. She browned them in butter in a skillet on top of the stove. Once the coating was crispy brown, she placed them in a covered baking dish and put them in the oven for thirty minutes.

She was just closing the oven door when Patrick pulled his car into the garage. She glanced at the clock. Six-thirty. He was right on time.

Mary Margaret blinked at the old wall clock, a green plastic shamrock-shaped monstrosity that one of the children had given her for Christmas in 1935. Or was it 1936? She'd redecorated the East Street house several times, changing paper, paint, and slipcovers, but she never got rid of the clock. How ironic that she couldn't remember which child had given it to her.

"It couldn't have been Sheilagh," she muttered to herself. "It must have been Michael."

Suddenly she stopped herself. Why had she immediately assumed that Sheilagh would not have been the gift giver? Was she still that angry with her daughter? Regrettably, she had to admit she was.

All Mary Margaret had ever wanted for her children were the advantages she felt she'd not received in life. From the day of their birth, she had sacrificed her own happiness and done everything in her power to insure a good social standing in the community for her daughters. She wanted them to make good marriages with men who were respected in Chicago. Most important, she wanted her daughters to be loved by their husbands. She never wanted them to make the mistake she'd made by marrying Patrick.

To Mary Margaret's mind, Patrick's lowly background had made him the man he was. If he had not suffered such dire poverty as a child, he might not have become so self-centered, so greedy.

She was only sixteen when she met Patrick Killian on New Year's Eve 1919. She knew nothing about his background or his family, only that he was the most handsome boy at Julia Marshall's birthday party. Julia's family home, an ivy-covered nineteenth-century town house on Fullerton Avenue, was the most tastefully decorated home of any of Mary Margaret's friends. For weeks she had been afraid she would not receive an invitation to the party, especially since she knew Julia only from their mutual participation in the choir of St. Clement's

Catholic Church. Mary Margaret's parents did not live in such a fashionable area, and many of their friends chided them for attending St. Clement's, which was located on Deming Street, rather than keeping to their own South Side neighborhood parish. Mary Margaret's mother made no secret about the fact that she loved the eleventh-century architecture of St. Clement's Church, with its dome of mosaic tile figures above the apse and transept. They made Mary Margaret's mother feel closer to God.

Every Sunday Mary Margaret and her parents would ride the train to the edge of Lincoln Park and walk two blocks north to Deming Street, where they would begin to meet up with other St. Clement parishioners on their way to Sunday mass. For years Mary Margaret complained about the pilgrimage that consumed nearly half their day. It was not until she was in high school that she began to appreciate St. Clement's and its socially prominent congregation.

Some of Chicago's oldest and wealthiest families attended St. Clement's in those years after World War I. As Mary Margaret blossomed into a petite and shapely young woman, she attracted the attention of many young boys on Sunday morning. She struggled to keep her head bowed demurely as the congregation filed up to the communion rail, but too many times she caught herself lifting her darkly lashed eyelids to sneak a peek at the boy kneeling next to her.

Once she was accepted into the church choir, and Sister Angelus proclaimed her a perfectly pitched soprano, Mary Margaret's working-class South Side world altered drastically. She was invited to canoeing parties, croquet matches, and summer picnics in Lincoln Park. Her mother was thrilled over her daughter's popularity, and spent her time sewing new clothes for her to wear. It was a magical time in Mary Margaret's life. She felt like a princess.

When she first met Patrick Killian, she thought he was one of Julia's lifelong friends. He dressed the same as the other young men, in a dark blue suit and starched white shirt undoubtedly purchased at Marshall Field's. His manners were impeccable, and he seemed to know nearly everyone at the party, though she did think it odd that he seemed more familiar with Julia's father than he was with the young people.

Mary Margaret had no idea until much later in their courtship that Julia's father was one of Patrick's clients.

What she did notice was that Patrick was not as reserved

as her friends. He seemed to grab more excitement out of the evening than the others did. He played the gramophone a bit louder, he sang along with more verve, he rushed, rather than walked, to get her a punch, and he gazed into her eyes with an intensity she'd never experienced. From their first encounter she knew that there was nothing dull or commonplace about Patrick. He seemed larger than life, and the way he talked about his dreams and ambitions made her feel as if she might have a chance to become queen once he became king.

At midnight when everyone counted down the seconds and then sang "Auld Lang Syne," Patrick held her hand, and then kissed her on the mouth. From what she could tell, none of the other girls were kissed on the mouth but rather on the cheek, as was acceptable at that time. She was stunned when he pulled his lips away. She blinked at him three times, feeling as if she'd just been anesthetized.

"What's the matter, hasn't anyone ever kissed you before, Mary Margaret?" he asked.

"Not like that!" she replied with indignation.

He leaned close to her, and she smelled his spicy cologne. "I intend to change all that for you, Mary Margaret. From now on, you'll be kissed a great deal."

Curiosity kept her at Patrick's beck and call. She'd never met such a forward young man. Patrick decided he wanted Mary Margaret, and he set about his romancing with a vengeance.

He sent her poems penned on long sheets of paper. She knew they'd been written by Longfellow and Keats, but she never accused him of passing them off as his own. During January and on till Valentine's Day, every Saturday night he brought her exquisite silk-covered wooden boxes filled with the most heavenly chocolates.

Each delicacy was hand-dipped and decorated with tiny icing flowers. He brought her bitter chocolate heart-shaped candies filled with raspberry cream, and milk chocolate bonbons with centers of ground hazelnuts and chocolate mousse. He asked her to provide him with a list of her favorite flavors and then went back to his father, who concocted batch after batch of chocolate creams fashioned especially to please her. When she was with him, she swore she could barely feel the sidewalk beneath her feet. She anxiously awaited the postman every day to see if there was a note from Patrick. She thought he was the most handsome, romantic, and exciting man she'd ever met. When he proposed to her on Valentine's Day while walking down State Street, Mary Margaret was so overcome by his earnestness that she agreed.

They were married on April 22, 1920, and it wasn't until after her honeymoon that Mary Margaret realized that Patrick had never told her he loved her, only that he wanted and needed her.

When Sheilagh was born the following year, Mary Margaret discovered what Patrick had meant by needing her.

"I just don't feel up to going to a party at the Marshalls'," Mary Margaret said after nursing Sheilagh and putting her back in her crib.

"We have to go," Patrick replied as he adjusted his starched collar and bow tie.

"Julia will understand. I can send her a card in the morning explaining about the baby."

Patrick shot his wife a sardonic gaze. "You will do no such thing. James Marshall is one of my largest clients, and I cannot afford to lose his account. He's opening six new stores this year from Racine to Green Bay. He likes you, Mary Margaret, and he will want to see you at this party. Now, get dressed!"

Mary Margaret tried all that night to suppress the hurt feelings she felt so acutely, but she failed. Later in the evening, when the guests had gathered in the drawing room to listen to a violinist, she noticed that Patrick slipped out of the room with James Marshall. When the music ended, Mary Margaret went in search of her husband. She found him standing on the back veranda smoking a cigar with their host. She started to call to Patrick, but James Marshall's words stopped her cold.

"I'm proud of you, Patrick. You took my advice and here you are now a married man, a family man. Didn't I tell you that your business would improve?"

"Yes, you did, sir. I am amazed at the respect I have received. I'm no longer just a kid scrounging for another sale. Why, I can go back through my files and pinpoint the day Mary Margaret told me she was pregnant, because that's the day I got the Carson Pirie Scott account."

The two men laughed and slapped each other on the back. Mary Margaret's knees were shaking as she slipped back into the house.

In the first year of her marriage, Mary Margaret had come to realize that Patrick was a single-minded man, a man of intense focus, and his only concern was his business. As the years passed, she seldom heard him tell her that he loved her, except on her birthday and their anniversary. He still brought her chocolates on special occasions and when she gave birth to another child. He provided a good home in which they all lived, and later, just before the stock market crash, he built the green-tiled house on East Street in Oak Park just two blocks away from Ascension Church.

Over the years Mary Margaret learned not to expect love from Patrick, because every time she slipped and let her vulnerability show, Patrick's indifference to her needs sliced through her like a razor.

Mary Margaret clung to her church and forced herself to believe that her marriage was blessed. She explained away her husband's ill treatment of her. She told herself that other husbands forced their wives to beg for attention. She was ashamed that she wanted him sexually and even more humiliated when he laughed at her gentle overtures and turned away from her. Patrick joked about her tears and belittled her growing ties to her tiny children. "They don't really love you, Mary Margaret. They're children. They have no intelligence."

Mary Margaret began keeping score in those early years of her marriage. She forced herself to remember every one of his malicious remarks. She counted each time he turned away from her in bed. She chalked up the missed birthdays for the children, their anniversaries, her birthdays, even holidays when Patrick was "tending to business." Mary Margaret was not sure when she would call up all his failures, but she sensed deep within her broken heart that the day would come and she would be ready.

A myriad of emotions went tumbling through Mary Margaret as she continued to prepare their meal. Sadness over a past she could never relive, anxiety over the poisonings and Clay's defection, and apprehension over the news that Sheilagh was coming home all caused her head to pound and her eyes to swell with tears.

It had been a long time since Sheilagh had left. Mary Margaret ached just thinking of the years . . . thirty of them. She rubbed her thin arms. Sheilagh had been such a wicked girl. Even Patrick agreed with her about that.

Sheilagh . . . my beautiful Sheilagh. Always testing my patience.

When she was young, it was the little rebellious acts that

unnerved Mary Margaret. In the fourth grade Sheilagh detested her school uniform and so she reversed her cardigan and wore it buttoned up the back so the boys could better see her budding breasts. In the sixth grade, she stole Mary Margaret's lipsticks and mascara, sneaked hosiery out of the house to wear with her saddle oxfords rather than the white cotton anklets that were part of the dress code, and always she unfastened the rubber band that held her thick hair in a ponytail and let it fall about her shoulders.

When Sheilagh was in the seventh grade, Mary Margaret caught her smoking cigarettes behind the garage with Nancy Kelly. In the eighth grade, Sheilagh met Brian Shaunnessy at Nik's Pharmacy and rode behind the sixteen-year-old boy on his black and chrome motorcycle up and down Van Buren, thumbing their noses at Ascension Church. This activity persisted for two months before Mary Margaret and Caitlin pulled up to the stop sign at Van Buren and East Street in the family Buick, and caught Sheilagh in the act. Mary Margaret grounded Sheilagh for a full month, but she always knew that reprimands had little effect on her daughter.

As she remembered it now, it was about this time that Sheilagh's behavior did alter. There were long periods of time in high school when Sheilagh was the model daughter. Good grades. A helper around the house. Dressing to modestly deemphasize her large breasts and tiny waist. Mary Margaret had never questioned Sheilagh's change in behavior; she'd simply believed that her daughter had "straightened up." At least until that day . . . the horrible day when Sheilagh did the unthinkable.

"I can't think about that . . . it's too awful," Mary Margaret scolded herself as she went back to her meal preparation.

The beans hissed in the pot. She glanced at the clock. It was six-forty. Patrick had been home for ten minutes, and she hadn't heard him come in.

How many times had that happened? When the children were young, he slipped in and out of the house like a night thief at all hours, and Mary Margaret never heard a sound.

He crept out to see his mistress when Mary Margaret was asleep with her rosary under her pillow, always hoping the new day would bring a change in her husband. But that day never came.

After Caitlin's birth, Patrick's drinking escalated from a nuisance to a problem. Mary Margaret performed her wifely duty by undressing him and putting him to bed; then she lied to herself and to the children about Patrick's condition. She denied his abuses to herself and created an illusionary reality by presenting to her children and society a portrait of the ideal family.

Things were different these days, she thought. Young girls now spoke of mental cruelty being as bad as physical abuse. The articles in her women's magazines spoke of birth control, the sexual revolution, women's lib, consciousness raising, equal pay, and divorce. The young girls now talked openly about everything inside and outside their marriages. They no longer pretended their husbands were loving when they were not. They did not believe they were failures when their husbands became alcoholics, beat them, or had affairs. These young girls did not keep secrets like Mary Margaret's generation; they had learned to rely on one another's friendship. Mary Margaret liked this new openness because it made her realize that she was not alone.

She sliced a ripe summer tomato and tossed the wedges into a bowl filled with lettuce and crisp young spinach. She thought about leaving Patrick, but she dismissed the idea. It was a sin to divorce. She'd be excommunicated. It might be a sin even to *think* about divorce.

So many things had changed in the Catholic church since Vatican II. Ascension Church had a guitar mass at eleven o'clock on Sundays. Kids from Wells Street, who looked like hippies sang unmelodic hymns she didn't know and didn't want to learn. She missed the Latin mass. She missed the days when moral issues were black and white, right or wrong. Everything was so confused now in the seventies, and the more she thought about it, the more fearful she became. Lately she had begun to realize she had made many bad choices in her life, and she was unaccustomed to thinking of herself in that manner. She was unused to accepting responsibility for her life. She'd always thought of life as something that happened *to* her.

Patrick thudded heavily into the kitchen carrying a stack of mail and wearing a look of dark depression. "Is it ready?"

"What?" she asked, her mind still caught up in personal quandaries.

"Dinner." He flashed her that condescending look that meant he thought her a fool.

She placed a wooden salad bowl filled with the tossed

greens in front of him. "It won't be long. We can start with our salad."

She sat opposite him and carefully placed a white linen napkin in her lap. Though they now ate in the kitchen for convenience' sake, she was reluctant to give up all the amenities she used to enjoy . . . when the children had lived at home . . . when they were a family.

Patrick stabbed his salad repeatedly and then plopped his fork down on the plate without taking a single bit.

"What's wrong?" she inquired politely, hoping to defuse his very visible anger.

"Goddamn bastards."

"Who?"

"The FBI. They think they can just move in and dictate how I run my business. I'm the president, for Christ's sake!" he bellowed. "I'll decide how I want to handle this . . . this fiasco!" He slammed his fist onto the wooden table. A tomato wedge jumped on the bed of lettuce.

Mary Margaret blinked. She tried not to react to his violent mood.

He glared at her.

"I think they can do just about anything they want. They're the law," she said.

"The law is the law. Those putzes are egotistical cops in business suits."

"Patrick, for heaven's sake, tell me what they've done today that has you so upset."

His arms went limp as he placed his elbows on the table and clasped his hands together. "They've ordered me to halt all production. They shut down the machines."

Mary Margaret gasped. She had not spent fifty years in and around the chocolate business without knowing that even a few days of a plant shutdown could cost them as much as an entire quarter's profits.

In the years since the children had grown and left home, Mary Margaret had not been idle with her time. She'd set out to learn the chocolate business, but she had done it surreptitiously. Knowing that Patrick would never give her an actual position in the company, mostly because he feared his wife gaining any kind of power over him, she had had to learn by a slow and careful process of observation and inquiry. Mary Margaret's women's magazines expounded upon the fact that a woman needed to know her husband's business and how to handle the financial responsibilities of a household, because even if her husband did not leave her, eventually she might be widowed. Mary Margaret wanted to know that when Patrick died, she would be competent enough to take over the company. None of this had she ever confided to her husband. It was simply another of her secrets.

"For how long?" she finally asked.

"Indefinitely."

"But that could ruin us," she said with a rush of breath. "It could be the end of Emerald."

"Don't I know that!"

"Why are they doing this?"

"They are convinced the murderer is connected to Emerald. If not one of the family, then an employee. They . . . they think whoever it is either wants to frighten me . . . or kill me." His face was ashen.

Mary Margaret stared at him. She couldn't believe what she was seeing . . . Patrick afraid. It was something she'd never witnessed before. She was even more curious about her own calm reaction to his dilemma. She stared at Patrick, wondering how she could feel so utterly unmoved.

Perhaps she should say something to encourage her husband. But the truth was that she was enjoying his moment of despair. She had not realized she had wanted, even needed, revenge against him all these years, but now that it was given to her, she accepted it as her due. This one moment had vindicated her. The fear in his eyes told her that God does exact a price for evil.

Mary Margaret fought back a victorious smile as she went to the oven and pulled out the perfectly baked stuffed pork chops and placed the hot dish on a wooden trivet in the center of the table. She picked up a double-pronged meat fork and stabbed one of the chops through its center and pulled it out of the dish.

"It's not goose, but it's cooked," she said with a laugh.

Patrick did not laugh along with her.

Chapter 8

$\mathscr{P}$ATRICK KILLIAN SAT in his easy chair pretending to watch television. His stomach churned with anxiety as it struggled to digest his evening meal. He reached over to the leather humidor on the table next to him and lifted the lid. The aroma of his favorite cigar, usually a pleasant sensation, only sent his stomach into another lurch. He clamped the lid down. "Shit."

How was it possible, he asked himself, for his business to be disintegrating before his eyes? He had worked hard to build Emerald into the success it was. At a time in his life when his trials should all be behind him, he was faced with ruin.

Patrick had played all the angles to get to this point, and yet, somehow, fate was telling him he'd miscalculated. But where?

He'd made certain over the years never to let anyone get too close. He'd kept his secrets. He'd used his employees, even his son-in-law, to his advantage. Patrick had always thought himself a winner.

How far back did he need to explore to ferret out his mistakes? he wondered. He looked to his childhood, a place haunted by specters of hunger, physical abuse, and hopelessness . . .

Before the turn of the century, Bridgeport was the name of the Irish village that sprouted on either side of Archer Avenue. The Irish back then called it "Archey Road"; it was a wagon route long before there was a canal at the South Fork of the Chicago River. Archer Road was one of the two original highways that ran straight southwest from Chicago. The other road was Odgen Avenue, which ran north of the river on the Des Plaines and was a main highway for stagecoaches to Ottawa. Patrick remembered stories about the days in the early to mid nineteenth century when Chicago was an integral part of the winning of the West. When he was a boy, Bridgeport was bounded by the river on the north and west, by West Thirty-first Street on the south, and by Halsted Street on the east. Bridgeport was unique from its inception, for it never followed the rest of Chicago streets, which were laid out along the cardinal points of a compass. This was where the canal workers lived, and later where the stockyard workers resided under the bridges and between the saloons.

The Killian house was small, like most of those around it, and was built of brick, with doorsteps, windowsills, and foundations fashioned from limestone stacked like layers of old parchment. Inside, the few meager furnishings revealed a lack of pride. Patrick did not know that the cold, damp air came more from the lack of love than from insufficient heating. Home to Patrick was a place to escape from rather than a retreat.

The only bright moments of his childhood that he remembered were spent listening to the stories of the bridgetender, John Quinn. The bridgetender was the man who worked the levers and cables that lifted the suspension bridge so that the larger, taller boats could continue down the river.

John Quinn puffed cheap tobacco in his white clay pipe and let the smoke snake up through his nostrils and down into his lungs. There were few luxuries in Bridgeport, which meant that tobacco and whiskey were common vices. John enjoyed both.

In the spring when the snow melted and made the river banks mushy and difficult to negotiate on foot, Patrick used to wander down the embankment and wait by a huge maple tree until he saw John Quinn's familiar battered brown derby hat emerge from the bridge house. John did not wear ordinary seafaring head gear. "No sailor's tam for me," he would say with a laugh. "I'm better'n that. Without my expertise, such as it is, ain't nobody goin' anywhere anyway. These fellahs need the likes o' me."

John walked with a limp and told Patrick it was from an injury in the Boer War, but Patrick knew this explanation was just another story, because John had never worked anywhere or been anywhere except along this canal. His limp was an accident of birth, a misfortune, just as Patrick had been born to two people who barely spoke to each other and treated him as if he'd been a mistake.

"Yer lookin' mighty low this mornin'," John said as he slid on a dying patch of winter snow and thick mud.

Patrick waited until John slapped him on the back in that old familiar way. He liked how the old man would not take his hand away immediately, as if burned by touching another human's flesh. John would grip Patrick's slender shoulder and massage the muscles along his clavicle and neck before folding his arms over his rounded beer belly. "What's got ye down?"

Patrick looked up into watery blue eyes and watched how the fading spring sunshine glinted off the gray and red hair that curled under the rim of the derby. A tapestry of lines and creases marked John's face, but failed to dim his elfin grin. Patrick could never resist that smile. "It's me pa. He's made a place for me at the meat plant."

John looked into the black water that emptied into the canal from the Bridgewater pumps. It didn't matter that sixty barges a day passed down this lane. It mattered that the water would never be the same as it had been when he'd been Patrick's age. John hated the slaughterhouses for that. He clucked his tongue at the disgusting ooze, but kept his head cocked to the side so as not to miss any of Patrick's words. "How much they payin' ye?"

"Ten cents a day."

"What about yer schoolin'?"

"It's over in a month. Till then I work th' afternoons, and Saturdays, o' course. Just like Pa."

"Don't care much for schoolin', eh, Patrick?"

Patrick's eyes narrowed. "I care about the money more."

"I s'pose that's about the truth of it. If Mr. Moody, the boss man, don't care if the Progressives find out 'bout you workin' there, if he don't care if the Socialist muckrakers print his name in a paper or put him in a book like Upton Sinclair did, then why should you?"

Patrick's nod was solemn. "All the kids in Bridgeport work. Everybody knows it. It's the way things are."

"Yep. 'Tis the truth," John agreed.

The truth was also that children in Bridgeport were taught early to obey their elders or burn in hell. When Patrick was seven, he learned two lessons. Now that he'd received his first Communion and the sacrament of penance, if he did something that was bad, the worst that could happen would be that he went to confession and was told by the priest that he was forgiven. For Patrick, hell had lost its fury. The second lesson was that the beatings he received from his father came not as a result of his own bad behavior but because of his father's unpredictable mood swings.

By the end of his seventh year, Patrick believed not in God, not in society, not in man; he believed only in himself. He learned to dodge his father's razor strap and to hate not being in control of his life. He longed to be old enough to leave home, and to learn how to command his fate.

It took Patrick less than a month to come to loathe his job. No amount of money could clean away the stench from meat and blood that ran seemingly in rivers down through the cracks in the plank floors of the packing house. For years, Bubbly Creek, that East Fork of the South Fork that began just below Thirty-seventh Street in the stockyards area, gurgled a greasy, thick, stinking sewage that many joked a steer could walk across without sinking.

But more than the sound of saws and hatchets breaking and snapping steer bones, or the sulfuric acids that assaulted his nostrils each morning, Patrick despised the sharp hunger pangs in his stomach. Day in and day out, they gnawed at his belly. They sapped his physical strength and later his resolve to make more of his life. Bit by bit, Patrick forgot about wanting an education. He forgot about John Quinn's caring ways and his stories of Chicago's early days. Patrick forgot about everything except killing the hunger. He learned to crave money.

For a long time, he believed his father when he told him his pay wasn't enough to cover the coal they needed to chase away the bitter Chicago winter nights and the rent for the brick house, the clothes on Patrick's back, or his mother's doctor bills. For a long time, Patrick was charmed by his father's Irish smile, his merry blue eyes and cherry red cheeks. He watched his mother grow thin, her skin turn from peach to pallid and her auburn hair lose its luster. For a long time, he blamed the owners of the meat-packing plants who got rich off the misfortunes of Irish families like the Killians. It wasn't until the night his mother lay dying, sucking only handfuls of air into her lungs, that Patrick learned the truth.

Cathleen was alive, but her hand was cold, frail, and it looked older than her forty years. Patrick held it to his lips and blew on it, trying to warm her skin. "I'll go to the plant and get Pa."

A tear crept out of the corner of Cathleen's eye and slid down the pasty slope of her cheek. "Patrick, yer pa is not at work."

"O' course he is, Ma. Tha's where he goes at night."

Cathleen closed her eyes, and Patrick could make out each vein on her eyelids, her skin was so transparent. He'd never seen a human being die, only animals, and that had been when they were healthy and fattened up for market. This was another kind of dying. This was more frightening.

"Yer fethur is at th' saloon on Dearborn Street where James McGarry is bartender. I don't know th' name o' the place."

"Are ye sure, Ma?"

Cathleen nodded.

Patrick donned his gray tweed tam and set out to find his father. He grumbled to himself as he walked through the sleeting rain and snow. Few houses were dark in Bridgeport at night. Gaslights flickered and warm fires burned in most of the homes of his Irish friends. He was nine years old, and for the first time he noticed that the Killians *were* different from the other Irish. Men who worked alongside his father and who had many children all seemed able to afford gas lamps and fire fuel. None of the children of Bridgeport had many clothes, nor were those clothes much nicer than what Patrick owned, but none of the other boys complained of being hungry. Patrick realized that he never spoke of his hunger. He wondered if they were all too proud to talk about such things. Was it Irish pride or foolhardiness that kept them all behind their lace curtains, their private lives a mystery to neighbors, denying their pains even to themselves?

Patrick finally stumbled stiff-kneed from the cold up the steps to the third saloon he'd found on Dearborn Street. This one was called McCleary's.

Patrick found his father standing at the bar tossing back a glass filled with a dark amber liquid. The frothy drink in the glass mug was beer, he knew. It was the first time he noticed his father's nose was as red as his cherry cheeks. He also noticed that there were two silver dollars on the copper-topped bar next to his father's hand. *Two silver dollars,* Patrick thought. That was enough money to buy bread, milk, and eggs for over a month. He watched as the bartender took one of those silver dollars and plunked it into his cash register.

"Anything else, Killian?" the bartender asked.

"Another round fer me pals!" Mike Killian listed to the left as he raised his beer mug above his head and splashed it onto his shoulder.

Patrick had never known that this was where their money
went. Cathleen had never breathed a word to him. She'd never
hinted, complained, or chastised. She had covered up the truth
all Patrick's life. She must have worked like the very devil
to keep Mike's comings and goings a secret. She had never
stopped him from drinking. She had never demanded she keep
the money for clothes, fuel, food, not even for new cleaning
rags. And at that moment Patrick had never hated anyone on
earth as much as he hated his mother.

He hated her more than the stench from Bubbly Creek. He
hated her more than the sound of the butcher's saw on animal
bone or the thick, syrupy blood that flowed around his brown
leather shoes on slaughtering day. He hated her more than
the pain in his stomach. It was all Cathleen's fault, he told
himself.

Had Cathleen been strong and stood up to his father, none
of these things would have come to pass. If Cathleen had left
Mike . . . if Cathleen had forced Mike to give her more money.
If Cathleen had gone to work for one of the fancy houses like
Timmy's mother did . . . if Cathleen had only gotten what was
hers. If . . . if . . . if . . .

Suddenly Patrick knew now what he must do.

His father was a weak man. There was only one way to
handle a weak man. He walked straight up to the bar, slammed
his hand down over the remaining silver dollar, and glared at
his father. "Put the beer down, Pa. Either on the bar or down
yer gullet. We're goin' home."

Mike peered at the boy through bleary eyes. "Who says?"

"I do. Ma's dyin'."

"She ain't."

"She is. I wouldna' be surprised if she ain't already passed.
You can see her if ya want. I don't really care."

"Na, tha' ain't no way to speak about yer elders."

"Ain't it?" Patrick's eyes turned to icy steel as they bore
down on his father's pupils. Years of frustration, anger, hunger, and hate whirled into a fiery ball in the pit of Patrick's
stomach.

This night, this was the time to take command of his fate.
Never again would he be afraid of anything. They were all
going to die anyway, so what difference would it make if he
disobeyed his father? What the hell difference would it make
if he were to grab the razor strap from his father's hand and
beat Mike Killian himself? What difference would it make to

anyone if one more kid from Bridgeport dropped dead from overwork? Nobody was going to save him but himself.

His spine went ramrod-straight as his chin jutted forward like a prizefighter ready to take on his challenger. "Then hear this, Pa. You ain't comin' here no more."

At that, the barroom full of inebriated Irishmen burst into raucous laughter. They shouted insulting epithets at Mike and taunted Patrick. Mike wavered. Patrick's expression remained like granite. "I ain't gonna allow ye to do to me what ye did ter Ma. Had I known this was the circumstances, I woulda come after ye with a shotgun. Ye deserve no less. But I won' be puttin' no guilt upon ye. Ma got what she gave. She didna' give a damn. I do. This is my money now. We're leavin' this life behind us just as sher as Ma is passin' tonight. I want somethin' better, Pa. Ye owe me."

Mike Killian stared at his only son, and with each angry declaration, Mike sobered. "Lead the way, son."

Cathleen was dead when they arrived home.

Mike Killian went into shock. Through that long, agonizing night, he came to realize that of all the things in the world that mattered to him, the most important was his wife and son. Sadly, he had neglected both of them, and now Cathleen was gone. Mike sat by Cathleen's bed until dawn, holding her hand and making one vow after another to his young son.

"I swear to you on Cathleen's body, Patrick, that I will never take another drink again for as long as I live," he said with genuine tears in his eyes.

Patrick had never seen his father quite so humble. He didn't believe him.

"I also swear that we're gettin' the hell outta that stink hole. I'm goin' ta make our life as sweet as I can. I'm thinkin' to fill our nostrils with the sweetest smell I know."

Patrick looked up into his father's very sober face. "Yeah? Like what?"

Michael looked down at Cathleen's lifeless face. "Chocolate. Yer mither used to beg me ta buy them for her when she was a-carryin' you. She used to make the finest fudge, so creamy it melted when it would touch the lips." Mike let the idea sink in slowly. "I think Cathleen would like that."

"And just how are we going to do this, Pa?" Patrick asked.

"Work and save our money for now. I'll visit all the candy makers in the city we can find and learn their secrets. It shouldn't be hard. People are always free with their secrets if you flatter them a lot. We'll read and learn. I can make the candy here in the house, and you can take it and sell it on the street corners."

"I don't know, Pa."

"It'll be all right," Mike said firmly.

And it was.

Patrick knew nothing about candy except what he'd learned from watching his mother make Christmas nougats for friends and, of course, her famous fudge. He left the candy making to his father, and he began selling fudge and taffy to every person he met. As the weeks and months passed, Patrick learned that the most important asset a salesman required was drive.

Patrick wanted success because he did not intend to die like his mother as a result of another man's selfishness. If anyone in the Killian family was going to be selfish, it would be him.

By mid-July of 1914, just two weeks before Austria-Hungary declared war on Serbia, Mike Killian's Emerald Chocolates were being consumed by most of the North Side upper-crust patrons his son, Patrick, called upon door to door. Mike had sold the house in Bridgeport and moved away from the stench of Bubbly Creek in favor of the growing Irish community on the near west side. In less than nine months, he quickly outgrew the storefront he leased with an apartment above for himself and Patrick. Mike bought a space on Cicero Avenue that he intended to turn into a real chocolate factory.

Now that he was sober, Mike found he was a quick study. He went to the Chicago Public Library on State Street to learn about chocolate. He learned that the best beans that year were coming from British West Africa, since America had joined the Cadbury family in their boycott of Portuguese cocoa to protest that country's unconscionable labor practices. By joining Cadbury's boycott, Mike endeared himself to many other American and British candy makers. He made a name for himself without even trying. Luck was on his side.

Mike knew that the conditions for growing cocoa trees in British West Africa never varied. The temperature seldom climbed above eighty degrees or dipped lower than sixty degrees. There was very little wind, which was good, because the trees are slender and could easily break. The soil was loose, the sunlight was filtered by dense forests, and rain was plentiful. Mike decided that the young trees planted in Ghana in 1913, descendants of the Aztec seeds planted by Cortez centuries earlier, would be his source of beans in 1920 and for generations of Killians to come. He threw his lot in with the Brits. The move was a good one.

Mike was fascinated with every phase of chocolate making. He wanted desperately to visit the cocoa plantations and watch the pods being whacked open by machete, to scoop out the pulp and taste it. He wanted to know if it was true that the pulp was like sugar, and the bean bitter. He wanted to watch the centuries-old method of fermenting the beans on layers of banana leaves. With the pulp still around them, the beans developed the first of the chemical elements called "flavor precursors." As they dried in the sun, the beans lost their bitterness and changed from lavender to white to brown. It took nearly a week for the beans to dry and ferment. Once this process was completed, the beans were packed in 140-pound jute bags, which Mike received at his back door. As he purchased machinery for his factory, made possible by a bank loan from Chicago Bank and Trust, he continued to pat himself on the back.

Patrick wondered where his father would be if he, Patrick, had not been able to sweet-talk every merchant on State Street, every resident up and down Michigan Avenue all the way up to Evanston and back down through the Irish families of the North Side, into buying Emerald Chocolates. Patrick had literally worn through four pairs of shoes in the last year. That was more shoes than he had owned in his entire life. Yet Chicago loved Emerald Chocolates. He didn't know why they liked his father's candy any more than their Hershey bars and Curtiss Baby Ruths, but they did. Patrick was not discerning in his tastes, like his father. Chocolate, like any food, served only to kill the pain in his belly.

Patrick became the sales manager and later created the marketing and advertising departments of Emerald Chocolates. He paid little attention to the product itself and kept his focus on getting the orders. At an early age, the natural division of the work between himself and his father taught Patrick to look solely for the incoming revenues. Before he was twelve years old, he was obsessed with money. Money saved him from hunger. Money gave him a new home in a respectable neighborhood. Money made people look at him in a new way. Suddenly he was part of a thriving business. He had respect. Despite his youth, his customers trusted him. He was making a place for himself in the world, and he liked it. Patrick learned very quickly that money was the only god that deserved to be worshiped.

Patrick no longer went to mass on Sundays as he had when his mother was alive. Sunday mornings he examined every entry in the company ledgers, noting the credits and debits. He set goals for the following week and listed the new customers he would approach, never allowing more than ten days to pass without contacting his old customers. His six-day work week stretched to seven. Ten-hour days became twelve, then thirteen, fifteen hours a day. He slept only from midnight until five, when he would rise and start his day. He taught his father to do the same.

The years passed, and father and son spoke of nothing but the chocolate business. There was little affection between them, simply a shared need to achieve. If Mike Killian possessed anything, it was the passion to produce a chocolate finer, smoother, richer, than Lindt or Suchard. Patrick, on the other hand, loved only money, both attaining it and using it to wield power.

As he matured into his teens, Patrick's respect for his father declined. He believed that his salesmanship made Emerald Chocolate Company all that it was. He gave his father no credit for his contribution. He thought his father foolish for spending his time with noted chocolatiers. He cared little about ganaches and the careful hand-dipping process that brought customers back for reorders. He knew little about the sorting, roasting, and winnowing of shells or grinding of cocoa beans. He couldn't tell the difference between a refining machine, with its three steel rollers that rotated over the chocolate and smoothed the tiny particles of chocolate and sugar to twenty microns each, and a conching machine, which stirred the chocolate again and coated the particles with additional cocoa butter. Patrick thought that cheap powdered milk was as good as regular milk, but Mike insisted on using Nestle's condensed milk, even though it was produced by his competition.

Early on, Patrick developed a way of looking at the world in which he was always right. If he found that things didn't go his way, he made them do so by lying.

At first they were small lies. He wrote an order from Mrs. Cuthbertson for two dozen dark-chocolate-covered peppermint bonbons. When he delivered the order, she refused it, stating that she'd requested milk chocolate. Patrick realized he'd made a mistake, but he refused to admit it. He argued with Mrs.

Cuthbertson for over forty-five minutes until the woman paid for the chocolates just to get rid of Patrick.

He had lost a good customer, but he didn't care. It was more important that he not admit his failure.

Each time he mistook an order, he blamed the customer and used intimidation to wheedle the payment out of the client. He was able to convince himself he was still a success, since he always came back with the money. He surmised he could always cover his lost clients by simply working twice as hard to garner new business. It never occurred to him to tally his losses. Patrick made it a practice never to look back, never to analyze his mistakes, simply to keep moving forward.

The Killians experienced the First World War as a footnote in their lives. Neither was unduly concerned about the day-to-day battles, only the outcome. If Germany won, there would be better access to German candy-making machines. If the Allies won, their supplies would be delivered more promptly. The war did not affect production time or quotas, and, in fact, it was a boon for sales.

Patrick paid no attention to his father as Mike became caught up in dreams of becoming one of the great names in prestige chocolate, like Lindt and Cadbury. Mike no longer drank nights; instead he buried himself in research about his competition. The Swiss and German candymakers were still tops in the chocolate world. Cadbury was a good second, as were some of the French. But not one single American could match the quality of European chocolate. Hershey experimented with mass production and produced average quality, yet none of the Chicago candymakers could do better. The premier chocolatiers were all Europeans. Mike Killian wanted to be the first American to break into that *grande luxe* circle.

He died of a heart attack in 1922 before he realized his dream.

His legacy was a working chocolate factory and his son, whom Mike had taught through example to spend all his energy and attention on building a business.

Patrick Killian learned well from his father.

In 1928 when the stock he owned was soaring, Patrick closed the small chocolate factory he had inherited from his father and built new facilities, keeping Brach's to the south of him and the soon-to-be-opened Mars factory to the north of him on Oak Park Avenue.

Always with the idea that Emerald Chocolates should be upscale, Patrick wanted his new factory to be fashionable. Never an innovator, he built a factory that looked just like that of his competition, Mars.

The building was made to appear like a sprawling California-style movie studio fashioned of white stucco and wrought iron. The tile roof, trim, and shutters on the arched windows were green. Twisted white Tuscan columns marked the double front doorway. Spanish-style roof pediments crowned the length of the building. The lawns were of meticulously manicured zoysia grass, the kind used on putting greens. There was even an automatic sprinkler system. The grounds were fertilized and aerated to keep them perfect. Sugar maples lined the street, and beneath their leafy shade grew multicolored snapdragons.

All employees passed through the front doors; the factory workers to the left, the office personnel to the right.

At the front of the building, which spanned a full city block, was the cafeteria, where employees could buy their lunch. Patrick was proud of this innovation and entertained his suppliers, retailers, salesmen, managers, and directors in the same room as his machine operators. No one was given preferential treatment. This ingenious setup kept employees happier; his staff always knew Patrick was easily accessible should problems arise. He prided himself on the fact that he had few labor disputes at Emerald. He never told anyone that the idea for the cafeteria had come to him when his then three-year-old daughter, Caitlin, had visited him at his father's old factory and commented on the separate dining areas for the factory workers and the office personnel, asking: "Who is more important, Daddy? The candymakers or the candy owners?" Caitlin had made him realize they were dependent on each other.

When Patrick made a killing on his sale of some AT & T stock he owned, he bought the newest machines from the same German manufacturer his father had used. Instead of discarding the old equipment, he had it repaired. The new milk tank was larger and made of stainless steel. He bought the newest molds from France and Switzerland. He sold his Ford stock and bought the best crop of cocoa beans from Brazil, Ceylon, Mexico, and Java. He struck a peach of a deal with Imperial Sugar. Patrick intended to make and sell a great deal of premium chocolate to Americans who in the 1920s were still spending, spending, spending.

He had made all the right moves, or so he thought. When the crash came, he had sold nearly all his investments and turned the cash into equipment and supplies. His mistake was not realizing the depth of the downturn and not redirecting his expensive chocolate line toward affordable candy such as his competitors produced. The public was buying cheap Hershey bars, not fifteen-dollar-a-pound Emerald chocolates.

Since premium chocolates had a short shelf life, Patrick had to destroy what he suddenly couldn't sell. Orders dropped even more. Patrick was out of cash and in the red. He blamed everyone and everything for his situation except himself.

He ranted against the politicians. He cursed his competition for settling for mediocrity and continued to do little to save his company. Patrick's long-held belief that he could always continue to bring in new sales, despite the customers he had alienated over the years, now proved wrong. He may not have tallied up his disgruntled clients, but they remembered him and refused to do business with him.

Irish pride told Patrick to keep his financial woes a secret. He had no male friends he trusted, nor could he possibly confide in his wife since she knew nothing about business.

Since the day of Cathleen's funeral, Patrick had put his faith and trust in money and success. He could stand outside his beautiful new factory and the new house he'd built in 1927 on East Street and know that he had finally made it because he had the tangible signs of success.

Not once as he began to consume bottle after bottle of Irish whiskey did he ever consider that his soul was just as empty as his bank account. He never listened to the priest on Sunday who spoke of heaven and hell being the outward manifestations of one's inner spiritual life. He thought it was a sign of weakness the way Mary Margaret tried to cajole love out of him. He thought of his children as necessary evils in a society that required a family for social status. Patrick believed now more than ever that life was a game and that people were pawns to be used in any way he saw fit, so long as he came out the winner.

While Patrick struggled to survive, the Great Depression put eleven million Americans out of work, despite President Hoover's announcement that the worst of the crisis was over. Made of tarpaper shacks and cardboard cartons, Chicago's "Hoovervilles" sprang up overnight on nearly every vacant lot. One of the worst was on Cicero Avenue and Thirty-first

Street, next to a garbage dump. The three hundred people who lived there took turns scavenging each new load of garbage that was dumped. They scalded rancid meat and sprinkled it with soda. They made soup from chickens' feet and ate the pulp from melon rinds.

Smokestacks that for decades had belched black plumes of industrial waste into the Chicago sky were shut down. Fewer trucks shot along State Street, and the sound of riveters was silenced. In 1932 Chicago suffered forty more bank closings. Hope was all but gone.

But, like a gift from God, Chicago was blessed by chocolate.

The chocolate and candy industry boomed during the Depression. For the price of a nickel, a candy bar provided a whole meal for many people. Chicago was the center of America's candy industry.

The Curtiss Candy Company, founded by Otto Schnering in 1916 in a back room over a plumbing shop on North Halsted Avenue, grew to four factories working twenty-four hours a day to make enough Baby Ruth bars to feed the city and the nation. Otto developed Butterfinger, Baby Ruth Fruit Drops, Baby Ruth Mints, Peter Pan, Caramel Nougat, Coconut Grove, and Buy Jiminy.

Mars Candy had moved to Chicago in 1929 and introduced the Snickers bar in 1930. The Reed Candy Company produced Reed's peppermint and butterscotch rolls. The Shutter-Johnson Company had Bit-O-Honey Bars; the Williamson Candy Company made the Oh Henry! bar and Choc-O-Nuts; The Ferrara Pan Candy Company made Jawbreakers, Atomic Fireballs, Red Hots, and Boston Baked Beans; and the E. J. Brach and Sons Company began by specializing in chocolate-covered candies.

Patrick Killian was poised for greatness. But he missed the mark . . .

Patrick leaned his head against the back of the easy chair and looked out the window at the June night sky. The moon was a silvery quarter hung low just over the tips of the sugar maple treetops. For a moment it seemed to him that he had been catapulted back to the past. The inner turmoil he was experiencing now was no different than it had been back in 1932 when his company had been on the verge of bankruptcy. He had pulled himself out of hot water then and he could do it again, as long as he handled the situation his way.

He had been right to trust no one all those years ago. He needed to remember that now, especially in the face of Clay's betrayal. There was Caitlin to deal with, too. No doubt she would press him to carve up his company and give her a stake in return for her loyalty.

"I'll see her in hell before I'll do that," he vowed.

Maybe this was what they were all waiting for. Maybe that was why they were all coming here . . . Caitlin, Michael, and yes, Sheilagh, too. Sheilagh especially. She would really like to see him burn, he thought.

Patrick clenched his fists and felt determination course through his body. No one was going to take control of his company. No one.

Chapter 9 ───────────────────────

June 8, 1971
Chicago

Armed with the knowledge that Sheilagh would support her, Caitlin faced her adversaries. Clay was no longer with the company, and his responsibilities had fallen on her shoulders.

Mary Margaret stood at the window gazing out at the gardens in front of the Emerald building. She was mumbling to herself, and Caitlin assumed she was praying until she made a comment about the begonias. "What was that, Mother?"

"I think I should have chosen the fuchsia impatiens again. The begonias are leggy already."

Caitlin was used to her mother's ramblings during times of crisis. When Caitlin was a child, Mary Margaret had turned a blind eye to Patrick's drinking, or at least so it seemed. For years she had mistakenly believed that her mother was being a good wife by always seeing to his needs, especially when Patrick gave Mary Margaret so little in the way of love or attention. Now that she was an adult, Caitlin realized that her mother had been an "enabler" and that her mother's need to be loved had been just as much a problem as her father's inability to give love.

Patrick spread his hands over his rotund stomach. His blue eyes were steely and his voice determined.

"I won't do it, and that's the final word."

"You haven't got a choice. We have to recall every piece of chocolate . . . nationwide," Caitlin replied, wondering why she felt so confident as she hammered these nails into the Emerald coffin. She shouldn't have felt such a sense of satisfaction, but she did. Power was a heady elixir, and right now, the power had been passed to her.

In the past twenty-four hours, Patrick's ability to command had faded. His eyes were rimmed in red. He was hung over again or still drunk, Caitlin wasn't sure which. He was running away from the family crisis, not trying to battle it the way she was.

"I've already put the order through to recall," she told him.

"Oh, ho! So, that's the way it is. Your husband abandons us, and you slip in to take his place."

"You bet I have."

"He's a shit."

"You pushed him too hard for too long. I don't blame him a bit."

"Watch your mouth, Caitlin. He might just leave you, too."

Caitlin tried not to let her doubts about her marriage show. Patrick aimed clear and true, but she was determined not to buckle. "He won't."

"Yeah? Why not?"

"Because he loves me. Really loves me. He may be confused right now . . ."

"How would you know what he is when you didn't even sleep with the bastard last night?" Patrick's eyes gleamed with intense ferocity.

"I . . . I . . ."

"You didn't think I knew about that, did you? Well, I've got eyes all over this city. I know that he never went home. Went to the Lake Shore Club and had dinner. I'll bet he was meeting some tart—"

"Shut up!"

Patrick laughed and rose from his chair. "Don't get smart with me. I'm still president of this company, and no orders are to be followed except mine. And I don't agree to a recall."

"Fine. Rot in jail."

"What are you talking about?"

"This!" Caitlin waved a white legal paper in his face. "The FDA has already stepped in."

Patrick grabbed the paper from Caitlin and quickly scanned it. He sank back in his chair as if someone had suddenly deflated him. His face aged before Caitlin's eyes. "The press releases and the reporters were bad enough. This really will put us under." He leaned forward in the chair, with his elbows and forearms on the desk. He splayed his hands out. "Everything I built . . . gone . . ."

Mary Margaret had not moved from the window. She looked over at her beaten husband for only a moment before turning back to the gardens. Caitlin saw satisfaction on her face. An eerie chill seemed to touch Caitlin's cheek.

In that moment she actually believed her mother could have killed innocent people just to see Patrick broken.

Caitlin wanted to flee the room. Never had she realized how intense, how raging, her hatred for her own father was. She, whom Sheilagh had called a saint, was capable of seeking his destruction, of doing anything to achieve satisfaction. Why? she asked herself. Why had she never known her true feelings toward her father? She loved him, had always wanted him to love her. Hadn't she?

Confusion assailed her. It stirred up the past, whirled it around the present, and flung it against the future. What was happening to them? What was happening to *her*?

She looked down on her father for the first time with no respect whatsoever. Now she knew exactly how Clay must have felt. For the first time, she knew what Sheilagh had meant all those times over all those years when she told Caitlin that she hated her own father. Caitlin had been so sure, so blindly cocksure, that hating was wrong. Right now, hating felt good. It felt very good.

Caitlin was *glad* her mother had this chance for revenge. She would allow her mother this moment of triumph without reprimand.

"You didn't build this company alone," Caitlin finally said.

Mary Margaret's head snapped around to face her daughter. Patrick's empty hands became fists. "The hell I didn't."

"Good God, are you so blind?" Caitlin moved closer to the desk and leaned forward. This time she was the hunter, and he the prey. She was amazed that her nerves had turned to steel. Cold, vicious steel. "Your father built the company. You only took it over. You didn't start it from scratch. We made it through the Depression, but then, so did every other candy man in town. It wasn't until Clay stepped in after the war that Emerald took off. Even I did more to expand this company and broaden its scope than you ever did. This was a family effort, and you know it."

"I should have known you would turn on me, too. You're selfish and ungrateful, just like your mother and your sister . . . hell, like everybody. Who fed and clothed you and sent you to college?"

"You did. I suppose in your mind you think that's enough, don't you? You've never given Clay or me credit for anything we've ever done for you. You can't see beyond your own needs, and you probably never will. I feel sorry for you."

"Now you're shoveling pity? Well, I don't want it."

"That's all I'm giving. It's your company, as you said. You figure out what to do with it."

Caitlin straightened slowly with newfound strength. She turned to her mother. "If he calls, I won't be home."

Mary Margaret looked tired and lost, but there was understanding in her eyes. She nodded and looked away.

Caitlin left the room without another word.

Since Clay had taken the Cadillac, Caitlin had driven her daughter's red Mustang in to work. She unlocked the car, got in, and sped away. She was not even a block away when she turned her thoughts away from Emerald Chocolates.

Caitlin had a marriage to save.

The Mustang shot around the winding curves of Sheridan Road at fifteen miles over the thirty-five-mile-an-hour speed limit. She passed her redbrick home with its white Greek pillars and manicured lawn, and raced toward the Lake Shore Club. She had not spoken with Clay for two days, and she was determined to put their differences to an end. Since this was the last place he'd been seen, it was the best place to start.

She drove through Glencoe until she reached the black iron gates of the club. For some reason, the sight of the Tudor-style country club brought back a feeling of security.

It was a beautiful June day, perfect for sunning, tennis, or golf. She saw many of their friends coming into the club dressed in Izod shirts and pastel slacks. Jim Harrelman stopped to chat for a moment, but all Caitlin wanted to do was cut him off and be on her way. She tried to be polite, but she knew Jim must be sensing her impatience.

Huge vases of summer blooms filled the reception vestibule and decorated the tables in the dining room. Caitlin knew there was only one man who would tell her about Clay and be discreet enough to keep her inquiries to himself.

Alan Johnson was fifty years old, blond, tall, thin, and tan. He was a former tennis pro and golf instructor and was now employed as the manager. Caitlin found him in his office going over the mail.

He rose with a bright smile and greeted her with a warm handshake. "How lovely to see you, Caitlin. How are you doing?"

"I'm fine."

"I read about all this mess you're having. Any word on who did it?"

"No. None."

"I understand," he replied, looking deeply into her eyes. "He's here again today."

"He is?"

"I saw him only a few minutes ago. He's having lunch at the bar."

Caitlin pumped Alan's arm enthusiastically. "Thank you. Thank you."

"Don't mention it."

Caitlin walked into the dimly lit bar and nodded to a couple they knew from the tennis ladder they'd played on two summers ago. She scanned the room. He saw her before she saw him. His face lit up when her eyes met his. It was a good sign.

He waved her over.

Caitlin sat on the barstool next to him. "How are you?"

"All right," he replied, the smile gone now.

"You don't sound like it."

"I didn't say wonderful."

"Oh," she breathed. It was another good sign.

"I'm sorry I didn't come home last night."

"I was very worried. I still am."

"I needed to be alone. To think about things." He touched her hand. "I thought you would be angry because I left Patrick in the lurch."

"No, you didn't," she said. "You thought I chose my father over you."

Clay's eyes widened in surprise. Then he really looked at her for the first time since she'd walked in. There was something different about his wife, but he didn't know what. She'd never looked like this before, felt like this before. As if she were supercharged with electricity. She was on fire. He sat straighter in his chair. "What is it, Caitlin? You seem . . . different."

"I am different, Clay. That's what I came to tell you. I found out things about myself today, but if I tell you about them, I'm not so certain you'll like them."

"Jesus! What are you talking about?"

"I know how you feel, Clay . . ."

"You can't . . ."

"I can and I do. Finally I know what it's like to want to hurt somebody. Especially somebody you're supposed to love. I found out a lot about myself today, realized strange emotions that I've never faced. I can't say any of them are good. In fact, most of them are bad, but oddly, I feel better."

Bafflement filled Clay's eyes. "I'm afraid you've lost me."

"I know. But that's okay. We have a lot to talk about, Clay. Things we've never discussed. We're going to have to start from the beginning, Clay, because I think I'm starting to know myself for the first time. And all I want to know is if you'd like to get to know me, too."

"I don't have any idea what this is all about, but I am willing to listen. And when you're finished, can I have my turn?"

She smiled. "You bet you can."

New York

Tony Vallenti was desperately in love. He'd never thought it would happen to him. At the half-century mark in his life, Tony had analyzed, scrutinized, and distilled love down to an insignificant pile of nonsense. Love was a device used by women to trap men into marriage, and by insecure parents to manipulate their children. Love was for fools. Love was blind. Love was the act of an organ, not the heart but the penis. Love for Tony meant disappointment. He refused to buy in to it.

Tony believed in acting. He was a consummate artist at his craft and spent most of his waking life perfecting his skills. When he was onstage he could be anybody he wanted to be, and best of all, it numbed the pain in his life.

Tony's father had died when he was ten, his mother when he was sixteen. He had felt no different as an orphan than he had all his life. His father, Rocco Vallenti, had been a cruel man. Tony could not recall a single moment of closeness between them. Rocco had worked all day as a cook on Mulberry Street in Little Italy and spent his nights hanging out with his Italian hoodlum friends. He was arrogant, sarcastic, cold, and scared to death of life. Rocco's "friends" arranged for his presence during a scuffle over a dice game in which a gang war broke out and Rocco was knifed to death.

Tony's mother never shed a tear during the funeral. Once Rocco was buried, it was as if he'd never existed; she never spoke his name again. Helen Vallenti was English and the fifth out of eleven children. Her parents were unaffectionate and emotionally distant from all their children. Helen grew up thinking that was the norm.

Rocco and Helen had seemed like negative and positive energy forces creating a lot of friction but little else. Somehow they needed each other, but all of Rocco's arguing and sparring and Helen's frigid indifference left Tony alone, afraid, and confused. For the most part, his parents were so consumed with each other, they barely knew their son existed.

Tony's childhood was loveless, and his adulthood taught him no differently.

As a young, penniless but talented actor, Tony met Ruth Anderson, a beautiful but not so talented chorus dancer, in an off-Broadway production. During the play's two-week run, Ruth fell in love and Tony fell in lust. When the play folded, Tony proposed to Ruth since his future seemed so uncertain and at least he could count his marriage certificate as a tangible achievement. As the newly married couple exited the courthouse after the eight-and-a-half-minute ceremony, Tony picked up the latest copy of the *New York Times* and read the only review given on his play. The critic had lambasted the director, the playwright, and the cast, but he had raved about Tony's performance. He looked at Ruth, who gazed up at him adoringly, and realized he'd made the biggest mistake of his life.

Tony spent the next two years auditioning for every serious part offered on Broadway, and landed two supporting roles. The critics liked what they saw in him. He spent less time with Ruth and more time taking acting workshops. He was obsessed with his career, and eventually it paid off. Tony achieved stardom.

His marriage lasted seven years, during which Ruth played the dutiful wife until she decided she wanted more out of life.

She told Tony he had mixed up his priorities by putting her last on the list and that he didn't know how to love. He did not disagree with her.

When Ruth left, she got the Lincoln Town Car, the brownstone in the upper east eighties, and the Fauvistic art collection.

For years Tony was bitter about the settlement and drowned his anger in alcohol. Eventually the habit caught up with him. Growing up was the hardest thing Tony had ever done, especially since he didn't start trying until he was forty. His reputation as a womanizer was eclipsed only by his drinking. His career plummeted. Yet Tony had been born under a lucky star. He always worked—even though he spent eight years bouncing from one television soap to another, Tony was still in the public eye.

Those were the hard years. His drinking showed in the bags under his eyes and the extra forty-seven pounds of girth that wrapped around his torso. Gone were the golden boy looks that had garnered him many choice roles. Tony looked like shit and felt like it. He and his agent, Sam Winerstein, went around and around. He lost his agent. He got his agent back.

Tony finally buckled the day Sam agreed to take him back on the condition that he quit drinking. He joined Alcoholics Anonymous and discovered that quitting the booze was easy compared to coming to terms with his battered childhood. Finding that love did exist in the world and that he'd never had any of it was the cruelest blow of all. It took him a decade to heal himself, to regain his nearly lost acting career, and to find love. Love came to him in the form of Sheilagh.

In all his years on and off Broadway, in and out of television soaps and a half dozen movie flops, Tony Vallenti had never met Sheilagh Killian. He knew of her, her reputation, her work, but had never actually met her.

He was reading for the lead in a new play in which Sheilagh had already been cast as lead. Tony wanted the part so badly, he ached for it. He lost weight, had a face-lift, worked out, became a vegetarian and a yoga enthusiast, and had his hair restyled at a swanky but offbeat hairstylist's in lower Manhattan. He was living only for this part. Tony needed a hit.

Concentrating on his reading, he paid no attention to the beautiful redhead who watched him from the wings. When he finished, it was her applause he heard in the silent theater.

Glancing to stage left, he took one look at Sheilagh and knew that his life had changed. He knew instantly that they would never be apart and that their life together would be nothing short of wonderful.

Sheilagh's broad, appreciative smile turned sultry as Tony approached her. She noticed that he didn't wait for the director's dismissal. She wasn't certain if he was acting out of complete confidence in his acting, arrogance, or her own appeal. It didn't take her long to find out.

"I thought you were good," she said in a low voice when he stood looking down at her with crystal-clear blue eyes.

"That's all?"

"Oh, no. Don't tell me you're conceited, too."

"Too?"

"Besides gorgeous, I mean." Suddenly she couldn't think of a thing to say to this incredibly handsome blond man. She'd worked with the best in the business, the sexiest men in Hollywood, and shallow pretty boys who were hot for a year or two and never heard from again. Tony Vallenti was different. Very different, and she couldn't wait to get to know him.

"I'm glad you think so."

"Doesn't everybody?"

"I don't care about everybody. I care what you think."

"Why?" She nearly moaned and checked herself as he took a step closer and allowed his eyes to bore into hers.

"Because I have a feeling that you are going to be very important to me."

Sheilagh felt her bearings slip away from her. She tried to tell herself she was accomplished, old by most standards, and extremely independent. She didn't need anybody in her life. Certainly not a man. She should have been cool and aloof. Instead, she felt transformed into the eager young girl she had once been back in Chicago. No longer did fame and position protect her. She was vulnerable and giddy. She wondered what it would be like to touch his cheek.

"I should hope so," she chided. "I have top billing."

"God," he groaned sensually, "you can always have the top."

His sexual innuendo was too much for her. She instantly knew his kind. He must have needed this part badly. She wondered how many other actresses had fallen prey to his charms. *Probably hundreds,* she thought. *No, thousands.* She would check him out for herself. This man was a heartbreaker extraordinaire. Somebody should have told him that Sheilagh Killian had no heart. It had been destroyed a long time ago.

Sheilagh whirled her protection around her like a cape and spun on her heel to walk away from him, but he grabbed her arm. She glared at him. "Just remember, Mr. Vallenti, I'm the star of this show."

"I wouldn't have it any other way."

"I'm not so sure about that."

Tony checked himself. "I'm sorry about that remark. It's just that you're so . . . so goddamn beautiful. You took my breath away. I'm sorry. Really. How can I make it up to you?"

"You can't." She looked down at his hand which held her upper arm in a firm, but not hurtful grip. "Perhaps you should consult with the director and find out if you even got the goddamn part."

"Huh? Oh! Yeah!" He shot away from her back to center stage.

The director was angry. "Have you finished your tête-à-tête, Mr. Vallenti?"

"Yes. I mean, I apologize. It was rude of me."

"Yes, it most certainly was," replied the long-haired, bespectacled man in his mid-forties.

Tony kept smiling at the empty theater seats, knowing that behind the stage lights was the ticket to his future. He poured on his little-boy charm. He continued beaming, then shuffled his feet a bit. "Well, sir? Do I get the part?"

"We'll call you," snapped the director, now secure in his role once again.

"I appreciate the opportunity to read for you, Mr. Waller. It was a pleasure." Tony walked off the stage with supreme confidence, knowing in the deepest pit of his guts that he had gotten the part.

The call came the next morning.

Games, Tony thought. *Let them play their games. I know the rules as well as anyone. I know I will win.*

What he was not quite as sure about was Sheilagh Killian. He'd started out on a sour note. So much for betting on one's feelings. He just hoped he hadn't blown it already.

When Tony saw Sheilagh the next morning at rehearsal, he didn't know that she hadn't slept a wink in the two nights since they'd met. He didn't know that she couldn't study her script, shop, eat, or converse with friends without visions of Tony's face swirling like a diaphanous presence around her.

She was sitting on a stool on the stage when he walked into the theater. She seemed to be studying her lines intently. Tony held his breath as he watched her. She looked like a goddess dressed in white slacks and a white turtleneck, her luxuriant auburn hair cascading over her shoulders. From this distance she looked half her age. It wasn't until he was up close that he could see the fine lines about her eyes that told him this was a woman who had both won and lost at life's battles. He found he wanted her more than he had two days ago.

He took his time as he walked over to her. He could smell her perfume, a musky, sensual blend of flowers and spices. She looked up as he drew near, and he almost drowned in the glistening green eyes that invited him to come closer. Tony's heart jackhammered in his chest. He was certain she could hear the sound.

"Good morning, Miss Killian," he said with mock cordiality.

"Good morning, Mr. Vallenti," she breathed seductively, without consciously knowing that she was already responding to him.

"I'm looking forward to this opportunity to work with you."

"So am I," she said honestly, never taking her eyes from his. She found that none of her ordinary defenses were working. "I think we have something that is essential for this particular play."

"And that is?"

"Chemistry."

Tony's spirits nearly hit the gold-painted ceiling of the theater high above them. "Oh, I hope so, Miss Killian."

"Call me Sheilagh."

"Tony." He leaned over and touched her hand. He wanted to kiss her right then and there. He couldn't take his eyes off her lips. He watched the way they parted, as if she were about to say something . . . or bite something. Tony struggled with himself to dispel the image of her in bed with him. It didn't work. Tony Vallenti was hooked. All he could do was hope it wouldn't take her a long time to know that they would be spending their lives together.

"When we break for lunch, could you . . . I mean, would you consider sharing it with me?"

Sheilagh smiled up at him, her eyes hot with desire. "I would like that very much."

"You would?" Tony wanted to leap for joy, but he thought it inappropriate since the director had just walked onto the stage.

"I would," Sheilagh said, sliding off the stool to greet Ben Waller. She held Tony's hand for an extraordinarily long time, and just as she was about to release it, she squeezed it firmly. Tony knew she was not aware of the gesture; her mind was probably preoccupied with Ben, her role, and the play. She had slipped into career mode. But only just slipped. There was a part of Sheilagh that Tony had claimed. He was one lucky son of a bitch.

Tony watched her as she glided over to Ben and shook his hand, then kissed his cheek. Tony took the moment to assess the rounded curves of her hips and the long, lean legs he wanted her to wrap around him when they finally made love. Tony smiled to himself. He'd come to this theater to win a part. Instead, he knew he'd won the heart of the only woman he would ever love.

Once, Tony would have taken an oath on the Bible that he didn't believe in love at first sight, or any of those mystical, spiritual, or romantic fantasies that had been invented to dupe humans into illogical thinking. Tony was a realist. But as the days passed, as he worked with Sheilagh and got to know her, as he finally did make love to her, and proposed on the very same night, Tony was glad that for once in his life, he had relied on his feelings.

Tony finished checking Sheilagh's luggage at the United Airlines counter and joined her at the pub in A concourse. She was sitting at a small table, oblivious to the noisy patrons around her who were watching the Yankees game on television. As Tony walked up to her, he was amazed that the very sight of her still made him weak in the knees. Theirs was more than a sexual attraction, yet he couldn't think of a time of day or night when he didn't want her. Somehow he knew it would always be that way for him . . . for them both.

"You're all set, princess," he said, brushing her luxurious hair away from her shoulder and kissing her cheek.

She nervously tapped her straw against the side of the glass. Tony could see the stress that creased the sides of her mouth and furrowed her brow. He took her hand and caressed it. "Having second thoughts?"

"I'm having a million and one second thoughts. But I know I should go."

"Yes, you should. But I should be going with you."

"I have to do this on my own."

"Bullshit. You don't want me to go because you don't want me to meet your family."

Her eyes flew to his and settled there in the deep blue depths. Every time she looked at him, she felt as if she'd come home at last. It was the most comfortable, familiar, and loving place to be.

She moved her hand to smooth an errant lock of his honey blond hair away from his forehead. He took her fingers and kissed them. She took a deep breath, as if drawing in his strength. "It's not that. I do want you to meet them. But . . ."

"But nothing. Damn it, Sheilagh, I'm your husband. I'm the one who loves you. *You.* Just you. Not your talent or fame or any of that other crap. I love you. I should be there with you. I hate this stubborn side of you." Then he laughed and kissed her. "You can be so obstinate sometimes."

Sheilagh was determined never to let him know her mother or father. Clay, Caitlin, and Carin, they were one thing, but her parents were another thing altogether. Sheilagh didn't want Tony to know about her past in Chicago. She couldn't unleash her demons and allow them to plow up the fertile fields of her marriage. Sheilagh was excruciatingly aware of how untested their love was. In New York she had been safe from the past, from her sins. No one knew the truth . . . except herself and her parents. Sheilagh knew she could lose Tony once Mary Margaret saw them together. She and Tony were too happy, too much in love; they were shark bait for her mother, who was an expert at hobbling souls.

"I guess it's my turn to grow up. I'll be all right."

"Very bravely said, princess, but I don't buy it. This is Tony. I know there's something you're keeping from me. I can see it in your eyes. You have to know, darling, that there's nothing you could ever have said or done that will stop me from loving you."

Sheilagh wanted to say, "Oh, yes there is," but she kept silent and smiled. She was acting again, and Tony wasn't fooled one bit.

He looked down at her hand as a melancholy mood came over him. "Why don't you trust me?"

"I do trust you."

"No, you don't."

She laughed, the sound high-pitched and nervous. "How could you possibly want another woman when you have me?"

His head jerked up. His blue eyes glittered with pain. "I'm not talking about sex, Sheilagh, and you know it. I'm talking about you . . . and that thing back there in your past that makes you tick. You keep stuffing it back and you think it's hidden, but I can see it. When are you going to love me and trust me enough to tell me?"

Sheilagh kept firm control of her expression, summoning up all her acting skills. "You're making a big deal out of this, Tony. There's no big, dark secret. It's just that my father is an asshole and thinks all male actors are gay, neurotic, or both, and he would put you down constantly. I don't want to hear it. And my mother is just as bad. I understand them . . . I think. Maybe I don't understand them at all." She looked down at her watch. "I should be going."

"You have twenty minutes left. Spend them with me."

There was so much sincerity and love in Tony's voice that Sheilagh could not refuse him. "All right. But no more talk about my family and these fantasies about my dark past. Okay?"

"Okay." He leaned across the table and kissed her.

Their passion for each other was not something they could hide. Sheilagh felt as if their souls were uniting every time he kissed her; every time he made love to her. She had always played with sex, had fun with sex, even tried to be wicked as her mother had accused her of being so long ago. But never would she ever, ever have believed that sex could be the spiritual glue that kept her bound to Tony.

Yet every time his lips met hers, Sheilagh floated away into another world. It was a place filled with light, love, and promise. She felt young again, with all the pain washed out of her heart. Tony accepted her totally, but that was because she never exposed the dark side of herself. He was her life now. He had become more important to her than acting, the fame or the money. She didn't want him to know that she felt utterly lost to him. But she was. She wouldn't have it any other way.

"If you keep kissing me like this, Tony, we're going to have to find the luggage room."

"Great idea," he said with a lusty twinkle in his eye. "Do you think there's time?"

"No. I really do need to go."

"I know. Say you'll miss me."

"Of course I will. Every waking moment. Every minute of the night."

"The nights especially." He grinned playfully.

"The mornings especially." She smiled back and touched his cheek. "I really do love you, Tony. More than anything in this world."

"I know, princess."

"You'll call me?"

"Every day . . . and you call me before you go to bed every night. How's that?"

"A deal."

Tony took Sheilagh's hand as they walked down the concourse in silence. The final call for boarding came just as Sheilagh walked up. She turned and kissed Tony one last time. He held her tightly, released her reluctantly. Just as she entered the jetway, she turned to take one last look at her love before she stepped into an uncertain future.

Houston

Michael Killian whisked his plane tickets off the check-in counter at Intercontinental Airport and stuck them in his suit coat pocket.

"I don't see why you won't go with me, Bridget."

"I don't see why you have to go at all," she countered tartly.

"I told you. I'm doing this for Caitlin."

"Caitlin could always take care of herself, if I remember correctly."

"Even Caitlin's tower can crumble sometime."

Bridget turned her dark shining eyes away from him. She hated always being the bad guy. She was jealous of Michael's love for his sisters. She was only trying to get a little of that love for herself . . . something Michael had been unwilling to give for a very long time. She was exhausted from the effort. "Do you want me to walk to the plane with you?"

"Don't put yourself out."

"Shit, Michael. Can't I ever do anything without you putting me down?"

"Sorry. Habit."

"I know."

Michael sighed deeply. He didn't want to get into another quarrel in the middle of the airport. "Walk with me if you want."

Bridget felt the sting of his words long after he'd slung them at her, but she was too proud to let him know it. She could never let Michael know that she was vulnerable to him.

"I'll call you," she said.

"I'll be hard to catch. Lots of meetings. I don't know if I'll stay with Caitlin or get a hotel room."

"You could call me and tell me where you're staying."

"I could."

"But you won't."

"I won't be gone long, Bridget."

They reached the gate. Michael checked in and found that his row had already been called. "I gotta go."

"I know."

He kissed her perfunctorily. She tried to hold him, but his arms were full with his attaché case and hanging bag. He didn't try to hug her back. Her arms fell limply to her sides. She stepped back. "I hope it's a good trip."

"Me, too," he said, and turned away from her, nearly rushing onto the jetway.

Bridget Killian watched the plane taxi away from the building. She felt cold and alone. It was a familiar feeling. This time something was different. Their marriage had reached a turning point, and she realized that they both knew it. They could not continue as they had been, bickering, fighting, placing the blame on each other and avoiding the necessary repair work. She hoped she had not pushed him too far this time. Something deep inside her warned that Michael might not come back to her again.

Even if he did, how long would he stay?

County Clare, Ireland

Carin clung to Richard, who kissed her through her tears. She was leaving Ireland and felt as if she were leaving life itself. Never had she been so at peace nor simultaneously filled with joy and wonderment. She was thoroughly, hopelessly in love. They stood in the greenhouse to say good-bye away from Aileen, Lidia, and Ian, who were packing their things and loading the Fiat. It seemed only appropriate that they should end where they began, Carin thought sadly. The problem was that she didn't want it to end. She wanted to stay in Ireland forever with Richard. She was in love and she should be happy, but her heart was breaking.

"How can it be that I feel as if I've never lived anywhere but here, and yet the days have raced past me?"

Richard held her closer, feeling her pliant body mold to his. "It's because we've been caught between heaven and earth, you see."

She pulled away from him to look into his eyes. "Oh, is that it?" She smiled up at him. "And I thought I was just having a good time."

He touched a lock of her hair and peered deeply into her eyes. "This wasn't . . . excuse me, *isn't* just a fling for me, Carin. I hope I mean more to you than that."

"You do, Richard. So very much more."

He kissed her deeply. His arms were tense and possessive as they held her to his chest. She could feel his need for her even now, and his effort to restrain himself was immeasurable. Passion raced through them both. It wove them together and spun a rapturous cocoon around them, sealing them off from the rest of the world. They were one in their hearts and minds. The hard taskmasters of time and space sliced at the fine emotional threads that bound them, and threatened to keep them apart. Carin nearly believed she could feel the cracks in her heart deepen.

"Say you won't forget about me," Carin breathed between kisses.

"Never. Never." He plunged his tongue into the honeyed interior of her mouth. He relished the silky feel of her lips and tongue.

Voraciously he devoured her as if wanting to fill her with his breath and flesh . . . with his soul. Carin lost herself in the spinning vortex of emotions. From within and without she was bombarded by hungry, greedy passion that threatened to strip her mind from her soul, logic from feelings.

For long moments, her breath could not escape her lungs, and then it rushed forth like a whirlwind. Her heart banged against her rib cage. She could never let him go. Tears ran down her cheeks, flooding them both.

"Please don't cry."

"I can't help it . . . I feel lost to you."

"Not lost, but found." He moaned and kissed away her tears.

Carin tightened her arms around him, hoping that if she held him close enough, circumstances could not separate them.

He kissed her earlobe. Carin could feel his emotion-laden breath slip inside her ear into her brain and burrow into the deepest recesses for safekeeping. His love was part of her now. They were one.

"I'll come for you, Carin," he said.

Stunned, she pulled away from him and gazed into his smoky blue eyes. "You will?"

"Of course I will. Now that I've found you, I can't let you out of my life."

A joyous smile beamed from her face. "Oh, Richard, are you sure? Are you very sure?"

"I love you with all my heart. I can't let you go."

"But how?"

"I have some matters I must take care of here, and then I will come to Chicago. You will wait for me, won't you?"

"Yes! Yes!" she exclaimed, and then kissed him deeply, with tender passion.

He touched her cheek and traced the edge of her jaw with his fingertips. He was trembling. A curious trepidation found him as he spoke again. "I haven't the right to ask you now . . . I mean, there are certain things here that will keep me from you, but only for a little while."

"Ask me what?" she prodded. She had to know . . . to really know. Did he love her as much as she already loved him?

"I think you know. But I can't say the words yet. The time isn't right. But it will be." He held her closely again. "It will be, my love. I promise. Believe in me. Trust in me. I will come for you."

"Then we will be together?"

"Forever and ever."

Richard kissed her one last time. It was a kiss of possession as his lips sealed hers. With his mouth and tongue he told her that she was the only woman in the world he would ever want. With his strong arms he held her to his chest and told her that she would never be alone again. She was his and she was not afraid.

The Fiat horn honked, signaling Carin's departure. Slowly they ended the kiss, but as Richard walked with her out of the greenhouse, he kept his arm around her waist and held her hand. He tried to smile, but his courage failed him. "It will be torture not to see you or touch you every day."

Aileen was seated at the wheel of the car. She had already said her good-byes to Lidia and Ian. She waited patiently as Richard opened the door for Carin and then closed it. He walked around to Aileen's side of the car and leaned in to place an affectionate kiss on her cheek.

"Take care of her for me," he said sadly.

"Of course I will." Aileen smiled warmly. "You're a very special man, Richard. I'm glad we came to your castle."

"So am I. More than you'll ever know."

Aileen winked at him. "I think I do."

Aileen started the car's engine and put it into gear. "Good-bye, Richard," she said.

Richard reluctantly moved away from the car and waved at the retreating Fiat for an inordinately long time after it was out of sight.

As they roared over the top of the hill, Aileen glanced back in the rearview mirror at the castle. She blinked twice, knowing she was not seeing what she thought she saw. Instead of seeing Richard still standing at the front doors to the castle, she believed she saw Patrick and Mavreen, dressed in their formal clothes and waving good-bye. When she looked again, they were gone.

Carin had come to Ireland and found love. Aileen had come to Ireland and found that love never dies.

Heathrow Airport was jammed with travelers. Clusters of Saville Row–suited businessmen inspected the contents of briefcases as if expecting something to be missing. Children nagged their parents for another stop at the fish-and-chips stands, and airline workers weaved their way through the chaos as they struggled to keep on schedule. Carin lugged her suitcase through the glass doors toward the ticket counter where Aileen was receiving their boarding passes. Carin checked the last of their baggage, and then in silence they headed toward the appointed departure gate.

Carin's mind was filled with visions of Richard. She replayed every second of their days together. She was so immersed in her thoughts that she did not see the newspaper headlines of the *London Times* as they passed the newsstand. But Aileen did.

She stopped stock-still. She moved toward the newspaper as if in a trance. She picked it up and stared at the words EMERALD CHOCOLATE KILLS.

Carin had gone nine paces past her grandmother before she realized Aileen was not by her side. When she turned around, she, too, saw the bold letters of the headline.

"It can't be true!" Carin said, snatching up a copy from the top of the pile. Her eyes scanned the story quickly, but it wasn't until she reread the ominous report that she believed. "I've got to call Chicago." She tossed the paper down and raced toward the pay telephones. She waited impatiently as the operator placed the transatlantic call to the Emerald Chocolate headquarters.

Carin felt beads of anxious perspiration on her forehead as Martha O'Boland transferred the call to her mother. Caitlin finally answered.

"Mother! I'm at Heathrow and just saw the newspapers. What's going on?"

"Darling, I'm so glad we finally made contact."

"It never dawned on me to call you. I was having so much fun . . . I'm sorry I didn't think to call."

"It's okay, really. There isn't much you could have done." Caitlin's voice was filled with despair.

"I should have been with you."

"It's been rough on all of us."

"How's Daddy taking it?"

"He quit—"

"He did what?" Carin interrupted. "How could he do such a thing at a time like this?"

"Carin, honey, a great deal has happened since you left. I'm backing up your father's decision."

"What?" Carin felt as if the world were spinning out of control and she desperately needed some kind of glue to keep it all intact. "But you're still there."

"Only temporarily. Until the crisis is over at least. But we'll talk about all this when you get home. By the way, your aunt Sheilagh is on her way here, too. So is Michael."

Again Carin felt shock waves nearly knock her off her feet. "Aunt Sheilagh is coming home?"

"Yes. To be with me."

Suddenly Carin sensed the impact of what her mother was saying. "I'm so glad for you, Mom. She must love you a lot."

"I never doubted it for a minute."

"So what you're telling me is that by the time I get there, the sparks ought to be flying."

"I'm bracing for explosions." Caitlin laughed nervously.

Carin didn't like the anxiety she sensed in her mother's voice. There was something her mother was hiding from her. It seemed Caitlin was always harboring secrets. Carin wished with all her heart that her mother would release her demons, expose them for what they were, and then go on. But Caitlin was more Killian than Burke, and Killians protected their own.

Just then, Aileen signaled that their plane was boarding.

"I gotta go, Mom. We'll be there soon. Hang tough and don't let Grandpa step on you."

"I'm working on that. I love you, dear."

"I love you, too, Mom. See you soon."

Carin hung up and looked into Aileen's expectant eyes.

"How bad is it?" Aileen inquired.

"I'm not sure, but I have a strange feeling that the worst is yet to come." Carin sighed heavily. "We'd better make that plane."

As they headed for the departure gate, Carin's sense of unease grew. Caitlin's penchant for keeping secrets had always kept Carin in the dark and distanced her from her own family. She wanted to be a friend to her mother. But how? What had happened in the Oak Park house thirty years ago that no one could ever talk about? What exactly were Sheilagh's sins? Carin had never heard the whole story; only hints and half-completed sentences that ended in evasive glances and then finally in excuses to change the subject.

Carin would give anything to know the truth.

Chapter 10

May 1932
Chicago

SHEILAGH STUCK TWO bobby pins into Caitlin's head to affix the Communion veil. "Quit squirming!"

"You hurt me! Ouch!"

"You're such a baby, Caitlin."

"You're not so grown-up either, Sheilagh," Caitlin retaliated, and pushed her sister away. "I can do it myself!" Caitlin tried to tame her long, brown, baby-fine hair, which spun with static electricity. It matted to the side of her cheek and got caught in the lace edge of the veil. "Ugh!"

"Fine, have it your way. But Mother told me to make sure

you were dressed, and I don't want her yelling at me because you don't like the way I did your hair. She's mad at me already."

Caitlin stared into the vanity mirror. "What's she mad about this time? What did you do?"

"Nothing." Sheilagh's hands shook, a clear sign that she was lying. "You're too young to understand anyway," she said with a sigh, regretting her sister's younger age. She wished *she* had an older sister who could give her counsel. She needed someone to talk to. Especially now.

"You always say that, Sheilagh." Caitlin screwed up her face into an ugly grimace. "Someday I'm gonna be even smarter than you! You'll see. Then it won't matter that I'm so young."

Sheilagh observed her nine-year-old sister's efforts to hide her tears, and realized that now she'd been the one to cause pain. "I'm sorry, Caitlin. I didn't mean it the way it sounded. This is your First Holy Communion day. You should be happy. Daddy sent you white roses. That's a special thing. I never got roses for my First Holy Communion."

Caitlin sniffed. "You didn't?"

"No. So you see? You're more special already, and you didn't even know it." Sheilagh smiled, hoping to cheer her sister.

Caitlin propped her elbows onto the vanity table, sank her face in her hands, and stared at her glum reflection. "That's because you're pretty and I'm not. You don't need flowers to be special."

Sheilagh's hands flew to her hips. "You make me so mad sometimes, Caitlin! You think you have it so bad . . . you don't know anything. It's just as hard being me. And Michael doesn't have it any better."

Caitlin considered this for a moment. "Maybe Daddy doesn't like any of us."

"Maybe Mother doesn't either," Sheilagh said under her breath. She had tried to avoid thinking about the ugly scene the day before between herself and Mary Margaret, but now it came swirling back to her.

Caitlin had been in the kitchen smashing up Emerald chocolate "bricks" to put in her oatmeal cookies. As usual, she seemed merrily oblivious to the undertow of emotions that swirled around the other members of the family.

Patrick leaned heavily on the wide kitchen sink, staring out the window, while Mary Margaret sat at the table cutting six-year-old Michael's sausage into bite-sized pieces. As Sheilagh poured the orange juice, she noticed that her mother's hands gripped the knife and fork much too tightly as she whacked at the meat.

The only other noise in the room was the *click, click* of Caitlin's wooden spoon against the tan crockery bowl. Tension weighted the air. Even Michael was quiet.

"I think you'll like this batch, Daddy. I changed the recipe," she said, and continued churning the butter and sugar.

Patrick barely turned around. "Huh? Oh, yeah. Fine. Fine." He dropped his head and stared at the sink.

Sheilagh noted the pasty look to his skin, his bloodshot eyes, and the lethargic movements of his body. He seemed to look this way a lot now, she thought. Like their next-door neighbor John Flannery after he'd been drinking all night.

Mary Margaret's lips were pressed into a line, as if they'd been drawn on her face with a fine-tipped Sheaffer pen.

"Eat something, Patrick," Mary Margaret said flatly. "You'll feel better."

"I'm not hungry."

Michael tugged on his mother's chenille robe. "What's the matter with Daddy?"

"The influenza," she whispered to her son, and then whacked away at a second pork link. "Did you have a late supper last night?" She didn't look at her husband.

"Yeah."

"How late?" Mary Margaret demanded.

"Not very."

"Who went with you?"

"Stop it, Mary," Patrick growled. "We'll talk about it later."

Mary Margaret glared at him with tortured eyes. "No, we won't. We never do."

Sheilagh should have noticed that something more than the usual "morning after" dialogue was taking place, but she didn't. She was young and naive.

Suddenly Caitlin came to life. "Daddy, if this recipe turns out, will you print it on the chocolate brick wrapper?"

"Huh? Sure, sure," he said, seemingly glad for the diversion. "What's in it, Caitlin?"

"Half a pound of butter, one cup of light brown sugar, one

cup of white sugar, two eggs, one teaspoon of vanilla, two cups of flour sifted with one teaspoon of soda, a half teaspoon each of baking powder and salt, two cups of oatmeal, a cup of pecans, and one cup of chocolate chunks." She smiled up at her father, seeking his approval. He stared at her with lifeless eyes. "Maybe one and a half cups of chocolate chunks?" she asked tentatively.

There was still no answer. He hadn't heard a word she had said. Caitlin felt like a piece of furniture. She realized she was nothing to him. Not a daughter to be cherished and loved, a nothing. She looked down into the creamed butter through a veil of tears. He couldn't see them, her tears, she thought. He would never, ever see her tears, she vowed. "One and a half," she said loudly with conviction. She began beating furiously.

Sheilagh finished pouring the orange juice. As she passed Caitlin on her way to the sink, she whispered into her sister's ear: "You're wasting your time on him. He's a heartless bastard."

"Shut up! Leave me alone!"

Sheilagh's heart went out to Caitlin, who only wanted to be noticed and loved. They all did.

Sheilagh deposited the glass pitcher in the sink and sat down at the table. They waited. It was something the Killians did well. They waited for Patrick to move, speak, breathe. They all kowtowed to him.

Sheilagh hated the feeling of impotence. She felt tiny and weak when she was around him. She decided she hated him, and then she felt better. The hate made her strong; it protected her from his abuse. But her hate did not stop him from hurting Caitlin and Michael. She felt closed off from her family, and she hated that most of all.

Patrick's mood determined the atmosphere of the household. In his absence, Mary Margaret dominated the children, but Patrick was always king. The family ate his favorite foods, dressed to his satisfaction, performed at school only to please him. But none of them, not the children or Mary Margaret, had become the replicas of himself that he wanted. Their fits of self-expression could not be suppressed no matter how hard he tried.

"I'm going to work," Patrick finally announced.

"I'm taking Michael to mass. Wouldn't you like—" Mary Margaret began.

"No! I wouldn't," he interrupted, furious as he shoved the

swinging wooden door open and stomped out of the kitchen.

Mary Margaret's jaw tightened and the vein at her temple jumped. Only Sheilagh noticed.

"Do I have ta go to church?" Michael whined as he inserted a too large piece of waffle into his mouth.

"Yes," Mary Margaret hissed.

"But I don't wanna." Michael's face crumpled.

Mary Margaret ignored him. Sheilagh picked up the steel-topped glass syrup dispenser. Suddenly Mary Margaret's assault was directed toward her. "Did you clean up your room yet?"

"Not yet."

"I told you to do it yesterday!"

"Caitlin was going to help me."

"I didn't ask Caitlin, did I?" Mary Margaret's voice rose to a high pitch.

"She messed up her side . . ." Sheilagh defended herself.

"Get upstairs right now!"

"All right. All right!" Sheilagh replied, knowing her breakfast would not be kept for her. That was part of the punishment.

Sheilagh left the kitchen, and the sounds of the wooden spoon spanking the sides of the crockery bowl faded away.

She went up to the bedroom she shared with her sister, flopped on the bed, and pulled out her latest issues of movie magazines. John Wayne was starring in the fifth episode of *The Hurricane Express,* and Paul Muni was portraying Al Capone in *Scarface,* but it was the erotic photographs of Johnny Weissmuller half-clad in his Tarzan costume that caught her attention. A three-page spread showed the new star from every angle. Sheilagh held her breath as she placed her fingers on the photograph, touching his biceps, triceps, pectorals, and gluteous maximus. She knew all the proper names for the different muscle groups and had gotten an A on her health class exam. Never had she been so glad she'd paid attention in school. A curious ache roiled just below her abdomen. She wasn't certain what part of the body it was. Maybe it was her ovaries.

Sheilagh had been acutely aware of her body ever since she'd started her period a year ago. None of the other girls in her class were anywhere near menstruation, but she had been going through many bodily changes since the end of the fourth grade. Now she was in fifth grade. She wasn't the only one in school who had noticed that her breasts were larger than even most of the eighth-graders.

The nuns had always liked Sheilagh, partly because she was a good student and partly because she was pretty. In the first grade she was chosen to carry Mary's crown in the May Day Procession. She was the unanimous choice of all the nuns at Ascension Parochial School to portray the Blessed Virgin in the Christmas Pageant when she was in second grade. Life had been great until her breasts burst into near full bloom by the fifth grade. Suddenly she went from favorite to outcast. All the girls hated her. She was never invited to slumber parties or birthday parties anymore. Only the boys liked her.

Boys from Our Lady of Sorrows flocked to the school yard on Good Fridays when extra recess was given, just to watch Sheilagh jump rope. Even the boys from the public schools were known to hang around Ascension to see Sheilagh Killian in her conservative school uniform of pleated plaid skirt, anklets and oxfords, white blouse, and navy cardigan.

While the other girls were doing everything they could to encourage their preadolescent breasts to grow, Sheilagh was trying to smash hers down. She made her mother buy blouses two sizes too big and then pulled them out at the waist, creating a balloon effect that hid her bosom. She wore tight undershirts, which helped to press the flesh flat. No amount of physical torture was too great to keep her from being called hurtful names.

Her endeavors were in vain.

Sheilagh Killian was a freak. She retreated inward and began living out fantasies in which she was always the heroine. She read movie magazines with a vengeance. Each month when the new issues of *Photoplay* and *Modern Screen* came out, she was the first one at the magazine rack in Nik's Pharmacy. She *had* to know what was happening in the lives of Mae West, Greta Garbo, Marlene Dietrich, and Jean Harlow. Always she read that their lives were exciting, glamorous, and productive. Month after month, year after year, Sheilagh became more addicted to Hollywood gossip and inexorably immersed in a world of make-believe.

She acted out her favorite screen roles in her bedroom whenever she was alone. She watched her face in the mirror as if she were the cameraman photographing her on a Hollywood sound stage. She taught herself to cry on demand and to laugh uproariously at the snap of a finger. She learned to weave magic with her expressions, creating facades to hide her pain.

By watching herself in the mirror, Sheilagh discovered exactly what she did and did not like about her manner and appearance. She discovered that she did not detest her body but rather the people who were jealous of her. She learned to throw her entire body into this new art, to elicit emotional reactions even from herself. She experimented on other family members, the kids at school, the nuns, the priests, and found that she could manipulate the responses she wanted by simply lowering an eyebrow, pouting a lip, or crossing her arms. The magic she found was acting, and she realized by the age of ten that she was good at it.

Sheilagh could still hear the sounds that Caitlin made as she banged around in the kitchen downstairs, and Mary Margaret's voice as she scolded Michael for spilling his milk. Sheilagh went to her mother's bedroom, opened the dresser drawer, and withdrew one of Mary Margaret's slips. She intended to play out a Jean Harlow role that afternoon, and she needed just the right prop.

The slip bore a Sears, Roebuck tag and was made of cotton batiste, not satin like the movie stars wore. It had no lace for decoration, only a small, powder blue rosette between the breasts. But the adjustable straps allowed her to hike up the bodice, bringing the swell of her breasts up and over the top of the slip. She pulled her long auburn hair provocatively over her shoulder then as sensually as she was able, slid her hand down her arm. The effect was startling. She looked grown-up. Sheilagh sobered and stood still, staring again at her reflection.

She went to the small phonograph and put on the new Cole Porter song, "Night and Day." She spritzed Evening in Paris toilet water on herself and into the air. Acting required setting a scene, she knew, and she picked up the magazine with Johnny Weissmuller's nearly naked body splashed across the center two pages. Her ears listened to the romantic words, her nostrils were filled with perfume, and her eyes scanned the length of the most beautiful man she had ever seen. Suddenly she felt a pleasurable plunge in her abdomen again. Very pleasurable.

She pursed her lips and tilted her chin upward, imagining what it would be like to kiss Johnny. She could nearly see him standing before her, naked, skin slathered with sweat because it was hot here in the jungle. He reached out his hand, and she took it. He pulled her to his chest, and she pretended to protest. She placed her hands against his pectorals and pushed at him.

He was insistent. He held her tighter and tighter against his chest, crushing her breasts.

Sheilagh felt the plunging feeling again. She stood staring into the mirror and watched as she parted her legs into a wider stance. Her breasts felt bigger, as if they were swelling in front of her eyes. She moved them inside the slip, liking the scratch of the cotton against the tips of her nipples. She moved again. Her mouth went dry.

She could no longer see her own reflection in the mirror. All she saw now was Johnny Weissmuller, and he seemed to be all around her, surrounding her like the music and the perfume. She touched him, wanting to feel skin against skin.

She raised her hand to her own breast, suddenly hating the feel of the cotton slip, and lowered just one side. Now she rejoiced in the touch of the smooth skin under her hand. Her stomach sank deeper within her. Her knees began to shake. She had to breathe in deeper and more rapid breaths.

The ache moved from her stomach to the area between her legs. It ached and itched. It throbbed. Her free hand slid across the flat of her belly and then slowly began inching the cotton slip up above her knees, then above her thighs to her waist. She needed to stop the throbbing.

She heard the words "You are the one" just as she put her hand down her cotton panties. It was wet down there, and she realized with an ancient female knowledge that this was something different. Sheilagh knew that this event marked her as a woman more than menstruation and more than the day when she would conceive a baby. This incredible feeling of surrender to her own body was what being a woman was all about.

Shock waves seared through Sheilagh's body as she moved her hand across herself. Reflexively she flung her head back. She massaged her breast with more vigor. Then she picked up a rhythm by coordinating the movements of both hands at once. She was on fire, a momentous fire that kept building and burning and shooting fireballs up and down her body. A mist of perspiration covered her forehead, then down the valley between her breasts. She was light-headed. She could hardly breathe. She didn't know what was happening, but it was the most incredible feeling she'd ever experienced, as if she were riding the roller coaster and the double Ferris wheel both at the same time.

There she stood, before the mirror, breast exposed, nipple

erect, legs parted, and her hands manipulating her body into her first orgasm, when Mary Margaret opened the door and saw her.

"God in Heaven! What are you doing?" Mary Margaret's heavy brown oxfords thudded against the wood floor as she moved into the room and shut the door behind her. "You wicked, wicked girl!" she screamed, and slapped Sheilagh across the face.

Sheilagh's neck snapped back. She yanked her hand out of her panties and shoved her breast back into the slip.

Crrraaack! Mary Margaret slapped her daughter again. "Answer me!"

"I was . . . pretending . . ."

"What? To be a whore? Is that what you've been doing up in this room all by yourself?"

"No . . . Mama . . ." Sheilagh flinched as Mary Margaret raised her hand again and again.

She slapped her across the face, throat, shoulders, and especially the breasts. She punched her arm hard enough to produce welts. "Harlot! You'll go to hell! Whore! Whore!" Mary Margaret continued to pummel Sheilagh until she sank to the floor and Mary Margaret became exhausted.

Anger possessed Mary Margaret like a demon. She was out of breath and covered in sweat as she gazed down at her sobbing daughter. "I ought to kick you out of the house for this. Killians are not sluts, Sheilagh. And I'll be damned if I let you become one. Not if I have to beat you every day and keep you chained up every night."

"Mama . . . please . . . listen to me . . ." Sheilagh coughed out the words over the phlegm in her throat. Tears streamed in torrents down her inflamed cheeks. She choked again and wiped her running nose with the back of her hand. "I didn't know . . ."

"You didn't know? From what I could see, you know all too well what to do. Where did you learn those things, Sheilagh?" She grabbed Sheilagh's arm with a rough jerk, lifting her halfway off the floor. "Has some boy been doing this to you?"

"No, Mama. No. I would never . . . never do that with a boy."

"I don't believe you. I've seen how they watch you at mass. I've seen how many of them follow you home from school. Oh, they stay their distance, but I've watched them watching you."

"But I don't want them to . . ."

"You entice them, Sheilagh. You have something about you that draws them like a magnet. All sluts are like that. They draw unsuspecting men into their webs and then they destroy their lives. This is all devil's work, Sheilagh," Mary Margaret said, her eyes becoming frighteningly wide and glistening with zeal. "Perhaps I should get the priest and have you exorcised."

Sheilagh was suddenly flooded with fear. "No! Mama, no! You can't tell a priest! Don't tell a man what I've done. I could never go back to school if you did that. Please don't, Mama. Please . . ." She sobbed piteously.

"You should have thought about that before you committed this heinous act!" Mary Margaret grabbed Sheilagh's shoulders and pulled her to her wobbly feet.

"You have to confess this, Sheilagh. It's the only way out for you. Otherwise, you'll burn in hell for all eternity. Forever and ever, consumed in flames."

"I can't tell the priest."

"You can and you will."

"Please, Mama."

"I won't hear any more about it. But I will make a bargain with you. You go to confession next Saturday and I won't tell your father. We won't tell anyone. Not ever. You hear me? It's too humiliating. If anyone ever knew that my daughter, my own flesh and blood, was a whore, I could never walk the streets of Chicago again. The shame that you have brought to this family could be ruinous."

Mary Margaret's eyes were white-hot and blazing with righteousness. In this situation she was omnipotent. Sheilagh could not imagine the final Judgment Day being any more shattering than this trial she was now enduring.

"I . . . I'll go see the priest."

Mary Margaret straightened and stuck her chin in the air as she looked down at her daughter. "Very well. And you are never to repeat this debaucherous act again."

"Never!"

"Wait here." Mary Margaret stomped out of the room, marched down the hall, and returned with a pair of shiny steel shears. She walked up to Sheilagh, jerked at the hem of the slip with one hand, and began cutting the fabric away from Sheilagh's body.

"What are you doing?" Sheilagh cried as her eyes filled with hot tears of humiliation.

Mary Margaret cut the slip away from her daughter, leaving Sheilagh clad only in her cotton panties and with her arms crossed over her breasts. The scissors flashed in the light that filtered through the venetian blinds as Mary Margaret cut the slip into a dozen pieces. Then she threw the shears on the floor.

"I don't ever want to see that garment again. Throw it in the trash," she said. With her lower lip curled in contempt, she added: "I don't want any of your smell on my clothing." She slammed the door behind her.

Sheilagh fell to the floor and cried for over an hour. Her sobs finally became whimpers. Then they, too, died. She wrapped the slip scraps in a brown paper bag and deposited them in the trash bin behind the house. Then she took a bath to wash away her tears, the bruises, and her smell, even though she wasn't sure what her mother had meant.

Sheilagh looked down at Caitlin clad in her pure white dress and Communion veil. *Innocence,* she thought. *That's what I've lost.* Suddenly she was very jealous of Caitlin for still being only nine years old. Sheilagh wished she could go back and start yesterday all over again, but she couldn't. She wondered just how long her mother would keep her word about not telling her father. She didn't trust her mother anymore. Mary Margaret believed she had a demon in the house. Such thinking could lead to some bad times ahead for Sheilagh. She knew her mother would never let her forget this.

"What's the matter, Sheilagh?" Caitlin asked. "You look kinda mad."

"It's not because of you." Sheilagh put her hand on Caitlin's shoulder. "I'm very proud of you, you know."

"You are?" Caitlin's smile was filled with love.

At that moment Sheilagh realized she needed Caitlin as she had not needed her before. Caitlin adored her, tried to emulate her in many things. Sheilagh knew she wanted that adulation to continue; it was essential to the rebuilding of her self-esteem. She would have to make a pact with her mother never to tell Caitlin. She could never let Caitlin know the truth—that her sister was a whore.

Chapter 11

RAYS OF SUN coming through the stained-glass windows bathed the First Holy Communicants of Ascension Church in a kaleidoscope of color. The first two pews were reserved for the members of Caitlin's second-grade class, who would all be making their first Communions. The next dozen pews were reserved for their respective families.

Caitlin kept her chubby fingers pressed firmly together, pointing reverently upward, just as Sister Constantine had instructed. She felt her veil slipping, but she dare not touch it, now that the two rows of girls had proceeded halfway down the aisle. She didn't want any of the parents to see her fidgeting. It would be another black mark against her. Caitlin already knew that her mother regretted the fact that she was not in front of the line with the pretty, petite girls with their Shirley Temple curls. She was the last in line, which marked her as the tallest, fattest, and clumsiest.

Caitlin was scared to death of this ritual even though they had studied the procedure long and hard with Sister Constantine. She remembered all too well the stories that Sister Constantine had told about the girl who spit out her Communion host into her handkerchief, and when she returned to her seat, the host had turned to mud. Billy Leary told her that the host tasted like human skin and the wine tasted like real blood. Caitlin knew it was a test of courage to receive Holy Communion, but she dare not let anyone know that she thought she'd puke right there at the Communion rail. Her mother did this every day of her life. The rest of the family went to Communion every Sunday and never flinched. It was a test of strength . . . of being a Catholic and a Killian.

"I can do it. I can do it," Caitlin repeated to herself like a litany.

Just as the children were all seated, the choir burst into a chorus of "Salve Regina." The bells on the altar were rung and the priest entered the sacristy. Caitlin raised her eyes to the round domed ceiling and gazed at the paintings of the apostles at the Last Supper. If she kept her head up, her tears might flow back into her head. She was scared. Really scared.

Sheilagh sat two pews behind Caitlin and wondered what her sister was looking at. She, too, raised her eyes upward, but Sheilagh found no solace in the paintings. The gold-edged words seemed to scream down at her from above. "Chastity. Charity. Modesty. Faith. Mildness. Long Suffering. Patience. Peace. Benignity. Goodness. Continency. Hope." Above these words she read: "He who is among the least of you is the greatest."

Sheilagh hung her head. Surely those words could not be meant for her. She was the worst of sinners, according to her mother. This church was the last place on earth she wanted to be. She couldn't look into the eyes of the priest when he spoke the sermon. She avoided the faces of the nuns who taught her classes. She wanted to crawl beneath the kneeler where no one would ever see her again. If she'd been Mary Magdalene, she couldn't have felt more unclean.

Everyone knelt for the offertory. Sheilagh was so lost in her thoughts, she didn't notice. Mary Margaret whacked her on the hip. "Kneel!" she commanded, and skewered her with a condemning look.

Sheilagh sank to her knees and kept her head bent.

"You can't go to Communion," Mary Margaret whispered in her ear.

"But I . . ." Sheilagh knew what her mother was saying. She had sinned. She hadn't been to confession to wash away her sin. All the families of the communicants were going to Communion today. If she stayed in this pew when everyone else walked up to the Communion rail, then everyone in the entire church would know that Sheilagh Killian had sinned. Worse, they would all be wondering what she had done. On Monday the kids at school would ostracize her even more than they already did. This punishment was too great.

Sheilagh's eyes shot to the upper dome above the burgundy marble walls that surrounded the white-pillared altar where Jesus looked down from the cross. She stared into his soulful, pain-filled eyes. She felt sick to her stomach. This was it, she was going to die. And she deserved it. What Sheilagh didn't understand was the bitterness she tasted in her mouth when she looked over at her mother.

It came time for Communion. Slowly each of the children marched to the white marble rail. Caitlin felt drops of nervous perspiration on her forehead. Her hands were shaking, so she pressed them more tightly together. She knelt and waited for the priest to come to her. She closed her eyes much too soon, but she didn't want to see the host as it was laid on her tongue. The priest's words were a jumble of Latin she didn't understand, but when she tasted the host, it tasted like Big Chief yellow tablet paper. She clamped her mouth shut, and her eyes popped open. Billy Leary was wrong! Billy Leary had lied to her. The wine was more water than wine, and not at all like blood.

Caitlin nearly jumped up from the Communion rail. She wanted to run back to the pew and shout out loud that she would strangle Billy Leary the next time she saw him. But she didn't. She kept in line with the other girls, completely forgot all the after-Communion prayers she'd been memorizing for weeks, and swallowed the Communion wafer. There was a very wide, mischievous grin on her mouth as she thought about how she would get even with Billy and watched her mother and father go to Communion. The smile disappeared when they passed her by without a wink or smile like the other parents gave their children.

Caitlin had accomplished something today. They had no idea of the courage she had expended. They still didn't pay any attention to her. She looked for Sheilagh. Sheilagh would seek her out and catch her eye. Sheilagh would let her know that she was proud of her. But Sheilagh didn't go to Communion. Suddenly Caitlin knew that something was very wrong. Her sister had been acting strange all morning. Now she hadn't gone to Communion.

Sheilagh kept her head down, pretending to pray so intently that she was oblivious to the mass being conducted around her. As the parishioners passed, she heard her name being spoken in the whisper of rumor. She would never live this down. Now she would have to find a lie to tell everyone. She could never, ever tell anyone the truth. Humiliation hovered over her like an albatross.

For the first time in her life, Sheilagh Killian prayed with all her heart. When she ended her prayer, she was hit with the thought that her humiliation had been unnecessary. Mary

Margaret could have dropped the matter, but in her righteousness, she had chosen to weaken Sheilagh. She wanted to see her daughter suffer.

Sheilagh looked into the eyes of the portrait again. Maybe Jesus could forgive, but Sheilagh never would.

By inviting up-and-coming politicians, society doyennes, and prominent businessmen to Caitlin's reception, Patrick and Mary Margaret hoped to better their social position. None of Caitlin's school chums had been invited, and she realized her Communion was only an excuse for her parents to entertain. Even her white roses, placed on the dining table as a centerpiece, matched the decor of white gladioli and pink peonies that her mother grew in their garden. The china, crystal, and sterling silver that Mary Margaret had bought at Marshall Field's before the crash gleamed against the white Irish linen tablecloth. All the Sheridan dining chairs had been removed from the dining room and placed around the living room. The silk draperies and sheers had been pulled back from the French doors to reveal the opulently blooming gardens where most of the party was to take place.

Sterling epergnes overflowed with Emerald chocolates. The deep, dark chocolates that Caitlin loved the best had been molded into tiny Bibles, crosses, and lilies. Caitlin knew these were from their Easter collection, but she felt warm at the sentiment. Maybe her father had done this just for her. The milk chocolates were in the shapes of bicycles, megaphones, baseballs, various seashell designs, seahorses, and flags. They were part of the upcoming summer collection.

Caitlin's face fell as she scurried into the living room. There on each of the piecrust mahogany pedestal end tables, next to the celery green overstuffed sofas, were the new tufted satin gift boxes Emerald was bringing out in June. One for graduation, one for weddings and bridal showers. There was even one hand-painted with a pink-bonneted baby on top for baby showers and christenings.

"At least it wasn't a boy baby on the top," she said aloud solemnly. It was clear to Caitlin that little had been done this day to honor her. Again she had to take the crumbs of affection her parents doled out to her.

The empty spot in her heart ached and so she lifted the cover of the wedding gift box, picked up a dark chocolate shaped like a wedding bell, and ate it. Then she ate one shaped like an orange blossom filled with orange-flavored filling. It was followed by two foil-wrapped chocolate-mousse-centered milk chocolates, three coconut balls, and a scroll-shaped solid piece of chocolate that was imprinted with the words "Just Married." Like all the premium Emerald chocolates, they melted like warm sunshine in her mouth.

Caitlin knew more about chocolates than anyone else in the family. She knew the history of chocolate as if it were a fairy tale.

Chocolate came to earth when the Incan god Quetzalcoatl appeared to his people to show them how to plant the cocoa tree seeds, along with giving them their calendar and telling them how to work with wood, feathers, and silver. Christopher Columbus was the first white man to taste the bitter cocoa drink, but he rejected the worth of the cocoa beans and left Mexico without taking them back to Spain. In 1519 when Cortés came to Montezuma's court, he was served a gold-chased polished tortoiseshell filled with a drink called xocoatl, a cold, frothy brew of cocoa, honey, spices, and vanilla. Cortés noted that Montezuma drank fifty flagons of the brew each day, especially before entering his harem. Cortés called it "the divine drink" and brought it back to King Charles I of Spain. For centuries chocolate was thought to build up resistance and fight fatigue. A cup of this precious drink was thought to permit a man to walk for a whole day without food, just as Hernán Cortés had originally stated.

The divine drink went on to captivate Europe as more ingenious ways were found to enjoy chocolate. Since the Spanish court was the European trendsetter of the seventeenth century, travelers to Madrid discovered the various chocolate drinks of Spanish nobility. Chocolate houses sprang up in London where chocolate was mixed with wine or brandy and enjoyed with tobacco pipes. The young bloods of London would gamble and carouse in the Covent Garden or St. James Street chocolate houses.

Then, in 1828, a Dutchman by the name of Coenraad van Houten invented a screw press that squeezed the cocoa beans until two thirds of the cocoa butter was removed, leaving only cocoa powder and a small residue of cocoa paste. The cocoa powder was immediately introduced into dozens of recipes. But the cocoa butter went unused . . . until much later.

In 1847 the Bristol firm of Fry and Sons introduced the first "eating chocolate." They didn't know that the grainy texture would eventually be smoothed out and the harsh flavor would be tamed. It took the Swiss to finally refine, invent, and reinvent chocolate confections. In 1845 Rodolphe Sprungli-Amman opened a chocolate shop in Zurich. Daniel Peter and Henri Nestle, Swiss-French brothers, invented milk chocolate, and Rodolphe Lindt of Berne developed "fondant" chocolate that began to melt upon immediate impact with the tongue. Heaven had come to earth.

Through the years chocolate grew more tasteful, more meltingly smooth, exotic, and even heady as liqueurs were added to ganaches and centers.

Caitlin's side of her bedroom bookcase was lined with old and new books about the history of chocolate, and she had devoured them as easily as she did the candy itself. Chocolate was her world.

Caitlin ate another chocolate and felt the ache in her heart subside. Chocolate always made her feel better, and for that she was grateful. As she looked around the pretty room, she again felt the sunshine on her face and the courage she needed to meet her parents' guests. She smoothed the lace on her veil and pushed back the errant locks of hair on her cheeks. If her parents were not proud of her, she would be proud of herself.

The Killians' white stucco and green-tiled house on East Street in Oak Park was only three years old, and it overflowed with people, flowers, and food. De Sotos, Fords, Buicks, and a conspicuous Stutz Super Bearcat lined East Street and wrapped around the corner on the way to Oak Park Avenue. Local aldermen and would-be politicians followed Patrick into the study, where he dispensed bootleg whiskey into their punch cups.

Sheilagh and Caitlin didn't know many of the people at the party except for the Murphys from down the street; John S. Clark, the alderman; the Learys from their parish; Father Troy; and Martha O'Boland, Patrick's secretary, who gave Caitlin a new white pearl rosary as a gift.

Caitlin cut a piece of white-iced vanilla cake for Michael and sat chatting with Martha at a table beneath the crab apple tree. The tree was in full spring bloom, and the tiny white petals fell like rain. Michael grumbled as he kept picking apple blossoms out of the thick icing.

"Thank you for my rosary," Caitlin said to Martha.

"You're welcome." Martha patted her hand.

Mary Margaret had once told Caitlin to be nice to Martha, because she was an old maid and had no children of her own. The Killian children were as close to her own as she would ever get. Caitlin didn't understand why Martha was an old maid. She was pretty in a quiet way. She had brown hair that she wore short with soft bangs. Her blue eyes were a soft color. But Caitlin did notice that she never seemed to smile with her eyes unless Patrick was around, which to Caitlin meant that her father must be nicer to office employees than he was to his family. Martha had beautiful skin with no lines or wrinkles like the ones that were developing around her mother's eyes. She had to be younger than her mother, Caitlin surmised.

"Are the pearls real?" Caitlin asked, sipping her pineapple-flavored punch.

"Not on my salary. Why? Do you wish they were?"

"Oh, no. I think the rosary is beautiful just the way it is. I'll take very good care of it." Caitlin gave Martha a hug.

"You've always been special to me, Caitlin." Martha smiled happily as she touched Caitlin's dark bangs and affectionately lifted a lock of hair from her face. "Your father and mother tell me that they think of me as one of the family, but to tell the truth, you're the only one who seems to care about me."

"I like you, Martha."

"I know. It shows. You always ask about my day and help me water the African violets on my desk. I know I have you to thank for my invitation here today."

Caitlin's eyes reflected Martha's sadness. "You're the only friend they would let me invite. I'm glad you could come." She squeezed Martha's hand.

"I wouldn't have missed it for the world."

Martha's gaze wandered away from the children as she watched the guests move into the house from the terrace and then back to the garden again. She seemed to be looking for someone. Then Caitlin noticed that Martha's face became quite stern and her eyes narrowed.

She followed her gaze and saw an expensively dressed man walk through the French doors onto the terrace. He was very young, with black hair, brown eyes, and a hawklike nose. Caitlin didn't like the way his eyes darted about the mingling guests, as if he, too, was looking for someone. He seemed nervous, and when Sheilagh bumped into him as she rose from a table, the man jumped a foot and whirled around to face her with a menacing frown. Then, just as suddenly, a false smile spread across his face. Caitlin didn't like the way he smiled at Sheilagh either.

Sheilagh excused herself and quickly scanned the yard, caught Caitlin's eye, and rushed over to her.

She sat down with Caitlin, Martha, and Michael. "Did you notice that creepy man? I never saw him before."

Martha nodded. "He came to the office last week. Your father seems to like him, though. Mr. Killian told me he's a new supplier."

Sheilagh noted the suspicion in Martha's voice. "You don't like him?"

Martha shrugged her shoulders. "It's business. I never ask questions."

Sheilagh didn't like the way Martha put her off, as if she were afraid of the man. She had overheard her father say that Martha was a loyal employee and would do nothing to upset him, and for that reason she was highly valued.

Sheilagh was intrigued with the man. He was handsome, though in a dark way. There was something in his gaze . . . an appreciation of her that she didn't quite understand except to know that he must think she was pretty. She'd seen that look on the faces of the boys at school. But with this man there was something more. She wanted to know what it was.

The man stopped Patrick as he was coming out of the house. He whispered a few words to her father, who dismissed him and headed toward the children.

Patrick stopped behind Michael and, without a word, lifted him out of his seat. His mouth full of cake, Michael squirmed in his father's arms, wanting to be released. Patrick would have none of it. Michael finally abated in his struggles and flicked his fingers at a piece of white cake stuck to the lapel of his father's suit.

"Everyone, may I have your attention," Patrick announced, and held his punch cup level to his face. "A toast. To all my children. First, to Caitlin, in whose honor this party is given." Patrick sipped the punch as Caitlin beamed brightly, basking in the adoration. Sheilagh frowned, wondering what was really in the punch cup. "And to my son, Michael. Heir to my factory and fortune. Someday he will be the head of Emerald Chocolates." This time everyone applauded.

Patrick downed the rest of his punch in one gulp and unceremoniously dropped Michael to the ground. Sheilagh's eyes shot to Caitlin and saw the admiration in her sister's gaze die quickly, as if pierced by a sharp arrow.

Patrick stood firmly with both feet spread. He was ready for another of his oratories. They bored his children because they had heard them many times before, but entranced the guests, for he spoke with the zeal of a politician.

"These have been hard times for Chicago, indeed for all Americans. I know what it is like to be hungry. So hungry that one would commit a crime just to eat. My father vowed to me shortly before he began Emerald Chocolates that I would never be hungry again. He was true to his word. I hope that I can be that impassioned, that earnest, in the years ahead for my children. Emerald is going through a rough period, but it will not last. We will rise stronger than our competition, though there will be compromises to be made. But I promise you, my children, that you will never suffer as I have suffered. And so, I would like everyone to join me in thanking God for His blessings."

Caitlin bowed her head, as did some of the guests. Michael stared at his father, who was obviously not in prayer because he was glaring at his son. Sheilagh observed them all, including her mother standing near the pot of geraniums with Ethel Fieldstone, the leading grande dame of Chicago society. Mary Margaret's prayer tripped over her moving lips. Sheilagh thought it a waste of breath and spirit since her father only used his religion as a prop to help him shine.

Someone from inside the house turned up the phonograph. A Gershwin tune floated out to the garden and broke the solemnity. People began chatting as Patrick left his children without a smile.

Sheilagh felt used again. It was becoming a tiresome feeling. Her gaze followed her father's steps. She was surprised when the dark man walked up to him again and whispered something. This time Patrick nodded in agreement, and the two men entered the living room.

"Excuse me," Sheilagh said, and rose to follow them.

Most of the guests were now outside, since the noonday sun had warmed the house enough to make it uncomfortable, and there was no one in the hallway outside the study. The door was cracked just enough for Sheilagh to see inside. Her father was sitting at his desk while the other man stood off to the side. Patrick wore a somber expression.

"The shipments will come in after hours now that you've cut the factory hours in half," the man said. "Our men will load the cases onto your delivery trucks, drive them out, and return by morning. You don't have to do a thing except unlock the gate."

"I don't like any of this."

"What choice have you got? You told me yourself you don't have enough time to redirect your company. You should have seen down the road, Pat. You owe my employer a great deal of money for his generous loan. The interest is mounting up. You do us this favor, and the debt and interest will be canceled. It's a simple deal, Pat."

Sheilagh watched as her father's face turned pasty white.

"What guarantees do I have that this will be enough to satisfy my debt?"

"None. That's the chance you took when you came to him bellyachin'. Take the deal, Pat. It's a generous offer."

Patrick looked up at him and swallowed hard. "Like you said, what choice do I have?"

"Precisely." The man tapped the palm of his hand on Patrick's cheek. The gesture might have been affectionate, but Sheilagh knew it was not.

Patrick rose from his chair and extended his hand to the other man, who ignored it. Then, without further words, they both started for the door.

Sheilagh dashed into the dining room and pretended to look for napkins in the drawer of the serving chest. She waited until she heard the front doors close and her father walk out onto the terrace once again.

She went to the French doors and pulled back the sheer white curtains. Her father looked nearly as bad as he had the morning before. She made a mental note to remember this look. Patrick was frightened, though she didn't know about what. Whatever it was, Sheilagh hoped she would never be that scared in her life.

Chapter 12 —————————————————

November 1933
Chicago

SHEILAGH TURNED THE dial on the RCA console radio to the CBS news correspondent whose voice crackled from the thunderstorm that hovered over Chicago. The repeal of Prohibition, voted upon last year, would be going into effect in only a month. It had been fourteen years since liquor had been made illegal. Mary Margaret had been indignantly self-righteous in her campaign against the repeal, and to the children's surprise, Patrick hadn't thwarted her efforts. Because he liked to drink and even served it in clear view of the children at home, Sheilagh thought he would be just as jubilant as the barkeeps on Cicero Avenue about the opening night they were all planning. Curiously, he was not.

Mary Margaret sat in her celery and rose floral chintz parlor chair knitting mittens for Christmas presents. Sheilagh had never understood her mother's practice of allowing the younger children to know about their Christmas surprises in advance. But that was just the way her mother was. She lacked any sense of fun.

Sheilagh had saved her money from baby-sitting for the new Leary baby in order to buy Michael a toy medical kit. He'd been asking for the one at Marshall Field's, and Sheilagh knew that neither her mother nor father would indulge him. For Caitlin she had already purchased a velvet hat trimmed in lace, but she knew that her sister would not get the one thing she truly wanted and needed . . . recognition.

These days, Sheilagh felt good about herself. She had turned twelve on November first, and her chronological age seemed to have caught up with her biological growth. Finally the rest of the girls in her class had begun to look like her. Almost. She still had the best figure, and for the past two years she had let her auburn hair grow until it now fell in luxuriant curls to the middle of her back. She wore her hair like a prize she'd won at the carnival, open, free, and gaudily extravagant.

Sheilagh was determined to play by the Killian house rules until the day when she could go off to college. Until then, she would study diligently and restrict her after-school activities to choir practice, piano lessons, and baby-sitting at a nickel an hour. The regimen nearly killed her. She wanted desperately to sneak out of the house, slip behind the garage, and smoke one of the Chesterfield cigarettes she had stashed behind the peony bush. But she'd been grounded three weeks ago for smoking. Mary Margaret's face had turned three shades of scarlet at the height of her reprimand.

Sheilagh glanced out the window hoping Bobby McCoy, who had turned sixteen this past summer, would come by in his dad's new Packard. They could drive over to Columbus Park. Maybe she could fool around with Bobby and drive him nuts with her kisses.

A car whizzed by outside, and the horn honked.

Sheilagh didn't get to the window in time to see the car or the driver. Feeling guilty for her rebellious thoughts, she glanced at her mother.

Mary Margaret gave her a quelling look.

Sheilagh banished her fantasies. *God!* she thought. *How can I live like this for five more years?* Graduation could not come soon enough.

Caitlin came into the room and sat on the Aubusson carpet, beating rapidly at the pan of fudge she was making. Sheilagh noticed that her little sister had put on a few more pounds since school had started. She knew how the boys and even the girls at Ascension made fun of Caitlin, calling her "fatso" and "bonbon." Caitlin never let them see her tears or revealed how much the barbs hurt her. But Sheilagh knew. She had heard her muffled whimpers in the night. Many times Sheilagh had held her sister in her arms, trying to soothe her pain. She knew that Caitlin's only solace was food. She wanted Caitlin to know that she loved her no matter what.

Caitlin had begun to go to the factory offices after school to help out. She found no job too menial. She took telephone messages, cleaned candy machines, helped stock supply shelves, and took out garbage. She told Sheilagh she was learning a great deal about the chocolate business, but her sister didn't believe her.

"All this work you're doing isn't getting you anywhere with Dad."

"I don't care," Caitlin said.

"Yes, you do. And you don't have to become a slave to him."

"I'm not doing that. Just leave me alone. Haven't you been listening when he tells us that we will inherit the company? I want to be ready."

"You're the one who isn't listening. He wants to give it to Michael, not to us girls."

"I don't believe you," Caitlin always said. Sheilagh wanted to hit her father sometimes, but she knew it wouldn't help.

Click. Click. Click. Sheilagh watched dully as Mary Margaret banged her knitting needles together. There were white ridges on her mother's knuckles, and she wondered why the knitting needles did not emit sparks.

Tick. Tock. Tick. The clock on the mantel slowly counted off the minutes. It was ten minutes after nine. Supper had long ago been served, consumed, and the dishes washed and put away. Still, there was no sign or call from Patrick. Sheilagh was as aware of the late hour as her mother, whose gaze darted to the clock every five minutes.

Pat. Splat. Pat. Splat. Caitlin's spoon hit the side of the fudge pan. She seemed lost in her work, but Sheilagh knew better, because Caitlin jumped at the sound of each thunderbolt. Sheilagh knew that her sister loved thunderstorms, and before the storm rolled in, she had stood out on the front lawn, her arms outstretched to feel the force of the wind, the cool air, and first pelting drops against her skin. Caitlin was always exhilarated by storms and usually had to be dragged into the house for safety. Sheilagh loved her sister's display of fearlessness, though Mary Margaret continually sought to stifle it.

Rat-a-tat-tat. The wheels of Michael's wooden truck clicked against the floor near the French doors. Even he watched the clock. They all knew that Patrick was drinking.

Sheilagh hated nights like this. After the children went to bed, Patrick would come home very late. Her mother's reprimands and her father's angry responses would fill the upper hallway and seep under her bedroom door and invade her sleep. Many times she had heard her father slap her mother, just as Mary Margaret had hit Sheilagh. Too many times Michael had been forced out of bed to endure beatings with a belt when Patrick had swung into a senseless rage.

Sheilagh's stomach would knot and her hands would shake, but she would never stir from under the covers. She could push her emotions down deep where they would be hidden even from herself. For long periods of time they would not surface, but sometimes late at night they would come up like demons to ravage her heart. She could not tell anyone about the suffering, because no one would believe her. Her mother kept her father's sins a secret from the public.

Sheilagh knew of no one else who was experiencing the same kind of hell as the Killians. She knew of no other kids whose fathers or mothers kept the family in a constant state of tension. Or maybe she hadn't looked outside her world hard enough to see it. She did not talk to Caitlin about Patrick's drinking because she let Caitlin pretend that nothing bad was happening to them.

Nights like this were what nightmares were made of. There were no such things as bogeymen or trolls or witches. But there was the demon of abuse. Sheilagh knew him well and she hated him.

In the morning the pattern would be the same. Michael would be drilled mercilessly about his bad math grades or his lackadaisical attitude toward his household chores. Caitlin would be ignored, and Sheilagh would glare at her father, daring him to attack her. He seldom did now that she was older. Mary Margaret would bury her red eyes in her handkerchief and tromp off to church.

Sheilagh looked at the clock. Her gaze met her mother's, suffused with pain. It was the first time Sheilagh had ever felt sorry for her. Suddenly she felt like a warrior preparing for battle. "Maybe we should call the office," she blurted out.

"No! Don't do that!" Mary Margaret exclaimed.

"What if something is wrong?"

"I don't want to know about it." Mary Margaret clacked the knitting needles back and forth.

"I don't mind doing it," Sheilagh said, rising from her chair, intent on pushing past the denial that engulfed them all. She wanted to know the truth.

"Sit down, Sheilagh. He probably has another meeting."

"Then why didn't he tell us? Why didn't he call and tell you before dinner?"

"It's his way. He forgets sometimes."

Pat. Splat. Pat. "I think my fudge is ready now," Caitlin said, and jumped up quickly, then disappeared into the kitchen.

Sheilagh sat down and listened as the radio announcer stated that the World's Fair would be closing for the winter months.

"I wish we could go back to the fair," Michael said. "I'd like to see the science pavilion again."

"You went four times this year, Michael," Mary Margaret said. "But I'll take you in the spring when it reopens if you still want to go."

"Good." He raced his truck across the floor and up the pedestal of the mahogany table.

"I'm going to bed," Sheilagh finally announced. She dutifully kissed her mother on the cheek and hugged Michael before going upstairs.

She went to the bathroom and brushed her teeth with Colgate Tooth Powder, washed her face, and brushed her hair. She donned a pink flowered flannel nightgown that was four inches too short and slid beneath the covers.

When Caitlin came into the room only minutes later, Sheilagh pretended to be asleep. She listened as her sister said her good-night prayers and got into bed. Within twenty minutes she was asleep. Sheilagh listened to the diminishing storm while the faint sounds of Mary Margaret putting Michael to bed filtered in from the hall. By ten o'clock her mother shut the door to the master bedroom.

Sheilagh had meant it when she told her mother that she wanted to know where Patrick was. If he could slip through the night shadows of their lives, so could she.

She rose, went to the closet, and took out her rain gear. She buttoned her raincoat and belted it, donned her hat, and quietly left her bedroom, carrying her shoes in her hand on the way down the stairs and out the door.

It was not far to the Emerald factory from their home. Sheilagh walked quickly down the sidewalks, darting behind a huge maple tree whenever a car approached. She didn't want her father, who might be driving home, to find her. She took the side streets over to Oak Park Avenue and approached the factory from the south.

She was surprised to see lights on in her father's office. She had truly expected no one to be around and thus confirm her belief that he was at some speakeasy drinking. Perhaps he *was* just working.

As she drew nearer, she heard voices coming from the loading docks. Four black trucks were parked there that did not belong to Emerald. Sheilagh had never seen them before, or the men who drove them. Two of the men were standing off to the side under a light, smoking cigarettes. The rain had stopped, but the caps pulled down low over their eyes hid their features.

She darted over the grass and hid around the corner, sighing with relief when no cry of alarm was raised. She slipped through the yew bushes toward the front doors. She pulled and found them unlocked. The light was on in her father's office. She kept in a crouch and moved around the receptionist's desk to the closed door that bore her father's name. She could hear voices coming from inside. Suddenly they stopped and the two men approached the door. Sheilagh darted behind the massive credenza in the reception area. She waited tensely.

"This gravy train is going to stop for you in a month, Patrick."

Sheilagh was astonished when she recognized the man's voice. It was the man from Caitlin's first Communion reception over a year ago. Her hand flew to her mouth to stifle her gasp.

"I know that," Patrick said.

"I'm not so sure you do. You've put away a handsome sum of money since we began doing business together. And you still owe my boss plenty. If you cooperate with this little favor, all debts will be forgiven. You can even keep your hidden money."

"How many times do I have to tell you that I don't have the money."

"Shut up, Killian!" the man exploded, and grabbed Patrick by the lapels of his coat. Their faces were so close that Sheilagh thought they must be exchanging the same breath.

"I can't do this."

"You can and you will. Ya know why, Killian? 'Cause you're the greediest bastard I've ever met. And you like the danger . . . you like it as much as I do. We're two of a kind . . ."

"No, we're not . . ."

"Don't pull that sanctimonious shit on me. We are, and you know it. You'd kill your own mother for money. That's why you're gonna be there and point him out to us. I'll pull the trigger. Don't worry, you won't mess up your Sunday suit."

"And when it's over?"

"Just like we agreed. You go your way. We go ours. Nobody knows about our business transactions, and they never will unless you spill your guts. Keep that Catholic conscience under wraps, Mick."

"I would never tell this to anybody. Not even the priest."

"See that you don't and everything will be fine. I wouldn't want anything to happen to your family . . ."

There was a very long pause. Then the man continued. "Since that threat didn't rattle your cage, maybe a little fire here at the factory . . ."

"You wouldn't dare . . ."

"I thought that would get your attention." The man loosened his grip on Patrick. He laughed, a menacing sound. "Like I said, you are one greedy bastard. All you Irish shits are."

"All right. All right. I'll be there. I'll set it up. But after I order my second drink, I'll head for the bathroom."

"That's all we ask. We'll take care of our business and be out of there before you get back from the head." The man slapped Patrick on the back. "Brighten up, Mick. It's not the end of the world. Now, let's go check on those deliveries."

The two men left the reception area and headed down the hall past the cafeteria, then turned right toward the candy machine area.

Sheilagh realized that she'd been holding her breath. She bolted for the front door and eased outside with not a sound. She hid under the bushes and watched as all the black trucks left, followed by a like number of Emerald trucks. One by one the lights were turned off. The gangster drove off in a Stutz Bearcat. Just as he left, Sheilagh saw their own Buick pull up in front. It was being driven by a woman.

She strained to see, but it was very dark, and the woman wore a hat that shadowed her face. The headlights flashed off and then on again.

Patrick exited the building, locked the front doors, put the key in his pants pocket, and went to the car. He got in on the passenger's side, something Sheilagh had seldom seen him do. The woman bent over and kissed him. Sheilagh counted the seconds. It was a twenty-one-second kiss. The woman was not her mother. The car drove off down Oak Park Avenue to the north, away from the direction of their house.

Sheilagh hit the sidewalk running. She had to get home before her father did. She nearly slipped on the wet autumn leaves, but she kept on. A million questions raced through her mind, and to nearly all of them she had the answers.

Her father was involved with gangsters. He had been bootlegging liquor for a long time. He was going to be an accomplice to a murder. She didn't know the victim, probably never would. And her father was having an affair. She shot down Euclid and raced to the back of the house, opened the screen door, and wiggled the loose doorknob until it clicked open. She'd complained about the faulty lock to her mother, but for once, she was glad her mother paid little attention to her.

She took off her raincoat, shoes, and hat and carried them up the stairs. She slipped into her room just as the light beneath her mother's door flipped on. She shoved her wet articles under the bed and hurried to get beneath the covers. She feigned sleep when the door to her room cracked open. Then she heard her mother's thudding footsteps return to her room. The door creaked this time when it closed.

Sheilagh let out a huge sigh of relief, but her nerves still dangled on a razor's edge. She had wanted to learn the truth, but she was not prepared for it. What kind of blood was it that ran through her veins? Would she grow up to be as heinous as her father? Would she feel no remorse in killing, like him? Would she not care one whit about her brother, sister, and mother the way he obviously did not? What was in him that made him want to protect his money more than his own family?

Patrick Killian had violated every law of both man and God. And yet he seemed to be the strongest of them all. He was destroying each of them daily, bit by bit. And God did not punish him.

Honest men starved with their families in shanties on Cicero Avenue, yet just tonight there had been porterhouse steaks on the Killian table.

Sheilagh turned on her side and let her tears soak into the pillow.

Two days later, Sheilagh went to Nik's Pharmacy with Bobby McCoy for a chocolate soda after school. As Bobby bragged to the Fenwick High kids about his dad's new car, Sheilagh's eyes strayed to a stack of the afternoon edition of the *Chicago Tribune*.

The headline made her stomach lurch and she lost interest in her chocolate soda. She slid off the stool and picked up a newspaper.

GANGLAND SLAYING, the headline read.

Sheilagh scanned the story twice. It was eerily familiar. Joseph Alvaranti had been murdered in a South Side restaurant just after finishing his evening meal. Witnesses stated he had dined with another man, who insisted the pair be seated by the window. Alvaranti's dinner companion left the restaurant, and less than a minute later, a car raced down the street and someone shot him through the plate-glass window with a .22 rifle.

Police stated Alvaranti had been set up by his dinner companion. The descriptions of this man were vague, though witnesses said he was of medium height with dark hair and blue eyes—probably Irish.

"That fits the description of nearly the entire male population of Chicago," one witness was quoted as saying.

Sheilagh's hands were shaking. She could barely believe what her eyes were telling her. It couldn't be true! The man the witnesses had described must be Patrick Killian. How fortunate for him he was so average-looking. Maybe that was why the gangsters had chosen her father for this evil deed.

Sheilagh told herself not to believe what she was reading. It was a mistake, a coincidence. That man couldn't have been her father. It was some other Irish man.

There had to be a way to discover the truth, she thought as she folded the newspaper, placed it under her arm, and deposited a dime on the counter in payment.

Sheilagh waited until the family, friends, and mourners of Joseph Alvaranti filed into St. Anthony's Church before she slipped in the back door, tiptoed to the far right, and sat in a back pew behind a marble pillar.

In the front pew sat a young woman, obviously Joseph's widow. She looked to be no more than five or six years older than Sheilagh. Next to her sat a little boy of about two years of age dressed in a pair of dark short pants, white shirt, and black bow tie. The little boy kept asking his mother why she was crying. He fidgeted, cried, and finally wailed: "I want my daddy! Where is Daddy?"

The young widow gathered the boy in her arms and broke into sobs. The white-haired woman next to her put her arms around them both.

Surely, Sheilagh thought, her father could never be the cause of so much misery. She must have made a mistake. There had to be some other explanation.

She listened to the priest speak the eulogy, then waited patiently while he blessed the purple-draped casket with incense and holy water. She bowed her head during the offertory. During Communion the church echoed with the sounds of kneelers banging, feet shuffling against the marble floors, and noses being blown into handkerchiefs. And finally Sheilagh found the proof she was seeking.

The back door barely creaked when it opened. A blast of cold incoming air swept over the mourners in the back pews.

Wide-eyed, Sheilagh watched her father edge inside the church and stand for only a brief moment, his hat doffed. He glanced at the bereaved family seated in front, then he turned and left.

Sheilagh eased behind the pillar, hoping he had not seen her. Her heart was beating like crazy. Until the moment she saw her father, she'd nearly convinced herself that he was innocent.

What threshold of evil had Patrick crossed? He had seldom showed love or affection for his family, but she'd just assumed that he wasn't cut out to be a family man. Now she realized it was more than that.

His selfishness knew no bounds. He took what he wanted when he wanted it. He craved power, and like a demigod, for him the ultimate power was control over life and death.

Sheilagh hid behind the pillar as the mourners filed out and formed a motorcade to the cemetery. She remained in the empty church for over twenty minutes before she slipped away. She didn't want another Killian to intrude into the Alvarantis' lives.

She was only twelve and she was learning about life, real life, very quickly. Playing by the rules wouldn't get her anywhere. Those who played by the rules were weak. Sheilagh would no longer obey anyone's rules but her own.

That day she vowed to be even stronger than her father.

February 1934

Michael lay awake in his bedroom snuggled beneath a heavy Dan River Indian-print blanket. Red-foil-covered hearts cut out of cardboard dangled from white strings over his bed. He watched them twist and then untwist. Perspiration trickled across his forehead as he kicked off the scratchy wool blanket.

He was burning up with fever from the influenza attack that had spoiled the family Valentine's Day dinner.

Sheilagh sat on a straight-backed wooden chair next to his bed, inspecting the thermometer she had just pulled from his mouth.

"What does it say?" he asked weakly.

"Not bad. Still a hundred three degrees."

"I feel awful. My head hurts."

"Here," she said, and handed him a glass of water and two aspirin. She poured out a teaspoon of belladonna.

"I hate that stuff!" Michael protested as Sheilagh shoved the spoon into his mouth.

"You have to get well, Michael, and this is the only way." Then she dipped a terry cloth towel into a basin of icy water, wrung it out, and placed it on his forehead.

The cool cloth felt good and stemmed the burning sensation in Michael's eyes. "Will you stay with me again tonight?"

"Of course I will." She tried to smile at him, but Michael could tell that she was very worried. "Do you want me to read to you again?"

"Uh-huh," he said. "But not that boring stuff . . ."

"I like Shakespeare!" Sheilagh exclaimed, affronted by his criticism.

"It's boring. And I don't understand it. Look under my bed. That's what I want you to read."

Sheilagh bent and retrieved a copy of Robert Louis Stevenson's *Treasure Island*. She smiled. "I suppose this would be more to your liking." She opened the book and began reading. She hadn't read more than a page when Michael stopped her.

"I think I'm going to throw up!" He jerked up onto his elbows.

Sheilagh quickly grabbed the bowl of ice water she'd used for the cloths and stuck it under his chin. "It's okay. Go ahead."

Michael retched. His face contorted and he retched again, tasting the bitter belladonna all over again. Sheilagh rubbed his back gently and continued soothing him with comforting words. When he was through, he lay back down, and Sheilagh went to the bathroom to clean out the bowl. She returned, and began reading again.

Michael watched her for a long time, not hearing any of the words. He'd been terribly embarrassed to have his sister see him vomit. That anyone would have to help him eat and get out of bed seemed impossible to him. But then, Michael had never been so ill before. He hated not being able to do things for himself. He couldn't understand how his body had become so utterly lifeless. It was an effort just to talk . . . just to breathe. He hated this feeling of dependency.

As Sheilagh continued with the story, he thought of the author of *Treasure Island,* what it must have been like for young Robert to be confined to his bed for most of his life. How awful to know that all one's days were going to be the same.

Michael couldn't play with his friends or go to school. He was quarantined from the rest of the family as if he were a leper. No one wanted to be around him . . . especially not his mother or father. If they caught the influenza, his father's business would suffer, and his mother would not make her bridge luncheon tomorrow.

His suffering frightened Caitlin, who had heard stories of people dying of influenza. She often talked to him through the closed door when she came home from school. It was Caitlin who had brought him all his valentines from his classmates and shoved them under his door.

But Sheilagh wasn't afraid. She skipped school to take care of him when his mother would not risk the chance of infection. Michael wondered if Robert Louis Stevenson had been so lucky to have a sister like Sheilagh. He bet not.

He wondered how many suffering children there were in the world. How many lived in a bed and never could go outside and play? He knew there were lots and lots. Millions maybe.

"Do you think anybody cares about them?" he asked suddenly, interrupting Sheilagh.

"Care about who?"

"All the sick people. I mean, you're taking care of me . . . but what about the others?"

"Nurses and doctors, I suppose. And families always help each other."

"Not always." The pain he felt came not from fever, but from a sadness deep within himself.

Sheilagh closed the book, ready to discuss the subject. That was what Michael liked about her. She always tried to help him understand. "That's true. Not all families help their own sick ones. Not all the time."

"I think I really do want to be a doctor, Sheilagh."

"I know, Michael."

"No, I really mean it now. Before, I just wanted to be a doctor because it was different from . . . well, Emerald and all that. You know what I mean."

"Yes, I do." She rubbed his feverish arm and lifted the wet hair off his forehead. "I know exactly what you mean."

Michael felt tears in his eyes and let them fall, because he knew that Sheilagh would not scold him for being weak. He'd seen her cry lots of times. "He wants me to be like him, and I don't want to . . ."

"I know you don't."

"I want to be as different from him as I can. He never asks what I like or what I think. Even for Christmas, he didn't buy me that telescope I wanted. He buys me things he thinks I should want. Things he didn't have when he was little. But I'm not him, Sheilagh. I never will be . . ."

Michael was sobbing profusely now, and Sheilagh gathered him up into her arms and rocked him back and forth. She said a lot of soothing things to him. Her arms were strong, her skin soft. His tears and runny nose wet her beautiful hair, but she didn't complain. She smelled like roses and lilies of the valley . . . like a spring morning. Sheilagh made him feel loved and warm, and later she made him feel terribly, utterly guilty, because he was never able to return the favor.

Chapter 13

June 1934
Chicago

THE NEW WORLD'S Fair of 1934, "A Century of Progress," boasted exhibits from eighteen countries around the world. Scores of old buildings had been demolished to make way for wondrously designed new structures. The exposition was constructed on 420 acres of land reclaimed from the fathom-deep bed of Lake Michigan. It was truly a testimony to man's conquest of nature. The most dazzling of all the exhibits was the Ford Building. It occupied eleven hundred feet along the lakefront and it depicted the story of modern-day civilization.

Caitlin, Michael, and Sheilagh walked through the main structure lit by specially designed units that reproduced sunlight. Michael was fascinated with the scientific exhibits that related to the intricacies of the automotive industry. Caitlin liked the historical displays of Henry Ford's original brick workshop and the collection of vehicles ranging from an ancient Egyptian chariot to the newest Ford with the V-8 engine. Sheilagh could not get enough of the Ford Gardens across the street where the Detroit Symphony Orchestra played two concerts daily amid the beautiful landscape. She sat on a concrete bench, listened to the music, and dreamed about her future on the stage.

Sheilagh's vivid imagination spun gossamer scenarios of herself playing lead roles in Broadway dramas and musicals. She leaned back on her arms, looked up at the brilliant summer sky, and watched the clouds skid across the sun. Someday, she thought, I'll make my own world, and it will be wonderful.

She didn't see the young, dark-haired boy watching her. She paid no attention to the gentle breeze that lifted her long auburn locks and twisted them in the sunlight. She could only hear the music as it caressed her ears and see the visions of the dreams she wove. She had no idea that she was the central character in someone else's daydreams.

Cleary "Clay" Burke was nearly fifteen years old and looked twenty. Like Sheilagh, he had blossomed early into manhood. A hundred years ago he would be married by now, probably settling some new western territory and making his mark on the world; or so it seemed to Clay. He had tried to imagine what the girl of his dreams would look like, but she'd always remained faceless.

He believed he would know her when he saw her. He imagined the sound of her voice and the gentle touch of her hand. He would kiss her pale pink lips and slide his hand over the abundant coppery gold curls. She would not protest, but only smile at him and lean against him in surrender. Somehow she would know that they were meant to be together.

As the music rose to a booming crescendo, Clay watched his dream girl rise and glide toward him. The breeze caught her gently flowing white summer dress. She was looking at him and yet did not see him. She smiled, and the sun burst over the edge of a huge cloud and illuminated the air around her. She looked like a goddess, an angel. Clay couldn't let her escape.

She moved closer to him. Closer. She was next to him. She still didn't see him. It was nearly too late.

Clay stuck his arm across her path. She stopped. And then she looked at him for the first time. His heart nearly stopped beating and he held his breath. She was more beautiful than words.

"Are you nuts?" she demanded with a furrowed brow. "Are you trying to trip me?"

Her perfect image was shattered. "I didn't want you to leave."

Sheilagh impatiently stepped around his arm and walked away. Clay bolted to his feet and started after her.

"What's your hurry? The music isn't over. I thought you liked the music."

Sheilagh, long used to handling confrontations with boys, ignored him. "Go away."

"I won't." He continued walking behind her.

Sheilagh picked her way through the crowd. She glanced back over her shoulder several times, only to find the boy still following her. He was very good-looking, she grudgingly admitted. In fact, she could honestly say that she'd never met a boy as handsome, or with such wide shoulders. She guessed he was much older than she was. She slowed her walk. She didn't have to meet up with the rest of her family for another twenty minutes. What could it hurt to talk to him? She might even have some fun with him since he was so obviously smitten with her.

She whirled about suddenly and faced him. "Are you some kind of pervert? What do you think you can gain by following me?"

Clay stopped when she stopped. He smiled. "Your name. I just want to know your name."

"Sheilagh. Sheilagh Killian."

"I . . . I'm Clay Burke. Nice to know you."

"So is that all?" she demanded with her hands on her hips. She had no idea how seductive she appeared with the sunlight shining through her dress, revealing the outline of her long, shapely legs.

"Uh . . . where do you live?"

"Why do you want to know?"

"I thought I might see you again. We could get a soda or something."

"I don't think so."

He moved a step closer. It took a great deal of courage to take that step. "Why not? I'm a very nice person. Wouldn't you like to know me, too?"

"Not especially," she replied, but her amusement was overcoming her ability to remain aloof. She didn't realize she was smiling at him.

"I live on the North Side. My parents are quite respectable. My father is Robert Burke, the alderman."

"I don't know much about politicians, though my father does."

"We're very nice people. Honest. I go to Queen of All Saints. I play football. Someday I'm going to be the captain of the team."

"Good for you." So, she thought, you aren't as old as you look. They certainly had that in common.

"You're not very talkative," Clay said, flashing her a friendly smile.

"You're a stranger . . ."

"I'm trying to change that. I'm an only child. No brothers or sisters. I wish I weren't, though. I don't have anybody to look out for me, or me for them. No one to talk to except my parents, and that's not the same, is it?" He looked at her pursed lips, which showed no sign of relenting. "So tell me where you go to school."

"Ascension. My father is Patrick Killian. He owns Emerald Chocolates. I have a sister and a brother. And someday I'm going to be an actress. A Broadway actress, in fact, and I won't be living in Chicago." She paused for a moment and then looked into his happy blue eyes. She did not see any pain as she did when she looked at her own reflection. Clay Burke could be dangerous for her, she thought, because if he got to know her and her family, then he might discover some of their secrets. Sheilagh would have to keep up her guard. "Now that I've told you everything you wanted to know, will you please not follow me anymore?"

"Why are you trying to get rid of me?"

"Because . . . I . . ."

Just then Sheilagh heard Caitlin calling her above the music. She looked around but didn't see her sister.

Clay cocked his head in the direction of the voice. He saw a chubby brunette running toward them, waving her arm frantically over her head. The little girl wore a red gingham dress, white socks, and black shoes. There were two plaid bows in her long braids, and horn-rimmed glasses perched on her nose. She looked nothing like the goddess who stood before him.

Caitlin was nearly out of breath when she reached Sheilagh. "I . . . have been looking . . . everywhere for you," she said, puffing. She glanced up at the handsome boy who was smiling indulgently at her. She quickly looked away. "Mother says you have to come with us to lunch." Caitlin huffed out the words between pants. Her lungs were burning from exertion. She glanced at Clay again. She moved closer to Sheilagh and whispered: "Who's he?"

"Nobody."

"I heard that!" Clay exclaimed, and stepped forward. He extended his hand to Caitlin. "You must be Sheilagh's sister."

"Yes," Caitlin replied meekly, and took his hand.

"What beautiful skin you have, Caitlin," he said, and turned her palm over in his. "Like velvet . . ." he muttered to himself.

Caitlin snatched her hand back as if she'd been burned. Never had anyone talked to her like that. At first she assumed he was just being nice to her to win Sheilagh's attention, but as she looked at the confusion on his face, she realized he'd actually meant what he said. Caitlin had never been complimented on anything but her accomplishments in her life. An odd sensation flitted across her stomach and she suddenly felt lighter. She didn't know if it was an attack of a stomach virus or the residual effect of her overexertion. She did believe that she liked this handsome boy whom Sheilagh had found.

"What do you say, Caitlin, when someone compliments you?" Sheilagh teased.

"Th–thank you."

"You're welcome." Clay looked at Sheilagh. "Now, that wasn't so bad. I didn't devour your little sister. Why not introduce me to the rest of the family?" He glanced back to Caitlin. "What do you say, little one?"

Sheilagh opened her mouth to protest, but Caitlin broke in too quickly. "Fine. You can come to lunch with us."

"Great. That's two votes to your one, Sheilagh. Where are we supposed to meet up?"

Caitlin was completely caught by his charm, and answered frankly and enthusiastically. "By the Avenue of Flags."

"Terrific," Clay replied confidently, glancing at Sheilagh, who was glaring at him. He took Caitlin's hand. "Come on . . ."

"Caitlin," she replied brightly.

"My name's Clay Burke, Caitlin."

"Nice to meetcha," Caitlin said as they started away from Sheilagh.

Unlike Sheilagh, Caitlin wanted to know everything about Clay. "How did you get to the fair?" she asked.

"By train. I've got a schedule right here in my pocket. I come down here at least once a week. You can't see all the fair in one day. I've learned a lot here. What about you, Caitlin?" He glanced over his shoulder at Sheilagh, who was following begrudgingly behind them.

"I like the fair just fine," she replied, tilting her face up at him. The sun glinted off the lenses of her glasses. She lowered her gaze, thinking, I like it even more with you here.

The trio found Mary Margaret and Michael standing beneath the flapping British flag on the Avenue of Flags. Patrick was nowhere to be seen. As they approached, Sheilagh was the first to sense Mary Margaret's tension. Her stomach knotted with anxiety with each new furrow in her mother's forehead as her eyes studied every inch of Clay Burke.

Mary Margaret's voice was raw with indignation as Clay approached. "And who is this?" she inquired more of Caitlin than Sheilagh.

"Clay Burke, Mrs. Killian," Clay replied easily. "I thought your daughters needed an escort. I'm certain you wouldn't want anything to happen to them."

"Of course not. Thank you." She paused icily. "You may leave now, young man."

Caitlin bounced toward her mother. "Can't he come to lunch with us, Mother?"

"I think not." She turned judgmental eyes on Sheilagh. "You haven't been properly introduced."

"I beg your pardon, ma'am," Clay said charmingly, "but no harm has been done. I can arrange for proper credentials if you wish. My father, Robert Burke—"

"Not the city alderman?" Mary Margaret's eyes widened with appreciation.

"The same, ma'am." Clay clasped his hands behind his back and rocked back on his heels.

A showy smile paraded across Mary Margaret's face. It was an expression Sheilagh and Caitlin both knew too well. The Burkes were obviously above the Killians on the social ladder, otherwise Mary Margaret wouldn't have shown Clay a smidgen of interest. They watched their mother preen before the adolescent boy.

Sheilagh's emotional walls went up. Two minutes ago Mary Margaret would have blasted her for enticing another boy. Now the situation was changed. Sheilagh could feel herself being bartered for the "proper" introduction to the Burke family. It would be a social coup for her mother, and somehow, Sheilagh and Clay would be the losers.

"Where's Daddy?" Sheilagh asked, bored with her mother's games.

"He should have been here by now. He was talking to some men by the doors to the Hall of Science. Sheilagh, why don't you go find him and tell him we're waiting for him. Tell him . . . tell him Caitlin and Michael are hungry." Mary Margaret patted Caitlin's shoulder. "You're always hungry, aren't you, dear?"

Caitlin didn't take her eyes off Clay. "Uh-uh," she said, not wanting her mother to know that the last thing on her mind was food.

Sheilagh did not find her father anywhere near the Hall of Science doors. Shielding her eyes against the brilliant sun with her hand, she scanned the area. She saw the black-haired, brown-eyed man first. As he moved to the side, she saw her father. Patrick's face was ghostlike and he kept looking away from the man, as if searching for a place to hide. Sheilagh darted over to the flag of Brazil and grasped the white pole. What was her father doing talking to this gangster again? Prohibition was over. He couldn't be involved in bootlegging anymore. What did this man want with her father, or Patrick with him?

Sheilagh watched as the man jabbed his finger into her father's chest. Patrick's face went red, but he said nothing. She could see rage and fury burning in her father's eyes. This man had an incredible control over him, and only Sheilagh knew just what it was.

For months she had spied on her father, watching his comings and goings. But since Prohibition had ended, Patrick no longer ventured out of the house much during weeknights.

Life had seemingly settled back into a normal routine. Now Sheilagh realized that nothing was as it seemed.

Patrick made a comment, and the man nodded. Then suddenly the man sidestepped him and blended into the crowd.

Sheilagh felt quite bold. She left the imaginary protection of the Brazilian flag and walked up to her father. She could tell by his expression that he knew she had been watching him. She felt angry and defiant. And reckless.

"Who was that man you were talking to, Daddy?" she asked, hiding behind the last vestiges of her childhood innocence.

"No one important," he said nervously. "Where's your mother?"

"She sent me to find you. We're to go to lunch."

They started walking. Patrick's power seemed to melt in the hot sun. "Didn't we see that man at the house?"

"No."

"At Caitlin's first Communion . . ."

"I don't remember it."

"I do." Sheilagh knew she had replied too forcefully, but she couldn't take back the words. She wanted to hit him in the face with her challenge. She wanted to blurt out everything she knew about the black-haired man, the scene at the offices, the woman in the car . . . the murder.

"You must be mistaken," her father countered with unconcealed vehemence. He grabbed her upper arm and squeezed it roughly. "You have a vivid imagination, Sheilagh. It will be the ruin of you someday. You're always making trouble, telling lies. I won't have it anymore! Do you hear me?" he hissed through clenched teeth.

Sheilagh was frightened. She had leaped blindly over the boundaries that kept her safe. "I must have made a mistake."

"Damn right you did. Now, drop it."

"Yes, sir," she uttered with soft repentance.

"That's better." He loosened his grip on her arm and began walking again. His eyes were steadily focused on the crowd ahead. Mary Margaret's black horsehair hat with red silk roses came into view. "Who is that with your mother?"

"It's a boy I met and—"

Patrick's fleshy cheeks turned crimson again. "Is that right? What nasty business have you done now?"

"Nothing!"

He was squeezing her arm again, pinching the soft flesh between his fingers. "I'm not a fool, young lady. Your mother has told me about you . . . and your ways."

The smack of betrayal stung Sheilagh. How could her mother have told her father when she had promised that no one would know? Would there never come a time when her family would not betray her? Sheilagh no longer felt wicked as she had on that day when her mother found her. She refused to feel guilty about anything she did since other Killians committed much worse sins than she.

How she wanted to tell him that. How she wanted to blast him with the truth. But she didn't. She bit her tongue until she tasted blood. She would continue to play by the rules. She would keep her mouth shut until the day came when she could leave Chicago. It was all she lived for.

"I . . . I didn't do anything except talk," Sheilagh stated with a double dose of abnegation. "Caitlin likes him. And . . . and Mother wants to meet his family."

"Why's that?"

"His father is a politician. Robert Burke, I think he said."

Patrick stopped dead still; Sheilagh was nearly jerked out of her shoes. "Are you sure?"

"Yes. Why?"

A menacing smile came over Patrick's face. "Perhaps you have done something right for once, Sheilagh."

Again she was yanked alongside her father until they joined the rest of the family. Patrick was effusive as he introduced himself to Clay. Sheilagh stood aside and watched as if she were viewing a play. Her father moved the pawns in his life from square to square to suit his needs and desires of the moment.

Clay seemed to be unaware of her parents' machinations, or if he was, he didn't seem to care. Sheilagh had never met anyone at any age as self-assured as Clay. He seemed to know who he was, what he wanted, and how to get it. Sheilagh was a purposeful person as well, but her identity was born of pain and necessity. Clay's self-concept had been instilled by love and security. There was a big difference.

Sheilagh watched as Michael fidgeted, Mary Margaret extolled her own social virtues, and Patrick massaged Clay with flattery. As the family stood on the Avenue of Flags that summer afternoon, she was aware of every nuance and exchange between the Killians and Clay Burke.

The only fact she missed was that Caitlin's life changed that day. Caitlin had fallen in love with Clay Burke.

Chapter 14 ──────────

October 1937

*I*N THE FALL of 1937, Sheilagh's junior year, she nabbed the lead in her high school's production of *Romeo and Juliet*. Sister Josephina had been jealous of Sheilagh's talent since the day the two met in the nun's freshman speech class three years earlier. Sheilagh had barely squeaked out a C from the thin, tall woman, the only "bad" grade she'd ever received in high school. But by her junior year, no one could outact Sheilagh.

Everyone from the surrounding parishes bought tickets to the play three weeks in advance once they knew that Sheilagh Killian was playing the lead. She had always known that she had been born with a special talent. Now other people knew it, too.

Sheilagh worked hard on her acting. She memorized her lines so perfectly that she recited them in her sleep. She went to the library and read history books about Italy during that period. She checked out a lengthy biography about Shakespeare. She studied how the great actresses had handled this part and even asked to take her costume home so she could wear it from time to time, hoping it would help her "become" her part. Sheilagh was no longer Sheilagh, she was Juliet.

Like Juliet, she fell in love.

The curtain fell for the final time on opening night. The auditorium was filled to overflowing with parents, teachers, and students who were all on their feet applauding so loudly that the cinder-block walls reverberated with the sound.

Sheilagh's smile was so broad and proud, her cheeks ached. Like a military general, she had laid her strategies well. She had sprinkled the audience with her special invited guests— theater critics from the *Chicago Sun Times* and the *Chicago Tribune*.

Since she had purchased their tickets herself and sent them gratis to the newspapers, she knew precisely the location of their assigned seats. Her eyes shot to each of their faces during each curtain call. Two of them were on their feet before the rest of the audience. Only the third, an independent writer for several area magazines who had been known to contribute to *The New Yorker* magazine, stood reluctantly. But stand he did, and he applauded just as energetically as the rest of the audience.

Sheilagh experienced her first taste of victory, and it was sweet.

Caitlin was the first to rush into the makeshift dressing room to congratulate her sister. She dodged costumed Italian peasants and merchants, rounded the corner between two rows of the girls' gym lockers, and found Sheilagh sitting on a stool in front of a mirror, smearing Pond's cold cream on her face.

"You were wonderful!" Caitlin squealed with delight.

Sheilagh blinked out at her sister from behind a thick, white mask of cream. There were only two round portholes where Caitlin could see her sister's eyes.

"Do you truly think so?"

Caitlin was nearly out of breath with enthusiasm. "Can't you tell? People were pounding their feet on the third curtain call. What more do you want?"

Sheilagh looked down, but only momentarily. "It didn't seem enough somehow. I wonder if it ever will . . ."

Caitlin thought Sheilagh looked sad, and she didn't understand it at all. But Sheilagh recovered her exuberance quickly. "Did you see Mother's face?"

"Yeah." Caitlin giggled snidely. "She couldn't believe it. I don't think she ever believed you really had talent. She was stunned. I was sooo proud of you, Sheilagh."

Sheilagh opened her arms to embrace her sister and held her tight. "That's what I wanted to hear." She closed her eyes, thinking: *I was right. There was more to come, and this is it.* "I hope you'll always come to me backstage and tell me that. Thanks."

Just then other female parents and family members burst through the outer hallway doors to congratulate the other actresses in the play. The men had to remain outside.

Mary Margaret's stern face seemed to loom ahead of her body. Sheilagh would never know her mother's true feelings about her conquest that night, because Mary Margaret would not allow herself to praise her children. But as she drew nearer, her thin lips pursed tightly across her face, Sheilagh could see tiny sparks of adoration in the deepest regions of her eyes. Then she saw a flash of jealousy before her mother gained control of her emotions.

"Sheilagh, how much longer must you be? Michael is getting hungry and cranky," she said, without absorbing any of the other parents' excitement.

Sheilagh had long prepared for her mother's reaction, but she still felt wounded. Somewhere deep inside, she had hoped . . . wished that it could be different between them. She had wanted her mother to fly into the locker room and declare her daughter the best actress in Chicago. But it would never happen. Not tonight. Not ever.

Sheilagh's spirits sagged. She struggled not to let anger win out, but she lost. "Michael is not a child anymore, Mother. None of us is."

"What is that supposed to mean, young lady?"

"That I doubt Michael said anything of the kind to you. In fact, my bet is that Michael wanted to come back here and be with Cat and me. He wanted to congratulate me."

"Congratulate you? For what? For some amateur high school night? You see, Sheilagh, this is precisely the attitude that I've tried in vain to tell you will inevitably be your undoing."

"My *what*?" Sheilagh was on her feet to defend herself, but Caitlin grabbed her hand and held her back. Sheilagh decided to let her mother have her say. She told herself it would be for the last time.

"You exaggerate everything," Mary Margaret went on. "You think this is Broadway. Well, it's not. It's never going to be. These foolish notions of yours about acting are simply that . . . foolish. When are you going to grow up and realize that you should go to college, get married, and raise children?"

"Just like you did?" Sheilagh replied, easing her body toward her mother.

"It's a woman's birthright to be a good wife and mother."

Sheilagh bent her shoulders and purposefully angled herself beneath Mary Margaret's nose. "Tell me, Mother, when do you intend to become one . . . a good mother, I mean?"

Mary Margaret's eyebrows shot up her forehead.

Caitlin threw her hand over her mouth and sucked in a deep breath.

Sheilagh waited for the crack across her cheek, braced for it, and when it didn't come, she jumped back and stood erect. Never had a declaration of independence felt so satisfying.

Mary Margaret pretended to eye her daughter, but, in fact, she surveyed the locker room through her peripheral vision. She could not make a scene, though she wanted to reprimand her daughter with a vengeance that frightened her. For months Sheilagh had performed the role of the dutiful daughter. She had done her chores, her homework, even kowtowed to all her mother's friends. Mary Margaret could see now that all this had been acting on Sheilagh's part. Lord in heaven! The girl was a better actress than any she'd seen. Mary Margaret had believed that her daughter had changed. She believed she had finally triumphed in the remolding of her recalcitrant child.

She had been wrong. Obviously she'd placed too much emphasis during the past years on her social connections. She'd risen to the top of Chicago society. She'd even gotten Patrick to buy a piece of waterfront property along Lake Geneva. Already she was mentally designing the fabulous home they would build there and the kind of boat they would buy. They would be spending summers with the McCormicks, the Harrises, and the Wrigleys.

She was almost there. But she needed Sheilagh to marry well, not to make a spectacle of herself on a theater stage. She needed Sheilagh to be afraid of her again, the way she'd been as a child.

As Mary Margaret glared into her daughter's glittering green eyes, she realized she'd never stop Sheilagh. It was Mary Margaret who had been living in the dreamworld. Sheilagh had only allowed her to believe that she was compliant and acquiescent. Something had happened on that stage tonight, something momentous, and Mary Margaret had missed it. She couldn't help asking herself, *What else have I missed?*

Her composure had barely slipped. She lowered her eyebrows and gazed calmly at her lost daughter. "After you have been a mother for seventeen years, you may pass judgment. Until then, you will do as I say." She turned to Caitlin. "Go out and tell your father and brother that I will be there in a few moments. I'll meet them at the car."

"I think I should stay with Sheilagh," Caitlin said bravely. This was the first time Sheilagh had needed any help. Sheilagh had always been defending Michael against their father or covering up for Caitlin when she'd eaten too much or had spent too much time at the factory when she should have been at home studying. Caitlin didn't want to let Sheilagh down.

"Go to the car, Caitlin," Mary Margaret said sternly.

"You won't be much longer, will you, Mother?" Caitlin asked.

"No, I won't, Caitlin. Now, go on, before I decide you are in on this with your sister. Or is that what you are trying to tell me? Hmmmm?"

"I . . ."

"No!" Sheilagh interrupted her sister before she could further incriminate herself. "Caitlin isn't trying to defend me." Sheilagh gave her sister a grateful smile. "Go on, Caitlin. Find out for me what Michael thought. Okay?"

"Okay," Caitlin replied, letting her mother know that she was going only because Sheilagh had asked her to. She squeezed Sheilagh's hand one last time. As she walked toward the locker room doors, she noticed that nearly all the other girls and their parents had already left. Mary Margaret and Sheilagh would be alone. *That's not good for Sheilagh*, Caitlin thought as she closed the doors.

Michael had been peeking through the frosted-glass window of the locker room door, hoping to get a quick look at one of the chorus girls as she took off her costume. When Caitlin opened the door, he pretended to be getting a drink from the water fountain, mounted on the adjacent wall.

Michael smiled sheepishly at Caitlin as she walked up to him.

"Pervert," she sneered as she folded her arms over her chest.

"Awww, Cat." He lowered his voice to a whisper. "I just wanted to see Doreen Massucci's breasts. I heard they're really big."

"Not as big as Sheilagh's," Caitlin grumbled as she scanned the hallway, noting that her father was speaking to Jimmy Kelly, a neighbor. She assumed they were either talking politics or scheduling a golf game for Sunday after mass. Suddenly she felt very sorry for Sheilagh, when only a few moments before, she'd envied her. Now she wouldn't want to be her sister for all the chocolate in the world. Patrick was just as unimpressed with Sheilagh's triumph as Mary Margaret was.

Caitlin was even disappointed in Michael. "Don't you care about what happened to Sheilagh tonight? What she did?"

"What did she do?"

"She brought the house down, bozo! She showed everybody in Oak Park that Sheilagh Killian has talent. She's gonna be somebody."

"I know all that, Cat. I just don't believe the part about her getting out of here. Away . . ." Michael's gaze wandered away from Caitlin's face and focused on a place off in the distance.

Michael was retreating again, Caitlin realized. He didn't talk as much these days as he had even a year ago. For a while she had chalked it up to the onset of puberty and his fascination with Doreen Massucci's breasts. She could now tell that it was more than that. Maybe she hadn't paid enough attention to Michael lately. She had been caught in her own dreamworld.

Thoughts of Clay Burke had hovered around Caitlin all evening. She had had no reason to think that he would come to this particular performance, though she had sensed he would.

Caitlin noticed that the number of Clay's calls had diminished once he'd entered fall classes at the University of Chicago. Now, in October, she no longer jumped across the hallway every time the phone rang on the off chance that she might have that one moment to hear his voice as he spoke her sister's name.

Sheilagh had never told her parents that she was dating Clay. Now she never even talked about him to Caitlin at night before they went to sleep the way she had in the beginning. Sheilagh no longer mentioned the names of any boys in particular. She talked only of acting; of going to New York; of being famous and of having enough money to take Michael and Caitlin out of Chicago. That was when they would all be happy . . . once Sheilagh was famous.

Caitlin didn't believe Sheilagh. It wasn't that she didn't believe *in* Sheilagh; it was simply that she knew it would all be much more difficult to achieve than her sister knew.

"It will be more than wonderful for us in New York," Sheilagh would say, pulling the white eyelet blanket up to her chin. "We'll have a driver to take us everywhere in a big, fancy black car with white sidewalls and leather interior. We'll go to the Stork Club and the Rainbow Room. We'll live in a fantastic penthouse on Park Avenue with white carpet and sofas so soft, you'll sink a half foot."

Sheilagh would sigh deeply as she continued to gaze around their bedroom with its new rosebud wallpaper, her eyes finally coming to rest upon the statue of the Blessed Virgin on the dresser. Caitlin always wondered why she got that curious look on her face then, as if she were waiting for the statue to speak to her or something. Then the odd moment would pass and Sheilagh would continue. "I'm gonna make up for everything . . ."

Caitlin usually humored her sister, but just last week, Caitlin had spoken up for the first time.

"What 'everything'?" she had asked.

"Freedom. Love. Control. All those things we don't have now."

Caitlin rolled over and propped herself on her elbow. "I don't think we have it so bad. I'm not so sure I want to go to New York. I like Chicago."

"You like it here with Mother and Father?" Sheilagh spit out the words. "Sometimes you make me so mad. Where's your pride? Your courage? You have to make your own life."

"I will make my own life, Sheilagh, but when are you going to understand that I *like* the chocolate business? I'll be fifteen in December, and sometimes I think I know a lot more about people than you do."

"Is that what you do at the factory? Learn about people?"

Caitlin stared through the darkness at her sister. It always amazed her that Sheilagh's beauty, her auburn hair and gleaming eyes, could glow in the dark like one of Michael's Captain Midnight decoder rings. "Yes, people. And marketing, purchasing, payroll, accounting. Lots of stuff. I bet if Father died tomorrow, I could run the business better than anybody."

Sheilagh began to hear what her younger sister was saying. She rolled her head on the pillow and found that a shaft of moonlight had lit Caitlin's face. She looked like an angel. Sheilagh smiled. "I know you could."

"You do?"

"Uh-huh. I guess I was being selfish thinking that you would want what I want."

Caitlin's smile was sweet and warm as always. "Oh, I don't think so. I think you just want me to be happy."

"Yeah, I do," Sheilagh said, and rolled over and went to sleep.

Caitlin watched Michael as she remembered that night. They were all changing somehow. It was becoming more difficult for them to stand up for one another, or hide secrets and escapades from their parents. Sheilagh was in that locker room right now, perhaps making plans that would alter her future forever.

Michael looked back to his sister. He'd popped a grin onto his face. "So what's Tallulah doin' in there, anyway?"

"I think it's a showdown."

"Damn," he replied with awe.

"Mother said we're supposed to go to the car."

"Not on your life. This I gotta see." Michael stood firm and said nothing more.

Caitlin decided he was right. She would wait until the bitter end. Even if they said nothing to their mother, their very presence would make a statement. Sheilagh would need their moral support. Caitlin prepared for a long wait.

She heard someone walk up behind her. She didn't need to turn around. She didn't need to hear his voice. It was Clay. She suddenly felt very much alive.

"Gotta see what?" Clay asked.

Michael's eyes widened in surprise and then he froze as if he'd been turned to salt. "I haven't seen you since this summer, Clay. Watcha doin' here?"

Somehow Caitlin had the presence of mind to turn and smile at Clay. *God*, she thought, *how could he possibly be more handsome than last summer?* But he was. His tan had faded, making his hair seem darker and his eyes a more intense blue as they smiled down at her. She wondered if her legs would support her. "Oh, nothing," Clay replied.

Michael glanced at his sister, who was gawking at Clay Burke like a lovesick puppy. Michael had thought Caitlin was over her infatuation. Now he knew he'd been wrong.

Caitlin turned to Michael. "Mother says for you and Daddy to meet her at the car."

Michael started to protest, but Caitlin screwed up her face in a grimace and rolled her eyes. He grabbed his cue to leave. "What about you? Aren't you coming now?"

"In a minute." She beamed up at Clay, who was still looking at her.

"Why not now?" Michael pressed innocently. He loved teasing his sister.

"Go ahead. I'll be right there," she said with exasperation. *Deliver me from little brothers,* she said to herself.

Michael nodded. "Right. Maybe I can get a driving lesson from Dad while we wait," he joked. "Nice to see you again, Clay."

"You too, Michael," Clay replied courteously, and shook Michael's hand before he sauntered down the hall and joined Patrick.

Clay couldn't take his eyes off Caitlin, and she knew it. It was the reaction she'd waited a long time to see. She'd done it. She'd finally gotten his attention. All the dieting, all the exercises, the brushing of her hair, the lemon juice on her freckles, the layers of Pond's cold cream and the development of a much-needed woman's shape had done the trick.

"Caitlin, I hardly recognized you. You've grown up," he said appreciatively.

Zingo. Bingo. The gods had flipped the fate switch to "on" position. *It's my turn*, Caitlin thought as she gazed dreamily into Clay's eyes. She did not know if she should thank the saints of heaven, her guardian angel, or take the credit herself. All she knew was that it was now or never. She was alone in the grandstand, and she had to make this play.

"I was wondering if you would notice."

"How could I not? You're as beautiful as . . ."

"As Sheilagh?" It was a loss of half a point, Caitlin thought. But that was okay. She wanted to stand on her own merit.

"I would never compare the two of you."

Because she is so exquisite, so perfectly beautiful, that no one could compare . . . even if I do come from the same gene pool, Caitlin thought. "You wouldn't?" was all she said in reply.

"You're so natural . . . so incredibly real, and yet . . . you remind me of this statue of the Blessed Virgin I saw once. Your dark hair . . . blue eyes. Uncanny."

Demerit of five points for the crack about virginity. Caitlin was losing her edge, and fast. But what could she do? "I'm not a statue, Clay."

"I know," he said with a gleam of desire in his eyes.

And in that moment Caitlin knew that one day Clay would be hers.

She didn't have anything concrete to base it on, but she knew. She knew from the depths of her soul, the way she'd known it was Clay she loved from the first moment she saw him. He would be her husband. The father of her children. Only she wasn't quite sure how she was going to convince him of that, especially since he was obviously here to see Sheilagh.

"How is college going, Clay? We haven't heard from you for so long. I guess we lost touch," she said, making an imperceptible move forward. She wondered if he would flinch if she touched his hand.

"Yeah . . . I got pretty busy this fall. My schedule was really full. Business law. Accounting. Two finance courses."

"I saw your picture in the University of Chicago newsletter."

"You mean when I crowned the homecoming queen?"

"I heard you were dating her," she probed, wanting to know the details of the gossip she'd heard, yet wishing now she'd never asked.

"She's pinned to an SAE now. He goes to the University of Michigan. Plays football."

"Did you like her?"

"She was okay," he said in unemotional tones, which told Caitlin everything she wanted to know.

She pushed her luck. "You sound a bit sad about it. Are you very sure?"

"I was thinking . . . how much I missed seeing you . . . the Killians, I mean."

Caitlin noticed that he didn't mention Sheilagh by name. That was a good sign. "I missed you, too."

"You did?"

"Uh-huh. I did."

"I suppose you were really busy this fall . . . Do you still go to the factory after school like you used to?"

"Every day," she said enthusiastically.

"Tell me about it. Tell me what you're doing that's new. I have new marketing courses, and I even took one in advertising. I tell you, Caitlin, every time my prof gets up there and starts talking about the way some guy marketed his product twenty years ago, I think . . . that was then. What about now? Especially, what about tomorrow. Funny, but I always think about chocolate when I'm in those classes."

"Chocolate?"

"Yeah. Not that I'm hungry for it, but how to market it. New ideas that just come to me in a flash. I think your father should think about foreign markets."

"Now? With all this talk about a war? Half of Europe doesn't know what the morning will bring."

"Precisely. It would be small scale, but if he could get in before war breaks out, it would be *his* chocolate on the black market . . . not Hershey's. Oh, well. It was a dumb idea. Besides, do you think there will be a war?"

"Yes. Chicago is so isolationist, but yes, I think there will be, and eventually we'll have to be in it." She looked up at him with new eyes. There was a chance, a real one, that she might lose Clay before he was ever hers. "Oh, Clay. Promise me you won't go to war."

He put his hand on her shoulder. "I don't think there's much chance of that."

"Hush!" She put her fingers over his lips. "Don't scoff at fate. If you do, you'll be the first to be taken."

"I didn't know you were so superstitious." He laughed and squeezed her arm affectionately.

"Now you're making fun of me."

"I think you're adorable."

"You do?"

"Yes, I do, little one," he said, and placed his forehead against hers for a moment.

In that instant, Caitlin felt her heart turn upside down. It was the first time a boy—a man, in Clay's case—had ever called her by a term of endearment. Love vibrations sang in her mind. She wanted to touch him the way she had dreamed. Boldly she reached out and let her fingers glide across his cheek.

An electric sensation went zinging through Caitlin's fingertips, and she quickly snatched her hand away.

"Must be dry in here," he said. "Static electricity."

"Yeah."

Clay again stood upright, and the precarious spell they had been weaving was rent apart. "Tell me more about all that's happening at Emerald."

Caitlin spoke easily enough, but as she continued, she realized that Clay was truly interested in the daily happenings. She was cheered by his interest and so she told him humorous anecdotes about Martha, the secretary, and the candy machines that had gotten stuck the day before.

"No one believed her at first. She's always been miss prim and proper. She keeps her mouth shut all the time. Martha is nice and all, but she's gotten to be such a fuddy-duddy these past years. I guess some of the workers just wanted to see her smile, is all. The joke just got out of hand."

"Tell me more."

"Well, Martha has been going around for the past two years with such a sour face. I mean really . . . scrunched up and puckered up . . . like this," Caitlin said, and forced her face into a distorted grimace that looked as if she'd just chewed a half dozen grapefruit rinds. "Well, anyway, every Monday morning the office personnel tastes the new concoctions and flavors of creams or what have you. Out of these tastings we may choose less than half a dozen recipes or mixtures or shapes that actually make it into the line."

"Your father doesn't like change?" Clay asked.

"Not at all!" Caitlin laughed. "If I ran Emerald, I'd make twice as many changes as he does."

"Me, too. Anyway, go on with the story."

"I don't know who really thought up the idea to pull this trick on Martha, and I probably never will. Somebody made up special creams . . . lemon creams in dark chocolate. Only there was no sugar at all in the cream or in the chocolate. The lemon had bits of rind and tasted like actually biting into a *real* lemon. Which, after I thought about it, wouldn't have been such a bad idea, as long as the chocolate had been creamy milk chocolate. But they put unsweetened chocolate on the outside of these heart-shaped candies.

"I guess poor Martha nearly choked on the chocolate, which was very dry in texture, and then to hit that sour lemon taste. Ugh!"

"I'd want to throw up!" Clay chuckled.

"She did! But not right then. She stormed out to the factory. She had a couple ideas about who might have pulled this joke on her, and she went over to their stations where they were wrapping the candies as they came off the machines. She started yelling and cursing and screaming, and I guess everybody in the shop was watching before it was all over.

"Poor Martha got so overworked, she threw up right on the machine!"

"Oh, God!"

Caitlin nodded. "That isn't the half of it. Everyone was so busy watching Martha blow up, which is totally out of character for her, that nobody paid attention to their jobs. Candies started backing up at the wrappers' stations. The conveyers just kept piling up chocolates and bonbons and ganaches and nougats and nut clusters. It was a disaster. I got there just as it was all happening. It was just so hilarious, I couldn't help laughing. Not once did I think to stop production. I just stood there laughing as chocolate came out of the machines, missing their nougats and toffee centers. It looked like an army of gremlins had come in and reset the timing devices on every machine we owned."

Clay was laughing hysterically. "What did your father do?"

"He was furious! Furious. And that made it even funnier to me, because now *he* was running around and cursing and yelling and screaming. Finally he shut down all operations, and then the cleanup began. He also docked everyone's pay. I felt bad about that."

"Did you ever find out who pulled the prank?"

"No. I'll probably never know. And I don't think it did one bit of good."

"Why not?"

"Because Martha seems more sour-faced now than ever before." She laughed again.

Clay laughed along with her. "I love talking to you, Caitlin. It's always been like this for us, hasn't it?"

"Like what?" *Dare I hope?*

"Easy. Natural. I hope you'll always be my friend."

Her heart sank. Why couldn't he tell her that he loved her? Why couldn't he see that she was the girl for him? Didn't he feel the electricity between them? Didn't he want to kiss her and hold her as much as she wanted him to?

What was the matter with him?

In the girls' locker room, Sheilagh had finished dressing while Mary Margaret tried to entice her into battle. Sheilagh was having none of it. She didn't care if her mother kicked her out of the house tonight, she would not bend to this woman.

She shoved her arm into a navy wool sweater. "Who is it?"

Mary Margaret prided herself on her control, but tonight her eldest daughter nearly had her sputtering and stammering. "Who is what?"

"This man you would have me give up my career for?"

"Sheilagh, don't overdramatize. You have only been in a high school play. You don't have a career to 'give up.' "

"Who is it? Surely you have set your sights on someone. Let me guess. A Ryan. Or a Wrigley? No? Too high up the social ladder. How about a Comisky or a Kirkpatrick? Is his mother on the Art Institute Board or is she merely a yachting friend? Who is he, Mother?"

"This is ridiculous. I don't have someone picked out like a steak at the A and P."

"Why not? We aren't talking about anything important here . . . only *my life*!"

Sheilagh hated to let Mary Margaret push her this far. She had planned for too long how she would handle her final days in Chicago, and this was not part of the strategy.

"I am simply saying that it is time we plan your coming out."

"Coming out? Coming out? You mean like one of those society cattle calls they call debutante parties? No, Mother. You hear me? I'm not going to let you do that to me. I will not be paraded around so that all your friends can tell you that I'm pretty, that you're a good mother, and that I'll make a man a good wife. I don't want to be *anybody's wife*! I want to be an actress, Mother. Nothing else. You got that?"

Mary Margaret nearly levitated off the floor, she was so shocked. "Don't you *ever* speak to me in those tones."

Sheilagh felt nearly seventeen years of defiance rise up in her like hot lava. She wanted to let it flow. *"I want to be an actress."*

Mary Margaret glared at the immovable force in front of her. She needed Sheilagh to make the proper marriage she'd always dreamed her daughter deserved. She truly wanted the best for Sheilagh, and she believed it was in the home as a wife and mother. She did not for one half a second understand, nor try to understand, her daughter's needs and desires for a crazy-quilt kind of life that an actress would live. She had always believed these notions and daydreams of Sheilagh's would pass as she matured. Instead, they had strengthened. Mary Margaret didn't want to admit that her daughter had turned out to be the wanton harlot she had seen evidence of those years ago, but now she had to admit it was true.

She knew that in the years to come, Sheilagh would scandalize the family with her antics, sexual independence, and yes, perversions. Eventually the Killians would be ostracized from parties, clubs; the country club set would spurn them, maybe even blackball them from other organizations. Her church friends would look the other way when they walked down the center aisle on Sunday to their favorite pew, third row, center front. Mary Margaret's life would be over. Everything she'd built, worked for . . . every sacrifice she'd made, every social connection she'd fused into that fine and precariously thin chain that bound her to Chicago's social elite, would be annihilated.

Mary Margaret knew it was time for her to use all the powers she possessed as a mother.

She consciously erased all emotion from her countenance and looked her daughter straight in the eye. "Over my dead body."

"Fine!"

Sheilagh picked up a round hatbox, which held her wig, makeup, and accessories, and went racing toward the locker room doors. Her mother was shouting something, but she couldn't hear her anymore. She never wanted to hear her. She wanted to do something to defy her mother, to set her mother in her place. She wanted to show the world that she was a person. She wanted to be free of Chicago; free of being a Killian; free of her mother's twisted need for her.

Sheilagh burst through the door as if she were breaking out of prison. Then she saw Clay.

She stomped her heels on the linoleum floor as she walked up to him. He was laughing about something with somebody else, but Sheilagh did not realize it was Caitlin. Her mind was in a fog that had affected her vision. She did not stop to hear what they were talking about. She did not care that she was being rude. She only knew that she was in pain. Her life and her dreams were about to be murdered by her mother, and she had to stop her world from spinning out of control.

"Hello, Clay," Sheilagh breathed as sensually as she knew how. How was it possible that he had sensed she would need him now, after so many weeks apart? Was Clay her savior after all? He looked like a hero dressed in varsity navy blue, his black hair gleaming. She had known Clay was handsome last summer, but when had he acquired this easy natural glow about himself? Maybe he was in love. Maybe he was in love with her.

Sheilagh was not the first to see the chills race down Clay's back when he heard her speak his name. Caitlin saw them, too.

Caitlin felt as if she'd been shot at close range.

He'll go to her, Caitlin thought. *I almost had a chance to win you, my love, but you still have her under your skin. I can't win this round*, her desperate heart told her.

"Hi, Sheilagh." Clay turned around. He was nearly struck dumb by her overpowering physical presence.

Sheilagh had never thought she would need a man. She had been wrong. Tonight she needed Clay. She held out her hand to him and smiled.

For Clay, it was as if the sun and moon rose together. She was gold and silver and light. She sparkled. She was a rocket on fire. Once again, she was the Sheilagh who wanted him.

"I need a ride home," she told him.

"I've got my dad's new Studebaker."

"I can't wait to see it."

"Do you have to go right home?"

"Not especially. Why?" Sheilagh breathed voluptuously through half-parted lips.

"I thought we might drive down the lakefront."

"It sounds lovely, Clay." Sheilagh slipped her arm through his.

It took the courage of Titans, but Caitlin made herself watch Clay leave with Sheilagh. He didn't say good-bye to her. He never looked back. He was too busy looking into Sheilagh's eyes.

Chapter 15 —————————

July 1938

SHEILAGH WATCHED MICHAEL and Caitlin playing catch from her second-story bedroom window. The day Dizzy Dean was traded to the Chicago Cubs, April 15, Michael decided he wanted to be just like his hero. He wanted to be a star. He had worked on his pitch all that spring of his twelfth year and on his batting most of the early summer. He was insatiable in his quest to be great. Sheilagh knew the feeling well. They all wanted to be somebody.

No one in the Killian household seemed to care what Michael wanted except Caitlin and herself. Caitlin was the good egg. She was forever willing to pitch to his hits, catch his fly balls, and be the father to Michael that Patrick would never be. Sheilagh was their cheerleader. It was a small role, but one she thought they needed.

"Hey, Michael! Great catch!" Sheilagh called. "I think you'll make the team."

Michael's impish grin broadened to a beaming smile. *God,* she thought, *how little it takes to make him happy. How little we all need.*

Caitlin worked the hardest at trying to please her parents. That year she had excelled so incredibly at her schoolwork that the principal had advised Mary Margaret and Patrick to skip her a grade. Caitlin took special tests and fulfilled most of her English, math, and science requirements. She only had one year of French to her credit, but she could write and speak the language better than many four-year students. All the teachers talked about how brilliant Caitlin was. "Caitlin Killian is nearly a genius," Mr. Forestall, the English Department head, had told Mary Margaret.

For weeks the family had listened to Mary Margaret praise Caitlin, but Sheilagh and Michael noticed that their father never congratulated their sister on the fact that she would graduate from high school when she was only sixteen and a half. Caitlin still looked up to him and hoped he would give her an accolade, but the praise never came. Patrick closed his ears to his childrens' accomplishments and turned his attention back to his business. Sheilagh hated his indifference.

Caitlin didn't stop at academic achievement in trying to win Patrick's attention. She had worked out a new recipe for chocolate Christmas cookies that Sheilagh thought was incredible. Patrick only waved his youngest daughter away, and Mary Margaret ignored all Caitlin's hard work. Undaunted, Caitlin persisted until her father agreed to print the recipe. Now that Emerald had come out with its own brand of baking cocoa, Caitlin wanted her recipe to be printed on the back of the green and gold tin can. Sheilagh knew it would be a hit. But, as always, Patrick would take the glory and flip Caitlin a cursory remark, which she would grab and cherish.

Sheilagh wanted to make it right for them, but she was only sixteen. There was only so much she could do.

She smiled back at her brother and Caitlin, who was feeling quite proud of her own athletic abilities. She had changed a great deal this year. She had lost the last of her "baby fat," let her dark hair grow nearly to her shoulders, and experimented with Sheilagh's secret stash of Helena Rubenstein cosmetics. Her emerging beauty had come as a surprise to most of them, including Caitlin herself.

"When are you going to call it a day?" Sheilagh called out.

Caitlin spun toward the window, flipping the ball into the air and catching it again. "When we're good and ready!"

"I think you'll both make the team!" Sheilagh laughed.

"Wouldn't that be neat?" Caitlin yelled back. "But I think I'll let Michael take the honors."

"If you meet me in the kitchen, I'll fix the lemonade," Sheilagh offered.

"That's a deal!" Michael called, and pitched the ball back to Caitlin without a second look.

Sheilagh pulled six lemons from the Frigidare, cut them in half, and squeezed out the juice into a pitcher of ice water.

"So, all in all, how do you think your practice went?" Sheilagh asked Michael, who plopped down at the kitchen table.

"Great! If I make the parochial team, I know I'll get better and better."

"And?" Caitlin said, sucking on a lemon rind and grimacing.

"I'm gonna get a baseball scholarship to college. Maybe I can be so good, I can get into medical school. When I'm old enough, I mean."

"Boys are so lucky. Don't you think so, Sheilagh?" Caitlin asked.

Sheilagh stirred a huge spoonful of sugar into the lemonade. "I don't think so. Of all the people in this family, I would never want to be Michael."

"Why not?" he asked, looking suddenly wounded.

Sheilagh refused to let her eyes meet his. She took glasses from the cupboard. "Because." She pondered the wisdom of telling him the truth. He was nearly thirteen, and maybe it was time. "Father will never let you go to medical school, baseball or no baseball."

"That's a terrible thing to say!" Caitlin exclaimed. "You don't mean that."

"Father means it. And Michael knows it, don't you, Michael?"

Michael hung his head. Sheilagh always had the ability to bring him back to reality. Sometimes he hated her for it. This was one of those times. "I don't know anything of the kind. I'll get so famous in high school that he won't have any say about it."

Sheilagh placed the glasses of lemonade in front of them. "I shouldn't have said anything."

Caitlin's enthusiasm dimmed. Sheilagh was right. She hated her, too. "Why do you have to make Michael feel bad?"

"I said I was sorry," Sheilagh defended herself.

"I know. But it's just that you're . . ."

"Right."

"Yeah." Caitlin sighed.

Sheilagh took Michael's and Caitlin's hands. "Which is better? To face the truth? Or to fool yourself into thinking something is going to happen that never will? All you two do is set yourselves up to be hurt again. Hit it right on. I do. That way, you're not hurt."

Michael and Caitlin stared intently at Sheilagh. For a long moment she thought they would both burst into tears, but they didn't. The acquiescing nods came slowly.

"What should we do?" Michael asked innocently.

"Stick together. Like we always have. But with more force. I think it's gonna take a lot of work on our part to beat the system around here.

"Let's make a pact. Right here. Right now. No matter what, we always stick up for each other. If one of us is in trouble, the other two have to come to their rescue. Any time. Any place. Is it a deal?" Sheilagh asked.

"Deal," Michael chimed in first.

"Deal," Caitlin echoed.

They stuck their hands into the middle of the table, topping one other's hands with their own.

"This is a sacred and solemn pact. Okay? Anybody ever, ever fails to live up to the pact, then they can be ostracized."

Caitlin and Michael nodded in unison.

Sheilagh beamed. "Done, then."

"Done!" they all exclaimed.

Just then the telephone in the front hall rang. Caitlin was the first on her feet. She raced through the kitchen door and down the Persian-carpeted hall to the telephone stand at the base of the staircase. She lifted the receiver off its cradle.

"Hello?"

"Hello," a young male voice said on the other end.

Caitlin's heart skipped a beat. There was only one person on earth with that voice. That voice was the reason she'd lost eighteen pounds in the last year. That voice was why she'd let her hair grow and permed it with a Tony perm. That voice was her reason for being in this sixteenth year of her life. It was Clay.

"Sheilagh, is that you?" he asked.

"No, Clay, it's me, Caitlin," her young voice responded much too quickly, much too urgently, and with too much interest.

"Oh, hi, Caitlin. Is Sheilagh home?"

Caitlin felt her dreamworld collide with reality. The explosion depressed her. She'd waited so long to hear his voice. She'd made so many plans that included him for the summer. Why was he calling for Sheilagh? But then, why *wouldn't* he call for Sheilagh?

"Just a minute, Clay. I'll get her for you." Caitlin's heart was split in two as she delicately laid the receiver on the telephone stand and went back to the kitchen.

"Sheilagh, you're wanted on the telephone," Caitlin informed her sister.

"Do you know who it is?"

"Clay Burke."

Sheilagh's eyes held surprise and pleasure as she dashed out of the kitchen. She didn't notice the crestfallen look on Caitlin's face Michael did.

"I thought Clay was Sheilagh's friend," he said simply, taking another swallow of lemonade.

"He is, Michael."

"Then how come you look so sad?"

"I'm not sad."

"Uh-huh, you are."

"Don't be silly. He's too old for me," Caitlin replied, and masked her emotions with an indifferent smile.

Michael watched his sister for a long moment. He realized that Caitlin didn't want him to know her secret. He also knew that Sheilagh liked Clay a great deal, even though they didn't see each other much. Michael had overheard Sheilagh talk about him from time to time. There were other boys who called for her, but when Clay called, her eyes lit up. Michael knew, too, that Sheilagh had no idea Caitlin had a crush on Clay. He knew Caitlin would tell him about her feelings when she was ready.

"You're right. He's too old. Besides, if you got all crazy over him, you wouldn't have time to coach me."

Caitlin grasped at the excuse Michael had given her. "And you're a lot more important to me."

Sheilagh returned to the kitchen, a whirlwind of giddy excitement. "He's asked me to go to the dance at the Columbus

Park Pavilion on Saturday night! I have to find something to wear . . . paint my nails . . . wash my hair. I wonder if I still have those red ribbons. Did I give them to you, Caitlin?"

"No." Caitlin stared down at the glass of lemonade.

Michael watched the interplay. Usually it was Sheilagh who was the astute one, but for some reason, she was oblivious to Caitlin's feelings. "What makes you think Mother is going to allow you to go to the dance? She always says that only the riffraff go there."

"I'm not going to tell her," Sheilagh said with flat defiance.

"How in the world are you going to manage that?"

"I'll think of something. But I'm going to that dance with Clay Burke if it kills me."

"Oh, yeah?" Michael grinned mischievously. "This I gotta see."

Throughout the rest of the afternoon, as she played catch with Michael and then going to Nik's Pharmacy with her fourteen-year-old girlfriend Sally, Caitlin's mind was filled with thoughts of Clay Burke. She never confided in Sally about her love for Clay, nor did she allow her brother or sister to see her concern. Knowing that Clay preferred Sheilagh over herself gnawed at Caitlin's heart. She felt empty and cold again, as she had when she'd been a child and her father had ignored her. She sat next to Sally at the soda fountain counter and leaned on the white marble as she watched Joey Kirkpatrick serve up a banana split for Sally.

"What'll you have, Caitlin? The usual cherry Coke?"

"No. I think I'll have a hot fudge sundae."

Sally's blue eyes shot open in her freckled face. "Caitlin! What about your diet? I thought you still wanted to lose another six pounds."

"What for?" Caitlin's reply was low.

"I don't know. You're the one who told me you wanted to be healthy," Sally said as she sunk her spoon into the creamy vanilla ice cream.

"I guess I just don't feel like it anymore."

"Well, I'm glad."

"You are?"

"Yeah. I was getting pretty sick of you telling me not to eat all the things I love. It was boring, Cat."

"I guess I was. But the thing is, Sally, you never get fat. You just eat and eat and stay skinny. I have to stick to celery, tuna, and iced tea just to maintain this weight. Then I run all over the backyard with Michael, and it never seems to be enough."

"My mom says it's just baby fat and that you'll lose it when you start your period."

"I already did that, too, and it didn't help much."

"Caitlin Killian. You never told me!"

Caitlin grasped the hot fudge sundae dish with a vengeance and filled her mouth nearly to overflowing with the cold vanilla ice cream and gooey hot fudge. She relished the nearly forgotten feel of the treat against her taste buds. She felt better instantly. Oddly, she took another bite and found that her responses had dulled somewhat. She began toying with the food. "I don't tell you everything, Sally."

"I know," Sally responded sadly. "Maybe you should."

"Why?"

"Maybe I could help. That's what friends are for."

Caitlin eyed her friend suspiciously. She'd never heard of such a thing. Her mother didn't have friends to whom she talked about her problems or desires. Sheilagh never had any girlfriends. Michael was a loner, too. Caitlin could barely remember having any other children at the big house to play. Mary Margaret always complained about them, their dirty habits, poor table manners, and the fact that it cost too much money to feed other people's children. Caitlin had never given the Killian household atmosphere much thought until now. She realized that her house was cold, empty, sterile . . . just like her heart.

Caitlin looked down at the melting ice cream. It was cold and hot both at the same time. Maybe that was the answer that Sheilagh was looking for in her life. Sheilagh wanted to heat up her life and enjoy her last days in high school. She was willing to risk being caught at her escapade, just as Caitlin was willing to risk her diet on this ice cream to find some excitement. She wondered if Sheilagh would find her romance with Clay Burke as empty and unsatisfying as she found her sundae.

"What are you doing Saturday night, Sally?"

"Nothin'. Why?"

"Good. We're going to break out that night."

"Break out of where?"

"Our old, boring selves, that's what!" Caitlin announced with a satisfied smile, and pushed the hot fudge sundae away.

* * *

Saturday night found Sheilagh with her fingernails painted with Revlon's Fire and Ice red nail polish, a rebellious gesture since Mary Margaret did not allow any colored nail lacquers on her daughters' fingers or toes. She wore her long hair pulled to the back of her head and tied up with the red satin ribbons she'd found in the bottom of Caitlin's sock drawer. Her red and white floral polished cotton chintz sundress fit her waist snugly and emphasized her full breasts and rounded hips. She looked like the kind of Hollywood siren she'd aspired to be since she was a young girl.

Caitlin sat on the bed chomping on an apple. "What excuse did you give Mother?"

"I didn't."

Caitlin nearly choked on a small piece of apple. "What?"

"She and Daddy went to the church fund-raiser meeting. Then I heard her say that they were going with the Kellys to Guioune's Paradise Ballroom afterward. They'll be out till after one themselves. It's perfect!"

Caitlin's eyes flew wide at the news. "Perfect!"

Sheilagh turned away from the mirror and faced Caitlin. "Well, what do you think?"

"I think every boy in the place will want to dance with you."

"All of them?"

"Every last one. Who could resist you?"

Sheilagh looked back into the mirror. She saw a pretty girl in a pretty dress, but she also saw the girl who'd been jeered at and taunted for having a womanly body when she was still only a girl. She could never forget those days, and realized that at seventeen, her world was a very different one. She hoped Caitlin was right. Sheilagh wanted to know what it would be like to have the same boys who had mocked her, now desire her. The anticipation of that scenario made her head spin with a new sense of power.

She gathered up her purse and headed out the front door. Caitlin picked up the telephone, placed a call to Sally, and informed her that she would be at the street corner in twenty minutes. Then she dashed upstairs to prepare for her own big night.

When Caitlin walked up, Sally barely recognized her. "You don't look like you!" Sally exclaimed. "Isn't that Sheilagh's dress?"

"Yes." Caitlin glanced down admiringly at the cotton full-skirted yellow summer dress. She liked the ruching of white lace at the rounded neckline and beneath the cap sleeves. She didn't have Sheilagh's breasts, but there was a tiny crevice between her own that hadn't been there a month ago. Caitlin was still giddy over the fact that, though the dress was tight, her waist was nearly as small as her sister's now. She congratulated herself again for sticking to her diet. "And these are Sheilagh's shoes, and I used her lipstick and rouge, too. But I don't look like Sheilagh."

"*Nobody* looks like Sheilagh," the skinny, freckle-faced girl replied. "I wish I did. Guess you do, too."

"No, I don't. I want to look like me, only grown-up, that's all."

"Oh." Sally nodded as they started toward Columbus Park.

The white stone and redbrick pavilion overlooked a shimmering lake upon which swans glided between moonbeams. Through the arched windows above the French doors that opened out onto the veranda, Caitlin could see the glittering, dancing lights that reflected off a mirrored ball suspended above the dance floor. The sultry yet lilting strains of the clarinetist wafted across the flower-edged walks, and through the trees toward Caitlin and Sally.

"Gosh! He sounds as good as Benny Goodman."

"Yeah. He does," Caitlin agreed as she headed toward the pavilion, looking for a sign of Clay.

Caitlin stopped at the entrance. Just as she was about to go through the doors, Sally grabbed her arm and jerked her back. "You don't mean we're going in there?"

"Of course we are. What did you think we were going to do?"

"Watch. From out here. Like we did last summer."

Caitlin's chin tilted upward purposefully. "That was last year."

"Oh, no, you don't. I'm not going in there."

"Why not?"

"I'm only fourteen."

"So?"

"You gotta be seventeen. We're not supposed to be anywhere near here."

"Says who?"

"My mother, that's who."

"Fine. Then go back to her. I'm staying."

"You'll never get past the pages."

"You wanna bet?" Caitlin shot back defiantly.

"Okay. Fine. Go ahead," Sally gave back with equal steadfastness.

Caitlin scurried past her friend, who circled around the corner to watch the confrontation between Caitlin and the page through the French doors.

Caitlin paid the quarter admission, then batted her eyes at the pimply-faced young man when he asked her age. The next minute she entered the ballroom. Sally watched as she ringed the room in search of Clay or Sheilagh. Sally, unused to this much excitement and daring, chose to retreat homeward.

After two complete unfruitful reconnaissance missions around the dance floor, Caitlin paused for a moment in front of the band as they played "Moonlight Serenade." She let the music fill her head and move her body. She closed her eyes and pretended that Clay was with her, holding her, dancing with her, whispering in her ear.

"What are you doing here?" he asked in those deep, breathy tones she always recognized on the telephone.

"I came to see you," she whispered aloud, as she often did when she daydreamed about him.

"Oh, I thought you came here to find Sheilagh." He laughed merrily.

Caitlin's daydream was so real, she felt his breath upon her face. Suddenly she realized she wasn't dreaming. Her eyes flew open. Clay was smiling down at her. "You!"

"Me!" He laughed again and touched her arm.

Caitlin's knees went all jittery, and she thought she'd collapse as she did whenever Michael tackled her in backyard football. She felt as if the wind had been knocked out of her. She sucked in with her lungs, but nothing happened, except that Clay was still smiling at her. He was talking to her. Now he was holding her hand.

"I suppose you want me to take you to Sheilagh. Well, she's been a busy girl since she got here. See that line of boys over there?" He pointed to the far left. "That's Sheilagh's stag line. Hers is longer than Rosemary Campabello's."

"I thought she was coming here to be with you."

"So did I. But it didn't work out that way. They were lining up before she even got through the door."

Clay looked down into Caitlin's blue eyes. She looked up at him. He held her gaze for a strangely long time. Caitlin wished he wouldn't look at her so intensely. She felt her stomach lurch. She thought it was indigestion, but it went away too quickly and then came back again, traveling to a deeper place she hadn't known existed until now. Clay wore an odd look on his face, as if he didn't know who he was looking at or why. Caitlin didn't like feeling as if she were a specimen of some sort.

"You look very pretty tonight, Caitlin," he said appreciatively. "Nearly . . . grown-up . . ."

"I *am* grown-up," she replied tartly.

"I can see that. Isn't that Sheilagh's dress?"

Caitlin was shattered. Sheilagh again. She could never get into Clay's mind when it was so filled with Sheilagh. All at once, she wished she'd never come here tonight. She had tried to be like her sister . . . daring, adventurous, sultry—or at least as sultry as Caitlin knew how, which wasn't much.

"Yes. It's Sheilagh's." Caitlin tore her eyes from Clay, hoping he wouldn't see her disappointment. She looked to the dance floor and saw her sister in the arms of a handsome blond boy. She looked regal, elegant, and sultry all at the same time.

Her sister was very, very different from the other high school kids at the pavilion that night. The most elite of Catholic families sent their sons to Fenwick High School, and these boys formed a ring around Sheilagh in the hopes that they could possess her. She looked like a Venus from another world who, through a merciful heart, was granting audiences to these mortal boys. There was a radiance about her that they craved, as if to be in her presence would bless them.

Clay was worshiping Sheilagh from afar. His eyes glistened each time she passed by in the arms of another boy. She would idly toss Clay a faint smile as she was whirled about the ballroom. He acted as if she'd bestowed an honor upon him, Caitlin thought.

Caitlin could see that Clay was one of the idolaters, and the realization made her heartsick. He was no different from all the other boys in that respect.

"I guess I'd better go," Caitlin mumbled.

Clay remembered that Caitlin was standing next to him. "What for? Why don't you dance with me?"

"Why?" Caitlin turned hot blue eyes on him. She hoped he couldn't see her anger or disappointment.

"Because I like to dance. Because you'd like to be dancing like your sister."

"No, I wouldn't," she replied, wondering which was more important, pride or Clay.

Clay grabbed her hand, and before Caitlin knew what was happening, she found herself in his arms, whirling around the dance floor. Except for her eighth-grade graduation dance, when she danced only once with the tallest and skinniest boy in the class, Caitlin had danced only with her sister and her girlfriends in each other's basements. Her senses reeled.

For months, she had spent long, sleepless nights wondering what it would be like to feel Clay's arms around her, his hand on her waist; what his breath smelled like, and just exactly how he would hold her. Would it be forceful? Were his arms strong? Would he look away from her or at her? Would the lights dance off his dark hair the way they did now, and would he want her to like him?

Everything was just as she wanted it except that he did not look at her, but at Sheilagh. She could feel his fingertips dig into the back of her waist, possessing her. But this night was an illusion, because Clay wished he were holding Sheilagh. Caitlin wanted to cry.

"This is nice, don't you think?" he asked, looking directly at Caitlin for the first time.

"Is it?" Caitlin thought it was torture to love someone who loved someone else. The emptiness in her heart was a burning ache.

"It is," he said slowly, looking more intensely at Caitlin. "In fact, I think you're a very good dancer. You follow well. Who taught you?"

"Sheilagh."

"Ah," he said, and started to look away, but didn't. He studied Caitlin again in that way he had of seemingly measuring her every pore.

Caitlin buried her face against his shoulder. She didn't want him to read her jealousy or sorrow.

The dance ended, and while the dancers applauded the band, Sheilagh glided past the myriad of couples now overheated from the sultry summer night and passed among the darting lights toward Clay and Caitlin like a beautiful vision emerging from the mist.

"There you are!" she said to Clay. Her smile cast a light on them both. Caitlin was amazed at her sister. It was the first time she realized that there *was* something special, something nearly charismatic, about Sheilagh. She was only sixteen, but already she had star quality. Then Sheilagh looked at Caitlin. "You didn't tell me you wanted to come tonight. I would have brought you."

Caitlin was dumbstruck. "You would?"

"You're old enough. I just didn't think you would want to risk the wrath of Witch Mary."

"It was worth it," Caitlin replied, now suddenly feeling the camaraderie they shared in their unity against the elder Killians.

Sheilagh laughed, a light, musical sound that made Caitlin envious. No one should be that lucky to be so gifted, she thought. She wondered what her sister was going to do with her talent.

Sheilagh's gaze turned back to Clay. "I guess I abandoned you."

Clay sucked in his breath, taken aback by the attention Sheilagh was giving him. He had brought her here tonight, but after sharing her with every other boy in the room, he had wondered if she even knew he was alive. He wondered no more. "I hoped I would walk you home."

"I had no intention of leaving with anyone else," Sheilagh said with a pleasant but noncommittal smile.

Caitlin watched them, Clay so transparently enamored of Sheilagh, and Sheilagh basking in his adoration. She wondered if Clay realized that Sheilagh treasured his veneration no more than that of any of the other boys. She needed the worship of many people, not just one. One set of hands applauding would never be a substitute for the multitude Sheilagh craved. Caitlin wished she had a chance to tell Clay that.

"You're welcome to walk with us," Clay said to Caitlin, but there was no conviction in his voice.

"No. Sally is around here somewhere. I guess I'd better go find her."

"Suit yourself," Clay said with relief. He looked back to Sheilagh.

Caitlin could tell by the star-struck look in his eyes that he was hooked, and she had no idea how to unhook him. She watched Clay slip his hand into Sheilagh's as they wandered off into the crowd.

She watched them disappear, thinking that in the space of a single night, her four-year-long obsession had come to an end. She was only fifteen, but she had found both heaven and hell in the arms of Clay Burke.

* * *

Clay and Sheilagh were halfway down Roosevelt Street when he pulled her into the shadows of the maple trees and kissed her. It was a youthful kiss of passion, all lips and urgency and no finesse. Clay's erection surfaced instantly, and when he pulled Sheilagh's hips next to his, he was surprised that she responded to him. She kissed him back. She pressed her hips into his, rubbing him up and down. She moaned, sending his mind reeling. He'd never prepared himself for so much passion. He didn't know what to do, but he damn sure wasn't going to let her know that. He did the only thing he could; he slid his hand over her right breast. Rather than jumping away from him and slapping his face, she moved into the caress. She seemed to want more of what Clay was doing to her. She moaned again.

"My God, Sheilagh," Clay finally breathed as he held her closer to his full erection.

"Don't stop, Clay." Sheilagh groaned and kissed him again. This time she parted his lips and thrust her tongue into his mouth. Clay had heard about French kissing, but none of the girls he had been out with would ever consent to such a lurid intimacy. He liked the feel of her soft, sweet tongue in his mouth. He touched the tip of her tongue with his, and in seconds he found he was quite proficient at French kissing. Clay couldn't get enough of it.

Sheilagh pulled the strap of her sundress down her upper arm and then peeled the polished cotton chintz away from her skin, exposing her melon-sized breast. "Kiss me here, Clay," Sheilagh commanded.

Like the worshiper he was, Clay genuflected before her and did as she wished. Her flesh was soft and pliant. His hands were overflowing with her breast as he trailed tremulous kisses across the mound to her nipple. He didn't know what to do with the taut tip and continued kissing it.

"Use your tongue, Clay, like you did with my mouth," she whispered seductively.

Clay thought he would lose his mind, so incredibly heady was the experience. He was older than Sheilagh. He was nearly a man, yet it was she who was teaching him about a woman's body. Sheilagh both fascinated and frightened him. He didn't want her to think he was inadequate.

Sheilagh's body undulated against Clay. She breathed heavily, then began panting almost like an animal. She clutched at his head, shoving his face further into the mound of satin flesh. Clay thought her heart would explode through her ribs. She moaned over and over. He was afraid that someone would hear them as they committed their sin.

Gradually Sheilagh's gyrations slowed, her breathing evened out, and she pulled his head from her breast. Clay was confused. He knew he must have done it wrong.

"Thank you, Clay," Sheilagh said simply. "It's much better when I do it with a boy."

Clay gulped down the lump in his throat. "You've done this before?" Suddenly he felt quite ordinary, not special at all.

"No, I haven't, Clay. You're the first. I meant not by myself."

Clay's eyes widened with shock. "I thought only boys did that . . ."

Sheilagh's smile was wickedly delicious. She looked like a little girl, but her lips were still swollen from his kisses. "Girls do, too. Some girls. I did. Some of us have needs that other girls won't know about for years to come. If they ever do."

Clay's eyes were swimming with admiration. He'd never been able to talk to a girl like this. "You're really different, aren't you, Sheilagh?"

"You'll never meet anyone else like me for the rest of your life, Clay Burke."

"I know I won't."

Sheilagh smoothed down her skirt and started to walk away.

"Wait! When can I see you again?" Clay needed to know.

"Soon. Very soon. We'll do this again, okay, Clay?"

"Okay," he breathed, knowing his fading erection was coming back to life already.

"I like you, Clay Burke."

"I like you too, Sheilagh."

"Call me tomorrow, okay?" she said over her shoulder as she walked away.

"I will! I promise!" He waved, but she didn't look back. Clay watched Sheilagh vanish into the night shadows. He could hear the sound of her heels clicking on the sidewalk long after she was out of view. But as the sound faded into the summer air, Clay was surprised that the eyes he remembered losing himself in were blue, not green. They haunted and confused him, because he knew they belonged to Caitlin.

Chapter 16 —————————————————

August 1938

*S*HEILAGH SAW CLAY nearly three times a week that summer, which presented a problem of logistics because of the distance between their houses. He had to travel the Lake Street el, which ran from downtown Chicago to Cicero Avenue. Then he would walk or take the bus up Oak Park. Clay fantasized that he was traversing mountains to be with his one true love.

His mother, Aileen, sat in the kitchen of their home in Evanston, watching her nineteen-year-old son prepare lunch. Aileen made no secret of the fact that she doted on her only son, but she was wise enough to know that possessiveness pushed children out the door.

She realized her son was infatuated with the beautiful Killian girl, but she knew in her heart it was an affair that would not last. They were nothing alike, Clay and Sheilagh. Aileen did not turn a blind eye to the matter, nor did she make the mistake of forbidding him to see her. Rather she watched . . . and waited.

Aileen pretended interest in a newspaper article about a new archaeological dig being planned near Quamrum in the Middle East. The sound of the WMAQ radio announcer's voice wafted through the open kitchen curtains. It was nearly time for her favorite program, "Club Matinee" with Ransom Sherman. Clay pulled the leftover roast beef out of the refrigerator, whacked off a thick slice, and stuck it between two slices of wheat bread. He chomped away at his lunch a bit too quickly. Aileen was immediately suspicious. She kept her eyes on the newspaper and her ears tuned in to her son's every movement.

"What are your plans for today?" she finally asked.

"The usual Saturday stuff," he managed to say around huge bites of his sandwich. "A baseball game this afternoon with the guys. The White Sox are playing a doubleheader."

"And after that?"

"I don't know."

"Another dance at Columbus Park Pavilion?"

Clay's blue eyes widened in surprise. *She knows,* he thought. *How could she know? I've been so discreet. I've covered my tracks.* Or so he'd thought. "How did you know about that?"

"You should quit asking Shorty McGuire to go with you. His mother called me and told me all about it."

Clay's face fell and his shoulders slumped. He sank into the bentwood chair next to his mother. "I'm sorry."

Aileen chuckled. "Sorry you got caught, but not sorry you're sneaking around to see Sheilagh Killian."

His eyes began to sparkle. Aileen frowned. This was a bad sign. But was it infatuation or true love?

"I like her, Mom. A lot," Clay replied. His eyes probed his mother's face, searching for her blessing. To have his mother's approval would be like receiving the ivy crown of a Greek warrior.

During that split second of eye contact, Aileen saw in her son's face all the anticipation of youth, the naive hopefulness and unspent passion of first love. There was an electricity about him that was nearly visible; a flush of heat wafted toward her from his body, and then she knew. Whether Clay was truly in love or not didn't matter. He thought he was. It was as if Aileen could see his future laid out before her like a road map. Clay was going to get his heart broken. It was the one thing Aileen had prayed would never happen to him. *A mother's love,* she thought, *can be as naive as a first love.*

Aileen took his hand and held it for a moment, hoping she could dam back her tears. "I'm happy for you," she finally said, wondering if he noticed the crack in her voice.

"Thanks." He blushed.

"Does she like you?"

"I think so."

"You don't know so? Why don't you ask her point-blank?"

"You think I should?"

"Yes, I do. Unless you're just using her affections and she doesn't actually matter that much to you," Aileen offered, hoping she might be right.

"She does."

"I would think that Mary Margaret Killian would like her daughter to be properly courted."

"C–courted?" Clay stumbled over the word.

Aileen had always prided herself on her finely tuned insights, and when she heard Clay's pause, his split-second hesitation, she clung to this glimmering ray of hope.

"You have met Mrs. Killian, I assume," Aileen said, side-stepping the real issue and deflecting his attention. Aileen was good at games, too.

"Well, uh, yeah. A long time ago. I don't see her much."

"Heavens! Why not?"

"I, uh . . ."

"I should think such formalities would be required in the Killian household. I know for a fact that Mary Margaret Killian is a stickler for good manners. I saw that when she was planning the Christmas party for the Chicago Yacht Club last year. It was beautiful and orchestrated to please every single one of her social-climbing friends."

Clay stopped chewing his sandwich as he peered at his mother. "You don't like Sheilagh's mother?"

"Not particularly. No."

"Great," Clay replied depressively.

"I hope the daughter is nothing like the mother."

All Clay could think of was Sheilagh's long legs and shapely breasts. "She isn't," he said dully, trying to hide his real emotions.

Aileen put her hand on Clay's shoulder and looked deeply into his eyes. "I love you, Clay. I want only the best for you. I want you to finish college . . ."

"I will, Mother. Nothing is going to stop me from getting my degree."

"Women have a way of doing that."

"Sheilagh isn't like that. She doesn't want to get married. She isn't looking for a husband. She wants a career in acting." Clay's thoughts suddenly seemed outside himself, as if he were seeing Sheilagh clearly for the first time. "I think she *needs* a career even more than I do. There's something that drives her . . . forces her to push for her acting . . . something I don't understand at all. We've always talked about my going to college as if it were expected, nearly like going to kindergarten. There was never any question about it. But Sheilagh, she's different. She says she never talks about her dreams around her family, and even when I've brought it up, she tells me that 'it's private' and then she changes the subject. Almost as if it were sinful even to think about her future. Don't you think that's odd?"

"Yes, I do," Aileen mused, now lost in observations of her own. "Not odd, however, if her parents are thinking her only future is a proper marriage." She looked back at her son, forcing herself to see him the way the world saw him; the way Mary Margaret Killian would view a prospective son-in-law.

Clay was handsome in that very black Irish way. Dark black hair, white clear skin, and flashing blue eyes. He was tall and muscular from his high school years in football and baseball. He was a politician's son, however, and not as socially elite as Mary Margaret would want. Since Prohibition, too many politicians were linked with gangsters in the minds of Chicagoans. Only time would show people like Patrick and Mary Margaret Killian that the Burke family was honest. Aileen wondered idly what time would write about the Killians.

As for Sheilagh's prospective marriage partners, Aileen's instincts told her that Mary Margaret probably had her eye set on the posh group of North Lake Shore Drive; the Wirtzes, who had acquired the Chicago Stadium in 1935, or the Wrigleys, the banking Mitchells, the Armours or the Wackers. A common Burke would never do, not for Mary Margaret Killian.

Aileen was unsure of her feelings about Clay and this unknown entity named Sheilagh. He showed some of the signs of being in love . . . that distant, faraway look when he was thinking about a girl; the more than usual use of the telephone, and the nights when he snuck out of his bedroom window and was gone till late at night. Clay was no longer a child. Aileen knew better than to play the role of an authoritarian dictator to him. He would do what he wanted. His summer job at the Cook County Records Office was boring, but he earned enough money to pay for the buses and trains that took him to Oak Park. She knew for a fact he saved half his money for his college expenses in the fall.

For the first time in her life, Aileen Burke wished she'd spent more time at charity and social functions than she had at her teaching and pursuit of Ph.D.s. Perhaps then she would have had more contact with the Killians or even met Sheilagh firsthand. She wondered if the daughter was anything like the mother. She couldn't imagine Clay being interested in a cold, unfriendly woman like Mary Margaret.

Aileen would never forget the first time she'd met Mary Margaret, at a benefit dinner for the Chicago Symphony at the La Salle Hotel. She remembered it well, because it was the first year that Chicagoans had started to wear their minks since the crash of twenty-nine. Still, too much guilt over the homeless and hungry prevented the rich from openly displaying their jewels in 1937. Oddly, it was the furs that Aileen would always remember. Hers was a black ranch mink three-quarter jacket she'd bought in 1928. It was out-of-date, thin, and looked its age. Mary Margaret Killian's mahogany mink coat was nearly ankle length and brand-new. Aileen thought it a brash move for a woman who was still trying to be accepted by Chicago's old money.

Mary Margaret had managed to be included on not only the invitation committee but also the seat-assignment committee. Naturally she was seated between the Marshall Fields and the McCormicks. The Burkes were in attendance because of their political connections. The food was ordinary, not the hotel's best, the music divine since the benefit was for the symphony, and the company at their table standard but amusing.

Mary Margaret Killian sat next to her inebriated husband and stood quickly when her committee names were called. Aileen noticed that she stood longer than the other women and looked around the ballroom at nearly every table, basking in the applause as if it were bread and water to her. Aileen's keen eye noticed, too, that the velvet of Mary Margaret's gown was not crushed from many wearings or creased from hanging in a closet. It was brand-new. She guessed she'd been to the couture department at Marshall Field's. Probably intended to keep the carriage trade alive single-handedly, Aileen thought.

In the hotel's lavish marble ladies' lounge, Aileen had encountered Mary Margaret firsthand. Jane Briskin, a friend of Aileen's, had introduced them.

"How do you do, Mrs. Burke," Mary Margaret said perfunctorily.

"Very well. And you?" Aileen offered a pleasant smile to the slender and striking brunette. Aileen was thirty-six, and guessed Mary Margaret was two or three years younger, but her face was harder, though not lined or creased by age. Rather, there was a set quality to her features, as if her eyes had been slashed into her face, and her mouth painted on with a steady hand. There were no human flaws to be seen. She could have been made of marble.

"Wonderful." Mary Margaret eyed Aileen's dated black shantung dinner suit. "You're the alderman's wife."

"Yes. That's right."

Mary Margaret kept her social smile in place, but her eyes went to the mirror, inspecting her coiffure, the drape of the back of her gown. She seemed to be unimpressed with Aileen and was obviously dismissing her. "What do you think your husband's chances are of winning the next election?"

"I'm not worried about it. His constituents know that he does a good and honest job for them. He'll always win."

Mary Margaret's lips curled into a smirk. "There's no such thing as always winning. Naïveté is attractive in novels and movies, but has no place in real life," she said, glancing back to the mirror and now checking her ruby red lips.

Aileen was so taken aback, she was unsure what this woman was trying to tell her. Or was she revealing something about herself? It was a question she would wonder about for years to come.

"I'm simply stating a fact," Aileen replied courageously.

"Good for you. Well," Mary Margaret said with a dramatic intake of breath that signaled the end to their conversation, "I must get back. My guests will be missing me."

Without another word, Mary Margaret dropped her lipstick tube into her expensive beaded evening bag and walked stiffly out of the ladies' lounge. Aileen noted that there was no sway of the hips, no swing of the arms, when Mary Margaret moved. *She's like a mannequin,* Aileen thought. *No emotions, no spirit, just the physical being that was all anyone would ever know of Mary Margaret Killian.*

Aileen believed Mary Margaret's drunken husband had stolen the life out of her. She had not paid much attention to idle gossip, but as the other woman disappeared from her view, she remembered stories that had filtered around town about his philandering and his "keen business acumen," which had kept his company afloat during the Depression. In the same breath she'd heard guffaws about his gangster connections and his failure to envision new trends in chocolate. Was Patrick Killian a genius or a fool? Who was this cold woman he had married? Had she always been that way? Aileen smiled to herself; there was nothing she liked more than digging for the truth, both in her chosen field of archaeology and into the human psyche.

Aileen knew she would never forget Mary Margaret Killian, but she never dreamed she would be entertaining the possibility that the two families might be joined one day. No two women could be less alike.

Clay had finished his sandwich, and now lifted the Borden glass milk bottle to his lips, and drained it.

"I do wish you'd pour it in a glass first, Clay."

He leaned down to kiss her cheek. "You've been saying that since I was eight. I gotta go."

"Think about what I said," Aileen reminded him as he opened the screened door.

"I will," he said jauntily, and raced out the door.

The doubleheader was over by six, the White Sox winning four to two against the Cleveland Indians in the first game and losing five to four in the second game. Clay hadn't cared about the game all afternoon. He only went with Harley and John to pass the time until he could meet Sheilagh.

Today she was trying out for a part at the Blackstone Theater, and he was to meet her at the back door. Then they were going to get a burger together. Then he hoped she would let him kiss her and touch her magnificent breasts the way she had all summer.

Sheilagh was a new experience for Clay. Never had he met a girl like her. She was independent and determined, and she was nearly as free with her body as he was with his. They hadn't gone all the way yet, but they could pet for hours and hours and she would never stop him. The odd part was that he never thought of Sheilagh as being a slut or loose like other girls he knew from high school. He knew she'd never done these things with other boys, and he didn't care how uninhibited she was, as long as it was with him.

The other oddity about Sheilagh was that she never demanded that he tell her he loved her. Because she had never pressed the issue, Clay had not spent much time thinking about loving her. He thought only of wanting her. Desire. Passion. Lust. Those all came to mind when he thought of Sheilagh. Yet, above all, he liked her as a person. He wasn't sure what love was, but this had to be close.

Marriage had never entered Clay's thoughts. When his mother started talking about courting and meeting the Killians, as if his future were already determined, he had felt his hands go clammy and his tongue turn to ice.

Clay stood at the back of the Blackstone Theater listening to the actors and actresses as they departed the building and hailed Yellow cabs. They seemed different from him somehow, a difference that went deeper than their bohemian dress, their flamboyant gesticulations. There was a fire in their eyes that seemed to be stoked by some internal furnace. They didn't walk, they floated. They seemed like gods to him, not of this earth. In contrast, he felt very ordinary and plain. His mood sank into a deep pit.

Sheilagh appeared in the doorway. As Clay looked up at her, a hot city breeze skipped across the alleyway and lifted a long tendril of coppery hair off her shoulder. She smiled at him, and it was like the sun bursting through a morning horizon. She was Sheilagh . . . a goddess. He was a mere mortal.

At that moment Clay knew that he had lost Sheilagh before he'd ever won her. She was not there for a man to have or possess. She belonged only to herself. He reached out his hand to her, and she took it. Clay knew it would be only for a little while. And then she would be gone. He could see it all as clearly as if it were happening today. Now he knew what his mother had meant when she'd told him about premonitions she'd had or "things" she had seen before they came to pass.

"You look wonderful . . . incredible."

"I got the part."

"You didn't!"

"I did!" She clasped her hands together and jumped down the steps. "It's not much, but it's a start. And it's at the Blackstone. A real theater. A real chance."

"I'm so happy for you, Sheilagh."

She put her arm around his waist and kissed him. There was none of the passion in her lips that he'd felt before. But there was caring. "You're the only one who will know."

"I'm honored. But why?"

"I can't tell my family."

"Why not? They would be proud."

"My mother would have me stripped and whipped," she said angrily. "My father would pack me off to some boarding school in Wisconsin. But I would only break out and run off to New York. That's what I would do." She said the words so fiercely that Clay nearly thought she'd planned her escape a long time ago. He wondered how close to the truth her words were.

"They wouldn't do anything of the kind."

"They would."

"Then what do they want you to do if you don't go into acting?"

"Get married, of course."

Clay gulped. His mother was right. "Do . . . do they know about me?"

Sheilagh looked up at him and burst into laughter. "You should see your face! You look as if you've been sentenced to a firing squad. Would it be so awful?"

"Well, I like you, Sheilagh, and all that, but I have college to think about. A career in business . . ."

"Calm down, sonny." She continued laughing, to his distress. "You have nothing to worry about, because I don't intend to ever get married."

"Not ever?"

"Never. Unless I'm old . . . like thirty or something. Maybe then. But he'd have to be an actor."

Clay thought of the young gods who had just walked his way, and he understood. "Yes. You should marry an actor."

"I already know what he's going to look like."

"You do?"

"Of course. I saw him in a dream. It was after Maria Bertillini's wedding. I not only caught the bouquet last summer, but I slept with a piece of Italian wedding cake under my pillow, and that night I had a dream of the man I was going to marry. He was quite tall and blond and had piercing blue eyes. He was definitely an actor. You can tell by the eyes."

"Yeah, I know."

"Are you sad because I don't want to marry you, Clay?"

"No."

"I still want to have fun with you. I like kissing you and touching you. It's all right."

"It is? I mean, I've never met anyone like you, Sheilagh. Other girls wouldn't do any of that stuff if I wasn't telling them I loved them."

"But you don't love me."

"How do you know? Maybe I love you more than I've loved anybody."

"No, you don't. You don't know what love is. You like to play with my body and you think I'm different. But that's not love."

"And I suppose you know what love is."

Sheilagh looked up into Clay's blue eyes and touched his cheek with more fondness than she'd ever shown him. "I know more than you do. Loving is very, very tough. You and I . . . we're easy. So, what do you say? Let's go have some fun tonight, okay?"

Clay allowed Sheilagh to lean into him, put her arms around his neck, and kiss him. She let him taste the interior of her mouth with his tongue. She let him push his erect penis against her hips.

"Maybe we should get a cab," she whispered through their kisses.

"Oh, yes," Clay groaned as he kissed her again. He was glad he didn't know anyone else like Sheilagh Killian. One was enough.

They necked in the back of the taxi, they stole breathless kisses beneath the oaks and maples of Oak Park Avenue, and brazenly, Sheilagh forced Clay to kiss the tip of her very taut nipple on the steps of Resurrection Church just as the midnight bells began to peal.

Sheilagh burst into raucous giggles watching Clay's discomfort. "It's only a building, Clay," she said, feeling his hands grow clammy and trembling against her breast.

"Why do I keep thinking we'll go to hell for this?"

"Don't worry. We won't."

"How do you know?"

"God invented sex to be enjoyed. If He didn't want us to do it, then why does it feel so good? It's a good thing we're doing."

Clay looked up at the stained-glass windows, the pillars and huge doors. He shivered. "It feels like a sacrilege to me."

Sheilagh boldly slid her hand down the front of his pants, searching for his lost erection. "It feels like nothing to me," she teased, and then took his hand. "Let's go. I didn't want to make you feel uncomfortable. I guess I'm the only truly rebellious one around here, aren't I?"

Clay grinned at her unabashed ease with her body, her sexuality, and her ability to flaunt them both in the face of her background. He liked her independence, her carefree spirit. He let her lead him away.

They raced down the empty sidewalks, slipping between moon shadows from the summer foliage overhead. The night air was cool and deliciously silky against their overheated skin.

Clay was perspiring as they ran faster and faster, jumping over the raised sidewalks where maple tree roots had flexed their long, gnarled arms. Suddenly they reached the corner where Sheilagh lived. He pulled her beneath the largest maple and slammed her back against the trunk of the tree. Only tiny pinpoints of light from the streetlight found their way through the leafy canopy. Sheilagh's eyes turned smoky and seductive as she watched Clay's lips move nearer to her mouth.

"Sometimes I think I'll never let you go," he said lowly.

"Yes, you will," she replied tartly. "But only because I wish it."

Then she kissed him with a hunger born of years of living in an emotional wasteland. She was young and desirous of all that life had to offer, and very, very impatient. She craved the attention and affection that Clay so willingly lavished upon her. But always she knew that he was exploring his own reactions, his mental illusions about what love should be and this new sense of his own sexual powers. Sheilagh gave herself to him because it pleased her and took her mind away from her troubles. Clay was an escape. Just like her daydreams. Just like acting. Sheilagh was using Clay, and she knew it. Clay was using Sheilagh, but he didn't know it.

Sheilagh took his hand and pressed it to her breast. "Take me, Clay. You know you want to." She slid his hand down her rib cage, over the bright brass buckle on her cotton print dress to her abdomen. With her other hand she lifted the full skirt and petticoats and guided his hand to the juncture of her legs.

"We shouldn't . . ." Clay breathed the words out hoarsely.

"We should. You've been dying to know what it's like. To feel the juices of your goddess . . ."

"How did you know I thought that of you?"

"It was in your eyes." She groaned and shoved his hand down farther into her panties, where his fingers separated her and suddenly entered her. "My God . . ." Sheilagh closed her eyes and rested her head back against the tree. "You don't have to do anything, Clay. I'll do all the work."

And she did.

She lifted her hips and lowered them onto Clay's hand. She undulated and gyrated and manipulated herself and him until her breath was coming in such quick, shallow pants that

Clay thought she sounded more animal than human. His head reeled as his rational thoughts succumbed to passion. He was suddenly all emotion, all feeling. The only thing he could smell was Sheilagh. All he could hear and see and touch was Sheilagh. It was as if she were part of him. He wanted to be part of her.

Clay unzipped his white cotton pants and let them drop to his ankles. In one swift though fumbling movement he pushed Sheilagh's panties to her knees. He clutched her buttocks in both his hands and brought her to him. But when he started to enter her, Sheilagh went instantly rigid.

"Don't, Clay. I . . . I didn't want it to go this far."

Clay barely heard her protest through the cresting waves of desire that filled his ears. "I want . . . to."

"I know . . . I'm sorry."

Clay's eyes rolled back in his head again as he brought his lips down on Sheilagh's luscious mouth. He rode another wave of need. "Please, Sheilagh. I love you," he blurted through wet and demanding kisses.

Sheilagh squirmed, put her hands on his chest, and pushed him firmly away from her. His eyes were open now as she looked deeply into their sensual depths. "Don't ever love me, Clay."

Clay was stunned. "Why not? Isn't that what every girl wants to hear?"

"Not me."

"I do love you, Sheilagh. You're everything to me. You're beautiful and fun and smart and not at all like anyone I've ever known. You aren't afraid of anything. I like that."

Sheilagh looked away from him and reached down to pull her panties back up her thighs. For a long, silent moment she occupied herself with straightening her skirts and bodice. She didn't want him to see the huge tear that fell when she bent over. She didn't want him to know how terrified she was.

She needed to be loved. She'd kept her emotional barriers up for so many years, she was exhausted from the effort. She wanted to love someone and have him love her back. But in the depths of her heart and mind, she knew it could never happen. She was destined for more than just a husband and kids. She wanted to be loved by many people . . . whole theaters full of people. She knew that Clay's love would never be enough for her and that someday she would break his heart. She already cared about him too much to let that happen.

She would have to let him go now, before she gave him her heart completely. She had to keep it for herself.

"Don't you see?" she finally said with an air of joviality.

"No. I don't," he replied angrily, pulling his pants up. "For weeks you've allowed me to do almost anything to you, except for . . . the real thing. Are you afraid of getting pregnant? Afraid I won't love you afterward? Well, I will. I know I will. Someday I want to marry you, Sheilagh. I want everyone to know that the most beautiful girl in the world is mine."

Sheilagh leaned against the maple tree and looked at him sadly. This time she could not keep the tears from welling up in her eyes. "You're not enough for me, Clay." She knew she was being painfully blunt, but she wanted to end it now.

"What's that supposed to mean? You don't like the way I was doing it?" Clay felt as if Sheilagh had crushed the broken shards of his pride beneath her shoes. He'd never experienced such cruelty from her. Why was she doing this? Why had she led him on for so long? Why had she let him build up such hopes and dreams? It wasn't just the sex. It was something else. Clay suddenly wished he were older and knew more about women so that he could understand. She made him feel inadequate in so many ways, and he hated her for shattering their idyll.

Sheilagh forced a smile. "Oh, no, Clay. You're a very good kisser, and the things you do with your hands . . ." She touched his cheek fondly. "I could love you, Clay . . . so easily. But I don't think that loving me would be so easy for you. You may be older than I am, but I know more about life. I know hurt and pain. I know suffering . . . long suffering. You don't. I hope you never will. I want to be your friend, Clay, but that might be more difficult than being petting partners." She chuckled softly. "I call us that because we aren't technically lovers, you know."

Clay felt a slow smile crease his face. "Yeah, I know." He glanced down at his crotch. "I was trying to change our status."

She smiled back at him. "I like us better this way. Let's just have fun. That's all I want. I can't give you more than that."

Clay's immediate reaction was to take her up on her offer, but he decided to proceed with caution. He didn't know whether to keep his goddess on her pedestal, destroy the pedestal, or replace the goddess with a new one. As moonbeams wove their way through Sheilagh's coppery hair, and her sultry green eyes peered up at him, Clay knew there would never be another goddess for him. She was in his blood. But he also knew that she was right. No matter what he did or said, he would never have her. Sheilagh would never belong to any man.

Chapter 17

April 1939

PATRICK WAS THIRTY-seven years old, and for a very long time, he had thought the excitement in his life was over. He was surrounded by sweetness at a time when he wanted nothing but spice.

He dreaded going to work, where the air was perpetually permeated with sugar. His employees were happy as they jauntily waved good day to him each morning. His secretary was overly accommodating, too willing to help him plan his social calendar, too eager to please him. Patrick didn't want Martha.

His friends were making money and playing golf again. He had a standing tee time of 8:30 A.M. every Friday. His children were suspiciously nice to him. Their grades were straight A's. Their health, clothes, manners, and attitudes were cloyingly perfect. What had happened to the pranks Sheilagh used to pull? Or Michael's lazy study habits or defiant attitude, which used to land him in the principal's office? Or Caitlin's inquisitive mind, which used to drive him crazy with twenty questions on every topic under the sun? Had they all become automatons?

These days Mary Margaret was getting what she wanted from her new society friends, her mah-jongg games with her church crowd, and the decorating and construction of the Lake Geneva house. She no longer argued with Patrick. In fact, she barely spoke to him as she dashed out the door, checking the seams of her stockings in the hall mirror one last time before she bounded into the new black Buick he'd bought her and sped down Oak Park. Always her smile was saccharine, vapid. Had her indifference always bothered him? Or was it that suddenly he'd begun to notice how unimportant he'd become to them all?

He knew that nothing had changed between himself and Mary Margaret. Not since their newlywed days had their relationship cost either of them very much emotionally. Mary Margaret took care of the children, the house, and her campaign to raise the Killian family flag over Chicago society. The children were almost grown, involved with their friends and school activities. His candy factory seemed to run itself. Nobody needed Patrick.

Spring was in the air on Easter Monday when Shannon O'Rourke walked into the Emerald Chocolate factory wearing one of the new shorter skirts that had been introduced in Paris the prior fall. She was an athletically built woman of thirty years with narrow hips, tiny waist, shapely legs, and a straight back. She held her head as if her face and brain were her most prized possessions, and they were. Her long chestnut hair was folded neatly into a chignon at the back of her neck, and she wore a tubular black hat and veil perched jauntily on her head. It was the only display of individualism in her perfectly groomed ensemble of black linen and shantung suit with black bag and kid shoes to match. Shannon O'Rourke looked more like a member of French café society than a secretarial applicant.

"Good day," she said pleasantly to Patrick Killian's executive secretary.

Normally a woman of restraint, Martha could not stop from surveying Shannon O'Rourke. She wasn't drawn by her alabaster-smooth skin with the hint of ripe peaches in her high-boned cheeks, nor the perfection of her figure, nor the panache with which she wore her clothes and carried her body. It was the fact that her eyes boldly told the world she was fully cognizant of all her attributes and intended for the world to know them, too. Shannon O'Rourke was the kind of woman who knew what she wanted and intended to get it. The ambitious gleam in her eyes was one that Martha had rarely seen in women. Martha found Shannon intimidating . . . and a threat.

I've seen her kind before, Martha thought. She's not here to find a job, she's husband-hunting. My guess is, she'll stop at nothing to get what she wants.

This woman would use all her tricks to get me fired, take my job, and no doubt sleep with Patrick. All my years here, my loyalty to the Killians, would mean nothing to her. I'll bet there isn't a caring bone in her body. God! She might even go so far as to get Patrick to divorce Mary Margaret and marry her.

I can't let that happen.

"Is there something I can help you with?"

"I'm here about the job as receptionist."

Martha did not miss a beat. "There have been several applicants . . ."

"I would hope so."

"Why is that?"

"I wouldn't want a job if no one else wanted it." A smile flitted across Shannon's fuchsia-painted lips.

"You'll have to fill out this application." Martha recovered quickly as she reached into the third drawer left for the file marked "Applications." She handed it to Shannon, who sat in a straight-back wooden chair against the wall.

Shannon pulled a Sheaffer fountain pen out of her purse and began filling in the blanks. She was finished in less than three minutes. "And who will interview me?"

Just as she spoke, the walnut door to the left opened. Patrick entered the room, his eyes still perusing a lengthy report; he did not see Shannon, but he heard her voice. It was a moment he would never forget, that sensuous voice with its careful pronunciation. Patrick put the report on Martha's desk and turned toward the woman.

Her appearance did nothing to unravel the mystery. Her clothes were proper, her eyes and mouth as sexy as hell. He felt as if he'd just wandered onto a surreal movie set. She was the celluloid goddess, and he was the bumbling mortal hoping for a crumb of her attention. He felt old, he felt young. He felt stupid and silly, yet strong and very, very virile.

"I will conduct the interview," he said, finding that his words flowed easily over the lump in his throat.

The beautiful creature smiled at him. "You must be Patrick Killian."

"I am."

"Good," she replied, uncrossing her long legs, making certain he could see up the side of her skirt to midthigh. "I like going straight to the top. I don't like wasting time."

"You don't, huh?" He smirked to himself, thinking he was picking up on her attraction to him.

"No. I don't have much of it to waste. You see, Mr. Killian, I don't want your job. I need it for now, but I have other ambitions, much loftier and more creative than simply spending the rest of my life as a receptionist or an—" she glanced disdainfully at Martha—"executive secretary."

A bit put off by her attitude, Patrick defended himself. "I'm not interested in anything but the best person for the job, Miss . . ."

"O'Rourke. Shannon O'Rourke." She squared her shoulders and took a breath. "I am the best receptionist you could ever hire, Mr. Killian. The point I'm making is that I intend to accomplish a great deal with my life. This is simply a necessary step toward my goals. Now, when can we begin this interview?"

Patrick raised a bushy black eyebrow as Shannon O'Rourke eased past him and walked into his office without a proper invitation. He noticed that her perfume was Shalimar . . . French and expensive. He'd bought it once for Mary Margaret at Marshall Field's for some damn anniversary or something, and his wife had never so much as lifted the stopper.

Patrick followed Shannon into his office. He was not only intrigued, he was fascinated. He hired Shannon O'Rourke that day to fill the receptionist's position.

It took her only one week to make Patrick Killian fall in love with her.

Shannon's ambitions were larger than life, but somehow, once he knew her, Patrick expected nothing less. At the age of twelve she had gone to Paris with her parents and learned about the world of fashion. She combed the Rue de Cambon, where the House of Chanel was only steps away from other famous houses like Callot, Schiaparelli, and Molyneux. She soaked up the styles, the fabrics, the cuts, the lay of the cloth as it rolled from the bolt, the precise placement of buttons, frogs, and fragile bugle beads. Shannon made use of her time in Paris and built upon it every day afterward. By the time she was twenty-five, she had completed a course at the Art Institute and could draw as well as any artist in the Midwest. But she wasn't interested in the arts. She wanted to make money from her fashion designs.

By the time she was thirty, she had discovered that it takes money to make money. The Depression was over and the moment was ripe for her to realize her dream. She'd worked for cheap tailors, in the elegant salons of Marshall Field's, and had designed clothes privately for women who were far too poor to pay her the kind of money she deserved and who did not possess the eye necessary to appreciate a Shannon O'Rourke creation.

Shannon needed a mentor.

She had seen Patrick Killian in church and known he was the man she was looking for. She had been to every Catholic church on the West and North sides over the prior six months in search of the rich lover she intended to use to fund her future. Shannon believed the best way to find an unhappy man was to observe him with his family while standing before his God.

She was beginning to think that *all* Chicago Catholics actually believed the crap handed out to them by the priests and nuns. Her investigations had produced more happy men and families than she'd thought existed. But then, she was looking for someone special. She wanted a man who accepted church dogma which said it was a sin to divorce. She would teach him how to bend the remainder of his morals to her advantage.

Shannon spotted Patrick Killian when he marched his family down the center aisle of Ascension Church, only moments prior to the processional. She noted that he looked to the left and right, making certain the congregation watched him as he led the way to the front pews. Patrick Killian was the kind of man who wanted to be noticed.

Though he dressed conservatively in a gray tweed overcoat that was at least seven or eight years old, judging from the narrow cut of the lapels and the longer length, his black felt hat was new and lined in pearl gray satin. He was a man who spent money on details.

After genuflecting and standing aside for his family to be seated, he chose to sit next to his son, not his wife. Shannon considered it a good sign. During mass, Patrick's thoughts seemed to be anywhere except on the service. This was another good sign. His faith, if he had any, was shallow. Shannon need not worry at his being too guilty about adultery. When the collection basket was passed, Patrick dropped a large wad of dollar bills into the basket. If he'd been poor, he would have given quarters; if rich, he would have quietly placed a twenty in the basket; if very rich, he would have given nothing. Patrick was nouveau riche and needed to show off, Shannon thought as she watched the thick wad roll around in the basket as it was passed from hand to hand.

Shannon watched the Killian family as they departed the church. Patrick made a big show of presenting his perfectly groomed children to his adult friends. There was much handshaking and hearty laughter, much like a politician who's running for an election he knows he's going to lose. Patrick Killian showed all the signs of being an unhappy man.

Shannon believed her plan to be foolproof. She put it into action.

Chapter 18 —————————————

June 1939

CAITLIN FOUND THAT a broken heart could be mended. It took threads of time, the sharp needle of reality, and a courageous hand, but it could be done. Caitlin tried to make herself give up her childish dreams of loving Clay and go on with her life.

Purging her brain and heart of the only boy who had ever meant anything to her was nearly too much for her. The more Caitlin strove not to think about Clay, the more she did. The problem was exacerbated by the fact that Clay was now a fixture in the Killian household. He came to call on Sheilagh every Saturday night.

Caitlin always made arrangements to be gone from the house from six o'clock on Saturday until nine. She didn't want to watch Sheilagh choosing her dress for her date, always one that would seduce even the most devout and chaste priest, much less a virile young man like Clay. Caitlin thought her heart would be torn from her rib cage every time she heard

Clay's familiar footsteps on the front porch. She learned to force herself not to answer the jangling telephone. Clay wanted to talk to Sheilagh, not to her.

After three months, Clay telephoned less, and it was all right for her to answer the phone. After six months, she had managed to catch only a glimpse of him twice, and she congratulated herself on the fact that she'd deftly avoided contact with him.

After nine months of her vigilant efforts to avoid him, she still thought about him incessantly. Caitlin would always love Clay, and it was Sheilagh who had him.

To ease the pain, Caitlin chose the sweetest route to recovery . . . chocolate.

During her last year of high school, her days ended at noon, which gave her all afternoon to spend at the Emerald Chocolate offices. Nothing could have pleased Caitlin more. She immersed herself into the world of chocolate.

Caitlin took it upon herself to reevaluate the molding machines and conveyer belts. Several of the workers had complained of breakdowns in the machinery and that some of the bar molds needed replacing.

It was Caitlin who took a checklist with her and walked down the production line past the pouring machine to the molding machine. She found that the molding machine was in perfect working order, but that three cogs had been ground smooth and were missing their catches on the vibrating machine, which removed the air bubbles from the chocolate in an early stage of producing Emerald's new line of cream-filled chocolate bars. The cooling machine was in good order, as was the packaging machine.

In the past weeks Caitlin had investigated filling chocolate bars with liquid liqueurs and fruit brandies, much as Cadbury had been doing since they'd merged with Fry company, which claimed to have been the first to fill chocolate bars in the 1870s. New and deeper molds would have to be purchased, new packaging chosen, a more aggressive advertising campaign begun, but all of these changes excited Caitlin. It had been a long time since anything innovative had been done at Emerald.

These days it seemed as if her father didn't care anymore. He had almost no interest in the company, which was a boon to her, because he allowed her to execute company policy and make decisions he might never have allowed otherwise. Caitlin overlooked the fact that Patrick took all the credit for himself. He stole her ideas and called them his own. He made her wait in his outer office to see him longer than his salesmen, directors, and even suppliers. His actions told Caitlin she was unimportant. But she didn't care, because she knew someday she would be important to him and he would have to come to her. She was willing to wait for that someday.

The problem was that Caitlin just plain didn't know what was going through his head. She'd never known her father to be so preoccupied. He'd started to keep the oddest hours. Some days he didn't come into the office at all, which caused Martha a great deal of extra work just to rearrange his schedule. He seldom returned his phone calls, handing them over to Caitlin or Martha. He encouraged Caitlin to run the sales meetings. This past week he had spoken of hiring a general manager.

"What would he manage?" Caitlin demanded.

"Everything you don't," Patrick boomed. He sank into his leather chair with a heavy thud, then drummed his fingers anxiously on the desk.

He'd told Mary Margaret he'd been playing golf two afternoons a week, but his skin was pale. Obviously he had not been outside. Patrick was restless, and Caitlin didn't know what to make of it. "You mean he would handle your responsibilities. Isn't that it?"

Patrick avoided her eyes. He was sick of the candy business. He needed more time with Shannon. "I'm getting on in years. I won't be around forever. I need to train someone to be ready to take my place."

All Patrick could think about was the last time he'd been with Shannon, when she had poured champagne down the length of him and then proceeded to lick it off his body droplet by droplet. *Yes,* he thought, *Shannon is my only reason for living these days.*

Caitlin stuck her hand on her hip. "I agree that something is wrong, but I hardly think you're ready for the family burial plot. You aren't even forty yet."

"Jim Kelly had a heart attack at forty. I can't believe the bastard is still alive."

"You could have a heart attack too." Caitlin made certain to emphasize with clear, loud, and distinct syllables every word she said. Her father was not listening.

"Did you finish that report on the repairs?" Patrick knew he could sidetrack Caitlin with talk of the company.

"Yes. And I have another report I worked up. About the filled chocolate bars. I was thinking orange liqueur in a vanillin fondant . . ."

"Fine . . ." he said, grabbing the manila folders she handed him. "I'll look them over." He glanced at his watch. Three weeks ago he'd fired Shannon, thinking that would keep their affair quiet. He'd been getting the evil eye from Martha about his "closed-door meetings" with Shannon. Every time he left his office, Martha had scrutinized him for telltale mussed hair, lipstick marks, or an unzipped fly. Martha had become the family watchdog.

It was nearly time to meet Shannon at her place for lunch. "Put an ad in the *Trib* for a general manager. But get him cheap. I don't want to pay an arm and a leg . . . especially since we have to train him to our way of doing business anyway. Maybe a college grad . . . you know, green around the edges, impressionable . . ."

Caitlin left Patrick's office and went to her own makeshift office. It was really a storage closet that she'd renovated by taking out half the shelves, installing a telephone, and erecting a pair of large wall brackets to hold a thick piece of mahogany that had once been a residential door and which was now her desktop. She had found an unwanted chair, painted it white, and made a blue and white toile-patterned seat cushion. The bare light bulb overhead gave hardly enough light to the tiny area, but it was officially hers.

Caitlin went to her desk and wrote three drafts of the ad she intended to place in the newspaper before she was satisfied with the wording. She placed a telephone call to the *Chicago Tribune* classified section and told the order taker that the billing should be sent to the Emerald offices.

Three days later, Caitlin picked up the *Tribune* on the front steps of the Killian house before she went to school. She never dreamed that her simple want ad would change her life.

Of the twenty-seven applicants for the job as general manager, only three were recent college graduates, and only five would accept the low pay being offered. None had any experience in the candy or chocolate-making business.

Patrick abandoned the office four afternoons that week, telling Martha and Caitlin he had meetings and his golf games. Martha never said a word. Caitlin questioned him incessantly, which angered him.

"If you're gone this afternoon, who's going to interview these applicants?" Caitlin inquired as Patrick jammed his arms into his tweed overcoat.

"This meeting is just as important as those interviews."

"Really? Then I'll put them off until tomorrow."

"No. Not tomorrow. Maybe Friday . . ." He patted the pockets of his coat. His eyes scanned the room. "Where are my reading glasses?"

Caitlin pointed to the round cherry wood table next to the leather sofa. "Over there."

"Thanks. Now, what were you saying?"

"It was your idea to hire a general manager. Now you act as if you don't remember."

"Fine. You interview them. You decide who to hire."

Caitlin took a step back. Patrick had given her many tasks to perform, some with more authority attached to them, but this was a major decision. If she chose the wrong person, the company would suffer. She was only seventeen. What did she know about the credentials necessary to run their company?

Suddenly Caitlin felt as if she were standing outside herself looking down at the situation with an objective and critical eye. Patrick Killian was abdicating his responsibilities. She, Caitlin, was the only one who gave a flip about what was happening within the walls of Emerald. *She* was concerned. *She* cared. At this moment she was probably the best-qualified person to conduct the interview on that basis alone.

"I accept," she replied with confidence.

"Good. I'll look him over after you make your choice." He glanced at his wristwatch. "Damn! I'm late."

Caitlin went back to her desk, picked up the telephone, and began setting up interviews.

By Thursday, Caitlin had interviewed all twenty-seven applicants and had liked none of them. Each had certain strengths and looked good on paper, but since she wasn't sure what she was looking for, she passed judgment based solely on her gut instinct. Nearly one-half of the applicants were incensed that a high school girl was interviewing them. One-third realized it was a family-run business, and therefore knew not to expect career advancement. None of them was particularly interested in devoting his life to chocolate, as Caitlin was.

She sat at her father's desk, still poring over the applications, lamenting the fact that she had not a single prospect to consider, when Martha tapped on the door.

"Yes?" Caitlin glanced up. For the first time she noticed the light flecks of gray that had begun to sprout in Martha's hair. How old was she now? Thirty-two? Thirty-three? And she had never been married. Mary Margaret always joked that Martha was married to Emerald Chocolates. Caitlin felt pangs of sympathy for the woman.

Martha had no children. No life. Only chocolate. Caitlin had never heard Martha talk about her parents or any brothers or sisters. She knew of only one girlfriend, Betty, who had recently married and moved to Des Plaines.

Martha worked overtime, even Saturdays. No wonder Patrick said that she did the work of two secretaries. She put in over sixty hours in a normal week.

It was a moment of instant revelation that Caitlin would remember for a long time to come. "I never want to live like that," she mumbled. "Yet that's exactly what I've been doing."

Martha said nothing about the queer expression on Caitlin's young face. "There's another applicant here. He doesn't have an appointment, but he begged me to coerce you into seeing him with no notice." She smiled.

"Begged?"

Martha's smile broadened. "Begged."

"Send him in," Caitlin said, and paused a bit before continuing. "Oh, and Martha?"

"Yes?"

"Mother is having a fish fry on Friday night after work. It's just the family, but we'd all like you to come."

Martha's eyes shone with gratitude. "I'd love that, Caitlin."

"About six-thirty. You . . . you can bring a friend if you like."

"Goodness, no," Martha twittered. "It'll just be me."

"That's fine, just fine." Caitlin smiled.

Her smile faded as Martha brought forward the new applicant. Clay Burke wore a dark blue gabardine suit, a white shirt, and a navy tie. His hair was slicked back with pomade and his bay rum cologne was too strong, which told Caitlin he'd just come from a fresh shower.

She nearly jumped out of the chair as images of Clay naked under the shower head . . . soap suds slithering down his chest, back, and thighs . . . assaulted her.

"Clay! I . . . never . . ."

"Never? Surely you knew I would like to be considered for this job. Haven't we always talked about chocolate . . . you and I?"

"Yes."

"I doubled up my classes two years ago and now have only two semesters at U of C to get my degree. I was thinking I could take night sessions this summer, fall, winter, and next summer. You see, I want this job, Caitlin. In my marketing classes, I couldn't help thinking about how to apply the principles I was learning to Emerald. When I had an advertising idea, it was always about chocolate. I can't explain it. I believe chocolate is my niche.

"Based on your previous knowledge of me and that I'm an upstanding, honest, decent, hardworking, and concerned person, I think you should give me the job."

"You do."

"I do." He smiled.

Caitlin was nearly knocked over by the force of him. She wanted to hire him instantly. Visions of them working together, day in and day out . . . building the company . . . being together, swept over her like the wind off Lake Michigan. But what would her father say?

All the angels and saints in heaven were not going to convince a stubborn Irishman like Patrick Killian that he should turn the management of his company over to the young man whom Patrick thought of as the boy who had been keeping Sheilagh out late at night, the boy Patrick was convinced needed to "go back to the North Side, where he belonged."

Clay flashed a second smile at Caitlin.

This time she did sink down into the chair behind her. "You're hired."

"Just like that?"

"Not exactly. I'll recommend you to my father for the job. He'll make the final decision."

"I think he'll agree with you that I can handle it."

This time Caitlin smiled. "We'll see about that."

"Yes, we will."

The next afternoon Caitlin sat in her office chewing on a pencil eraser head while Clay met with her father behind closed doors. She couldn't remember the last time she had been so nervous.

Her first surprise had come when Patrick actually agreed to

see Clay. Her second came when twenty minutes passed and they weren't finished. After thirty minutes together, Patrick buzzed Martha and requested that coffee be sent in. Caitlin peeked around the corner and watched as Martha carried in a tray. Through the crack in the door she saw that both men were laughing as if they were old friends.

How was this possible? Patrick didn't like Clay. Or so she had thought.

After forty-five minutes, Clay Burke walked out of Patrick Killian's office, the two men shook hands, and Clay stated that he would be reporting to work Monday morning at seven-thirty when the factory officially opened.

Caitlin waited for Clay to leave before she rushed into her father's office. The door was still open, but she tapped on the doorjamb.

"It went well?" she asked expectantly.

"Surprisingly so," Patrick conceded. "I can't tell you when I've been so impressed. And I have to admit I had preconceptions against him. That boy has vision. But I guess you saw that in your interview with him." Patrick's blue eyes probed his youngest daughter.

Caitlin remembered her interview, all right, but for some reason, she had never gotten past the smell of the bay rum and the imaginary soap suds. "Yes, I did," she lied.

"Damn! Such moxie! Reminds me of myself at that age, he does." Patrick paused for a reflective moment. "Clay thinks I should put in a government bid for war rations. He's heard that Hershey is trying to take the contract with a new Ration D . . . which is no more than the old Ration D with more chocolate in it. I never would have thought of that."

"You think we have a chance? Hershey is awfully big."

"Who gives a shit about Ration D? I just like the idea that this kid would go to the moon for this company." Patrick crossed the room with a zing to his steps. He took his new charcoal gray fedora from the coat rack. "I'll see you at home tonight, then."

Caitlin was rocked back on her heels by her father's reaction. She was so thrilled about Clay being a part of Emerald that she never stopped to wonder where her father was going on a payroll Friday afternoon.

Patrick Killian kept Shannon O'Rourke in a two-bedroom brick bungalow just off Washington on Kildare Avenue. She had worked at Emerald Chocolate Company for less than three weeks before she took him to her bed. She used her hands, lips, tongue, and teeth to bring him to the climax of his life. They made love on the pink and blue flowered sofa, in the claw-footed porcelain bathtub, on the rose point rug in front of the green-tiled fireplace, and on the kitchen floor. At dawn they still had not made it to the bedroom. Shannon was saving that for later.

The following day, Patrick was flooded with fear that his passion for Shannon would be obvious to anyone who saw them together at work. So he fired her. She called him a son of a bitch and departed his office almost like a lady. But there was much too much sway to her hips.

The next day Patrick showed up on Shannon's doorstep with his Buick filled with empty packing boxes. He carried a gold-foil-wrapped box of Emerald's prestige line of chocolates and two dozen red roses.

Shannon's eyes gleamed with triumph as she peeked through the white curtains at him. She stopped at the hall mirror to smooth her pompadour hairdo and adjust the silver barrette at the back of her head. *Just remember, he needs you. There are plenty like Patrick Killian around,* she told herself as he impatiently rang the bell again.

That very afternoon Patrick insisted that she move from the tiny, weathered apartment in Hyde Park to be closer to him.

"I like the view here," she protested.

"All I saw was a bunch of Negro children playing around Lorado Taft's statue."

"I like 'em. They're friends."

"This is too close to the stockyards. It stinks here."

Her pretty bow mouth pouted. She licked her upper lip.

Patrick couldn't take his eyes off her tongue. Perspiration sprang up across his forehead.

Shannon shifted her weight onto her left foot. Her hip curved outward. She ran her hand over the swell of her buttocks, then let her arm dangle expectantly at her side. She took a very slow, deep breath and pushed her breasts against her sheer white linen blouse. Patrick's eyes took in each movement. He could see a pair of taut brown nipples through the fabric. He dropped the flowers and candy to the floor and in one stride, crossed the area between them. He took her into his arms and kissed her with more passion than he knew he possessed.

"I said it stinks."

"Then where am I going?" she breathed, and surrendered her body to his. They fell to the floor, and she let him take her there on top of the flowers and Emerald chocolates.

Clay hiked Sheilagh's skirts up to her waist and sank his hand into the fertile valley between her satin-smooth thighs. She grabbed his face with both hands and pulled him to her until their tongues met. Clay leaned into the kiss and slowly edged Sheilagh onto the backseat of his father's new Cadillac.

He kissed her throat and traveled farther down her breast-bone through the open neck of her cardigan before he stopped at the row of tiny pearl buttons. It was Sheilagh who unfastened each one. Her movements were torturously slow, causing both anticipation and excruciating need in Clay.

Finally the cardigan opened like the parting of the seas. She pulled her slip strap down her arm, and a full breast glistened in the moonlight that filtered through the windshield. Clay could resist most things in this life, he thought, except Sheilagh's breasts. With his lips and tongue he devoured the nipple and as much flesh as he could suck into his mouth. But he could never get enough of Sheilagh.

She smelled like roses and hyacinths. Her long, coppery hair spilled over her shoulders and onto his head as he moved lower on her body. He wanted all of her and was determined that this time he would get it. He was celebrating his good fortune. He was now on the payroll of Emerald Chocolate Company.

He had intended to formally ask Sheilagh to marry him tonight, before they'd started petting, but as always with Sheilagh, words didn't seem to be important. In fact, they got in the way.

Sheilagh's hand slid down Clay's back and moved around to his chest. She unbuttoned his white cotton shirt. She moved her hand across his chest, then lower down his hard, flat stomach. She unbuckled his leather belt. She unzipped his slacks.

"Sheilagh?" Clay's head popped up. He stared into her smoky green eyes. For the first time, he saw acquiescence. He'd wanted to see surrender. He wasn't sure what that would look like, but something told him this wasn't quite it.

"I want you to do it to me, Clay."

"You do?"

"Oh, yes. I think it's time we grew up."

Since the first time he had seen Sheilagh five years ago, he had wanted her. He had dreamed about her. She had alternately been his goddess, his tease, the bane of his existence, and Mecca all rolled into one. Now that the moment was upon him, it was Clay who suddenly felt as if something were wrong. "I . . . I don't think we should."

Sheilagh's mouth dropped open. She peered deeply into his eyes. "You're scared."

"I guess I am."

She touched his cheek with such tenderness, he thought he would crumble . . .

"I don't want to feel so alone, Clay. Please . . ."

"You? Alone? You have a big family . . . all your friends at the theater. Your life is full."

Sheilagh looked away so that he wouldn't see the tear that slid down her cheek. It was an honest tear, not an acting tear. It was the kind that came from a wounded heart. "I've always been alone. I'm afraid I always will be."

"Never."

"It's time for me to move on, Clay. My family isn't a family anymore. Everybody is off in one direction or another. When I do see Mother, we inevitably fight. Except now I know how to play her game more effectively. I don't get as caught up in her tirades. Caitlin is consumed by work. Michael lives for medicine, which is why he and Father don't speak much anymore. Michael has ignored everybody ever since he got that volunteer job as an orderly. I think he'll be a fine doctor someday and I'm happy for him."

"And your father? He's at work. I saw him just today."

Sheilagh nearly glared at him, but she decided now was not the time to bring up the subject of her father's infidelity. Sheilagh was certain she was the only one in the family who knew about her father and Shannon O'Rourke. Her mother might know, but she doubted it. Mary Margaret was too busy looking for a husband for Sheilagh. "My father is a busy man."

"Obviously. He's hired me to be his general manager."

"What!"

"I was going to tell you later . . ." He leaned down and kissed her deeply.

Sheilagh needed to lose herself in this kiss, just as she did in her acting. She didn't want to think. She only wanted to feel. She kissed him back. She laced her tongue around his.

He moaned.

She pulled him on top of her. There was a great deal of fumbling with his trousers and briefs. He was eager and she was compliant. He tried to keep his weight on his elbows, but the seat was too narrow and he got the band of his wristwatch caught in her hair. He fumbled again for a moment, but then Sheilagh reached up and touched his penis.

Clay moaned again and entered her. Sheilagh's breath caught in her throat and nearly choked her. She felt the tissue of her hymen tear as he broke through and penetrated her fully. It was supposed to be excruciatingly painful, she'd heard, but it wasn't. She waited for his smooth stroking to become pleasurable, but it didn't. For long moments between his puffs of breath against her cheek and the guttural utterances that escaped his lips, she felt as if she were removed from herself, as if her consciousness left her body and she could look down upon the scene like a sports fan in a stadium. She was completely detached from her physical responses. Her emotions, tiny and feeble, had fled from her like insects fleeing from a raging fire.

Tears stormed the edges of Sheilagh's eyes and hung there suspended. All those stories, the movies and the romance novels she had believed in, had deceived her. She had been trapped by some ancient hoax. There was no clashing of cymbals, no great union of two lost souls, no ascension to the heavens, no music, song, or dance. All these years of playful experimenting with Clay . . . and others . . . with herself . . . She had "saved" the best for last, or so she had thought. She realized now it had all been a waste. What was that old saying? The best part of life was in the playing? Well, she had played, and she didn't feel good at all.

Clay ground his hips into Sheilagh's pelvis. He thought his heart would explode right out of his chest. He could barely catch his breath. Not since the time he played tennis for three and a half hours had he expended so much energy. He was seeing white lights, rockets, and fireworks behind his closed eyelids. He had never "done it" with anyone, and he was glad that Sheilagh was his first. It seemed fitting that she had always been his goddess. He was flattered that despite the rumors he'd heard about her in high school, she had not lied to him. She had been a virgin. To him it was a sign that she truly loved him. He needed to know that she had given her virginity to him because she had wanted him so much.

He liked the way he felt inside her, all slick and smooth and throbbing. He liked the way her breasts filled his hands and seemed to overflow his splayed fingers like honey oozing out of the comb. He liked the floral scent that wove up into his nostrils, obliterated the smell of the Cadillac's upholstery, and conjured a fantasy of country meadows. Clay pushed, pressed, and probed inside Sheilagh, never realizing how forceful his gyrations had become. He panted and stroked. He kissed and licked her ear and throat, her lips and teeth. The pit of his stomach seemed to fill with hot lava.

Clay felt the rush of semen as he exploded inside her.

Surfeited in sexual release, Clay collapsed on top of her.

Sheilagh stared at the gunmetal gray wool that covered the roof of the Cadillac. She inspected each silver chrome strip that held the material in place, wondering how the manufacturer had hidden the screws. She cast her eye down to the back of the seat and noticed that there were two ashtrays built into the back. She wondered if lighters were included in both trays or just one. She crooked her left arm behind her head while her right arm restly limply on Clay's shoulder. Force of will dried her tears as he dropped tender, bite-sized kisses on her breasts.

"I love you, Sheilagh."

"I told you never to love me, Clay."

"It's different now."

"Yes, it is." Sheilagh sighed as Clay rested his head on her breast once again. The weight of his body made her feel trapped, but it was his words that nearly suffocated her. Wresting her body away from him was a simple task. Forgetting their past together seemed nearly impossible.

Clay had been a part of her childhood and now her sojourn into womanhood. She could forget him no more easily than she could eradicate her own brother or sister. She had been wrong to have sex with Clay. It gave him false hopes. She had always shot straight with him, and prided herself on never letting pretenses stick to her as others did, like wads of bubble gum on shoe soles.

She didn't know how she would do it, what words she would use, but she did know she was going to miss him when she left.

Chapter 19 ─────────────────

$\mathcal{S}$HEILAGH DID NOT have to knock at fate's door to find her escape. Fate came to her.

His name was Abe Meindel. He was a short, pudgy German Jew from New York with the face of a Greek god. He had thick, curly black hair that he wore cropped close to his head. His eyes were nearly black but shone like expensive black pearls. They were deep-set with heavy lids that gave him a seductive, mysterious look when directed toward a female, and a jaded, suspicious air if the onlooker was male. Abe was all of these things.

His jaw was stronger than his nose, and his lips were full and sensuous. Had he been six feet tall, he would have been the hottest thing this side of Clark Gable, and Abe knew it. But he wanted to be more than just another pretty actor. Abe wanted, desired, and craved immortality.

Abe produced plays off Broadway which he hoped would someday run on Broadway. Abe liked Chicago theater because he found that midwestern talent seldom "went Hollywood" on him. As a rule, they were a humble bunch, itching for a chance to do well, which made them malleable and easy to govern. They also respected theater more than their western counterparts. At least that was how Abe explained his forays into Chicago. Bald truth of the matter was that he'd always gotten lucky whenever he came to Chicago, and found just the right actors and actresses for his plays.

Not as lucky as I coulda been, he thought. He had always believed he'd been born too late. He was twenty-eight years old and was probably the only man on earth who wished he were older . . . much older. If he'd been ferreting out talent fifteen years ago, *he* would have found Carl Sandburg playing guitar and reading poems in a little theater on North Avenue. *He* would have seen first runs of Ben Hecht and Sherwood Anderson's *Benvenuto Cellini*. *He* would have produced Kenneth Sawyer Goodman and Ben Hecht's repetoire of one-act plays. But nooo. He had not been lucky in his accident of birth.

Abe Meindel knew he would spend the rest of his life making up for all his missed opportunities.

He sat in the backseat of a Yellow cab, grumbling to himself. He hated stalled traffic. He hated it in New York, he hated it in Boston, but he especially hated it in Chicago. The windy city was his lucky place. He could almost hear the fur falling off his rabbit's foot as he squirmed impatiently on the dirty plastic seat.

The cab driver flipped on the radio and turned the dial to WMAQ, where "When You Wish Upon a Star" was playing for the umpteenth time that month.

"Turn that shit off!" Abe growled.

"Youse dint like *Pinocchio*?"

"Not particularly, no."

The cabbie shrugged and turned the dial farther down the line, hitting upon a Glenn Miller tune. "How's that?"

Abe shook his head. "All those band guys sound alike."

"Not Gene Krupa."

Abe shoved his hand out into the air, as if to push the cabbie, the music, and the remark away from him. "I don't care."

Like a wounded inchworm, the traffic moved up East Balboa Drive to number 60. The stone and granite Blackstone Theater loomed before him. The mansard roof with its dormer windows on the top floor, the two-story Ionic columns on the facade of the second and third floors, and the art nouveau ironwork on the flat canopy over the five sets of entrance doors all made the theater look as if it had been plucked off the cliffs of some southern French resort town where only rich European dowagers and flashy Texas oil men vacationing with their nubile mistresses would go.

To Abe this was Mecca. The Celestial Kingdom. In this Paradise Lost Abe found the boys and girls whom he could pay minimally, and from whom he could expect to receive maximum returns. Some had talent, but not all had the tenacity and fortitude to make it in theater. Abe liked to think of himself as the "make it or break it" guy.

Abe gladly paid the driver and scrambled out of the cab. He checked his wristwatch and found that he was right on time after all.

"Luck." He smiled to himself and walked into the theater.

It was audition day. Abe was able to attend the auditions because he had many friends in Chicago. One of them was Will Gardner, who was producing Ibsen's *A Doll's House*. Abe was extremely interested in the women who would try for this role about a woman who becomes financially and emotionally enslaved to her husband. Abe also knew Will Gardner well enough to know that he was not a good judge of talent. A good pair of legs, yes. But never talent.

Abe would have his eye on Will's castoffs.

Sheilagh was early for the audition, which gave her time to size up her competition. She was not the youngest hopeful in the group, she thought as she watched a doughy-faced sixteen-year-old cross the stage. She hadn't thought the girl could possibly be as ugly as her first assessment, but as she watched the young girl's wide hips and thighs waddle past her, she changed her mind.

There were several local actresses she recognized from previous auditions at the Blackstone. One was Janet Parker. She was thirty-one but had told every director and producer for the past two years Sheilagh had known her that she was only twenty-seven. Nobody seemed to mind. She had that pure, natural Kansas down-home look, with lots of freckles, cornflower blue eyes, pale lashes, and a shock of blond hair that looked like vast wheat fields blowing in the wind. The out-of-town crowds loved her.

Susannah Blake, on the other hand, looked like she'd just stepped off a yacht, with her million-dollar smile, precision-cut pageboy tied with a French silk scarf, white pleated sharkskin skirt, blue and white spectator pumps, and navy linen double-breasted blazer. Susannah spoke with an affected Boston accent offstage but always had trouble with her Chicago nasal twang onstage. Susannah had fine bone structure with a thin nose, high cheekbones, and slender jawline. With the exception of her riveting blue eyes, which reportedly had brought more than one Broadway producer and two leading Hollywood top-billing-type actors to their knees, Sheilagh believed that Susannah's looks were a bit too pointed, a tad too witchy.

Susannah caught Sheilagh looking at her and gave one of those quick, sophisticated waves that looked to Sheilagh as if she were swatting gnats. Sheilagh smiled back but knew her antipathy showed. Susannah was always a favorite to win the best parts.

Sheilagh quickly scanned the room to see Eddie Foster, Joe Larson, and Hal Hanover. The last was Morey Lefkowitz's stage name, and it had never gotten him a part, because the truth of the matter was that Morey couldn't act.

There were a half dozen newcomers, some students and bored housewives. The band of amateurs who performed in community theaters on the North Side tromped in together, four women and three men. None of them took acting seriously; it was a game to them, a night out on the town, yet they were all talented. Any of them could be chosen.

The stage lights went up. The theater lights were brought down. Footsteps were heard out front as several men shuffled into their seats in one of the first rows.

"Shit. This is it," came a male voice behind Sheilagh.

She gulped and tried to drown the flutter of winged creatures in her stomach. She broke out into a sweat and used the back of her left hand to scrape away the tattletale bead of moisture that signaled to her fellow actors that this part was important to her.

Why was it, Sheilagh wondered, that she could pretend she was Electra, Ophelia, even Hedda Gabler, but during auditions, when it was paramount that she keep her composure, she got visibly nervous? Sheilagh needed this part to make her final break from her mother. To move out. To move on. To move up. Maybe even New York. Please, God, especially New York.

"Number one." A voice called from the darkness out front. Sheilagh recognized it as Will Gardner.

She propped herself against an upright piano, with one arm draped across the top and her head resting on her arm. She waited impatiently as each actress was called. The role of Nora was critical to the play. Nora's role *was* the play. Sheilagh wove her fingers around themselves so many times, they looked like a ball of spaghetti. She watched Janet perform and knew instantly she was not up to her usual style. But then, the psychological depth of Ibsen's play was out of reach to wholesome, straightforward Janet. Several of the "troupe" actors auditioned, but Sheilagh didn't think any of them would win, not because of a lack of talent, but because none of them had performed at the Blackstone before. Sheilagh knew that Will Gardner was looking for a "name."

On Sheilagh's tally sheet, that put her one up on most of the actresses, but two behind both Janet and Susannah, who had performed at the Blackstone at least half a dozen times, compared with Sheilagh's very shaky two inconsequential roles. She clutched her hopes around her.

"Number nine," Will called out.

Sheilagh, lost in her thoughts, did not respond.

"Number *nine!* Sheilagh!" Will called with exasperation.

Sheilagh snapped her neck up. Her long auburn hair flew around, and a long strand clung to her cheek. She brushed it away with her left hand and marched forward to her mark. With each step she moved into the character of Nora. She pretended she was wearing a very tight corset and dress with a bustle in back. Her carriage became that of a stiff-backed woman who held her throat much too tightly around the words she had taught herself never to utter.

Sheilagh's eyes refocused. She was no longer in a theater auditioning, but in the house, the doll's house, Nora's house. She began her reading without waiting for the cue.

Abe could not believe what he was seeing on the stage. The unknown girl he was watching had talent written all over her. She moved and gesticulated perfectly, and though the lighting was horribly inadequate, this girl had not a single awkward angle. She was beautiful in motion. She was beautiful in repose. She wore little makeup, but even from his seat he was aware she'd mastered the ability to turn her skin to ashen, to blush and then go pale again. She was amazing. Her gestures were superb, none too dramatic or too subtle, yet each blended with her words, creating the character the way the playwright had intended.

Abe was astounded. This was not an actress bent on projecting her personality onto the character, but rather an actress who had *become* the character. Quickly he looked to his pencil-scribbled roster, which the script girl had given him. Number nine was Sheilagh Killian.

"Never heard of her," Abe mumbled to himself. He looked back to the stage. *All the world will know you, Sheilagh Killian. I can feel it in the marrow of my bones.* Abe smiled inwardly. So this was how it felt to unearth a star.

Abe watched her continue. Sheilagh had suffused her own psyche so deeply with that of Nora that every breath, every tremor of her lips, every arch of her brow, had significance. When Nora slammed the door to her house, it was like the sound of Nora's broken heart. No actress, no human being, had ever pierced through the steel wall that Abe Meindel called his heart.

"Shit," he mumbled to himself, "I gotta have her. I gotta."

He was spellbound.

Will Gardner cleared his throat when Sheilagh finished. "Thank you, Miss Killian. We'll call you. Next."

Abe's heart slammed against his chest like Dizzy Dean hitting a homer out of Wrigley Field. He copied Will's non-chalance and leaned his head back on the seat, pretending disinterest in Sheilagh Killian's performance. Abe thought he had the tightest nerves in the business, but Will must either be blind or the best goddamn actor Abe had ever seen. As far as Abe could tell, Will didn't appear to be interested in Sheilagh. He had made no notes. He didn't light up his Havana cigar, which he was known to do once he'd made his decision. Word around Chicago was that when Will Gardner pulled the golden band off the cigar, he was already strategizing how he would negotiate the terms of the contract.

But Will had not so much as reached for the cigar. Now it was Susannah's turn onstage.

The way Abe figured it, Susannah must have improved a lot over the past year for Will to pass up Sheilagh. Abe sat back and prepared himself to be moved off his seat.

Susannah went through her lines, doing a damn swell job with Nora's part. But in Abe's eyes, she was no Sheilagh Killian.

As Susannah's voice filled the empty theater, Abe watched Will's hand slip into the breast pocket of his tweed jacket and pull out a Havana cigar.

"Jesus!" Abe nearly choked on his good fortune. It didn't get any better than this.

Will pulled off the gold band.

Abe ticked off the seconds. His eyes shot to stage left. Sheilagh stood just behind a sandy-haired boy with teeth too big for his mouth, her eyes rivetted on Will's every movement. Abe watched Sheilagh watch Will as he put the cigar to his mouth. Her eyelids fell as they closed out the pain. Her chin dropped ever so slightly.

Will held a cheap Zippo lighter to the end of the cigar. He sucked greedily, inhaled the expensive smoke, then blew it cautiously into the air.

Abe barely breathed during the process. He waited for

Susannah to finish. He watched her eyes light up when she saw Will's cigar.

"Thank you, Susannah. I'll call you."

Will began auditions for the role of Nora's husband. He called out, "Number one, please. Whenever you're ready."

Abe moved next to Will. "You're gonna hire Susannah, aren't you?"

Will threw Abe an arch glance. "How did you know?"

"Jesus, Will. You gotta leave the Havanas at home. Everybody knows. What I don't know is why?"

"She's a name. I need a name."

Abe's palm flew to his forehead; he drew it slowly down his face. "Ethel Merman is a name, Will . . ."

Will only smiled. "This is Chicago, not New York, and I don't want any of your patronizing carp about it. It's *my* show, okay?"

"Fine. Super. No problem, Will." Abe counted. One. Two. Three. Four. "You gonna use that Killian kid for anything this time out?"

"Nah. She's too young. Needs more experience. She's pretty good, though."

Pretty good? *Pretty good? What a putz you are, Will,* Abe wanted to say, but didn't. Thank you, God, if there was a God, and maybe this proved there was one, for making *idiots* like Will Gardner believe they knew theater and actors. Yessireee. This is your lucky day, Abe Meindel.

"Mind if I audition her for one of my shows?"

"You think she could do New York?"

Abe's nerves jangled. Maybe he had shown his hand too soon. "She's a little green, I know what you're saying, Will. And I want you to know I appreciate your caring about me like that."

Will placed his hand on the shoulder of Abe's wool jacket. He barely touched the fabric, which told Abe that Will was insincere. "Ours is a scary business. I wouldn't want to see a pal o' mine get hurt."

"Thanks for the advice, Will."

"Anytime." Will puffed again on the cigar and dismissed the boy onstage. "We'll call you. Next."

Abe left Will and took a circuitous route backstage. He got there just as Sheilagh was about to exit. She bent down to pick up a cranberry-colored duffel bag with black straps, and slung it over her shoulder. He was surprised that she was carrying such a bohemian-looking piece of luggage when all the other girls carried their makeup and clothes in round hatbox-type pieces. He liked that. Sheilagh was not one of the crowd. She was above it.

When she straightened, he noticed that she was above average in height. Probably about five feet seven, if he had to guess, but Abe never guessed. She drew her arm back to lift a huge cluster of shimmering coppery hair away from her face. The duffel bag was obviously heavy, though he could not guess what she had stowed in it.

"Let me help you with that," Abe offered as he walked up to her.

She glared at him, as if to say, *Keep your distance*. This time when it fell, the capricious hair nearly covered her right eye. "I can manage."

Abe felt his mouth go dry and his hands tremble. The Venus de Milo didn't hold a candle to Sheilagh Killian dressed in black capri pants, white flats, and a short white cropped blouse with middy collar. The blouse was slightly ajar, and with all her gyrations with the duffel bag, her shoulder had poked through the large, square neckline. Abe couldn't take his eyes off that pearly white shoulder. He swallowed nervously.

"I would like to talk to you."

"Really? About what?"

"Your acting." His eyes were still glued to her shoulder. He was almost afraid to look into her green eyes. Something told him he'd never escape her if he did.

"My acting? You want to talk about my acting. Sure. Well, I gotta go." Sheilagh started for the back steps.

"Wait!" he finally said, jolting out of his sexual reverie. "I'm serious. Very serious. I'm Abe Meindel."

Sheilagh looked down at him the way Helen must have looked down on the foot soldiers of Troy. "I never heard of you."

"Then we're even. I never heard of you either, and I said as much to Will."

Sheilagh chewed her bottom lip and sucked in her cheeks. "You know Will."

"We're old buddies."

"Sure." She didn't buy any of it.

"Look. This is getting us nowhere." He reached into his pocket, withdrew his card, and handed it to her.

Sheilagh took it with a too brusque movement. She realized

the truth when she felt the expensive cream paper and saw that the card was engraved. "New York?"

"Yes. I produce shows. Original shows for off Broadway. Someday . . . soon . . . I think . . . with your help, I'll be on Broadway."

Sheilagh rolled her eyes. This guy was too much. "You think I should believe you? Anybody can spring for some fancy cards."

Incensed at her disdain, Abe snatched the card away. "Fine. Don't believe me. Don't take a chance on your own future."

Sheilagh grabbed his wrist before he could pocket the card. "I was just testing you. There's a coffee shop near here I like a lot. Great cappuccino."

Abe paused for a moment, pretending to be momentarily lost in thought. "I can't make it right now. I have a meeting uptown shortly. But we need to talk. Come with me." He said it more like an edict than an invitation.

"I guess it would be okay," she agreed as he gave a slight bow, indicating that he would follow her down the steps to the alley in back of the theater.

As she exited the Blackstone, Sheilagh felt a prickle of chills on her back. Something told her that her life had drastically changed. This was the day she had been preparing for, and now that it was here, she felt oddly calm.

Abe Meindel needed Sheilagh Killian as his leading lady, but he *wanted* her as a woman. He began romancing her at the Michigan Avenue Bridge in the backseat of a Yellow cab, but it took a Fauvistic sunset behind the Wrigley Building and Tribune Tower to convince Sheilagh that he believed in her talent enough to bankroll her in his New York stage production.

"I'll make you so famous, the sun will never set on your name. 'Sheilagh Killian' will be lit up on the best marquees from London to New York." Abe continued with his sales pitch, not noticing that Sheilagh was already weighing her options.

Her eyes moved from the purple and red skies to Abe's face and then to the river scene before them. Her gaze followed a trail of vacationers as they boarded a steamship bound for Minneapolis.

The women who were dressed in cool white summer dresses and the men who wore tropical suits, Panama hats, and white buck shoes had their minds on escaping the city heat, just as Chicagoans had done for over fifty years. Little of the world turmoil invaded the average Chicagoan's life. Politics in Berlin, the capture of another Chinese village by the Japanese, even the splitting of the atom at the University of Chicago, all failed to attract more than a ripple of attention. Robert McCormick and Charles Lindberg had formed the America First Committee, dedicated to the antiwar movement. Chicagoans were well known to burnish the gold of their isolationist crowns, Sheilagh thought, as she continued to watch them crowd onto the steamship.

"Your play is about Jews?" she asked, wondering what would happen if America were captured by Hitler. How would life change? Would there even *be* a ship to Minneapolis anymore? Or would these people be refugees as she'd seen on the newsreels at the Marlboro Theater on Madison?

"Yes." Abe also stared at the scene on the steamship. Sheilagh was starting to slip off the pedestal he'd built for her. What am I doing? he asked himself. Why didn't I get a New York actress? Sheilagh probably didn't even know he was a Jew.

"Good thing it opens in New York. It'd bomb here." She looked at him momentarily, but long enough for him to see contempt in her eyes. Then she looked back at the steamship. "Ten bucks says not one of them thought about the fact that Paris fell just two weeks ago."

Abe cocked his head and spun his eyes to Sheilagh. Mentally he scrambled quickly to rebuild his image of her. "It could bomb in New York, but I'm willing to take that chance. It's a different kind of show, Sheilagh."

"How different?"

"It's politically unpopular. I wrote it myself. You see, my mother is still in Berlin. She's in hiding. The Jews over there are being persecuted . . . even murdered. But our government and the good citizens of America refuse to believe the truth. Somebody's got to do something!"

Sheilagh folded her arms over her chest. "And you think you're this somebody?"

"Yes."

"And you're gonna change the world?"

"I hope so."

"And you want me to star in this play—I'll probably be laughed out of town before I even get a chance to be known."

"I do."

"You're crazy." Sheilagh laughed, and the sound was like raindrops falling on expensive crystal. Abe was hooked.

"I *know* that." He sat up straight, stretched his neck, and elongated his spine so that he peered down at her. "But you can carry this play."

"I don't look Jewish."

"It doesn't matter. Helda must be sensual, beautiful . . . magnetic. All the things you are. Remember she is Hitler's first love. She dumps him. He's heartbroken, and then to avenge himself, to validate himself and prove to himself that she has no power over him, he begins his insane anti-semitic campaign, which has now lasted for over ten years and led to this war. Eventually this country will be in it too. Then you won't be saying I'm so crazy."

Sheilagh's gaze bored into him, expressing contrition for her own obstinancy. Her eyes spun fine webs of pride and ambition for them both. "I'll never say it again. And neither will anyone else. I believe you, Abe. I believe in what you're trying to say. I'm honored you want to give me this chance."

"Don't say yes until you read the script."

"Okay. When do I get a copy?"

"Tonight. If you'll have dinner with me."

She smiled, thinking Abe moved quickly from business to personal matters. "Of course."

"I'll send a driver for you. Seven o'clock. I'm staying at the Sherman House."

Sheilagh nodded and began rummaging in her duffel bag for a pencil and paper. She wrote down her home address and telephone number. Abe took the paper and shook her hand. "Until tonight."

To the left of the Randolph Street entrance of the Sherman House was the Dome Bar, where Abe sat on a barstool so that he could watch Sheilagh as she walked into the room. A man could tell a lot about a woman from the way she walked when she didn't know she was being observed. It was as accurate a barometer of character as any he had ever read about.

Sheilagh entered the room with the ease and grace of a woman of accomplishment. She could be mistaken for being twice her age. Men and women stopped to watch her, creating one of those monstrously awkward moments when time seems suspended and a lesser personality could become self-conscious. Sheilagh simply accepted their attention as her due, smiling at the women and tossing cool glances to the men. By the time she reached Abe's side at the bar, the soft buzz of intrigue was skipping from mouth to mouth.

Abe was grinning widely, and his black eyes danced. "They're all wondering who you are." He took her hand. "Are you ready to go down to dinner?"

"Yes," she said, and let him escort her to the basement, where he had reserved a table in the Great Panther Room of the College Inn.

The maître d' led the way down two tiers of booths covered in panther skins to the third tier, located two steps below the dance floor. All the booths were arranged in a horseshoe shape around the dance floor so that the sound of the Benny Goodman Band—or tonight's attraction, the Jimmy Dorsey Band—could be heard by all the patrons.

The Negro waiters were all attired in pantaloons and short Persian jackets, turbans with brilliant plumes, and Persian slippers with turned-up toes.

Sheilagh listened to the music and watched a clown dressed like a tramp go up to the dancers, tap a man on the shoulder, and take his partner away. Each time the clown "stole" a girl, his red, bulbous nose lit up. Intent on the floor show, Sheilagh did not see their waiter approach.

"What would you like to drink?" Abe asked her.

Sheilagh had never been to an expensive hotel dining room like the Panther Room. And she had certainly never been to an expensive bar. She realized Abe had no idea just how young she was, or that her level of sophistication was at ground zero when it came to night life. What should she say? She had read about all the popular cocktails, but which one would be appropriate? Rob Roy? Sidecar? Manhattan? Martini?

Abe noticed Sheilagh's consternation.

"You don't drink," he said.

"Of course, I do."

"May I suggest a champagne cocktail?"

"That would be lovely." She smiled back.

"A champagne cocktail for the lady, and I'll take an old-fashioned."

"Very good, sir," the waiter said politely, and left.

Abe turned to Sheilagh. "Just exactly how old *are* you?"

"Twenty-three," she lied.

Abe's top lip curled up. "Bullshit. You aren't even twenty-one yet."

"It shows that much?"

"Not so much." He leaned close to her, his face only a breath apart from hers. "Truth time."

"Seventeen."

"Shit." He blew out a deep breath of admiration and leaned far back on the stool.

"Is that a problem?" She felt her stomach become instantly queasy as she saw her chances for her life in New York spill from her hands like a deck of cards.

"I was just thinking how good you're going to be after I get you trained. Besides, twenty years from now, you'll be lying about your age anyway. So it's not a problem."

Sheilagh relaxed. "Now it's your turn to fess up."

"Shoot."

"Are you sure you can afford dinner here?"

A throaty guffaw tumbled out of Abe's mouth. Abe was moved by Sheilagh's concern. "Yes," he said, and patted her hand affectionately, "I can afford dinner."

Chapter 20 ───────────────

July 1939

ABE SENT SHEILAGH a one-way train ticket aboard the New York Central steel streamliner that would take her to Grand Central Station, New York City. She held the ticket up to the light, then inspected it back and front.

"It's real!" she exclaimed. "No looking back this time. It's really going to happen for me." She wanted to dance around the room, buy a bottle of champagne, and have her entire family toast her good fortune. She wanted to savor her elation, but she knew better. Patrick and Mary Margaret Killian would not support her decision, and she dreaded telling them.

She knew she had to break the news tonight. It was how she was going to do it that caused her consternation. Should she just pop into the kitchen before dinner and breezily inform them that she was off to New York to make her fame and fortune? She could see her mother now coming up with a million reasons to delay her trip, and most of them would be the sons of her socially prominent friends.

"No one will ever stop me again," she said aloud, hoping she could imbue herself with courage. But time was of the essence. Abe wanted to start rehearsals next week. Her ticket was for Saturday morning. Today was Tuesday.

Perhaps she should go to her father first, Sheilagh thought, and envisioned herself standing in his office answering a barrage of questions for which she did not possess the answers. No, she didn't know where she would live. Nor did she remember the name of the off-Broadway theater. She had not "checked out" Abe Meindel, nor would she know how to go about doing so. She did not have a signed contract. She had not talked to the family attorney. All Sheilagh had done was dream of leaving Chicago, leaving the Killian house, and working onstage.

She even tried to imagine telling Caitlin and Michael. They had heard her tales of moving to New York for so many years, they would probably think she was making it all up. It *did* sound too good to be true.

Sheilagh felt her innards churn at the thought. Maybe it *was* a sham: Abe, his play, his talk of her becoming internationally famous.

Her stomach churned again. She held her breath. The pain passed.

Had she fallen for some con man's game after all? She, Sheilagh, who had been defensive and aloof when it came to directors? Had she been dreaming of an acting career so hard that she would do anything, anything to make it all happen? Was she a victim of her own illusions?

She tasted bile as it rose in a nervous wave into her esophagus.

Should she keep believing?

Anxiety punched her stomach with pugilist's hands. She lay back on the bed until the wave of nausea passed. Finally she turned her head to the wall where she had tacked up black-and-white photographs of her favorite movie stars. Tears flooded her eyes, and the photographs waved in and out of her vision like desert mirages. She lifted her arm and stretched her fingers out to them as if the illusory figures could save her. With a pang of regret, she dropped her hand to the bed.

"Only I can save me. And I will!" Sheilagh vowed, and sat upright with renewed determination. The movement sent a rush of nausea over her.

She clamped her hand to her mouth and raced to the bathroom, where she vomited into the porcelain toilet.

One hour later when the telephone rang, Sheilagh was still feeling weak. But her condition had greatly improved once she had made the decision to inform the entire Killian family of her departure at the evening meal. Sheilagh had decided it would be best to take them all on at once.

She lifted the receiver. "Hello?"

"Sheilagh, it's Clay."

"Oh, hi," she replied, realizing that not once in the past two days had she thought about Clay. She had not included him in her plans to move to New York. She realized that she did not consider Clay a part of her life. She was surprised by the feeling of sadness this revelation brought her.

"You don't sound very glad to hear from me."

"I'm sorry, Clay. I was thinking about something else."

"Really? I was hoping you would be thinking about me."

"I know you do."

"Can I see you tonight?"

Sheilagh felt that odd twinge in her belly again. "Tonight? There's a lot I have to do tonight."

Clay sighed. He didn't like her answer, she could tell. "Look. I haven't bothered you for days. I know you were anxious about your audition. I thought maybe you would call to tell me how it went. When I didn't hear from you, I figured it was because you didn't get the part."

"I didn't."

"I know. I read about Susannah in the *Sun-Times*. But I wanted to hear it from you. So what's the matter? Have I got the plague or something?"

"Of course not."

"Then what is it?"

"I think maybe tonight would be good after all. We need to talk."

"You make it sound so ominous."

"It's not really. How about nine o'clock? We could go for a Coke or something after supper."

"Great. I'll pick you up then."

"Good-bye, Clay," Sheilagh said, and replaced the receiver lovingly. Clay was a good friend, but Sheilagh knew he was already part of the past.

The Killian family sat down to dinner at precisely seven o'clock. There were exactly four pieces of stemware at each plate, running in proper Emily Post fashion from the right to the left. Sheilagh thought it idiotic of her mother to set the table like this when only Patrick and Mary Margaret were allowed to drink wine, and even then only the red wineglasses were used, never the white and never the dessert champagne. It was all part of Mary Margaret's campaign to prepare her children for a more sophisticated world, one that Mary Margaret intended to drag them into, kicking and screaming if need be.

Sheilagh scanned the faces of her family and wondered if any of them knew what the others were thinking. Michael's thirteen-year-old face was flushed and glowing from playing basketball with Tim Farley and Billy Murphy at the Resurrection School gymnasium all afternoon. Michael whisked the perfectly pressed damask napkin into his lap with a snap. Sheilagh did not miss the brief snicker he uttered just loud enough for his mother to hear but low enough to be mistaken for clearing his throat.

Of them all, Michael reveled in his psychological warfare against their mother. He kept his daily schedule filled with studies, athletics, his friends, and dreams of becoming a doctor. He never talked to his father about Emerald, and Patrick and Michael were estranged, though they lived in the same house. Michael played cat and mouse with his mother, and usually he won. For that, Sheilagh greatly admired her younger brother.

Caitlin sat gracefully in her chair, bemusedly playing the sterling forks with her left hand like piano keys. First the cocktail fork, then the dessert fork, up the tines of the salad fork, and lastly she laid her hand on the dinner fork. She wore a mask of self-absorption that Sheilagh was unable to probe. The light from the crystal chandelier made dusky shadows beneath her long, dark eyelashes and in the hollows of her high-boned cheeks.

Caitlin's hair had grown past shoulder length over the winter and spring, and the light left copper shimmers as it scampered down the slopes of the curved pageboy. Sheilagh wondered idly what thoughts occupied Caitlin's mind. Was she thinking about the chocolate business again? Was there a boy in her life whom Sheilagh didn't know about? Who was he? And why hadn't Sheilagh thought to ask about him? How long ago had it been when they had made their pact with one another to stick together? When was the day they had stopped confiding in each other? When had they grown apart? And whose fault was it?

Sheilagh realized with a jolt that she had taken Caitlin and her good nature for granted for a long time. Sheilagh had always thought of her sister as good old dependable, predictable Caitlin. She was guilty of thinking Caitlin was still a child. For the first time Sheilagh realized that her sister was sixteen and a half, and nearly as beautiful as Sheilagh.

A pang of loss seared Sheilagh. She was about to leave, and she was going to miss her brother and sister very, very much.

No one said a word as Patrick ritually recited the blessing. "Bless us O Lord and these thy gifts."

Sheilagh kept her head bowed and pretended to pray, but she surreptitiously observed Mary Margaret. Her mother's head was bowed low and her hands placed neatly above her plate in full view of onlookers. Her fingers were intertwined and held so forcibly together that the knuckles had turned white. The same chandelier light that flattered Caitlin hit Mary Margaret's face like blaring sunlight on jagged rocks.

There were deep stress lines across her forehead. Her lips were tightly pursed, which created fine cracks around her mouth into which her ruby red lipstick had seeped. Her skin appeared lifeless underneath a thick layer of Revlon powder, and the color had been stripped out of her hair. She was still a handsome woman, dressed impeccably in a "smart" navy linen suit and "tasteful" costume jewelry. Her hair was tightly controlled in an elaborate chignon that was all the rage that summer. But as Sheilagh observed her, she saw nothing natural about her, nothing to suggest her mother was capable of spontaneity. It was as if she were only half-alive.

A statue, Sheilagh thought. *She's become like a statue in the church.* Sheilagh wondered what had happened to her mother's fiery self-righteousness.

". . . which we are about to receive from thy bounty through Christ our Lord. Amen." Patrick ended the prayer with the sign of the cross.

He picked up the carving knife, sank it into the pork roast, and sliced off five pieces, which he passed around the table. He grabbed the gold-rimmed serving dish of mashed potatoes. He lobbed a spoonful onto his plate, passed the dish to Michael, and quickly covered the meat and potatoes with a ladle full of smooth gravy. The steamed broccoli and tossed salad were passed. The butter, salt, and pepper made their rounds. Patrick drank half his red wine and refilled his glass. No one said a word.

Sheilagh smiled at Michael, who sat next to her, thinking she should break the silence with her announcement. Then she thought better of it.

They ate in silence like strangers aboard ship the first night at sea. Sheilagh prayed for the segue she desperately needed before she began her soliloquy. "How was the basketball game, Michael?" she finally asked.

"Fine," Michael said, and shoved in a mouthful of potatoes.

"Who won?"

"Nobody. We just did lay-ups."

Sheilagh frowned. Michael wasn't helping a bit.

"I suppose you'll be trying out for the team in the fall," Patrick interjected. He took another large swallow of red wine.

"I wasn't planning on it," Michael replied with a sharp edge to his voice.

"Why not?" Patrick inquired as he sawed off another hunk of roast and washed it down with wine.

"There are too many injuries in team sports. I don't want to hurt my hands."

"Your hands?" Patrick stopped chewing. "What the hell is the matter with your hands?"

"Nothing. I intend to keep it that way." Michael's jaw clenched. His cheeks burned red like a brushfire. His eyes narrowed and then focused squarely on Patrick.

Something was wrong, Sheilagh thought as her gaze raced back to her father. He pressed his back into the chair. They looked like cats squaring off for a fight.

"I played football in high school," said Patrick. "Was pretty damn good at it. Team sports can be valuable to your character, Michael."

Oh, God, Sheilagh thought. *Here it comes.*

Michael ground his teeth. "I'm not you."

Whew! Sheilagh sighed. It could have been worse. Michael could have hit lower, but he had wisely chosen not to.

"That's obvious," Patrick retorted.

Michael put his fork down. "Surgeons have to be careful about their hands. I'm going to be a surgeon."

"Are you still on that goddamn kick?" Patrick shouted.

"It's not a 'kick'!" Michael yelled back. "Ask Caitlin. Ask Sheilagh. Ask anybody. They'll all tell you that I've wanted nothing else since I was a little kid. You can't talk me out of it. I don't want to be *you!*" Michael shoved back his chair, threw down his napkin, and stalked from the room.

Mary Margaret's mouth was agape. "Michael! You come back here! You didn't ask to be excused."

Sheilagh and Caitlin spun their heads around to look at Mary Margaret. Sheilagh wanted to burst out laughing, but she held herself in check. The peals of laughter came from Caitlin.

"I think that's Michael's real problem, don't you, Sheilagh? His manners are atrocious." Caitlin smirked.

Sheilagh rolled her eyes. *Oh, no,* she thought. *Not you, too.*

"Just what are you implying, young lady?" Mary Margaret demanded.

Caitlin kept her mouth tight and ran the tip of her tongue over the top of her teeth the way she always did when she was calculating her next move. She tapped the tines of the dinner fork against the gold rim of the bone china plate.

Sheilagh watched her sister, knowing that Caitlin was trying to apply logic to emotion. She was more controlled than Michael. She had more at stake than Michael, who characteristically chose to cut and run, because she wanted Emerald Chocolates and this life in Chicago.

"I only meant, Mother, that Michael is thirteen and he doesn't know who he is right now. That's all. He was thinking about himself, not his manners right then. Just be patient with him."

Patrick gnawed away on his pork roast. He poured another glass of wine. "Goddamn kids today. They act like they own the world. Michael is the worst of the lot."

"No, he's not," Sheilagh blurted out. It was now or never. "I am."

Patrick's blue eyes shot to his wife for the first time during the meal. They exchanged a baffled look.

Sheilagh nearly lost her courage. She glanced at Caitlin for a smile of approval.

"I've been offered a leading role in a play in New York." *There,* she thought. *I've said it.*

"What?" Patrick's voice blasted loudly like a wounded moose.

"What?" Mary Margaret's voice hit high C.

"What?" Caitlin's voice was loving.

"I didn't want to tell you until I knew for certain. I've worked out all the details. I'll be leaving on Saturday."

Caitlin's eyes shone with excitement and then suddenly were filled with pain as the full meaning of Sheilagh's words hit her. "So soon."

Mary Margaret shot to her feet. "You can't go. That's all there is to it. You simply cannot go traipsing off to New York unescorted. And what about the party the McCormicks are giving? What about the housewarming plans I had for the Lake Geneva house? You were supposed to help me with that. I thought a dance on the flagstone terrace in the fall. It will be catered, of course. I thought you would arrange a band for us. Nothing elaborate. A trio would be acceptable, I'm sure. And then we have to discuss the plantings in the gardens . . . Near the waterfront we'll want plenty of geraniums and petunias. The draperies. Heavens! How could I have forgotten those? You see? You see? This is impossible."

Mary Margaret's hands fluttered up and down. Her eyes darted from face to face, as if she were looking for answers or trying to avoid them. Her voice rose an octave. She seemed close to tears, though no one in the family had seen her cry in years. Her voice cracked. She cleared her throat. There was a vibration to her body that looked like the onset of palsy. "You should go to Marygrove College . . ."

"No, Mother," Sheilagh said with conviction.

"St. Mary's, then. It's not far to South Bend. You could take the South Shore home every weekend . . ."

"No, Mother. I'm not going to college. We've had this discussion before."

"No, *we* haven't had any such discussion." Mary Margaret's voice cracked again. "*You* keep deciding these things. You lied to me."

"No, I didn't."

"You just graduated from high school. Now you should go full-time to college." Mary Margaret wrung her hands so forcefully, it looked as if she would wear the skin away.

"Mother, that was something you dreamed up in your head. I never intended to go to college."

"I suppose you don't intend to meet the McGuire boy, either."

"No."

"He's very wealthy. He will take care of you."

"Good God, Mother!" Sheilagh lost patience. "I don't want to be taken care of. I want to take care of myself. I want to be an actress. Don't you understand?"

"Never! I will never understand. Only harlots want to be actresses. I've read about what they do out in Hollywood. Vile, lecherous things. They are wicked, wicked people, Sheilagh. I've tried to keep you from destroying yourself, but you're bound and determined to race straight to hell, aren't you?"

"I'm not going to hell . . ."

"You are. Just like your father!"

Mary Margaret's eyes suddenly burst into round orbs as she clamped her hand over her mouth. Silence hung in the air like a heavy sword.

Michael, who had heard the shouting, stole around the corner and stood in the archway. Caitlin held her breath.

Patrick continued to stare at his wife. "You think I'm going to hell, Mary Margaret?"

Mary Margaret dropped her hands to her sides and lifted her chin. "Don't you?"

"Probably." Patrick didn't blink an eye. He looked back to Sheilagh. "I think you should let Sheilagh continue."

It was Sheilagh's turn to be shocked. Not once had she suspected that her father would champion her cause. She didn't know if it was wise to trust him now, but she had no choice.

"The play is a contemporary one about the Jewish people in Germany—"

"Oh, for God's sake!—" Mary Margaret expelled an exasperated breath as she sat once again.

Michael eased his way back into the room and sat next to Sheilagh, but he might as well have been invisible for all the attention he received.

"This play is important to me. If enough people are made aware of the plight of the situation under Hitler's regime, then maybe we—Americans, I mean—could stop him."

"We'd have to declare war," Michael interjected.

"I know . . . I know . . ." Sheilagh replied. "But this is my chance to get work on Broadway."

"Wait a minute." Patrick stopped her. "I thought you said you were *going* to Broadway."

"No, I said in New York. This play is off Broadway."

"Where?"

"I'm not sure exactly. Cherry Street Theater, I think."

"She thinks!" Mary Margaret blurted disdainfully.

"Damn it, Mary Margaret! Let her finish." Patrick was good at issuing rules to everyone else, though he never followed them himself, Sheilagh thought.

"My producer, Abe Meindel, has already given me a train ticket. I have to give it a try. If this play doesn't make it, then I'll find another one. Then another. There's always the chance it will be a hit. Then my worries will be over."

Michael was staring at his plate. When he looked up, she was shocked to see revulsion on his face. "I think Mother is right. You're a girl. You shouldn't be going to a city like that alone. All kinds of bad things could happen to you."

"Michael?" Sheilagh couldn't believe what she was hearing. What had happened to the pact they had made so long ago? Michael had known since they were children that she dreamed of acting on the New York stage. He used to force her into making up stories about what it would be like. Now that her dreams were becoming a reality, he was turning on her.

His eyes were pleading with her, but she didn't understand. She sensed that he wanted to cry or make her cry; hold her or have her hold him. There was such confusion in her mind over Michael's reaction that she nearly missed Caitlin's sad voice.

"I'll miss you, Sheilagh," she whimpered.

"We'll all miss you," Patrick said, not realizing they were the first loving words he had uttered to his eldest daughter since she was a tiny child. He picked up his wineglass, finished off the remainder, carefully replaced the glass on the snowy linen cloth, rose from his chair, and looked at his wife. "I'm going out," he said, and left the room.

Stunned at the emotion she felt at her father's words, Sheilagh felt the sharp blade of hot tears sear her eyes. She looked to Michael for support.

He withdrew into himself. "I won't be going to the train station on Saturday," he said defiantly, as if his decision might change her mind. Then he, too, left the room.

Caitlin was about to speak when the front doorbell rang.

Sheilagh looked up. "That must be Clay."

Caitlin's nerves ignited instantly. "Clay?" Her heart soared. "Here?"

Sheilagh nodded. "We have a date. I thought I should tell him tonight. I didn't want him to think that I was keeping anything from him."

Sheilagh went to answer the door.

"Clay . . . here," Caitlin muttered to herself. "Sheilagh is going to New York," she said aloud, but did not realize that Mary Margaret heard her statement. Then Caitlin, too, rose from her chair, folded her napkin properly, and placed it on the table. She turned to her mother. "May I be excused? I'd like to say hello to Clay."

Mary Margaret continued to stare blankly at the crystal bowl of summer roses in the center of the table. She nodded, saying nothing.

Mary Margaret noted that only Caitlin had asked to be excused. Michael's manners were deplorable. Patrick had left to fornicate with his mistress. Sheilagh had chosen to abandon her mother.

Mary Margaret bit her tongue, a trick her mother had taught her to keep her tears at bay. She tasted blood. Drop by drop, she died a little bit more.

Chapter 21

THE MOON STRUCK the surface of the Columbus Park pond and illuminated the strolling lovers like stage lights. A summer breeze lifted the low-hanging branches of the oak, maple, and walnut trees as Sheilagh and Clay finally sat on the cool grass. Sheilagh's stomach was still tied in knots from the confrontation at the dinner table that evening.

"I heard the shouting when I got to your front porch. I waited until your father came out before ringing the bell. You can tell me about it, you know," Clay said, not looking at Sheilagh.

"I'd rather not," she replied defensively.

Clay kept his eyes on the moonbeams as they danced on the water. "We're lovers now, Sheilagh. We should be sharing things . . . thoughts and problems. That's the way it should be. But you never want to talk to me, do you?"

Sheilagh knew she was hurting him, but she couldn't help that either. She had made a terrible mistake, having sex with Clay. She could see that now. It was not that the act was morally wrong or against some God- or man-made law, it was the fact that now Clay felt he had a claim on her. She didn't like giving away those parts of herself.

"No."

"I don't understand you, Sheilagh. You exasperate me. I swear, I feel closer to Caitlin than I do to you, and I've never touched her!"

"Maybe you are," Sheilagh replied too quickly, then she searched his face more deeply. She could see the man whom Clay would someday become, and what she saw, she liked. He was no different from the rest of them, reaching out for love and not finding it. She liked Clay, but she couldn't be his everything.

"But you're the one I want," he countered, and put his arm around her shoulders.

Sheilagh put her hand on his knee, a sisterly gesture.

Clay stiffened at the ominous sensations that coursed through his body.

"Clay, I'm leaving."

Shock rattled through his brain like an old, familiar freight train that had been expected, but was long overdue. "Where are you going?"

"New York."

"When?"

"Saturday morning."

"That's why they were yelling at you . . . your family . . ." Clay felt a thousand emotions wrap around his chest like barbed wire, and with each revelation, the stranglehold was tightened.

"Yes."

"They don't want you to go any more than I do."

"But I *am* going. I have my train ticket already. I met a man . . ."

Clay swallowed back tears, and they felt like chopped glass in his throat. "A man?"

Sheilagh patted his leg again to comfort him. "He's a producer. He has a fabulous play I'm going to be in. I got the lead role. Not only that, Clay, but it's an important piece. This play says something. It's about the political situation in Germany and the Jews . . . and . . ."

"Jesus Christ!" He started to sob, but he checked himself by swearing again under his breath. "Jesus . . ."

"I've never lied to you, Clay. Never. I always told you I wouldn't be staying in Chicago. I always told you I wanted to go to New York."

"But it's different now. You're my girl."

Sheilagh tossed back her hair and looked away from him. The moon had risen halfway in the night heavens. "I'm nobody's girl, Clay. I will never belong to anyone but myself. It's not you, Clay. This has nothing to do with you. We want different things, you and I. We could never be anything more than what we've been."

"Which is?" Clay swallowed hard again.

"Kids. We grew up together, and I like to think we helped each other."

Clay stood up, thinking that maybe if he didn't sit in the moonlight, she might turn into the monster he suddenly felt she was. But when he looked down at her, the moon caressing her skin with silver light, he fell in love with her all over again. His eyes swam in tears, but he turned his head so that she could not see what a fool he had become.

Sheilagh slowly stood, giving him a moment to compose himself. Guilt flayed her back like a cat-o'-nine-tails. "I'm so sorry, Clay."

"No, you're not."

"Yes, I am. I'm sorry we did what we did. I'm sorry I led you on in some respects. Mostly I'm sorry because I do love you . . . just not the way you want."

"I'm sorry, too."

Clay took a deep breath and felt the pain abate for the moment. Then he turned to her. This time he saw her charisma and the determination to make her dreams become reality. He was even more awestruck than before.

"You really will be famous someday . . ."

"I hope so." She smiled genuinely at him the way friends do.

"It's all over you. You'll make it happen."

"And will you be glad for me, Clay?"

"Yes, Sheilagh. I will."

Caitlin was late for work the next day. She had overslept,

and it was one of those summer mornings when everyone in the house had left early without bothering to check on the whereabouts of the others. Patrick had a golf game. Mary Margaret went to mass, as she did every day of her life, and Michael had planned an outing to the Field Museum with Tim and Billy. Caitlin threw on a starched white cotton blouse, red linen straight skirt, red pumps, and a wide white leather belt to accentuate her trim waistline, which she had finally whittled down to twenty-five inches without giving up her maple nut dark chocolate bonbon each day at lunch. She grabbed her white purse and gloves and raced down the stairs.

Caitlin went whizzing through the vestibule, dining room, and kitchen so quickly, she did not stop when she heard the odd sounds coming from the downstairs bathroom off the kitchen. She grabbed a banana out of the fruit basket on the kitchen table, opened the back door, and dashed down the back steps. She didn't lock the back door, nor did she hear Sheilagh emerge from the bathroom, go to the kitchen window, and call out her name. Caitlin had only one thing on her mind . . . getting to work as quickly as possible so that she didn't miss a minute with Clay.

Clay sat at his desk poring over the midyear sales records. He checked the previous six-month report against that of the first half of 1939. It was just as he thought. Sales were flat. Emerald was doing better than most of its competition, but nothing aggressive had been initiated in years. Most of the sales force had become order takers, failing to seek out new territories or develop new retailers.

The further Clay dug into Emerald's business, the more impressed he was by its untapped potential. He was excited.

"Good morning, Clay," Caitlin chimed breezily as she walked into his office bearing two cups of coffee.

"Mornin'," he replied, not taking his eyes off the files in front of him.

"I brought you some coffee," she said, moving to the side of his desk and holding out the cup and saucer.

"Huh? Oh, thanks," he replied, finally lifting his eyes.

She held the Haviland pink floral cup and saucer waist height so that the first thing he saw when he raised his head was the white leather belt cinched around her small waist. He took the cup and slowly, purposefully lifted his eyes to her rib cage, then to her breasts (when had they become nearly as large as Sheilagh's?), then to her throat, and up her chin to her radiant smile. Her eyes looked into his with more love in them than he'd ever known in his life.

Clay nearly dropped the coffee cup. He forgot all about the sales reports as the revelation hit him.

Caitlin was in love with him.

How long had she felt this way? Was it a recent development? And why had he not seen it yesterday? Or the day before? Or anytime in the two months he had been working at Emerald? So much love didn't happen overnight. How she must have felt watching him pursue Sheilagh while she had these feelings for him.

Clay had wanted to keep Caitlin as a friend who always listened to his woes and quandaries over Sheilagh. Now that Sheilagh had dealt him the final blow, he needed a friend more than ever. He couldn't lose what he and Caitlin had. It was too important.

"Don't tell me you've changed your mind and now you want cream?" Caitlin joked to ease the tension of the moment. Clay was looking at her with the oddest expression on his face. She read the conflicting emotions of desire and loss, hope and pain.

"No! Uh, no. This is fine," he replied quickly, and took a sip. "Great."

"What are you doing?" Caitlin inquired, looking down at the reports.

Clay glanced at the papers on his desk. His mind was still on Caitlin. "I was envisioning the future . . ."

Caitlin's smile fell away. She had expected him to talk about Sheilagh's New York plans. She had expected to hear him say he would follow her to the ends of the earth. She had expected anger and outrage; or impassioned excitement over his decision to leave Chicago and Emerald. She had never once thought Clay would be so calm.

"The future, Clay?" Caitlin waited. Five seconds. Ten seconds. Clay did not answer.

"Emerald's future," he finally said. "We need to make a great many changes . . . be more aggressive. Nothing creative has happened here in years."

"I beg your pardon?" she said aloud. In her mind she was lighting fireworks to celebrate the fact that Clay was not leaving Chicago. Sheilagh had not convinced him to go to New York with her. Caitlin was not going to lose Clay. Suddenly the thought struck her that perhaps Sheilagh had not asked him to go with her. Had Sheilagh rejected him, too?

Caitlin looked down at Clay's head and saw where the hair seemed to grow out of the scalp in a swirl. She felt his vulnerability. She reached out her hand and touched his head.

Clay jerked. She had startled him, but rather than wrench away from her touch, he lingered beneath it, accepting all the empathy from her fingertips that she had to give. He moved his head beneath her hand, rotating his head so that her fingers swirled into his hair.

Clay was overcome with emotion. He turned his head and rested his face against her abdomen, his forehead against the white leather belt. Caitlin put her arms around his shoulders and pulled him to her. He put his arms around her waist and hips.

"She's going away."

"I know."

"She's never coming back."

"I know that, too."

"I'm going to miss her."

"I know you are," Caitlin said, feeling tears well in her own eyes. They were tears of joy, but she couldn't tell Clay that.

"I couldn't sleep last night. I kept thinking what it would be like to be in New York with her. And you know what, Caitlin? I don't think I would like it very much."

Caitlin did not know how to respond to this news. Sheilagh was so beautiful, she imagined men doing nearly anything just to be with her.

"Why wouldn't you like it, Clay?"

"Because I have to do something of my own. And I know this is going to sound crazy to you, but I know my future is here at Emerald."

"You do?" Caitlin's joy caught in her throat.

"Yes. I know this job isn't important like Sheilagh's play. I mean, I'm not going to change the world. And I don't have aspirations to be a doctor like Michael. But I think it would be exciting as hell to get in here and turn this business around." Clay's voice became self-confident. "I see all kinds of holes that need to be plugged. New markets to tap. New strategies I'd like to try. You know what I mean, don't you, Caitlin?"

Clay's eyes were filled with expectation.

"Oh, yes, Clay. I do know what you mean. You want the same thing I've wanted all my life. I just had the misfortune not to be born a boy. If I had, Father would have groomed me as his heir."

"But I thought he did do that."

"I groomed myself. I came here when I was the last person he wanted to see. I shoved myself on him. I demanded to know the ins and outs, all about production, buying, bartering for sugar, cocoa beans, and nuts. I learned on my own."

Clay smiled at her. "You see it just as I do. And I have so much to learn yet."

"I'll teach you, Clay. Anything you want to know. We're friends, after all." Caitlin put her hand back on his head and luxuriated in the silky feel of his hair against her splayed fingers.

"Yes," he said happily. "Friends." Then he gave her waist a big hug and released her.

Caitlin smiled down at him and nearly leaned over to kiss his upturned face before she checked herself. This was not the time to push herself to him. Sheilagh was obviously not as much of a threat to her future as she had imagined. For now, she was glad that he was not bitter or maudlin. She admired him all the more.

"So, friend," she said lightly, "is there anything I can help you with right now?"

"As a matter of fact, I would like to know what Emerald's position on mass-appeal candies is."

"What do you mean?"

"There's a tremendous market in cheaper, fun candies. Like Jujubees, Dots, chocolate-covered raisins and peanuts. You know, all the candy people buy at the movie theaters."

Caitlin's eyes sprang open with interest. "That *is* a new market for Emerald."

"What I was thinking would be to offer a slightly more expensive chocolate alternative, but not our top-of-the-line quality, and then hit all the movie theaters. We would need to produce everything bite-sized, of course."

"Of course," Caitlin interjected, catching Clay's enthusiasm. "Not just raisins and peanuts but almonds, maybe hazelnuts and pecans."

"Right. I was even thinking about a bite-sized peanut butter candy covered in chocolate. You know, like miniature Reese's peanut butter cups."

Caitlin screwed up her face. "Nationally their sales aren't that strong. I doubt that bite-sized peanut butter candies would sell."

"It was just an idea."

She smiled at him. "I like the rest of your ideas."

"You do?"

"I think you should write it all up and let's take it to Father. Make a formal proposal. I'll back you up, for whatever it's worth."

"That's really swell of you, Caitlin."

"Anytime," she replied, and allowed her eyes to linger on his. Realizing that she was making him feel uncomfortable, she picked up the coffee cups. "I guess I'd better get some fresh coffee if I'm going to help you with your proposal."

Caitlin stretched out her arm as she leaned over to retrieve the Haviland cup. She had turned around, her back to him, when she felt his hand on her elbow.

"Caitlin?"

She turned to face him.

Clay's grin was spread mischievously wide across his face. "I sure am glad you didn't turn out to be a boy." He laughed. "You wouldn't be nearly as much fun."

Sheilagh waited for Julie Riley at Nik's Pharmacy. She sipped a chocolate soda, hoping the seltzer water would calm her nausea, but nothing seemed to help. She had devoured over a dozen saltine crackers, and they had done nothing either.

Sheilagh chose to face her unwanted pregnancy head-on. Maybe if she loved Clay, she could pretend for a while the way some girls did that this child was conceived in love. Maybe if her life's goal were to be a wife and mother, she could even be happy about it. But she felt none of these things. Her pregnancy was a big mistake. She'd made a wrong turn on her path in life. She knew it would be easier to correct her error now than ten months or ten years from now.

Sheilagh's eyes went to the black-and-gold-lettered front windows, but there was no sign of Julie.

Julie Riley was the class sleep-around. Slut. Whore. Gang-banger. She had rightfully earned all those titles, and she was proud of it. Sheilagh had never associated with her when they were at Ascension. None of the girls in Sheilagh's crowd had. Sheilagh had always wondered about Julie. Why she seemed to work so diligently at being so wicked was beyond her.

But there had been times when Sheilagh's eyes had caught Julie's as they pretended not to see each other in the halls or in line at the cafeteria, or when they'd inadvertently spied each other after Communion on Sunday when one or the other was supposed to be praying. And Sheilagh had thought: "She knows all my innermost sexual secrets." Sheilagh had looked quickly away.

Julie breezed into Nik's wearing a tight summer dress with an off-the-shoulder portrait collar, the top button of which she had "accidentally" not buttoned so that her ample bosom was freely visible to the passing eye. Sheilagh noticed that the dress was cheaply made and ill cut. Julie looked like a tawdry clown, and Sheilagh felt sorry for her.

"She-lag," Julie drawled over her Bazooka bubble gum as she hauled herself up onto a stool at the soda fountain.

"Jules." Sheilagh used the name she'd heard the football players use when they spoke of Julie.

Julie popped her bubble gum and smiled broadly at Sheilagh. The nickname obviously did not offend her.

"To what do I owe this pleasure? I mean you callin' me." Julie crossed her legs and let the man standing at the magazine rack look up her skirt.

"I need your help."

"Huh?" Julie popped her gum again. "I dun't belief this. You? She-lag. You want *my* help?"

Sheilagh nodded.

Julie spun her stool around as she scanned the pharmacy. She made a display of getting off the stool, looking under the stool, down the counter, and over to the door. Then she hopped back on. "This is a joke, right?"

"No."

Julie's eyes narrowed in suspicion. She stopped working her gum over. Her face turned to granite. "You and your kind didn't get enough grins pokin' fun at me in high school? Now youse wanna pull a trick on ole Jules."

Julie started to leave again when Sheilagh grabbed her arm imploringly. "That's not the way it is at all." Sheilagh peered deeply into Julie's hard hazel eyes. "Really, Julie. I needed to talk to you."

Julie stopped herself in midaction and balanced herself half on and half off the stool for over thirty seconds before she reseated herself. She took the gum out of her mouth, whisked a paper napkin out of the chrome napkin holder, and wrapped the gum in the napkin. "There's only one reason you could wanna see me."

"Yeah?"

"Yeah." Julie lowered her voice so that the man at the magazine rack could not hear her. "You got knocked up."

Sheilagh fought the tears in her eyes. "You are quite right."

"So tell me, Miss Rich Fancy Lady, what makes you so goddamn sure I know what to do?"

"They told me you did."

"You asked somebody about this? What kind of a nut case are you?"

"Well, I didn't exactly ask anyone. What I mean to say is that when we were in school . . . everybody knew that you . . . well, that you . . . fooled around. I just assumed, and, well, I suppose so did everyone else, that you had been in this situation before. And, well, you never dropped out of school . . ."

"I never got pregnant."

"Right."

"So all you rich don't-touch-me bitches thought I musta had an abortion somewhere down the line. Isn't that about the size of it?"

Sheilagh felt the force of Julie's anger hit her like a blast of heat from a furnace. "I guess you could say that."

"You're damn right I can say that. 'Cause that is exactly what all you prick teasers used to say about me. But you know what?" Julie leaned over to whisper conspiratorially to Sheilagh, and there was unveiled maliciousness in her eyes.

Sheilagh should have been afraid of the evil she saw in Julie, but she wasn't. Julie's eyes were too thickly rimmed in pain. Sheilagh reached out and touched her forearm. Julie snatched it back. Sheilagh pleaded with her eyes. "No, Julie, I don't know."

The sharp edge of Julie's anger ran up against Sheilagh's compassion and became dulled. "I seen nearly every one o' you rich-bitch hypocrites for the same reason. You was the only one left. You and Cindy Applebaum, but that's because she was so dang ugly, nobody wanted her ass." Julie guffawed.

Sheilagh did not have time to moralize on her friends or herself. She was in need of action. "So?"

"So you think this is an easy thing to do, what you want? You gonna do it yourself?"

"I . . . I hadn't thought about it. I don't really know . . ."

Julie screwed up her nose and lifted it above Sheilagh's face. "How far are you?"

"Three weeks."

"The good thing is that you're catchin' this early. You won't have to see an abortionist or have to do it with a kniting needle like Lucy Hailey."

"Oh, God . . ." Sheilagh moaned and turned pale. "Is that what was the matter with her last year? Her mother said it was infectious mononucleosis."

"You bet it was infectious, all right. She botched it but bad and got a real bad infection. Went to the hospital. I told her to take care of it in the beginning. But she kept thinking it would 'go away.' She told me that straight to my face. But don't you worry none. Your situation is much better. You can take some stuff they got right here in Nik's. It's called Ergotrate."

"I never heard of it."

"Why would you? It makes the uterus contract. Which means you get un-knocked up. But you gotta be careful not to take too much, because Andy Kiley's mother died of this stuff when we were in the fifth grade. I'd take like half of it maybe. If it doesn't do the trick, take a little more until the job is done."

"I can't just walk up to the counter and ask for this stuff, can I?"

"Whew!" Julie exclaimed, and lowered her head. "And I thought I was dumb. You might want to go someplace else . . . you know, where they don't know you. Then you find a time when just the clerk is there, like when the pharmacist is out to lunch? Then you slip the clerk an extra five bucks, ten if you got it, and get the Ergotrate. They use this stuff in doctors' offices and hospitals all the time because it stimulates convulsions in blood vessels, too. So lots of pharmacies have it."

Sheilagh looked away from Julie as the impact of her situation hit her full force. She was pregnant . . . out of wedlock . . . soon to become an abortionist. She didn't know if any of what Julie was telling her was the truth. Why had she called Julie in the first place? She was just a young girl like herself. What kind of sound medical advice could this uneducated girl give her?

Sheilagh was desperate. Desperation had led many a fool to their grave, she told herself. "So tell me, Julie, what happened when you used Ergotrate?"

Julie took out a brand-new piece of bubble gum and methodically unwrapped it and plunked it into her mouth. She chewed thoughtfully with her lower chin rotating in circles. She placed her hands on the counter and then spun her stool around and slid off so that her skirt rose up above her knees to nearly midthigh. She watched the man at the magazine rack nearly drop the new June issue of *Popular Mechanics* during her seductive dismount. Julie placed her left hand on Sheilagh's knee while she smiled voluptuously at the man at the magazine rack. Then she spun her head back and looked at Sheilagh with an impish, satisfied grin.

"I told you, She-lag. I never used the stuff myself. I never went to Mexico and had that loco seaweed stuffed up inside me. I never used a knitting needle or a coat hanger or a Coke bottle like Margaret Mary Durbin, either. I never used a lye douche either. You see, I never got knocked up. I'm smarter than that."

"You mean you used birth control of some kind," Sheilagh replied knowingly.

Julie's eyes gleamed with triumph. "Naw. Not that either. You see, I'm a virgin. All those stories you heard from the boys in school? Lies. Every damn one of them."

"But . . ." Sheilagh's eyes were round as saucers.

"I like the attention. That's why I dress the way I do and act the way I act. I want a guy to want me so damn bad, he'd jump fences for me just like a stallion in heat. That's what I want. Damn hard to find that anymore. I like a little romance with my seduction, too. Nope. The way I figure it, She-lag, is that I'm gonna make a guy pay plenty for me. I can only give it away once."

Julie picked up her cheap leather purse. "I gotta go. Good luck, kid. You're gonna need it."

Stunned by Julie's revelations, Sheilagh forgot to thank her before she left.

Sheilagh slid a quarter over the marble counter for her soda and left Nik's Pharmacy. It was blindingly sunny outside, and a lake breeze swept down the street, ruffling oak leaves and cooling pedestrians. Sheilagh felt like an automaton watching the businessmen rush into the corner grill for lunch, and women with children in tow buying new summer sandals and shorts for their jaunts to the lakefront beach. A particularly rushed middle-aged man raced around the corner and bumped into Sheilagh. He excused himself, but Sheilagh hardly noticed his presence. As he dashed away, Sheilagh couldn't help wondering how many of these people were not what they seemed, like

Julie. How many of them wore masks to deflect their pain?

Sheilagh had called on Julie for help, but instead she had learned that her predicament was worse than she had imagined. She knew little about pregnancy, miscarriages, or things medical, biological, and gynecological. Worse still, Julie had made Sheilagh feel ashamed.

Sheilagh had felt ashamed of her father for his drinking, his mistress, and his part in Joseph Alvaranti's death. She had been ashamed of her mother's relentless climb up the social ladder. But Sheilagh had never been ashamed of herself or her sexuality. She had prided herself on the fact that she had a healthy attitude toward her yearnings. Julie made her feel worse than the sinner her mother would accuse her of being. She made her feel stupid.

Sheilagh had given away something valuable, and she was hard-pressed to justify her own actions. Had she been swept away by strong feelings of love for Clay, it would have made sense. She had known exactly what she was doing and why she was doing it. She had been curious. She had also been angry, hurt, and rejected by her parents.

"God! How could I be so dumb?" she admonished herself as she watched the traffic light turn green before she crossed the street.

Now she needed to be smart. Very smart.

Sheilagh decided to take the train to the Loop. Once there, she would go to a pharmacy where no one knew her. She would ask for the Ergotrate, abort her baby, and get to New York before anyone in her family discovered the truth.

Sheilagh stood beneath three overly large apothecary urns filled with colored water in blue, red, and yellow. They were ornate jars with gold bands around the bottom, middle, neck, and bulbous stoppers. She waited behind an elderly woman who was complaining about the high price of pharmaceuticals.

"It never used to be this way, Judd. Half the time my mother would mix up some roots and herbs, make a poultice, and I got well. Now I've got to take these newfangled pills. And you're sure they won't make me vomit like last time?"

"No, Thelma, they won't. Just eat a little piece of bread when you take them."

"Does it say that on the bottle?"

"No, Thelma."

"It should say that, Judd. It's part of the prescription."

"Thelma, just take the medicine and get well so that you can continue to bother me like this for another ten years." Judd laughed.

The old lady shuffled away, still complaining under her breath.

Sheilagh stepped up to the pharmacist, wondering why every druggist she knew stood on a riser behind the counter. She looked up to this man who had power over her life.

"May I help you?" he asked.

"I would like some Ergotrate," Sheilagh said simply, as if she were asking for aspirin.

"You would." His eyes scanned the length of her, lingering too long on her abdomen.

Sheilagh's hand slid unconsciously across her belly. Her gesture told him everything he needed to know.

"Yes," Sheilagh replied firmly.

"What for?"

"I beg your pardon?"

"What is the ailment?"

"My mother told me to get some for her. She wouldn't tell me what it was for. Why do you need to know?"

"This is my stock-in-trade," he quipped superciliously. "It's my job to know what my customers need. Perhaps she sent you for the wrong thing. I wouldn't want to give out the wrong drug, now would I?"

"No, you wouldn't," Sheilagh replied, her hopes dimming quickly.

"Do you know what Ergotrate is? Hmmm?" His eyes nearly bulged out of his sanctimonious head. "Well, I'll tell you. It's most commonly used for abortions. Yes, that's right. You heard me correctly. Now, why would your mother need to abort herself? Is she a Christian woman?"

"Yes. Catholic," Sheilagh blurted, not knowing where he was leading.

"I'm Mormon myself. And I can tell you she surely did not send you in here for Ergotrate. A good Catholic woman would never go against her church in such a dire manner. She would be condemned to eternal damnation, young woman." He paused only briefly to assess both Sheilagh and the situation. Thoughtfully, he looked down at her. "Maybe our church can help you. What did you say your name was?"

Sheilagh watched as his cheeks flamed with indignation and

his eyes sparked with self-righteousness. She had never seen such a display even from Father Riley, who was without a doubt the most devout priest she had ever known.

Sheilagh knew she had not fooled this man for a minute. He knew she wanted the Ergotrate for herself. "Perhaps I should go back home and double-check with Mother. I must be mistaken."

"Yes, you must," he said.

Sheilagh walked decorously out of the pharmacy. Once she hit the outdoors, she raced down the sidewalk, weaving in between pedestrians. She ran and ran. Her lungs burned and her head pounded, she ran so fast. She ran even faster. She wanted to put as much distance between herself and her secret as was humanly possible. If Julie and Judd, the pharmacist, had discovered her condition with such apparent ease, how long would it be before Caitlin knew? Or her father? Her mother?

Sheilagh's calves ached from the merciless pounding they received from the hot pavement. She fled down State Street. She crossed Madison, then Monroe, Adams, and Jackson. She thought of taking a circuitous route home, but none came to mind. She did not want to meet up with anyone she knew. She would take the train at La Salle Street Station all the way out west to Oak Park.

Sheilagh ran as if there were banshees on her heels. Her mind screamed a hundred epithets. Harlot. Whore. Abortionist. Murderer. Wicked. Wicked. Wicked.

By the time she seated herself on the train, sweat pouring from her face, her hair a wild tangle of red locks that made her look like a broken Raggedy Ann doll, Sheilagh gulped for air and swallowed back the lump of panic in her throat.

She had failed to return with the Ergotrate. She was certain she would encounter similar attitudes from all the other pharmacists. Her options were diminishing rapidly. She racked her brain to remember everything that Julie had told her. She remembered that her mother kept lye underneath the kitchen sink.

Sheilagh leaned her head on the window and began to cry.

Chapter 22 ————————————

SHEILAGH SCREAMED AS she clutched herself and fell to the floor. The lye burned and seared away the delicate membranes of her vagina and cervix. She felt as if she had been impaled upon a red-hot metal sword. Tears filled her eyes. Her screams were dammed behind the torturous pain, where they doubled and redoubled and then exploded into the silent house.

Sheilagh had carefully planned her day so that no one would be home. Now she wished Caitlin would find her. She knew she was going to die.

"Please, God. Help me."

Sheilagh could barely breathe, the pain was so great. Shallow breaths. Deep breaths. Neither lessened the excruciating torment.

The lye water trickled out of her vagina onto the soft skin of her inner thigh and burned the flesh away. Then she saw blood. Blood on her thigh. Blood on the floor. The pain intensified. The lye sliced away at her insides like razors. She screamed continuously against the attack, but she was powerless to stop what she herself had started.

"God . . . help me . . . I'm sorry . . . I'm so sorry . . ."

Her tears came in heavy droplets like giant pearls and melted on the floor, mixing with her own blood.

She grew weak as she fought the pain. She knew she had to get out of the bathroom. She should clean up the mess. She couldn't let anyone know what she had done.

Her head pounded and then dropped against her chest. She propped herself against the toilet bowl, but she slumped to the side of it. The pain sucked her energy like a hungry cannibal.

"Fool!" she chastised herself. How could she have been so naive as to think that her heinous deed would not be painful? Her sin gripped her soul and flogged her body. Her mother had been right all along. How she hated admitting that to herself. Sheilagh surrendered herself to the admission and finally succumbed to the pain. Her eyes rolled back in her head and she passed out.

Mary Margaret found Sheilagh forty-five minutes later. When she saw her eldest daughter sitting half-slumped in a pool of blood, she acted on instinct.

Dashing from the bathroom, she went to the telephone and placed a call not to their family doctor, Sean McLaughlin, but to Saul Eberman, a man she had never met but had heard about from her society friends.

Saul was a man of discretion. He had to be. He was an outsider in Chicago. He made a great deal of money off the Irish Catholic wives of the city's millionaires, politicians, benefactors, builders, and merchantmen. Saul repaired broken arms, legs, and jaws, and stifled internal bleeding caused by the drunken rampages of the city's finest husbands. He gave birth control to cheating wives, aborted babies of not so naive debutantes, and repaired the bodies and psyches of homosexual husbands and sons of the stiff-backed, controlling, frightened Irish wives and mothers. He kept prominent Irish names off the hospital lists, the police records, and out of the society columns. Saul Eberman knew more family secrets than God.

Mary Margaret knew little of Saul's secrets; she only knew that he was a good, caring doctor who kept his mouth shut.

She did not know Saul's private number and thus simply telephoned his office. The nurse tried three times to put her off. Incensed, Mary Margaret finally exploded: "This is an emergency. I wish to speak to him *now!*"

The nurse immediately put her call through.

At first Saul wanted to meet them at Cook County Hospital, which housed the city's finest trauma unit.

"It's too public," Mary Margaret retorted. "And it's a long way to Damen Street." She continued to protest. Finally she arranged to meet Saul at his office, which he instructed her to enter by the back alley. No one in the waiting room would know of her presence.

Mary Margaret returned to the bathroom and shook Sheilagh by the shoulders to wake her. She groaned and half opened her eyelids.

"Get to your feet," Mary Margaret demanded. "We have to clean you up and get you to the doctor before it's too late."

Sheilagh's head swam in a sea of pain. "Oh, God. Mother. I didn't want you to know. Why couldn't it be Caitlin?"

Mary Margaret's already strained mouth tightened into a line as thin as piano wire. "Because God didn't want it to be that way."

Sheilagh grabbed her mother's forearms and tried to haul her tortured body to a standing position, but as soon as she did, a new onslaught of pain seared her insides, and her knees buckled. "God . . ."

"God has nothing to do with this sin. Better you call on the devil. Now, get up!"

Sheilagh hated herself. She hated her mother. She tried to feel compassion in her mother's arms, but all she felt was dry skin. Her vision was blurry, but Sheilagh could see the indignation in her mother's eyes. She was trembling, but she stood.

Mary Margaret ran cold water in the washbasin and dunked a washcloth under the spigot. She handed it to Sheilagh. "Clean yourself." She started to leave as Sheilagh leaned against the basin for support. "I'll get a change of clothes."

Mary Margaret looked back at her daughter for a moment, watching Sheilagh lift her skirt and wipe away the rivulets of blood that had trickled down her thigh. She saw where the lye had burned off the top layer of skin. She shivered with revulsion.

At that moment Sheilagh lifted her head and looked into her mother's face. She knew she would never forget that look of utter repugnance and censure. She believed that God on Judgment Day would not look upon her with as much repudiation as her mother did that day. A new wave of tears billowed in Sheilagh's eyes.

Mary Margaret instantly turned from her daughter and left the room.

She returned with a three-year-old summer sweater and skirt outfit that she had purchased from Marshall Field's when Sheilagh was entering her junior year in high school. It was mint green angora with a Peter Pan collar, short sleeves, and a mint and silver-gray cotton skirt to match. Mary Margaret loved it. Sheilagh hated it.

"Thank you." Sheilagh breathed out the words carefully, hoping they would not cause another rush of pain. She placed her arms in the sleeves. She stepped into the skirt gingerly.

Mary Margaret collected handbags and white gloves for them both. Sheilagh lay down on the backseat of the 1939 silver-gray Studebaker. She stuck a huge towel between her legs.

They said nothing as Mary Margaret sped through the streets of Oak Park. Fortunately, they did not have to travel far to Saul's office, located in the Jewish community on the near West Side.

Mary Margaret steered the car off Roosevelt onto Kedzie and then to the address on Lexington the doctor had given her.

It was a blond brick building, only recently finished. The trim was newly painted black, as were the wrought-iron handrails on either side of the four concrete front steps. There was a large picture window in front, but the interior was hidden behind drawn venetian blinds. Sheilagh sat up long enough to see the two cheap crockery pots filled with geraniums and English ivy on either side of the door.

They drove around to the back alley, just as the doctor had instructed. The back steps were new, but there was no handrail. The screen door was locked, to enable the nurse to inspect all patients and visitors before entering.

Mary Margaret grabbed her square leather handbag, got out of the car, and rushed up the steps. She banged on the screen door with her fist.

"I'm coming!" yelled an impertinent female voice.

A huge woman the size of both Sheilagh and Mary Margaret combined came to the door. Her face looked pockmarked, Sheilagh thought, until she realized it was the shadow from the screen falling on her skin. The woman had a thin wave of spiky gray hair she wore slicked back and twisted into a topknot no larger than the size of a nickel donut. She wore a white uniform that strained across her ample bosom, wide stomach, and enormous hips. She folded her arms in front of her like two pink hams. The nurse's mouth was set in an odd squiggle across the lower third of her face like a crawling earthworm, and was the only part of her anatomy that moved during the confrontation. Finally Mary Margaret moved away, the nurse unlocked the door, and Sheilagh was allowed to enter the doctor's office.

In less than three paces, Sheilagh realized that she had deluded herself into thinking that the pain had abated on the trip to the doctor's office. On the bottom step she stumbled and was forced to lean on her mother.

"I'll help you," Mary Margaret said stiffly.

Sheilagh wanted to shove her mother's arm from her sight, but she was forced to take it as they walked past the nurse's condemning gaze.

Sheilagh took her cue from her mother and kept her head down, as if she was shamed by the situation. It made her stomach burn nearly as much as the acid in her vagina. They turned in to a small room on the right.

"Strip," the nurse ordered indignantly. "And you'll have to leave," she ordered Mary Margaret.

Mary Margaret started to protest, but instead, she started for the door. She stopped. Her back straightened as she turned her neck to the right, placing her face in profile to her daughter. Her eyes remained downcast.

"I'll be outside in the car."

Don't go! Sheilagh wanted to scream at her mother. *I'm afraid. Don't leave me with these strangers. Tell me you care about me . . . even just a little bit. Don't leave me!*

But Sheilagh didn't say any of that. She maintained her Killian dignity. "Yes, ma'am."

Sheilagh turned away from the callous nurse and stepped out of her shoes, then unbuttoned her sweater. Every movement sent a streak of new pain through her. She neatly folded the sweater, then the skirt, then her slip. She wore only her bra and panties.

"All of it," the nurse commanded.

Tears trickled down Sheilagh's cheeks as she unhooked her bra. The nurse's condemnation filled the room like an evil presence. Mental anguish lacerated her heart more painfully than the lye had burned her skin.

The elastic on her panties had crusted to a piece of raw skin, but as she ripped them off, Sheilagh didn't utter a sound. *I'll be damned if I'll give this monster the satisfaction of seeing me squirm,* she thought. Slowly she stepped out of the panties. She turned to face the nurse.

"I'm ready," Sheilagh said defiantly with her shoulders back and her head erect.

Judgmental eyes scanned Sheilagh as if she were a prized breeder at a slave auction. "Here." The woman thrust a thin, worn sheet at her. "Put this around you."

Sheilagh took the sheet and ceremoniously slipped it under her arms as if she were being garbed for a high Roman banquet. She tucked the ends under themselves and fashioned the sheet into a gown just as she knew hundreds of this woman's patients had done ten times a day every day of her career. The difference was that Sheilagh went to the examining table as if she were royalty.

She would not allow this narrow-minded woman to rob her of courage. Though this woman was trying to cast stones at her, Sheilagh continued to deflect them. She would never let anyone, not this nurse or the doctor or her mother, ever know how much she was hurting. She didn't want them to know that she hated herself for what she had done. She didn't want to hurt Clay or the baby. She just wanted to leave Chicago. She knew she was selfish, but she was also right.

Sheilagh stepped up to the table and sat on it. She had never had a pelvic exam and had no idea what the steel and chrome apparatus was at the foot of the table. It looked like a medieval torture device, and she had a sick feeling that was precisely what this exam would be—torture.

The door opened and the doctor walked in. He reminded her of Abe, only much taller and older. Saul Eberman possessed kind brown eyes and the most gentle hands she'd ever felt. Before he introduced himself, before he inquired anything of her, he gently laid his hand on her forearm and patted it.

"Everything is going to be all right, Sheilagh. I wish you had come to me first. Perhaps I could have helped you."

His kindness fell on her like a gentle rain. She burst into tears.

"I didn't know . . ."

Saul's voice was like a friend's caress. "I know you didn't, my dear. That's the problem I face every day. No one ever tells you girls. Not your mothers, not the schools. There's no place for you to go."

Sheilagh covered her face with her hands. "I'm so ashamed. And I hurt so much . . ."

Saul held her hand. "I'll do the best I can for you."

Sheilagh let her hands slide slowly away as she looked up into his eyes. "Nooo . . ." Her sobs felt like gravel in her throat. She laid her hand on her heart. "I mean that I hurt here . . . inside."

Saul bent over very close. "I know that, too, but only time will heal that. I wish I could help there, too, but that you'll have to do yourself. Now, I'd better get to work."

Gently he placed her hand on her chest and walked to the end of the table.

"You'll have to slide down toward me, Sheilagh. That's good," he instructed. "Now, raise your knees and put your feet in the stirrups. I know they're cold . . . Now, take deep breaths as I examine you."

Saul sat on a short stool and disappeared behind the tent that the sheet and her knees had made. Sheilagh could hear clicking and clacking metal sounds. She heard mumbles between the nurse and Saul.

Sheilagh didn't like their ominous low tones. She heard not a word, but she picked up on their concern, alarm, and then acceptance.

"As I begin to work, start breathing, Sheilagh," Saul said.

Sheilagh felt some kind of soothing salve on her thigh. She felt the blood and lye being cleaned away. Saul was a gentle and thorough man, but even he could not eliminate the pain completely.

Sheilagh clutched the sides of the examining table and tensed. She felt some metal apparatus being inserted into her vagina, which sent sharp pangs racing through her lower extremities. Her hips jerked away from him. She wanted to cry out, but she would never give that woman the satisfaction. She bit her lower lip to keep her moans at bay. Her nails dug into the table. She swallowed back another painful moan. Tears slid out of her eyes at breakneck speed. She squeezed her eyes shut and breathed deeper.

Instinctively she realized that the deep breaths made the pain more intense, and so she began shallow breathing.

Another pain sliced through her.

Sheilagh's eyes flew open and she counted the ceiling tiles through the tears in her eyes. She heard more clicking and clacking. She heard scissors as they clipped away pieces of her burned skin.

She bit her tongue. She counted another twenty-three tiles and then slammed her eyes shut when Saul probed more deeply inside her.

Sheilagh's tears wet the old sheet that covered the examining table. Her moans grew into groans. Her groans threatened to become screams. She waged a silent war with herself. The screams raced up her throat and were about to burst into the room when Saul suddenly stopped.

"That's it, Sheilagh. You can relax now," he said, and stood. His smile was warm and caring as he looked at her. "I'm going to give you some salve to soothe the skin. I want you to double up on vitamins, no baths only showers, and let's both hope that there's no infection. Unfortunately, the most you can do now is wait, rest, and pray." He walked around to the side of the table. "I need to explain what you've done."

"I know what I've done . . . I've killed my baby."

"No, you haven't. I know . . . you girls go to each other to get information, but lye douches do not abort a fetus. The infection that follows, if it becomes severe enough, aborts the fetus, but not the douche itself. That's why it's important that I monitor your progress very carefully. I'll do all that I can to keep the infection from harming your baby or you."

"The baby is alive?"

"The fetus is not damaged."

"But you could abort it for me?"

"I could."

"But you won't."

"No."

"Why?"

"Do you really want an abortion? You may think you do now, but you may feel otherwise later."

Sheilagh could only nod her head. He was right.

"You, I still worry about. There's a possibility that the infection could kill you. I don't want to alarm you because you weren't burned as badly as some I've seen. I have every reason to believe that you will come through this in perfect condition. There's nothing we can do until you heal. That will give you some time to think this over. Promise me you will take care of yourself."

"I will," she replied feebly.

"I can teach you about birth control so that this won't happen again . . ."

"You don't have to worry, it won't," Sheilagh said sharply.

Saul shook his head. "It will take a long time for your body to repair itself. The lye burned very deeply in some spots. You won't feel like doing much of anything for a long time. Please, take care of yourself. None of this was necessary. You have options . . ." he was saying.

Options. Options. Sheilagh heard the word as if it were the clash of two cymbals. Disgrace? Chastisement from her mother? Marriage to a boy she didn't love? The end of her dreams? More pain in Caitlin's eyes every time she looked at Sheilagh or her baby? To bring a baby into the world that would never be loved? Options? Sheilagh was enough of a realist to know that her only option was abortion. But she couldn't take it.

"There are great Catholic adoption agencies in the city. All over the country if you want to go away," he droned gently, and Sheilagh indulged him the way one does an elderly aunt.

"I want to go away . . . to New York," Sheilagh whimpered. How could she tell him that she had been stupid and foolish and self-centered? How could she tell him she had put herself before her baby? How could she tell him she had needed to go to New York for her career . . . a career that she had burned up just as the lye had burned her skin? How could she tell him that nothing . . . nothing . . . nothing mattered anymore?

"Come back and see me in four days, Sheilagh. It's important." Saul went to the door. The nurse stood behind him.

"Thank you, Saul," Sheilagh said with pointed familiarity, knowing the nurse had never addressed him as anything but "Dr. Eberman."

"You're welcome, Sheilagh." He smiled, and they left.

Sheilagh painfully put her clothes on.

Mary Margaret was waiting for her, Sheilagh knew. She had no idea what she would say when she faced her, only that she would have to take every abuse her mother doled out. Sheilagh was to blame for her mistake, and she did not mind assuming the burden. What she feared the most was the rising tide of guilt that threatened to suck her under.

Chapter 23

CAITLIN STOOD IN the kitchen and unpacked the wicker picnic basket.

This was going to be her summer. It was her turn to shine. Today was the happiest day of her life, because today Clay had told her that he loved her.

Caitlin had chosen the lakefront on the North Shore for her Friday afternoon picnic with Clay. It was nearly balmy, with huge, cottony clouds leapfrogging across a brilliant blue sky. The air was hot, the lake breeze cool, and the water still cold from the latest spring thawing in Chicago's history. Every green tree, every vibrant red geranium, each grain of sand and rolling wave, seemed put there by nature to enhance Caitlin's carefully planned afternoon of playing hooky from work with Clay.

High school kids the same age she was rode past them on bicycles, arguing with one another about the Cubs game that afternoon. The curb was lined with Packards, Buicks, Chevys, and Studebakers whose radios were tuned in to the baseball game. From far off another radio played Tommy Dorsey tunes, and another played "Green Eyes," sung by Helen Morgan.

Clay carried the picnic basket as they walked across the grass to a shady area beneath a huge sugar maple tree.

"How's this?" she asked him.

"Great!" His smile reached his eyes and made them shine. It was the way he used to smile when they were younger.

Caitlin's heart swam in a sea of warmth. She smiled back. "No peeking," she teased as she took the basket from him, placed it on the ground, and bent over it.

"I wasn't trying to look in the basket," he said as his eyes swept the length of her.

Caitlin pretended not to notice his appreciative gaze, though she chalked up another point for herself. She was tempted to hope that this time he might do more than just brush her hand with his the way he did in the office. Perhaps this time she would take the risk of believing that Clay might be looking for more than simply friendship from her.

She was a hopeful person, but she had been disappointed too many times by the people she loved. Experience had taught her to keep her emotions in check. Clay was still nursing his wounds over Sheilagh and her departure tomorrow from Chicago. Caitlin did not want to be second prize to Clay. She wanted to be his first choice. She was afraid she wanted too much from him.

She withdrew a blue and white checked tablecloth, spread it on the ground, then whirled around and sat upon it. She took out two metal tumblers and a bottle of chilled champagne.

"Where did you get that?" he asked, knowing she was underage.

"I bought it, silly. I told Mr. Chilton it was for my father, like I always do."

"And what are we celebrating?" he asked as he sat next to her.

Caitlin smiled at him. "Your genius."

"My what?"

She delved into the basket and pulled out a glittering gold-foil-wrapped box. "Open it."

"This is the new packaging for the Christmas line I wanted."

"I know." Caitlin's grin grew wider.

Clay lifted the lid. Inside was another box, smaller and wrapped in deep hunter green moire taffeta fabric. "The upscale line?" His blue eyes gleamed brighter.

Caitlin nodded anxiously as her own anticipation grew.

Clay opened the green box, and inside, caught between gold-ribbed paper, were the four chocolate combinations he had suggested in his report only a few weeks ago. The champagne truffle rolled in finely sifted bitter cocoa. The maple pecan bar with its waffled cookie base, all surrounded in smooth milk chocolate. The peanut butter clusters of peanuts and peanut butter cream, all covered in milk chocolate. And last, a tart lime cream with dark chocolate molded to look like a lime.

"You had them all made!" he exclaimed, and exuberantly grabbed her face and kissed her soundly on the lips. At first, it was like the kiss a contest winner gives a judge at the county fair, but then his lips turned soft and pliant, as if they had found a better prize. And then they were probing, as if he knew the treasure was yet to be discovered.

He pulled away with a sharp jerk. His eyes were filled with uncertainty. He gazed at her for what seemed to Caitlin like an eternity.

Kiss me, she wanted to say. *Kiss me like you mean it.* She wondered if it were possible to think something so strongly that Clay could read her mind. He continued to look at her. There were a million questions and a dozen emotions whirling in his head.

Caitlin looked down at the chocolates. She had wanted him for so long; all those years, all the nights she had dreamed about him. She remembered when she had tried to run from the thought of him, but the dreams, the yearnings, the thoughts, had become a prayer, a litany. Sometimes she thought the only rosary she prayed was the one for Clay. She didn't want him to see the tears in her eyes.

"Cat . . ." Clay touched her cheek again.

His fingers were cold on her inflamed cheeks. They were both afraid, she realized with a jolt. She tried to turn away. In a moment he would see her tears. She was embarrassed. She was wanting. Yet she felt as if this was her last chance. "Clay, don't."

"I'm afraid I have to," he said, and brought his lips to hers once again. This time the kiss was soft, like the flutter of an angel's wings. She could feel his breath as it fell on her cheek and slipped into her hair. She felt his uncertainty in the tenuousness of his lips. It was as if he were kissing a girl for the first time, yet she knew he'd kissed Sheilagh plenty.

Damn, she thought, *I will not allow Sheilagh to steal this moment from me.*

Caitlin slipped her arms around his neck and let herself become lost in the kiss. She caressed him with the one part of her that she knew Sheilagh had never given him. She touched him with her soul.

With only her fingertips on the nape of his neck, she held him gently. She held him to her as no woman ever would before or after her. Clay was hers, and Caitlin had known it since the first day she'd met him at the World's Fair. She wanted to mark her claim on him, imbed herself into his psyche, and strike chords that would resonate until the day he died.

Caitlin knew little of sex and nothing of kissing as Sheilagh and her other girlfriends did. She had not "saved" herself for Clay the way other Catholic girls thought of "saving" themselves, because she knew that the day she finally saw her own love for him returned, she would give him everything. She would be a fool for him, and it wouldn't matter. She would crawl through glass for him, die for him, live for him, and it wouldn't matter. Though she had no basis for her beliefs through acquired knowledge or church doctrine, she believed that Clay was the other half of herself.

Caitlin kissed Clay back with all the tenderness and tumultuous passion he'd hoped to receive from Sheilagh but never had. His arms could not hold her close enough. His tongue could not probe deep enough. His breath came in pants . . . he thought his lungs would explode. But still he could not get enough. Caitlin gave and gave and gave. And every bit of it was innocent, joyous, and exciting to them both. She circled his lips with her tongue. She pulled his head closer to hers. She forced him to take her tongue into his mouth. She was at first gentle, then forceful, then exhilaratingly desperate. Her lips smothered his, then allowed him to seek her lips again. She laughed between breaths, and then when he kissed her again, he tasted salty tears.

Clay slid his lips to her cheek but refused to let his mouth leave her skin. "What is it?"

"I love you, Clay. I've always loved you. Why haven't you known?"

"Stupid. I was just so stupid."

"Blinded by Sheilagh . . ."

"Don't . . . don't talk about her. Kiss me again."

She did. Only this time she leaned against him and forced him to the soft ground. She lay close to him, her breast to his breast, her thigh wrapped over his thigh. She couldn't get close enough.

"You can touch me, Clay."

"No . . . it wouldn't be right."

Caitlin shook her head and smiled at him. "It will be a sin if you don't. You love me, Clay. You know you do."

"I do now. That's why I don't want it to be like this for us."

"Like what?"

"I want us to take our time. I don't want some quick romp in the park and then you feeling bad and me feeling bad and it all coming to nothing."

Caitlin placed her hand on his heart and peered deeply into his blue eyes. She saw pain there, pain over losing Sheilagh. But she also saw truth and honesty, and best of all, she saw love. "Tell me everything you want, Clay."

He took a deep breath. He didn't want to hurt Caitlin. Of all the people in the world, he had always liked her. She had been his friend, his little sister, his refuge. She had grown into a beautiful woman. She was everything he had wanted, only he had been too blinded by lust for Sheilagh to see it. Caitlin was his rock.

Clay looked up into the sky and watched the fat clouds sail away like giant pirate ships with tall sails. "I can't remember my life without the Killian family in it. I guess that's because all of you were very important to me. When I started working at Emerald, I was only there for a week before I realized that the most exciting part of my job, the part that I anticipated the most, was working with you." He turned to face her and smiled.

Caitlin's eyes brimmed with happy tears, "Truly?"

"Truly." He kissed her deeply once again. This time they both felt chills blanket their bodies. Clay put his arm around her shoulders and pulled her close so that her head was lying atop his chest. He wanted her ear close to his heart so that she would know he was telling the truth.

"I know now the horrible pain you must have felt each time I called for her. It wasn't until just now that I realized I liked hearing your voice as much—no, even more—than hers. You were always so happy to hear from me. You always asked about my studies, my friends . . . about me and how I was feeling. Except for my mother, I don't know anyone who simply said, 'How *are* you?' and meant it."

"I did mean it."

"I know. And I loved you for it. Then I realized that we not only worked well together, but we were on the same wavelength somehow. You would think of new chocolates or new promotions at nearly the same time I did. Then I realized that sometimes, not all the times perhaps, but sometimes, I worked extra hard and long to please you. Your praise was essential to me. The extra hours with you were becoming more and more important to me. I guess what I'm saying is that I was pretty dumb not to see it for myself a long time ago."

"It's okay, Clay. I've always known."

He picked up her head and caressed her silky hair. "You did? How?"

"I don't know how. I guess you were in my dreams when I was very young. Or maybe it was a premonition or something. I just always knew. But the question now is not whether you are the one for me, but am I good enough for you?"

"Of course you are," he reassured her with a smile and a kiss on her forehead.

"I can never be glamorous like Sheilagh. I don't even want to be."

"I don't want you to be, either. Sheilagh is driven by demons, and I don't fully understand them or her."

"Maybe she doesn't understand herself," Caitlin offered.

"No," he said. "I think Sheilagh knows herself very well. She has no illusions." Then he laughed. "I, on the other hand, have been plenty confused. But I think I'm resolving my confusion very quickly." He pulled her on top of him. "Yes," he said with sultry eyes and a raspy voice. His lips moved closer to Caitlin's mouth. His eyes were downcast as his lips parted just before they captured her. "I know I've found what I want. And this time, I'll never let you go."

Caitlin surrendered to his kiss, meeting him as if on some mystical plane, their souls uniting and becoming one. For the first time, her world was made whole.

The shouting from the front parlor of the Killian home brought Caitlin's thoughts back to the present and ripped away her smile. Her parents were arguing.

"They can't be married in the sacristy!" Mary Margaret yelled at Patrick. "It's against canon law."

"Fuck the canon law. I'll give Father Morley a thousand bucks for his new roof!"

"You can't buy morality, Patrick," Mary Margaret blasted back, and this time her tone was one note higher, signaling her distress and the fact that she had just lost the argument.

"You blew the whole damn thing by telling the priest that Sheilagh was pregnant. We could have posted banns and had a wedding."

"And lie about it?"

"Why not?"

"I could never lie to a priest!"

"Christ, Mary Margaret. A priest is no different than anyone else. And you lie to people every day."

Mary Margaret's eyes were filled with hatred. "Only because I have to cover up the truth about *you!*"

"If living with me is so goddamn difficult, then divorce me."

"You'd send me to hell with you? Never in a million years. Never, Patrick."

"Fine," he uttered. He took another deep swallow of bourbon. "They can go to the justice of the peace," he said with finality. He poured himself another straight bourbon. He downed it quickly and poured another.

"Where? There's a waiting period."

"Only a short one. We can send her to Reno or Mexico or wherever these things are done. I'll ask around."

"You'll have to. None of *my* friends would ever be caught in such a predicament."

"Bullshit, Mary Margaret. They've all done the same thing. You just don't know about it. Besides, most of their daughters probably paid Saul enough money to do the job right."

"Well, he won't now."

"Yeah? That's because you botched it. You shoulda given him some money. Now you've got Sheilagh all upset and she doesn't know what to do. I say she should still get the abortion."

Mary Margaret's face was scarlet with indignation. "You would. I will not have you helping your own daughter through the gates of hell. It's bad enough you're going there yourself."

Patrick finished off the bourbon, and this time when he refilled the glass, he placed a half dozen ice cubes from the silver bucket in the lead crystal tumbler. He hated arguing with his wife. She insisted she was right no matter what the consequences to anyone else in the family.

He sipped his drink, then looked at his watch. He was half an hour late for his meeting with Shannon. He had promised to take her to a quaint inn up in Wisconsin for the evening. He had told Mary Margaret he would be leaving town on business.

"I'm going to miss my train. Handle this however you feel is right. Just let me know how much you need for her expenses. I'll write a check."

"Don't you always?" Mary Margaret folded her thin arms across her chest. She glared at him. "When will you be back?"

"Tomorrow." He stopped himself. "Uh-hem. That is . . . if it goes well and we land the account. If not, I'll have to stay another day."

"Don't you want to say good-bye to Sheilagh?"

Patrick lifted his eyes toward the ceiling. "I think not. She needs her rest."

"Coward."

"Precisely. You handle it."

"Don't I always?"

Patrick did not look back at his wife as he left.

Caitlin stole up the stairs before Mary Margaret could see her. Her legs were trembling, her skin cold and clammy. Her world was coming apart, her happiness destroyed.

She knew she should talk to her sister, but she was too angry. He wanted to seek out Clay, but his betrayal sank deeply into her soul.

What kind of sick game was he playing? And how long had he been playing it? What did he intend to gain by making love to both her and Sheilagh?

Caitlin stumbled on the stairs. She blamed the ragged carpet and not the tears in her eyes. She was strong, she told herself. The strongest in the family. She didn't need Clay to make her happy. She didn't need anybody. She would make a life for herself in her father's business. She would be okay. She would. She had to.

She faltered again on the last step.

Agony held her in a vise. She started down the hall toward her room. As she wiped away her tears, she saw that the door to Sheilagh's room was half-open.

She saw Sheilagh lying on the bed. She looked sick. There was no color in her face, and her arm fell lifelessly over the side. Her eyes were closed, but the lids were dark, making the sockets look hollow. Her dull russet hair, unbrushed and snarled, snaked over the pillow. Caitlin had seen Sheilagh less than twenty-four hours ago, but now she looked suddenly very thin and small.

Caitlin blinked her eyes, thinking it was not Sheilagh but someone else who had stolen into her room and occupied her bed. When she looked again, Sheilagh's head moved slightly on the pillow so that the gold and pink rays of sunset outlined her perfect profile.

"Sheilagh." Caitlin spoke the name of her rival aloud. *Sheilagh.* Caitlin wanted to hate her. For some reason, Clay and Sheilagh had conspired against her. They had played Caitlin for the fool.

Rage whirled inside Caitlin like an imprisoned demon clamoring for freedom. It twisted and impaled itself on her fears and then rose phoenixlike to overtake her.

Caitlin's last steps toward Sheilagh's room were sure and determined. She put her palms up and slammed them into the door, shoving it aside. The brass doorknob banged against the plaster wall. Sheilagh's eyes flew open. Her face was filled with pain.

"Oh, Cat," she said in a low voice. Tears brimmed in her eyes, suffusing the bright jade orbs. Tears spilled onto the pillow, followed by still more tears.

Sheilagh tried to lift her arms and beckon her sister to her, but they fell back to the bed. "It hurts . . ."

Caitlin was suddenly confused as pity strangled the demon of anger. "What hurts?" *The fact that Clay is going to marry you? How long have you planned all this? Why is he trying to hurt me?* Caitlin had a million questions, none of which she could articulate. She remained mute.

"Everything. Life." Sheilagh blinked away another wave of tears and regarded Caitlin more closely. She saw the questioning look in her sister's eyes. She also saw a terrible, terrible pain she had hoped she would never see. "They didn't tell you?"

"Tell me what?" Caitlin gulped. She didn't like the care and concern she saw in Sheilagh's eyes. It was easier to hate, to be jealous.

"Where . . . where I was today? What I did?"

"No." Caitlin bit off the word sharply. "I heard Mother and Father arguing. I came up here instead."

"Oh, God . . ." Sheilagh groaned as the physical pain began beating at her insides once again. "It's all my fault. I've made a mess of things. For me, for Clay. Especially for you."

Caitlin willed herself to remain aloof. "Me?"

Sheilagh wiped away more tears. Her voice was gravelly. "I didn't want anyone to find out. Ever. I thought I could keep it a secret and go away, and no one would be the wiser. But it didn't happen that way. Mother found me . . ."

"Found you?"

"In the bathroom. I tried to do it myself, but I botched it. She had to take me to the doctor. I was stupid. So stupid. Now Clay has to know. They're going to make him marry me."

Caitlin felt as if the blood had been drained out of her body. Her thoughts raced in a million directions. "Clay doesn't know?"

"Not yet. Mother is going to meet with his parents, or so she says."

"Oh, my God." Caitlin backed up against the doorjamb for support. "Clay doesn't know about the baby?"

"No."

Silence hung between them. Sheilagh had had barely enough time herself to accept the fact that she was pregnant. Now she was tormented by the knowledge that Caitlin must bear the pain of Sheilagh and Clay's sexual affair. "Cat . . ."

Caitlin fought her tears like a relentless warrior. She would not let her rival see her vulnerability. "How long ago?"

"Cat, please. Don't do this to yourself. I'm sorry. I'm so very sorry."

Caitlin clenched her teeth. "How long ago?"

"Almost four weeks." Sheilagh watched her sister. She watched their lifelong bond unravel like a used piece of hemp. "It was only once."

"Sure." Caitlin's spine cemented itself against the doorjamb. She felt incredibly tired. She should leave. She and Sheilagh were lost to each other. Why was she staying? Why was she torturing herself like this?

"Did he tell you that he loved you?"

"Cat . . . don't do this!"

"Did he? Damn it, Sheilagh! Tell me."

"Yes," Sheilagh whispered.

"Do you love him?"

"No."

"Liar."

Sheilagh found the strength to raise up on her elbows. The tears dried. Her eyes flamed with zeal. "You want the truth, well, here it is. Down and dirty. As God is my witness, I did not and do not love Clay. I told him so. He thought he loved me, but you see, Caitlin, he didn't. That's the truth of it. I was pretty, and that was all he saw. Nobody has ever loved me for me. Not even you. You came as close as anyone has ever come to loving me, but Clay got in the way.

"You love him. I was too blind to see it for a long time, but you do. You can't help it. You will always love him. That's something you've got over me, and I know it. I think he loves you, too. But now I have ruined all our lives. Yes, I have. You can't have the man who loves you, and he can't have you. I still want to go to New York and work in Abe's play, but that can't happen now. And you know why? Because it says so in the rule book. And who do you think wrote that book that destroys lives like this? God? Jesus? The good old U.S.A.? Or maybe it was one of mother's hoity-toity crowd? Who do you vote for, Cat?"

Caitlin shook her head and did not answer.

Sheilagh's voice faltered, but only for a moment. "Go ahead and hate me. I deserve it. I really do. I wouldn't blame you a bit. I'd hate me if I were in your shoes."

Sheilagh peered deeply into her sister's eyes, waiting for her condemnation. She braced herself for the final cut.

Caitlin parted her lips to speak, but her words became a painful bellow. "Ooohhh, Sheilagh . . ." Caitlin went to the bed and knelt on the floor. She flung her arms around her sister and held her. "I don't hate you. I could never hate you."

Sheilagh let her sister's sobs rush over her. "It will be too hard to love me in the days to come."

Caitlin wanted to tell Sheilagh she was wrong, but she couldn't. She knew it would be hell for all of them. She felt empty, useless, and afraid.

They clung to each other, both knowing in the deepest, darkest realms of their souls that they would never again be the innocent, loving sisters they had once been. Their pain was mutual as they cried for each other and for themselves.

Soon they would go on to formulate a plan by which each would live out her life, doing what society expected of her. But for this moment the pieces of their shattered dreams mingled together and bonded them in a pain-filled embrace.

Clay had arrived home after his picnic with Caitlin thinking that finally his life was on course. He could see now that he and Sheilagh were mismatched, just as she'd tried to point out to him. But he and Caitlin—they were two halves of a whole.

Clay was whistling as he stepped into the living room and found his mother and father seated on the sofa. Their faces were etched with worry and concern.

"Mom? Dad?" Clay asked as he crossed the room and sat in the overstuffed club chair opposite them. He could feel the tension in the air.

"We just received a very disturbing phone call," Robert Burke said, his gray brows knitting together.

"From whom?"

"Patrick Killian," Robert answered. Clay was instantly on his feet. "It's Caitlin! Something has happened to her."

Aileen's eyes flew wide. "Caitlin? It's Sheilagh you should be concerned about." Aileen stopped abruptly to regard her son's face. Suddenly she realized that part of Clay's enthusiasm for his job at Emerald was due to his feelings for Caitlin. Upon the mention of Sheilagh's name, his face had a bewildered look. She realized it was true that he knew nothing of Sheilagh's pregnancy; and sadly, he was now in love with Caitlin. The tragedy of her son's situation hit Aileen full force, and her heart broke.

Robert spoke. "Clay, there is no way to say this gently. Sheilagh is pregnant. She tried to abort the child today, but she failed."

Clay's face went ashen from the shock, sweat broke out on his brow, and his hands were shaking as he slowly sank deeper into the chair. "Is she all right?"

Robert nodded. "Yes, son. She's resting at home. Naturally Patrick wouldn't go into detail over the phone."

"Of course," Clay replied.

Robert continued. "It's your baby, Clay, and the Killians feel you should do the right thing, as Patrick said, and marry Sheilagh. Give the baby your name."

Clay stared at the concern and caring in his parents' faces. Guilt stabbed him as he realized how much he had disappointed his parents. He had ruined not only his life, but Sheilagh's and Caitlin's as well.

"Oh, God!" he groaned under his breath. *My sweet Caitlin. What have I done to you? Now you have to know the truth. I would have continued pretending that Sheilagh and I had not made love. But now there is proof that we did. What a cruel reminder.*

Earlier that day with Caitlin he had felt as if he were at the crest of a fabulous roller coaster ride. Now his life was traveling downward at breakneck speed into a valley he was not sure he would ever escape. He felt his life was over when it should be just beginning. The dream of him and Caitlin being together shattered around him.

He wished he could cry, but his father might not approve. He swallowed his pain. Fear filled his eyes as he looked at his parents. How ironic, he thought fleetingly. For years he'd prayed that Sheilagh would be his. Now she would be.

Clay's mouth had gone dry. He barely croaked out the words. "I'll marry her."

Chapter 24

MARY MARGARET HAD long ago put away any hope of having a close relationship with her husband. Once she turned away from Patrick, she tried to bond with her children, but she knew that children grow up and leave home. She had tried to control and shape them in their early years, and as they got older, she tried to influence their career choices. Mary Margaret had become a desperate woman in her attempt to keep Sheilagh from moving to New York.

For the rest of her life, Mary Margaret would never forget the image of Sheilagh lying on the cold, tiled bathroom floor. Her beautiful child had mutilated herself, and Mary Margaret blamed herself.

Not once did she think of the moral implications of the abortion. Not once did she think of the unborn fetus, the condemnation of the Catholic church. She thought only of saving her daughter's life.

She was angry at Sheilagh for jeopardizing her health. She knew she'd been too abrupt with her, but she knew that every lost second could make a difference for the rest of Sheilagh's life.

When it was over, Mary Margaret wanted to forget it all; the lye, the terror, the doctor, the baby.

Over the years, she had developed an effective denial system. If her daughter was a good actress, Mary Margaret was an even better one. She convinced herself she could mend her world by pushing for this marriage between Clay and Sheilagh.

She wanted Sheilagh to be a responsible person, but more important, she wanted her to remain in Chicago, near her home. The two of them had battled mightily over this point. Sheilagh still insisted she would one day get to New York and Broadway. Mary Margaret vowed to do everything in her power to keep her from that bohemian life-style. She believed that she knew what was best for her daughter. Sheilagh would discover that happiness in life was simply finding the right husband. If only Mary Margaret could convince her.

All these years Mary Margaret had bragged about Sheilagh's achievements to her friends and played down her rebelliousness. She wanted her friends to think Sheilagh was a prize to be captured, hopefully by one of their sons.

Sheilagh's sudden marriage to Clay Burke would come as a shock to everyone. Mary Margaret hoped not too many of her friends would guess the cause for the sudden nuptials. She had an explanation ready. She was filled with anxiety as she prepared to defend her position to her friends. What if they didn't believe her? What if they ostracized her? What if Sheilagh didn't cooperate? She was so headstrong.

For the first time in her life, Mary Margaret had doubts. Sheilagh was an adult now. She might acquiesce for now, but what about in a year or two? Had Mary Margaret really won? Or was her victory an illusion?

Mary Margaret spread the lie she had concocted for her society friends as they gathered for luncheon at the South Shore Country Club and in the couturier fitting rooms at Carson Pirie Scott and Company. The story was told and retold, and no one believed it.

Women craned their necks over the pages of *Native Son*, the best-selling novel of the year by Richard Wright, pretending they understood a black man's experience, and clucked their tongues. "Dahling, you don't believe a word of it now, do you?" a middle-aged society doyenne inquired of her younger counterpart as they lounged on wide-striped canvas chairs amid the aroma of coconut oil on hot summer skins and fresh-cut limes for icy vodka gimlets.

"Nevah," the young matron proclaimed affecting an eastern accent, which was all the rage that year. "Sheelah Killian nevah had any interest whatsoevah in marriage."

"Mary Margaret Killian would have thought nothing of booking St. Peter's in Rome for the nuptials, I can tell you that," replied a minor league meat-packing heiress. "Instead there is no mention of a wedding ceremony. Only this reception at the Sherman House."

"Sheelah must have gohtten huhself pragnant." The young matron pronounced everyone's suspicions aloud as she sucked on the pearl-tipped mouthpiece of her black onyx cigarette holder.

"Do you think we ought to attend?" the heiress inquired.

"Nevah. How in good cohnscience could we pohssibly allow Mary Mahrgret to think we condone huh buhavior?"

"That's right," the middle-aged woman said. "She's been told, discreetly, of course, how to handle such unfortunate situations. She should have packed that daughter off to Switzerland. Instead, she has the effrontery to think we could be hoodwinked. I vote for the boycott. Mary Margaret needs to be taught a lesson."

The reception at the Sherman House would be a disaster, Mary Margaret realized as envelope after envelope arrived in the mail, all of them regrets.

"I've gone to so much effort! I ordered the flowers from Hazel Bodkins, paying double what they're worth because she's the only 'accepted' florist in town!" Mary Margaret wailed to Sheilagh one afternoon as they sat on the terrace.

"I wouldn't worry about it. They aren't your real friends anyway." Sheilagh sunk her teeth into a crunchy kosher dill pickle.

Mary Margaret's eyes formed horror-stricken circles. "Of course they're my friends. If I don't have them, I have nothing!" She wrung her hands and fled the terrace, the folds of her chiffon morning gown flapping about her heels.

As Sheilagh gazed around the ballroom the night of the reception, she marveled at their Catholic friends. She would have thought they'd see through her mother's lie and not dare to mingle with the Killians for fear that the taint of Sheilagh's sin would stain their own lives. Such was not the case. Sheilagh was certain every name from the roster of Ascension Church was present. Mary Margaret had fought Patrick when he had insisted his employees, clients, and salesmen be invited. Patrick had won the argument since he was paying the bill.

Sheilagh hid her pain. She retold her mother's lie of her and Clay eloping in New York and her supposed realization that her life was to be found in Chicago and not on the stage as she had always thought. She lied to employees, she lied to her high school friends. Mary Margaret even forbade Sheilagh from confessing her sin of attempted abortion in the confessional, which was fine by Sheilagh, because she did not believe in sin or confession or God anymore. She believed in pain; the pain she felt and the pain she had caused.

Sheilagh could barely look at Caitlin without wanting to cry. A wide chasm of anguish kept them apart. Caitlin retreated into work or closeted herself in her room and read. Sheilagh kept her distance, hoping that time would heal them all. In the end, she knew that was a lie, too.

Mary Margaret had arranged for Sheilagh and Clay to be married by a justice of the peace in Milwaukee. The ceremony was over in five minutes. They did not kiss. There were no flowers, no music, no friends, and no joy. Caitlin and Michael remained at home. Only Mary Margaret and Patrick, and Aileen and Robert Burke, attended. After the ceremony, Clay drove his parents' car to an inn south of Milwaukee where they would spend their wedding night.

When Sheilagh walked into the room decorated in Wedgewood blue and white, with a four-poster canopy bed, oval braided rugs, and chintz settee by the fireplace, tears welled in her eyes. A dozen yellow roses filled a country crockery vase. There was a bottle of champagne chilling in a copper bucket filled with ice.

She looked over at Clay, who was putting her suitcase on the luggage valet.

"It's beautiful, Clay, but . . . you shouldn't have done this."

"Why not?"

"I don't deserve it," she said, and finally let her tears fall.

Clay put his arms around her and held her as she sobbed her heart out. "This is all we have, Sheilagh. Let's try to make the best of it."

She felt her stomach knot. "I can't, Clay. You love Caitlin."

"I know," he said softly. "So do you."

Sheilagh felt a new wave of tears coming on. Clay walked her to the bed, where they sat on the edge while she cried.

Clay didn't make love to Sheilagh that night. Instead, he held and comforted her until dawn. He said very little. There were too many of his own tears in the way.

Now they were officially man and wife, and were expected to live together. In Sheilagh's mind, they acted more like a couple who had just divorced. Clay telephoned her from his office at Emerald to discuss the apartment he was renting for them. He kept his conversation polite but to the point and unemotional. There were no words of endearment, not a single note of recrimination. He felt just as guilty as she and was willing to accept his part of the responsibility. For that and that alone, Sheilagh loved Clay.

She watched him as he crossed the ballroom toward Caitlin, who stood with her back to him. His strides were purposeful and anxious. She watched as Caitlin's shoulders straightened and her head tilted to the side, as if she intuitively felt his presence. Sheilagh could see her sister's cheeks begin to glow and her mouth turn upward, as if only he could ever make her smile. Even in sadness Clay's eyes gleamed. There was an electricity between them that seemed to bounce from one to the other. They were more bonded in their souls than she and Clay would ever be through this child she was carrying. Sheilagh slipped beneath the lead mantle of guilt once again. She should give them their private moment, but she was compelled to spy on them.

Michael was talking to Caitlin.

"Hi, Michael," Clay said. "Mind if I speak with your sister alone for a minute?"

"Naw. Go ahead." Michael slurped the last of his Filbert's root beer and used his empty glass as an excuse to leave them alone.

"We haven't had a chance to talk since all this happened."

"I know," Caitlin said, faking a blithe attitude. But her raspy voice revealed her emotions. "I've been so busy."

Clay took a deep breath and put his hand on her shoulder. Caitlin shrugged it off. "Please, Caitlin. Please don't hate me."

Her chin fell to her chest. She stared down at the richly patterned carpet. "I could never hate you. That's the problem."

"I love you, Cat."

"Clay, don't . . ."

"I have to say this. We're going to be working together, and every time I see you . . . I'll go crazy. I want to hold you. I want to talk to you. Just like we did before. I've never felt so alone in all my life. And I'm scared, Caitlin. I had plans for us. Real plans. I couldn't tell you . . . I thought I was too young to be married. Too unprepared."

"Clay." Caitlin was crying now. She bitterly thought that she was getting used to tears. She carried two handkerchiefs with her at all times, and an extra compact of powder to cover her red nose. She opened her purse and withdrew one of the Irish linen handkerchiefs. She dabbed at her eyes. "I . . . I can't work with you anymore, Clay. It's too hard for me."

He grabbed her elbow. "You can't mean that!"

"It's the best thing. I've told my parents. I didn't tell them why . . . I don't think they know that I love you."

"Patrick hasn't said anything about firing me. I don't understand."

Caitlin lifted her head and faced him. His eyes filled with love and concern. She had spent five years dreaming and wishing that one day she would see that love in Clay's eyes for her. Now she did, and it was hell.

"Father's not going to let you go, Clay. You have to stay here and work for Emerald and make a life for you and Sheilagh . . . and the baby. I'm the one who's leaving."

"What?" Shock riveted Clay's body. "But Emerald is your life, too. You want it more than I do. Where are you going?"

"College . . . for now. After that, I don't know. I'll probably meet someone and get married. Just like my mother has planned for me all along." Caitlin looked away from him at that moment and saw her mother speaking to the wife of one of the Emerald salesmen. "She got her wish after all. Incredible, isn't it? The power she has." Caitlin's derisive words spilled from her mouth. "No matter how much each of us dreamed and worked and planned, Mother's vision overrode all of us. All that hope. What good did it do? No wonder people become cynical as they grow older."

Clay clamped his hands onto Caitlin's shoulders, and he shook her slightly to get her attention. "Listen to me. Don't you ever talk like that. I don't care if the whole world is jaded as long as I know you still believe in—"

"In what, Clay?" she said angrily, like an attacking tiger. "Love?" Her face distorted into a painful grimace.

"Yes."

"Why? So I can just get hurt again? Haven't you figured it out yet, Clay? We grew up this summer. All of us. We found out what the real world is all about. We aren't children anymore. This is life. This is why my mother is the way she is and my father is the way he is. It hurts out here in the world, and I can only make the best of it. Any way I can."

"Oh, Cat. What have I done to you?"

"It's not you, Clay. It's the way it is. Now I just have to go on with my life, too." Caitlin started to walk away from him, then stopped and looked into his eyes one last time. She forced a smile. "Make Emerald the best damn chocolate company in the world for me. Will you do that?"

"Yeah, sure," he replied, and swallowed a groan. He watched her walk away and wondered if anyone else noticed how the lights dimmed once Caitlin was gone.

September 1939
South Bend, Indiana

ST. MARY OF the Woods College was an all-girls Catholic
school, but Caitlin wouldn't have guessed it on the first
day of admissions, because everywhere she looked, she saw
boys. Men. Notre Dame men. They rode in "woodies," eight
and nine to a car. They walked across the highway to gawk
at the freshmen girls and to pick out their dates for the year.

Mary Margaret drove Caitlin to South Bend that first trip,
but they agreed that Caitlin would ride the South Shore train
home to Oak Park for the Thanksgiving and Christmas holidays. She was not but two hours from home, and suddenly she
felt as if she were on another planet.

Mary Margaret parked the car and helped Caitlin with her
suitcases, which held the latest fall fashions. She had a dozen
new skirt and sweater outfits, new saddle shoes, gloves, hats
for daily mass, dress pumps, a new tweed coat, and a new
black leather purse. Caitlin had never owned so many new
things all at once. Mary Margaret had taken her on a shopping
spree to Marshall Field's, Carson Pirie Scott, and I Magnin. It
didn't take Caitlin long to realize that Mary Margaret intended
for her to shop for a husband between her midterms and
research papers.

Caitlin looked at the Notre Dame boys, who looked back
at her. Twice she heard wolf whistles and realized they were
directed at her. In an odd way, they did make her feel good.
One red-haired boy came riding by on a bicycle and tipped his
British tweed touring cap and winked. She smiled at him. The
boy turned the bike around and was about to speak to her when
an approaching nun ran him off.

Caitlin looked to her mother and was surprised to see a
satisfied smile on her face.

"I think you're going to have your own stag line this year, Caitlin." Mary Margaret continued to survey the well-dressed young men who rode in nice cars up and down the highway. She saw brothers of sisters who came to St. Mary's and knew that even if Sheilagh had ruined her chances for a good marriage and a proper wedding, Caitlin would regain her position with her society friends.

"Come along, Caitlin. I'm wasting time."

Mary Margaret carried hatboxes while Caitlin lugged two huge suitcases into her dorm room. To her surprise, she found that her roommate had already been to the room and gone.

On one of the twin beds were two giant pandas of the county fair variety, one black and white, one pink and green. The far wall adjacent to the window wall was covered in pennants of nearly every Ivy League college. Caitlin instantly noticed that the Notre Dame pennant was not represented. On the desk was an array of perfume bottles that would put a department store to shame. Evening in Paris, Shalimar, Ambush, Chanel No. 5; they were all there.

Caitlin opened the closet. Over three-fourths of the storage space was filled with clothes, shoes, hats, scarves, and jewelry. "Just where am I supposed to put my things?"

"It's simple, dear. Take some of her things out, put them on her bed, and let her worry about it."

For once, Caitlin thought her mother had made sense. She immediately set out to do just that.

"I'll get the last of your boxes out of the car," Mary Margaret said. "And then I'm afraid I must start back. I have an art gallery opening I promised Linda Falladay I would attend with her."

Caitlin nodded her assent as she came out of the closet with an armful of her roommate's dresses still on the hangers. She had just plopped them on the bed when a silver-haired girl dressed in a red blouse and black houndstooth skirt came bouncing into the room.

"Hey! What are you doing?"

Caitlin spun around and came face-to-face with the most beautiful girl she'd ever seen. "I'm cursed." Caitlin laughed to herself.

The girl pointed to the bed. "What's your period got to do with my clothes?"

Caitlin laughed again. "I meant it must be my fate to have to live with beautiful sisters and roommates. Hi, I'm Caitlin, your roommate. I was making room for my clothes. You're a closet hog."

The beautiful girl with the heart-shaped face, alabaster skin, jet black eyes, and thick, smoky eyelashes giggled to herself. "I'm sorry. I guess I didn't think. I've never shared a room with anyone. I've never had to share anything. I'm an only child."

"I'm not."

"Good." The girl stuck out her hand. "I'm Anne Darling of the New York Darlings. My mother died when I was three, and I've been spoiled rotten by my daddy ever since."

"Oh, God." Caitlin rolled her eyes as she realized she had seen plenty of Anne's type amongst her mother's Gold Coast friends. She suspected Anne's father had sent her here for the nuns to "straighten out."

"I know what you're thinking, and it's all true. He is trying to get rid of me. He could have sent me to Vanderbilt or Radcliffe, but my grades weren't good enough, and besides, it would be too easy for my boyfriends to find me there. Now I'm stuck in the cornfields of Indiana and should stay out of trouble."

"Does he know that Notre Dame is across the street?"

"Yeah, but he thinks good Catholic boys will leave me alone."

"Is he kidding?"

"No. He's Methodist. I lied on my application."

Caitlin burst out laughing. "I think I like you, Anne Darling."

"Good. I like you, too. Now, what do you say we find a place to put all this stuff?"

After hurdling the challenge of storing two complete wardrobes in a closet that had obviously been constructed for the meager belongings of novitiates, Caitlin and Anne plunged into life . . . academic and social. Caitlin pressed Anne to study; Anne pressed Caitlin to play.

Caitlin did not tell Anne about Clay or the baby. She kept Sheilagh's secret and pretended to herself that none of it had ever happened. She forced herself to look at the world through a new pair of glasses. She went to the Notre Dame football games and rode the bus with other St. Mary's girls to the away games. Plenty of boys asked her out for a hamburger or a study date, and she felt sorry for them when she turned them down. She couldn't tell them she was already in love. She wrote home to her parents once a week, went to daily mass, studied, and like the rest of America, followed the growing crisis in Europe.

Caitlin talked little about her life in Chicago except when someone inquired if it was true that she was the Emerald heiress. After two months at college, she was dubbed "the chocolate queen." Once in a while she would expound about chocolate, particularly when the school kitchens tried to shave their costs by cutting back on the cocoa in the brownies, a foreshadowing of the rationing to come.

Caitlin never telephoned Clay and seldom called home. Michael placed a call to her twice without his parents knowing, until the bill came and he was grounded for a week. Mary Margaret insisted that only letters be exchanged, to cut costs. Caitlin never understood this since her mother was spending freely on the nearly finished summer home in Lake Geneva. She could only guess at her mother's motives, which usually involved wanting to maintain control.

The summer leaves turned to gold and scarlet in October. By the end of November the trees were bare, the leaves had all been burned, and the last of the pungent smoke had left the cold Indiana air. Thanksgiving arrived, and Caitlin packed to go home.

"Well, matey, are you sure you won't change your mind and come with me to New York for the holiday?" Anne asked.

"My mother would have a cow. Thanksgiving is a big deal at the Killian house."

Anne looked at the forlorn expression on Caitlin's face as she folded a black angora sweater and placed it in her suitcase. "You look like you're going to an Irish wake. What's back there that's got you so spooked?"

"Nothing." Caitlin ground her teeth.

Anne sat down next to the suitcase so that Caitlin could not escape this confrontation. "Tell me."

Caitlin folded a tweed skirt. "I don't know what you're talking about."

"You don't, huh? Well, it's like this. I've been living with you for three months, which is a record in my book since most people bore me to death after an hour or two, especially boys, but that's a different subject. You're smart and ambitious. You take this college thing pretty seriously, which, of course, I don't. You go through the motions of campus life here like a machine. You laugh when you're supposed to laugh, study, eat, sleep, and even go out when you can't think of anything else to do. You keep your mouth shut so tight, I'm amazed any air escapes at all. I am horrendously intrigued by you. Nobody is this controlled. Not once have you ever lost it . . . not even when Sister Angela gave you that C on your Greek mythology report, which we all knew was the best in the class. How do you stay so perfectly in control? And better yet, why?"

"Why must you always be so outrageous? Why so many boyfriends? You collect them like charms. Why isn't one enough?"

"Why not, is my answer." Anne laughed. "I like the attention. It makes up for the fact that my father never gave me enough of his time. There was always plenty of money, new clothes, new anythings . . . but never any of him."

"Big deal. Lots of us never got any attention from our fathers. That's just the way it is." Caitlin did not realize how forcefully she shoved a pair of wool trousers into the suitcase.

Anne watched the quick, jabbing movements. "What are you going to do about it?"

"Nothing."

Anne shook her head. "Don't kid a kidder. We all *do* something to get their attention. I studied all the options before I decided. I could become valedictorian, homecoming queen, marry a Rockefeller, take over Daddy's business, eat too much, drink too much . . . all those things. I chose Outrageous Behavior. It's not fattening and it's a lot of fun."

"Fine," Caitlin said, searching her drawer for her new black leather gloves. "You live your life your way and I'll live mine my way. Okay?"

Anne heaved a resigned sigh. "That's one of my faults too. I try to fix things. I just wanted to be your friend."

Caitlin closed her suitcase. She wished with all her heart she could tell Anne about Clay, but her loyalties were with her family. "I have to go. I'll be late for my train." She put on her new tweed coat and adjusted a charcoal gray French beret on her head. She forced a smile. "Have a great time in New York. I'll see you Sunday." Caitlin gave Anne a hug and left.

Anne sat cross-legged on the bed, her chin in her palm, contemplating Caitlin's behavior. "You are a riddle, Caitlin Killian. What makes you run so hard? What makes you so tough? If it takes me all year, I'm going to find out what makes you tick."

November 1939

"The Newport of the West," Lake Geneva had been home to the Potawatomi Indians until the 1830s when the white man stumbled upon the edge of a glittering body of crystal water and laid claim to it. Shortly after the Civil War, the first of many mansions was built by Sheldon Sturges. As early as 1873, Lake Geneva was becoming a summer resort, and the first Lady of the Lake side-wheel, double-decker steam launch began its daily excursions around the lake. By the turn of the century, Lake Geneva was home to the finest Chicago families. The mansions bore names like Snug Harbor, Green Gables, Wychwood, the Swift home at Villa Hortensia, Wadsworth Hall, and Glen Fern, built by the Sears family.

By 1939 the heyday of Lake Geneva was over, but no one could have told Mary Margaret Killian that. She had been obsessed with the area ever since she overheard one of her rich classmates in elementary school talk about going to an aquatic meet at Lake Geneva. Mary Margaret had heard tales of huge schooners, yachts, and boating parties. She envisioned the inside of the mansions her classmate had seen, the lawn tennis, the afternoon teas and luncheons under stately oak trees. There were dinner parties and wedding receptions attended by elegantly dressed women and handsome men. Wagnerian opera recordings were played on Victrolas on the aft deck of a yacht called *Passaic*, owned by the Crane family. Huge English roses were cultivated in the lavishly planned gardens and glass-domed conservatories and then arranged in opulent bouquets throughout the mansions.

Week after week Mary Margaret would listen to her classmate tell stories of their visits to Lake Geneva. Month after month Mary Margaret dreamed of one day living on the shores of that crystal lake. To her, Lake Geneva was a place of elegance, manners, and money. She was willing to pay any price to own her dream.

After the debacle of Sheilagh's wedding and the loss of her society connections, Mary Margaret especially needed to make her childhood dream come true. Lake Geneva and the glorious mansion she had built there was her last chance to snare a position for herself in the elitist circles that she believed would bring her happiness.

By Thanksgiving the house was finally completed. She took Michael out of school on the Tuesday before Thanksgiving and drove up to the lake with everything she would need for the holiday. She stopped at the A&P and bought the turkey, potatoes, butternut squash, dinner rolls, the ingredients for salad, dressing, and pumpkin pies. There were cranberries to sweeten and boil until they popped and oozed a thick, jellied syrup, cookies to bake, and dates to fill with pecan halves and roll in sugar. Mary Margaret wanted this holiday to be picture-perfect. Then maybe she could pretend she didn't feel the loss each time she went to the mailbox and found it bereft of charity and social invitations.

Sheilagh and Clay were to follow the next day with Patrick. It was Sheilagh who arranged for them to drive to Lake Geneva with her father. Though her relationship with Patrick was strained, she sought his company as a buffer between herself and Clay.

What Sheilagh and Clay shared these days was guilt and resentment. They blamed themselves for hurting the other. They loaded guilt upon their shoulders whenever the conversation turned to Caitlin. Over the months they talked less and less.

Sheilagh pretended to enjoy the time she shared with her mother decorating the Lake Geneva house. She found she could go three, maybe five hours at a stretch without thinking of her lost career. But she could never erase her dream completely. And she knew Clay resented her for denying him Caitlin.

They were both hiding behind masks of pretense, struggling to move forward in their lives, but what they actually accomplished was an ever-widening chasm between them.

Their lack of communication led to withdrawl from each other. Their lovemaking had been infrequent from the start; now it was nonexistent.

Sheilagh had planned and executed all the Thanksgiving decorations. She had made two pinecone wreaths for the back door and over the fireplace, and had decorated grapevine garlands with dried fall flowers, cones, and pods to hang around the double front doors. She had made an enormous cornucopia out of papier-mâché and filled it with moss, ribbons, gourds, Indian corn, squash, and dried golden yarrow and German statice. She wanted the house to look as festive as she possibly could for Caitlin.

She missed Caitlin more than she had ever dreamed possible. There were times when she would roll over in bed and see Clay alongside her and wish that he were Caitlin. She couldn't talk to Clay, couldn't share secrets and feelings and emotions with him. Mostly she couldn't dream with him. She'd always dreamed with Caitlin. Her sister used to egg her on and make her expand on her visions of acting on Broadway. Caitlin made her probe more deeply, asking what entreé Sheilagh would order if she went to Sardi's. What would she drink? What color was the negligee she would buy if she ever went to Saks Fifth Avenue? Clay never thought to ask such questions. The pain of separation from her sister drove deeply into Sheilagh's heart. She intended Thanksgiving to be nothing less than perfect for Caitlin.

Caitlin took the train directly to Lake Geneva and hired a cab at the train station. The cabbie was a talkative man who had worked in Chicago for twenty years before moving to the area. She allowed him to rattle on while her anticipation grew. For three months she had marked off the days until her homecoming. She had drawn the picture of her family reunion a thousand different ways in a hundred different mediums. And in all of them she had painted herself happy. Now that the moment was upon her, she was suddenly frightened. She could no longer dream. This was reality.

As they came down the drive from Manning's Point, past Buttons Bay toward the Lake Geneva Golf Club, the surrounding homes were huge Queen Anne and Victorian monstrosities built in an age when servants were cheap and dependable. Huge expanses of glass looked out across the bay to Kinney's Point and across the narrows to other similarly constructed manses. Caitlin had been up to Lake Geneva only twice and remembered little about it, except that it was too far from her beloved chocolate factory in Chicago . . . and Clay.

The cab dropped her off in the brick-paved driveway of the new Killian summer home. She paid the driver with a ten-dollar bill, though she never took her eyes off the house in front of her.

"Here's yer change, miss," the man was saying. Caitlin was so busy taking in the beautiful architecture that she did not hear him. He scratched the gray and red stubble on his cheek. "Doncha want yer change?"

"No. Keep it," she said as she picked up her suitcase and started up the front walk.

The desiduous trees had long since lost their leaves and bore a gossamer-thin cloak of frost on their branches. The sky stretched silver and gray above her, with no sign of sun or warmth to kill the gloom. The air was cold and brittle and smelled of pungent smoke from wood-burning fireplaces within the ostentatious houses. The placid lake reflected the sky like a mirror. Inside the house, lamps were being turned on, fires lit, while outside, lanterns welcomed visitors and enticed them to come inside.

Never before had Caitlin felt so much like a stranger. She looked at the house, with its long verandas that wrapped around the front and back; huge dormers on the third floor with crisscross sheer curtains and enormous blue and white delft urns filled with yellow and rust chrysanthemums. Caitlin had had no part in the planning, executing, or decorating of this house. She'd never seen the blueprints or the carpet selections or the furniture. Mary Margaret had never inquired what kind of wallpaper she would like for her bedroom on the second floor with its view of the bay. Caitlin had decided to go away to college, and it was as if she had been excommunicated from the family.

The house was built of brick and wood, solid, massive, and imposing. On the road side was a three-car garage, which sat at a forty-five-degree angle to the back door. The "back door" entrance was just as formal as the front door, which opened onto the sprawling lawn that sloped down the hill to the water's edge. On either side of the back door were Ionic columns that supported the semicircular portico. Above the door was a fan-shaped window in leaded glass. As Caitlin walked up to the door, light from within bled through the beveled panes and spilled onto the concrete steps, making tiny puddles of dancing light.

A huge pinecone wreath with a gold and green velvet bow hung on the door. Caitlin lifted her gloved hand and touched one of the lacquered cones. "Sheilagh."

Her heart caught in her throat. Immersed in the pages of Greek mythology, theology, and math, she had nearly forgotten about her sister. About Clay. Suddenly she realized she was home. Home . . . where all the pain was.

She knocked on the door.

How odd, she thought, *knocking on my own door. I should go straight in. It's my house, too, isn't it?*

She knocked again.

She could hear voices within. Her father. Her mother. Michael. Was it . . . Sheilagh? Yes, she thought. Sheilagh was there. It was her footsteps skipping toward the door with that light toe and heavy heel walk that caused her to swing her hips seductively.

The heavy brass door latch clicked. The door swung open with a rush of wind that lifted Sheilagh's luxurious hair off her face. Since there was no sun to cause the radiant glow around Sheilagh, Caitlin assumed the light emanated from her sister's eyes.

"Caitlin! You're here ! You're finally here!" Sheilagh threw her arms around Caitlin and pulled her into the house with a huge bear hug.

Caitlin drew back and looked at Sheilagh's abdomen.

"You're huge!" she blurted, then tried to correct herself. "I mean, I had forgotten that you're five months along now."

Sheilagh saw the pain in Caitlin's eyes. She wanted to wipe it away. "Oh, I know," Sheilagh said lightheartedly, hoping humor would make Caitlin forget. "I'm as fat as a pig. It's rather a shock to me, too."

Caitlin's laugh was strained as she took her cue from Sheilagh.

"I told Clay he should go down to the station and meet your train, but he's still poring over some damn report. Paperwork . . . that's all he does. Boring, isn't it?"

"Yeah," Caitlin breathed between Sheilagh's exuberant chatter.

"Here, let me help you with that suitcase." Sheilagh bent over to grab the handle, but Caitlin pushed her aside.

"No. You shouldn't lift it. It's too heavy."

"Gawd. You sound like Clay. I can't drive anymore, you know. That's why I couldn't come down to the station myself. It's such a pain in the ass, Cat. It really is. Everybody makes such a big deal about this pregnancy thing. But come on. Everybody is waiting to see you. We want to hear all about college . . . Tell us everything. Every tiny detail," Sheilagh said, closing the door behind her sister.

Caitlin didn't know what had happened to Sheilagh that she would be wanting to know about dull campus life. Not

Sheilagh, whose conversation had been sprinkled with famous names and places as if she'd known them all personally and visited each exotic city at least once. What had happened to the Sheilagh Caitlin had left behind?

Caitlin felt like a midnight traveler coming to the last vacant hotel after a long journey. She did not know her way down the hall to the kitchen or breakfast room. Nothing was familiar to her, since her mother had not moved a single item from the Oak Park house to inhabit the new summer home. The furniture was new. The drapes were in the latest flowered chintzes; the flooring was new linoleum; the plants, vases, china, pictures on the walls, were all new. They were simply items that had been tastefully chosen but had no connection to the family.

Caitlin was unbuttoning her coat in the back hall when she heard muffled steps on the carpet that ran up the wooden staircase in the front vestibule. They were the sounds of her father's feet, even and strong. Michael's footfalls came hurriedly from the dining room. The light, precise steps were her mother's. But it was the slow steps, the halting steps, that she had waited three months to hear . . . Clay's footsteps.

He was the last in the room, and his presence filled it. She caught glimpses of him between hugs from Michael, a pat on the shoulder from her father, and a stiff embrace from her mother. Voices chirped animatedly about dinner preparations, the house, the view from the living room, the neighbor's boat they had sailed on that afternoon. But Caitlin heard none of it, only a dim buzz in her ears. She looked at Clay, and he looked at her. She thought she could detect the very intake of his breath when she smiled at him, her ears were so acutely tuned into him.

Clay's smile was wan. Gone was the light in his eyes and the glow in his skin. His shoulders slumped, though only Caitlin would notice. There were stress lines in his forehead and around his mouth. He looked as if he had aged fifteen years.

"Hello, Caitlin," he said, as if he were greeting the milkman. He moved past Sheilagh, leaned over, and brushed the crest of her cheek with his lips. It was the first time Caitlin did not feel that spark of electricity between them.

He stood and put a hand on Caitlin's shoulder. "You look . . . wonderful," he said hoarsely, and then went back into the living room and continued stoking the fire he had just built in the hearth.

Sheilagh instantly put her arm around Caitlin. "I can't wait to show you the house!"

Still stunned at her reaction to Clay and his lack of reaction to her, she turned to her sister. "I'd love it."

Mary Margaret's smile was wide and powerful. She gazed down at her daughters like a Greek goddess. "Sheilagh has been such a help to me, Caitlin. I always knew she would take to domestic work like a champ. She not only helped select and design the draperies, but she sewed everything you see on the second floor. She learned to wallpaper and did a fabulous job on the nursery."

"Nursery?" Caitlin's eyes went to Sheilagh.

"We added another room. It's a fact of life; we're all getting older and the grandchildren will be a-comin'." Sheilagh laughed good-naturedly.

"Of course. Good idea," Caitlin replied hesitantly.

She followed Sheilagh to the dining room and listened with half an ear as she described the silk draperies, the frescoed paintings on the walls and ceiling, and the Hepplewhite table and chairs. "Mother paid a fortune for this Persian rug, but the ends keep curling up, and twice Mother has nearly tripped over it. She tried to take it back to the dealer, but he's being really nasty about it. He says it was a consignment rug and he's already paid off the owner, and the only way he'll take it back is to resell it. Anyway, its the only snag we ran into while we were decorating, so I guess we didn't do too badly." Sheilagh smiled and then continued on with her tour.

Caitlin felt as if the world had tipped ever so slightly out of balance. Everything and everybody were different somehow, yet she could not see exactly how they were different. Perhaps it was she herself who had changed. Suddenly she was no longer part of the family. Their daily lives did not include her. She was the observer, and for the first time she saw all the Killians as the outside world saw them.

Patiently she went from room to room and up the stairs. She *ooohed* and *ahhhed* at the appropriate moments. Every painting, vase, bedspread, and rug was designer-perfect. The house was a vision of grace and charm. From the bottle green leather chairs clustered around the fireplace to the complete set of shiny French copper cookware that hung above the stove in the modern kitchen, the house was Mary Margaret's dream come true. As Caitlin went through the rituals of unpacking, making up her bed with clean linens, helping make pumpkin pies, and setting the table for the evening meal, she found that, oddly enough, she had never seen Mary Margaret quite so genuinely happy.

The family was forced to remain indoors as the temperature dropped below freezing that night. Michael brought out a jigsaw puzzle after dinner, which the men began assembling while the women washed the dishes. The radio announcer read the news report about the crisis in Europe. Caitlin could hear her father's voice grow slurred and thick as he drank his after-dinner Manhattan. She ground her teeth as she dried the crystal goblets with a dish towel. For the first time she realized how much her own attitudes and behaviors were cut by family patterns.

Sheilagh put down her towel. "I think I'll see how the puzzle is coming."

As she entered the living room, where Patrick, Michael, and Clay were working on the puzzle at a card table, her foot caught on the edge of the Persian rug and she lost her balance. "Auughhh!"

Without thinking, Clay was on his feet to catch her.

Caitlin dashed through the kitchen, with Mary Margaret right behind her.

Michael bolted out of his chair so fast, he jostled the table and sent half the puzzle pieces sailing to the floor.

"Sheilagh!" Clay yelled.

"Sheilagh!" Caitlin cried out as she dashed for her sister.

None of them reached her in time. She landed on the floor stomach-first with a heavy thud. Caitlin halted in her steps.

At first Sheilagh thought it was the surprise of the fall that kept her from breathing. Then she realized the wind had been knocked out of her. A look of panic shot across her face. She gulped at the air, gasped, and then finally caught her breath. She could nearly feel the rush of oxygen into her numb body. Her trembling hands became still.

Sheilagh's maternity top was yanked up nearly to her breasts, revealing the stretched skirt fabric over her protruding abdomen. She remained calm as the rest of the family hovered around her, helping her to her feet, fussing over her.

"Are you all right?" Clay said, his eyes filled with concern.

"Yes, I'm fine."

"How do you know? Maybe there's been some internal damage," Mary Margaret said. "We should call the doctor.

A fall like this is no trifling matter."

"Mother, puuleeeze," Sheilagh groaned. "I'll be fine. I think I hit face-first, not stomach-first."

"Your mother is right, Sheilagh," Clay said.

"Oh, God, will you two stop? You'd think no one had ever had a baby before." Sheilagh laughed and gently laid her hand against Clay's cheek. She looked up at him with nearly adoring eyes.

Caitlin felt her stomach lurch—once, then twice. She felt as if she herself had hit the floor. *They're married,* she told herself. *They love each other. It's in their eyes. Clay probably never thinks of me at all. Sheilagh looks as if she likes being a wife . . . just as mother predicted she would.*

What had happened? Sheilagh seemed not to feel a single ounce of grief or remorse over losing her acting career. How could she change her mind so quickly? And Clay . . . he seemed to dote on Sheilagh now, and she accepted his attention as if it were her due. Obviously Caitlin's first impression had been wrong when she had seen them at the back door. They were in love. They were going to have a baby. Everything about their situation was natural and expected. The only misfit in this scenario was Caitlin.

"Sheilagh, you must be more careful," Mary Margaret scolded as she patted the folds out of Sheilagh's skirt.

"I will be, I promise."

Caitlin watched as they moved like a flock of geese into the living room, leaving her behind. Suddenly she understood. Sheilagh was the center of their lives now, still onstage, perhaps still acting out a role or perhaps sincerely feeling the emotions for Clay that Caitlin had read on her face. Maybe Sheilagh did not know herself what she was feeling. Caitlin could only hope that she did . . . for all their sakes.

Thanksgiving Day was much the same as the day before. Food was prepared and consumed. Dishes were washed. Fires were built and burned down to embers. Clothes were washed in the new Maytag washer and hung to dry on the clothesline in the basement since it was too cold to hang them outdoors. Sheilagh complained of being tired, which was unusual for a woman in her fifth month of pregnancy. Mary Margaret telephoned the local doctor and interrupted his holiday meal, but she would not be put off this time. Because Sheilagh was not in pain, nor was there any bleeding or sign of contractions, the doctor told Mary Margaret that the fall had not harmed mother or baby.

Despite the doctor's advice, Mary Margaret worried about Sheilagh all day.

Clay made several business calls to his salesmen to wish them a happy holiday. Patrick went for a long walk, came back, and drank two martinis while poking at the oak logs in the fireplace. His thoughts seemed a million miles away. Michael anxiously awaited a phone call from his friend Tim.

Caitlin watched Michael jump when the phone rang. He raced to the alcove in the hallway where a padded bench had been built into the wall. Caitlin flipped through a *Vanity Fair* magazine, then tossed it onto the pile of crumpled copies of the *Chicago Tribune* and picked up the latest copy of *Look* magazine. Michael came back to the living room and heaved himself onto the overstuffed down sofa.

"What's the matter?" Caitlin asked, not taking her eyes off the article about Cary Grant.

"Another wrong number."

"Another? How many have there been?" Caitlin inquired.

"Three today. Four yesterday. How can Tim call me if somebody is always tying up the line?" He threw his hands in the air, then clutched them on their descent and let them land together in his lap. His gaze did not waver from his folded hands as he contemplated his dilemma.

Patrick, who was sitting in the leather wing chair reading about the Italian invasion of Greece and the British warships that were now aiding the Greeks, lifted his head. "You didn't say anything about these calls yesterday when I asked you, Michael."

"You said: 'Were there any calls for me?' That's what you asked me. And there weren't," Michael replied.

"Goddamn it, Michael!" Patrick shouted, and rose from his chair, slamming the *Tribune* onto the mahogany coffee table. "When I ask you a question, I expect a truthful answer, not some qualified crack. From now on, I want the truth!"

"I *did* tell the truth!" Michael yelled back with equal force. He felt a flash of omnipotence.

Patrick glared at his son as his cheeks burned with rage, but he held himself in check.

Caitlin watched them both, not knowing what to make of the scene except that somehow the tables had turned in the relationship between father and son. Patrick was impotent against Michael, and they both knew it. There was a cat-and-mouse game going on here that she did not understand. But Michael did.

Patrick finished off his martini, put the glass on top of the *Tribune,* and stalked out of the room.

"Where's he going?" Caitlin asked.

Michael leaned back on the sofa. "To his bedroom, where he'll lock the door and make a telephone call from the other phone."

"What's the big deal?"

Michael's lips formed a cynical pout. "All this time he thought his girlfriend hadn't called him. He goes crazy when he doesn't talk to her. So I made sure I was the one who answered the phone all the time. That way I know she'll hang up. Maybe I can start another fight between them. Maybe then she'll tell him to drop dead."

Caitlin's jaw fell in shock. "What the hell are you talking about, Michael Killian?"

Michael folded his arms behind his head and leaned all the way back against the sofa. "Geezo peezo, Cat. Don't you know anything? Where have you been? Sheilagh knows about him and Shannon . . ."

"Shannon? You even know her name?"

"Yeah. I thought you did, too."

Caitlin felt her stomach lurch. Her sense of security was toppled as if an earthquake had just knocked it on the floor. "No."

"Don't look so shocked, Cat. He's a son of a bitch, and that's all there is to it."

"Oh, God."

"But don't worry, he won't leave us. He'll never break up the family."

"How do you know?"

"Because I've been listening in on his phone calls to her. He's told her that. Says it would cost him too much money. This stupid girl loves him, or says she does. She takes whatever he dishes out. He's got a good thing going. He won't screw it up. That's why he needs my help." Michael smirked.

"He knows you know?"

"He guesses."

"And that's the power you have over him."

"Yep. And I like it. Love it."

"You really hate him, don't you, Michael?"

"Yes, Cat, I really do." He sighed deeply but with too much satisfaction. "I figured out a lot of things while you were gone. I know I'm not gonna ever take any crap from him—or her." He pointed to the kitchen, where Mary Margaret was reading recipes. "I'm gonna do precisely what I want every day of my life. I'm gonna trash this idea of his that I join the football team. I'm taking art instead. I like medicine, and I'm gonna do it if I have to put myself through college by washing dishes and pumping gas. I don't care. I'm gonna get away from that asshole if it's the last thing I do."

A wave of angry heat rose from Michael like a demon. His eyes were glassy and his mouth tense. Caitlin had never seen him like this before. "But yesterday, this morning, everybody seemed so loving . . . so close . . . *I* was the one who felt like a stranger . . . I don't understand."

Michael spun toward her. "Damn . . . sometimes I can't believe you're my sister. You're smarter than this . . . It's a game we play to fool the outsiders, Cat. You know that. Maybe you've been away too long. You forgot how to play."

"What about Sheilagh and Clay?"

"What about 'em? What choice do they have? They're stuck with each other. They might as well have fun playing their game, too."

Silence stretched between them. Michael was right, Caitlin told herself. It was time she moved on to play her own game of life. She had been away from her family long enough now that she was discovering who they were as people and not just her family. They all had more problems than she did. Of them all, she thought perhaps she was the one with the best chance to mend her damaged heart and make some sense out of life.

In that split second Caitlin decided that she wanted to change. She wanted to start over, if that was possible. Mentally she was tossing out all that was old to her. Just as the family had accepted this new house, she would build a new house for herself. Perhaps she would change her major. Junk the liberal arts degree and go for a major in math. She could use math and accounting. She still wanted to run Emerald Chocolates someday; that much she knew. Maybe she could never have Clay, but that didn't mean she couldn't have the other half of her dream. She would find a way to make Emerald world-famous if it was the last thing she did. If Michael could figure out how to manipulate Patrick, then she could, too. She would not ever put limitations on herself again.

She stared into the dying flames in the fireplace and realized she was suddenly homesick for St. Mary's. She missed Anne's kooky antics and the sound of her caring voice. She missed the rush of anticipation before the mixers on the weekends with the Notre Dame boys. She even missed the stimulation that her studies gave her. She was ready to go back. She was ready to create Caitlin Killian any way she saw fit.

Michael blew out a long, resigned breath.

"Guess I'll go get a Filbert's," he said. "You want one?"

"Huh?" She looked at him. Gone was his anger, his aloof, calculating attitude. He wore the mask she'd seen when she came home yesterday.

"No," she said. Then she smiled at the brother she was only just beginning to know.

Chapter 26

*C*AITLIN STARED OUT the dirty window of the South Shore train as it passed through the South Side of Chicago, Whiting, Hammond, past the Gary steel mills, and then stopped at the junction in Michigan City, Indiana.

The passenger car was filled now with Notre Dame and St. Mary's students, a few businessmen, and one woman with three small children, all headed for South Bend after the Thanksgiving holiday.

The only seat open was the one next to Caitlin.

"Do you mind?" a young male voice asked pleasantly.

"Huh?" Caitlin was still watching the boarding passengers through the window. She turned her head and looked up into a pair of sparkling dark eyes.

"This seat. Is there someone sitting here?" he asked with the widest, most pleasant smile Caitlin had ever seen.

"No," she said, sweeping her textbooks and notebook into her lap. "I . . . I guess I didn't realize the train was filling up so quickly."

He plopped down next to her. He lifted his hand and jauntily tossed his blue and black plaid muffler over his shoulder. His straight nose was cherry red from standing in the cold. He wore a black knit cap with the Notre Dame logo pulled down over his hair, and it wasn't until he yanked it off that she realized he was blond. His lashes were black, and so were his eyebrows. With the juxtaposition of his light hair and dark eyes, the light from the incandescent bulbs overhead seemed to bounce up and down on his face. He had straight, even white teeth, which he revealed often through smiling full lips. His cheekbones were high and his jawline strong. He was handsome, but she did not feel the kind of electricity that she had with Clay. This boy was fun-loving and had none of the serious look about him that Clay wore.

"Matthew Lindsey," he said, then clamped his teeth down on one of his gloved fingers, pulled the glove off with his teeth, and shoved his hand toward her. "What's your name?"

"Caitlin Killian." She smiled back at him.

He folded his arms across his chest and leaned back against the seat, adjusting his body so that he faced her more fully. He blatantly scanned the length of her from head to toe. She wore a beret over shoulder-length chestnut hair. Her chesterfield coat was still fully buttoned, and he could see a pair of expensive kid gloves poking out from the welted pockets. She wore a black wool skirt, bobby socks, and black and white saddle shoes with no boots or rubbers. "I'll call you Kit Cat," he announced with a grin.

"What?"

"I have to have a nickname for you."

"Why?"

"Because I like you a lot."

"You don't know me!" Caitlin folded her arms over her chest and mimicked his slouched position. She met his probing gaze. Matthew wore a navy pea coat that fastened with wood and cord frogs across the front. His chinos were tan, his leather oxfords protected by black rubbers.

"You will get to know me, and I will get to know you. Besides, I know a lot about you already."

"Oh, yeah?"

"Yes. You come from a well-to-do family. You live in Chicago. You're Irish. You go to St. Mary's. You left your boyfriend back home . . . maybe even had a fight with him, but that's okay, because I'm here now, so you don't have to worry about him anymore. You're a freshman and you're majoring in liberal arts."

Caitlin glared at this audacious boy. "Besides the fact that you're observant and looked at my textbooks, you just made lucky guesses, that's all."

"And the boyfriend?" He pushed his face closer to hers.

Caitlin backed away from him as she peered deeply into his ebony eyes. "I don't have a boyfriend."

"Liar."

Caitlin turned away from him back to the window.

Matthew touched her shoulder and leaned over to whisper in her ear. "It's okay. I won't ever mention him again if you don't. I want to be your friend."

Caitlin felt tears well up in her eyes. Where had they come from? Why should she want to cry now, in front of a stranger? Why did his compassion touch her? Why was she making a fool of herself? "Why?" was all she could say aloud.

"Because you're probably the most beautiful girl I've ever seen."

"You never saw my sister."

"I'll bet she's not as beautiful on the inside as you are."

"How do you know what I'm like . . . on the inside?" She wiped away a tear before it fell.

"My mother taught me what to look for. Your beauty is in your eyes, Kit Cat."

"Don't call me that."

"Why not?" He touched her hair. It was even more silky than he'd thought.

"Because I'm never going to see you again after today."

"Yes, you will."

"Why should I?"

"Because you need a friend, Kit Cat." He let his hand fall down the length of her arm to the end of her sleeve, banded in black velvet. He touched her hand. It was warm, and his was still cold.

Caitlin felt a hot ball of pain in her throat. She had swallowed it back for a long, long time, and now it wouldn't recede anymore. She *did* need a friend. But she was afraid to trust this Matthew Lindsey, who seemed to have fallen from the sky. She wanted to turn to him, feel his arms around her, and cry her eyes out. She wanted to tell him about Clay, but she couldn't. She could never, ever reveal her secrets.

"If . . . if you're really my friend, then you won't ask me any more questions about him."

"So you did break up over Thanksgiving?"

"Yes." It wasn't really a lie, she told herself. She had come to some grave realizations. In a way, she had finally broken her emotional bond to Clay.

"I'm so sorry, Kit Cat," he said with concern. In a hushed voice he added: "I think he was the biggest fool on earth to let you go."

"He loves somebody else."

"Impossible. What more could he want?"

Finally she turned to him. "Why are you saying all these nice things to me when you don't even know me?"

"Because you need to hear them."

"Is that what you always do on trains back to school? Pick up girls and try to mend their broken hearts? Or is it just that girls are easy pickin's when they're vulnerable?"

"You're smart, too!" he said jubilantly. "I like that."

"You haven't answered my questions."

"Honestly, I've never done this before, but I've seen other guys do it. Some of them are real masters at it. Took me four years of observing them even to try it. You're my first . . ." His voice trailed off as he gazed into her eyes. He touched her cheek, then quickly jerked his hand back. "Soft skin . . . like your heart." His face was serious and deeply earnest. "You'll be the last . . . I hope."

She smiled at him. "I don't believe a word you're saying, you know."

"That's okay. In time, you will." He smiled back.

Matthew Lindsey spent the following thirty days proving to Caitlin that he meant what he said. It was the easiest task he'd ever undertaken, since all he had to do was be himself. He was not a liar, not a cheat, and not a heartbreaker.

He took her out for hot chocolate, went skating with her on Saturday afternoons, and rode the bus with her into town to do their Christmas shopping. He never kissed her or pressed himself on her sexually. He wanted to win her friendship and trust. Day by day, phone call by phone call, outing by outing, Matthew won Caitlin to him. For the first time she found she could go for days without thinking of Clay. Her dreams of him had ceased.

Instead, she thought of Matthew. She thought about herself and what she wanted for herself and not about others' expectations of her. When she signed up for the winter semester, she switched her major to math and science. When she went to the library, she went to Notre Dame's library and met Matthew there. She let him kiss her between the bookstacks and let him fondle her breasts beneath the shelf marked "The Complete Works of Shakespeare." She slept through her eight-o'clock theology class and signed up for a noncredit art appreciation class. Caitlin had begun to live for Caitlin, and she liked it.

As Christmas approached, she received two letters from her mother filled with holiday plans and schedules. The thought of being in Oak Park again, surrounded by Clay and Sheilagh, was more than Caitlin could stand. She was just beginning to heal. If she went back now, she would undo all the work she had accomplished thus far. Matthew wanted her to come to Michigan City with him, but she knew that she needed to spend her holidays without a man. She wanted to know what it was like to be without a father, a brother, a boyfriend, or the man she loved.

Three days before Christmas break, Caitlin turned to Anne, her roommate, and made her boldest move yet.

"Could I go with you to New York for the holidays?" she asked.

Anne spun around in her desk chair. "You'll have to beg harder than that."

"Please?"

"Harder. Try bended knee. That always works. A little groveling doesn't hurt either."

Caitlin sank to the ground. "Please don't make me go back to Chicago. It's so boring and awful there. I've never been anywhere, and you've been all over the world. Please take me with you. Let me see the wonders of the world. Please, please take me with you, O Glorious One." Caitlin gave a mock full-body bow.

Anne burst into laughter. "Adoration . . . nice touch." Anne motioned with her hand for Caitlin to rise.

"So, what do you think?"

"Yes," Anne replied, and turned the page in her biology book.

The next day Caitlin was sprawled across her twin bed, belly-down, her head hanging over the edge, reading her American lit book, which was opened on the floor. The door opened and she saw Anne's black suede high-heeled boots come into view. There was a ring of wet snow around the edges. A Western

Union envelope dropped onto the American lit book.

"Your tickets."

Caitlin picked up the envelope. Inside were two train tickets on the New York Central that would take her to New York City.

Caitlin scrambled off the bed and gave Anne a hug. "Thank you."

"Thank *you*," Anne replied with an emotion-filled whisper.

"I'm coming with you," Matthew said when Caitlin told him of her holiday plans.

"You can't do that. I want some time by myself. I don't want you around."

"Jeez. Thanks a lot," he replied with hurt-filled eyes.

Caitlin sighed. "It's not you, per se. It's just men in general. I just want some time to think about things. My life. You and me. All this stuff. Can you understand that?"

Matthew took her hand. They were sitting in the chapel, which was the safest place for couples to be since hardly anyone came there except during mass. Bob Binchley had told Matthew that he'd gotten his first piece of ass in the chapel. Matthew hadn't believed it at the time, but now that this was the fourth time he'd met Caitlin here, he believed it. Even the seminarians never graced the inside of these doors so far as he could tell. Matthew's only problem with the chapel was that every time he came here, he was preoccupied with visions of marrying Caitlin first . . . then of laying her across the third pew from the back. "I do understand, Kit Cat. I'm three years older than you, so I know a lot more than you do. If you say you need this time, then it's okay. Just don't go to New York and find some other guy and run off with him."

"I'm not going to do that."

"Promise?"

"I promise."

"Good, because I love you, Kit Cat." There, he thought, he'd finally said it. What a relief. She needed to know. He needed to tell her . . . for himself even more than for her.

"You do?"

"Yes. I think I fell for you when I first saw you on the train. I was going to tell you on Christmas Day. I was going to come to Chicago and surprise you. But now you won't be there."

"You were going to come to my house?"

"Sure. Why not? It's not so far. You would have been surprised, huh?"

Caitlin thought of her family. Of Michael and his anger. Of Patrick and his drinking. Of Sheilagh and Clay's pretenses, and of Mary Margaret's constant meddling. Caitlin had not told anyone about Matthew. He was her secret, not theirs.

No, she would not have liked Matthew to surprise her on Christmas Day. Perhaps if he met her family, saw her father drunk or her own face when she looked at Clay, maybe she would lose Matthew. Like a flash, Caitlin realized that he was more precious to her than she had thought. She didn't want to hurt him. She had begun to love him.

"Real surprised," she replied. "Will you call me in New York if I give you the number?"

"Of course I will," he said, and kissed her mouth. "If you want me to."

"Oh, yes, Matthew. I want you to."

This time when he kissed her, he finally allowed his emotions to rush over him. He put his arms around her and drew her to his chest. His kiss became insistent. He touched his tongue to her lips and forced them apart. He began to unbutton her coat. She put her arms around his neck and sank her fingers into the hair at the nape of his neck. He slid her overcoat down her shoulders and let it drop onto the kneeler. She unbuttoned his coat. It fell atop hers.

She pulled him to her as she lay back in the pew. Matthew scrambled on top of her. Caitlin kissed him with equal ardor, and both of them felt a burst of sexual need course through their bodies. Matthew ground his erection into her pelvis. She touched her tongue to his, then probed the inner lining of his mouth.

She moaned.

He unbuttoned the tiny white pearl buttons of her powder blue angora sweater and pulled it apart. He slid his hand over her white cotton bra until he felt her nipple harden at his touch.

She moaned again.

He jerked as shock waves of passion whipped through his body when Caitlin kissed his lips, then his chin, and then breathed into his ear. She rimmed the edge of his ear with her tongue and suckled his earlobe.

"Oh, God, Cat . . . you drive me crazy."

"Matthew, I think I love you, too," she said without thinking.

Then she kissed him again, and when she did, she tasted salty water. He was crying. He stopped kissing her and simply held her to his chest.

"What's wrong?" she asked.

"I don't want it to be like this. I thought I did, but I don't. I think I really do love you, Cat," he said with surprise.

"I know you love me."

His tears were huge and glistening as he looked at her. "No. I mean I really do. I want to marry you, Cat."

"But . . ."

"I mean it. When you come back, I want you to tell me that you'll be my wife. That's what I want you to think about over Christmas. Promise me you'll think about it."

Caitlin smiled at him as she touched the pad of her forefinger to his bottom lip. "I'll think about it."

Matthew cradled her head on his shoulder. "This is just nuts . . . you and me . . . like this . . . so fast . . . just nuts."

Caitlin stood with Anne, gazing up at the Christmas tree inside the newly built Rockefeller Apartments, where Anne lived with her father. Anne had explained that her father was convinced this area would "take off" someday, but the Sixth Avenue el had been a grim obstacle for nearly a decade now. Even though the el was being demolished this year, there were still vacancies in the two back-to-back apartment buildings that had been built around a central garden. Anne was an expert on the area and the proposed Rockefeller Center, which was to eventually encompass seventeen acres of shops and restaurants, an ice rink, and office buildings. Anne knew all this because her father was one of the developers.

"What do you think?"

Caitlin pursed her lips as she gazed at the flocked white spruce tree with its all-blue lights. "I never saw a tree with pink and silver glass balls before."

"I'll bet all your trees were plain green with red ornaments. Traditional stuff."

"Yeah." Caitlin sighed nostalgically, wondering if she'd done the right thing in coming here.

Anne slapped her on the back. "Just think of the new perspective I've given you! Who said Christmas has to be red and green? Is it written in the Ten Commandments?"

"No."

"In the Baltimore Catechism, then. Point out that rule to me."

Caitlin laughed. "It's not there."

"Then Christmas should be pink, silver, and blue."

"What about gold and purple?"

Anne plopped down on the floor and pulled out a long sheet of silvery paper. She opened a bag with pink satin ribbons. "Now you're getting the hang of it. Experiment. Broaden those horizons. Think a new way."

Caitlin sat down next to her. "That's what I've been trying to do."

"I know. And I'm helping you. At least my life is not for naught." She laughed. "Who said that? Robert Burns?"

"I dunno."

Anne took out a silver-topped powder jar, placed it in a box, and began wrapping it. She glanced up at her melancholy friend. "What's wrong, Cat?"

Caitlin toyed with the pink ribbon. "I thought I wanted a Christmas without any men in my life, yet all I do is think about Matthew. And home. I wonder what Michael is doing. I wonder if he liked the sweater I got him. I wonder if there's a big turkey or a small one."

"Oh, bullshit," Anne retorted as she whipped the ribbon out of Caitlin's hand and deftly tied it around the silver-wrapped box. "You're still thinking about that guy."

"What guy?"

"The one back in Chicago who broke your heart. You never talk about him. How come?"

"I told you there is no 'guy,' as you put it."

Anne shook her head forcefully and pulled a man's tie box out from under the overstuffed club chair with the gold fringe. "I don't believe you. Look, I'll give you all the privacy you want. Just don't lie to me. You don't have to tell me about him. Just don't deny him. I've been there, believe me."

"When?"

"I was sixteen. I fell head over heels for this boy. We went steady for a year. I gave him my heart and soul, and he took my virginity."

"You what?" Caitlin's eyes grew round with surprise.

"There, that's my big, dark secret. I loved and lost," Anne said with a catch in her voice. She smiled, but Caitlin could see her pain. Anne's sometimes brittle attitude was her own way of covering grief.

"I'm sorry." Caitlin covered Anne's hand with her own.

"He was the only one. I never did it with anybody else, if that's what you're thinking."

"No, I didn't."

Anne gazed up into Caitlin's compassionate eyes. "I'm not a slut. But I will never love anybody again like I did him."

"That's why you have so many boyfriends?"

"Yeah. There's safety in numbers. You remember that. They can't hurt you if you don't give them the power. To thine own self be true!" Anne said, and tied another bow.

Caitlin pondered Anne's words and thought about this funny, offbeat girl who wanted her father's affection so much, she was willing to sit in this apartment alone, wait until he came home, and do damn near anything he asked just for a few lousy moments with him at dinner. It was pathetic.

It was real.

It was exactly the kind of crumbs she'd taken from her own father. Perhaps it was that kind of neediness that had caused Caitlin to fall in love with Clay . . . a man she could never have. Family patterns, Caitlin thought.

The more she thought about Matthew, the more she missed him. When he finally called on Christmas Eve, Caitlin found herself nearly screaming with delight into the phone.

"Matthew, I miss you."

"Really, Kit Cat?"

"Yes, really."

"Good. 'Cause I miss you. I can't wait for school to start. I have so much to tell you."

"Like what?" she breathed longingly into the phone. She wondered if he could hear her heart rattling against her ribs.

"Like how much I love you. Like I want to marry you. Like I think you should go shopping with me and we should pick out an engagement ring."

"Oh, Matthew! Are you sure?"

"I'm sure if you're sure."

"I . . . am." It was only a hairsbreadth of hesitation. Matthew didn't catch it, but Caitlin did. She was learning to be afraid of herself.

"I think I'll call you again tomorrow. Would you like that?"

"Oh, yes, Matthew."

"I love you, Kit Cat. 'Bye."

" 'Bye."

Christmas with the Darlings was what *rich* was all about. James Darling played Santa Claus not only to his daughter, but to Caitlin as well. The flocked white tree with its nonconforming blue lights and silver and pink glass balls was circled Christmas morning by a knee-deep stack of gifts.

Caitlin had to blink three times as she stumbled into the all-white living room dressed in her robe and slippers. "Is it real?"

Anne stood next to her wearing white satin mules, a quilted blue satin robe, and a very wide grin. "Santa has struck!"

James Darling heard squeals of delight, and padded across the thick carpet in bare feet. He ran a hand through his dark hair and tied the fringed black satin sash of his velvet robe around his protruding stomach. He sat on the modern sofa, rested his folded hands on his knees, and watched as Anne dove headfirst into the pile.

There were identical presents for both girls. Gold compacts with jeweled flowers on the covers. Lipsticks in silver cases. Perfumes from Macy's and Saks. Gloves, purses, pearl bracelets, boxes of expensive stationery, bath oils, drawer sachets. There were lingerie sets, blouses, sweaters, and record albums. Caitlin had never seen so many gifts. It was obvious James had not taken the time to find out any of Caitlin's tastes, and thus, he'd simply bought two of everything. But she was touched that he had considered her on a par with his only child.

"You are much too generous," Caitlin said. "How can I ever thank you?"

"Be a friend to Anne. She needs you."

"That's easy." Caitlin smiled at him.

Anne picked up a huge blue-foil-wrapped box with a white pom-pom bow. There was not a duplicate of this gift for Caitlin, so they both knew it was special.

"I hope you like it," James told her.

"Did you pick it out?" she asked as she tore into the paper.

"I had some help," he replied with a parental smile on his lips.

Anne halted in midmotion. "Who?"

"Now, don't get your dander up. Just a sales clerk. I wasn't sure about your size, that's all."

"Oh," Anne said contritely. "I thought . . ."

"I *Know* what you thought. No, Mercedes and I are not that close. You're my number one girl."

Anne forgot all about the huge box and the furry contents that Caitlin could see through the white tissue. She scrambled across the room on her knees and scurried up into James's arms as if she were three years old. She threw her arms around her father's neck and hugged him. "I love you, Daddy."

James put his hands on Anne's and started to take her arms from his neck. "Here, now. That'll be enou—" Just then he looked over at Caitlin, who wore a stricken look.

She shook her head at him. She glared at him, warning him that he was about to do the wrong thing. She mouthed the words *I love you* to him. Then she smiled.

"I love you . . ." he said to Anne. He followed Caitlin's instructions and dropped his hands and then held his daughter close.

"Oh, Daddy," Anne said into his shoulder. "I've waited so long to hear you say that."

"But I tell you all the time that I love you."

"No, you don't."

"Of course I do. I bought you that new watch you wanted at Thanksgiving . . ."

"No! Daddy! You *bought* me something. I just want you to *tell* me that you love me. That's all. That's all . . ." Anne was crying now.

James turned to Caitlin with a lost look in his eyes. She motioned to him to tighten his hold on Anne. Again she mouthed the words *I love you*.

"I love you, Anne, dear. I always have. Why, you're the most important thing in the world to me. I thought you knew that."

"No, I didn't." Anne was crying harder.

"Then I guess we need to start over, don't we?"

"Yes, Daddy."

"Then we will."

Anne pulled away from him and sniffed. "I guess I'd better blow my nose." She rose and went to the bathroom.

James looked to Caitlin. There were tears in his eyes. "I think you have given me the greatest gift I've ever received . . . my daughter. How can I ever thank you?"

Caitlin chuckled. "Just be a good dad."

James laughed and wiped his falling tear. "I guess it is pretty easy after all."

Christmas in New York was spent shopping, eating at the 21 Club and Café Francaise, hitting the matinee at Radio City Music Hall, and staying up late talking and dreaming with Anne, not doing the work they *should* be doing on their term papers.

Matthew called Caitlin every day. Anne and James spent time alone every night together after he got home from work. Life was moving ahead and away from the Killian mold for Caitlin. Only once did she write home, and it was to Sheilagh. She told her all about New York, the plays she'd been to at the Shubert Theatre, the shopping, the new construction that James Darling was planning, and the people she'd met who were friends of the Darlings. It wasn't until the day after she mailed the letter that Caitlin remembered how badly Sheilagh had wanted to live in New York.

But then, that was long ago, before Sheilagh had Clay.

They all had new lives now. As for Caitlin, as long as she did not think about Clay or home, it wasn't so bad after all.

Chapter 27 ————————————

March 1940

SHEILAGH SAT IN a bentwood rocking chair gazing down at her enormous belly. She was nine months pregnant. She laid a hand on the tight skin and found another stretch mark that had popped into view since last night.

"That's three of those damn things," she complained to herself as she rose and went to the tiny kitchenette of the apartment she shared with Clay. She snatched the jar of cocoa butter off the counter. She waddled back to the rocker, laboriously lowered her massive body into the seat, and pulled up her dress.

Every time she looked at her grotesque body, she nearly burst into tears. She unscrewed the black metal top and sunk her fingers into the cocoa butter. She pulled away the elastic of her cotton maternity panties and began to rub the cocoa butter on her skin. Her mother, the pharmacist, and a jillion other women had told her that cocoa butter would prevent stretch marks, but Sheilagh did not believe it. As far as she could tell, it only helped to ease the itching and sometimes painful stretched feeling she felt.

"Please, God, let this baby come today. I'm sick of this torture." She leaned her head back on the rocker and let her daily tears begin again.

The Christmas holidays had been lonely without Caitlin. New Year's Eve was a disaster since she fought with Clay all night because she wanted to go out and have fun, and he wanted to stay home. Valentine's Day had been a real joy for her since they had been invited to her parents' house for a prime rib dinner. Mary Margaret forgot that Michael was going to a high school basketball game that evening with his friends, which soured her disposition considerably. Patrick forgot the family dinner completely, and came home after ten o'clock, drunk and stumbling. Clay had to undress her father and put him to bed. Sheilagh and Clay left feeling stiff with embarrassment.

Sheilagh had tried to redirect her life into domestic chores, and for a while the tactic had succeeded. But once the Lake Geneva house was decorated, the last flower arranged, she found she couldn't fool herself anymore.

Sheilagh still dreamed of acting.

Since the beginning of the year, she had found herself spiraling into a depression. Clay retreated by delving into work and following the war in Europe. He spoke of enlisting. Sheilagh thought she should talk him out of it, but she never said a word. He was as miserable as she was. She hated that he felt he needed to go to war to escape her, but at least he had something to run to. She did not.

The baby moved, and Sheilagh placed her hand on her belly to feel it. Her stomach was very hard. She felt the sides. They were hard, too.

She leaned her head back on the rocker. Of all that she had lost in the last few months, she missed Caitlin the most. The only letter she had received had come from Caitlin in New York.

Sheilagh groaned, and choked back a stab of remorse for the death of her dream. "New York." What irony fate liked to play with humans. Somehow it was poetic justice, she surmised, that Caitlin should be the one who got to see New York first. Sheilagh had Clay. Caitlin had New York.

"Ahhhggghhh," Sheilagh groaned again, this time with surprise. The pain she felt was not in her heart but across the upper portion of her abdomen. She rose and went to the mirror. The baby had dropped last week, but the doctor had told her she would have to wait another week before she could expect labor to begin. She could only surmise that this was false labor. She shrugged her shoulders and went to the battered wooden coffee table she'd bought at a yard sale for two dollars. She sat on the dirty sofa, cursing Clay and his pride for wanting to live within their budget. He believed that he already took enough charity from the Killian family by working for them. He refused to let Mary Margaret and Patrick buy them the furniture they needed.

"The only reason I work for your father is because I like Emerald and I believe that I am an asset to the company!" Clay had told Sheilagh one night over a dinner of macaroni and cheese. "Otherwise, I'd get a job someplace else."

"All I'm saying is that I want a decent place to live. For the baby."

"For you, you mean," he spat back angrily.

"Yes. Me, too. And you. There's no reason why we can't take this offer of Mother's to get some new furniture, and then when we have the money later, we can pay her back."

Clay jumped to his feet. "No fucking way, Sheilagh."

"Clay!"

"Goddamn it, I mean it. I'm bustin' my ass going to work every day, which is more than I can say for your father, who breezes in whenever he goddamn well feels like it, stays an hour or two tops, and then dumps his shit on my desk and takes off. I have night classes three nights a weeks to get my degree, plus I have to worry about you and the baby . . ."

"Just stop right there!" Sheilagh exclaimed, and shoved her face right up into his. "Don't you ever worry about me or the baby. We're just fine without you. This wasn't my idea . . . None of it was."

"Fine. I won't worry about you."

"Fine!" Sheilagh crossed her arms over her swollen breasts, and as usual, Clay stomped out of the house and went to the library to study.

He had returned about midnight, long after Sheilagh was asleep.

Sheilagh felt another pain in her abdomen and wondered if these were contractions. She had heard all the stories about labor. That it could take twelve, fifteen hours. That she wouldn't be able to eat anything. Her eyes flitted to a bunch of bananas on the counter. She broke off two of the largest ones, just in case the doctor would indeed not let her eat.

As she munched on the banana, she realized that she and Clay were as wrong for each other as two people could be. They did the best they could around other people. They put on quite a show for her family and an even better performance for his mother and father. Sheilagh was pretty sure they were fooling everyone except Aileen Burke.

Yes, Sheilagh thought, her mother-in-law was a wise, tough lady. Aileen had a sixth sense that Sheilagh truly hadn't understood until Aileen's last visit, when she had brought over a coconut cream pie.

Aileen wasn't in the apartment ten minutes when she said: "You aren't very happy, are you, dear?"

"What makes you say that?"

"Clay looks like last year's tire retreads, and you look even worse. Do you want to talk about it?"

"There's nothing to say. Nothing to be done."

"There is always an answer to a problem. Sometimes it's just that you might not have considered all the possibilities yet."

Sheilagh looked down at her swollen belly. "This is a problem that won't go away."

"I understand that. But what is it that you want, Sheilagh?"

Sheilagh gazed out the window onto the rooftops of other apartment buildings. "I want to be an actress."

"Then be one."

"What?" Sheilagh spun around and gaped at Aileen.

"Don't look at me as if I just stepped off a spaceship. What's stopping you?"

Sheilagh heaved an exasperated sigh. "I'm going to have a baby . . . in case you hadn't noticed."

"I know that. What's that got to do with you not having a career? I had a child. I have a career. And I don't mind saying, I've handled both of them quite well." She paused and patted the sofa next to her. "Sit down here and listen to me."

Sheilagh reluctantly left the window and sat next to Aileen, who took Sheilagh's hands in her own.

"After the baby is born and you give the child, say, six months or so to get used to this world, start auditioning again.

Go back to the Blackstone. See what happens. Clay is doing what Clay wants to do. Why shouldn't you do what you want to do?"

"I just never . . ."

"You thought you had to punish yourself. Probably some of that crap your mother dishes out to you."

Sheilagh's hand flew to her mouth to stifle a laugh.

"I'm right, aren't I?"

"Yes. But how did you know?"

"I pay attention. Always do that, dear. It will get you much further in life than those who don't." Aileen cleared her throat. "Now, where was I? Oh, yes. You see, Sheilagh, you and Clay are never going to be happy if you aren't happy all on your own. You have nothing to do, so you blame yourself and Clay. When he comes home, you both argue because, believe it or not, he feels guilty because you aren't doing what you want to do. Does that make sense?"

"Yes. It does," Sheilagh replied thoughtfully.

"Try that. See what happens." Aileen rose to go.

Pondering Aileen's suggestions, and without realizing she was speaking out loud, Sheilagh said: "And what do I do about the fact that Clay loves Caitlin?"

Aileen halted as if frozen. "I didn't know you knew about that."

"Has Clay talked to you about it?"

"Never a word."

"Then how do you know?"

"I'm his mother. I know my son and I love him. I've been able to read him like a book since the day he was born."

Sheilagh choked back a stinging sob as her heart broke for the two people she loved most. "Then it's true. I only guessed."

"It's true. Better to face the devil up front. And I don't have an answer for you there. You love him, too, though."

"Yes. But not the way Caitlin does."

"Hmmm." Aileen nodded, knowing it was best not to say anything one way or the other. "I'd pray on it if I were you. Maybe you'll get an answer."

"I don't believe in prayer anymore," Sheilagh said bitterly.

Aileen smiled fondly. "You will again." She picked up her square leather handbag from the table. "Think about what I said. I'll call you in a few days. Take care, dear," she said as she brushed Sheilagh's cheek with a kiss.

Sheilagh's reverie was broken by another strong pain. This time she watched her stomach tighten for nearly a minute before it relaxed. She started to rise off the sofa when another pain stabbed her in the back. Suddenly there was a rush of water down her legs.

"Oh, my God. The baby . . . it's coming!"

Caitlin received the telegram at school on March 2, 1940. Andrew Burke had been born at 6:30 A.M. Central standard time and weighed five pounds one ounce.

"That's kinda small for a baby, isn't it?" Anne asked as she read the telegram over Caitlin's shoulder. I was over seven pounds when I was born."

"It does sound rather little at that. Maybe I should call home and find out if they're okay."

"Yeah, maybe you should," Anne said nonchalantly, and went back to the letter she was writing to her father.

Caitlin's thoughts swirled around a vision of Clay with his newborn son, a child she had dreamed for years would be theirs. She chased the vision away with thoughts of Matthew. Everything was different now. She had Matthew. Her future had taken a new path, and she had been earnestly walking down it for a long time now. Then why was she suddenly so sad?

For months Caitlin had denied many things to herself. Because she was away from home, she was not exposed to the everyday reality. To her own detriment, she had pretended that some miracle would occur and there would not be any baby and that somehow all the wrongs in her life would be righted. Now truth struck her like a thunderbolt . . . Life was unfair and it hurt.

She stood staring at the telegram and made no move to gather the coins she would need to call home. Anne glanced at her, then did a double take when she saw the tension in her face. She moved her eyes lower and studied Caitlin's hands clutching the telegram. She watched as the paper trembled under the strain of Caitlin's grip.

Anne whirled around and put her arms around her friend. "What is it, Cat? You can tell me."

"I c–can't." Caitlin squeaked out the reply, nearly choking on her despair. She looked into Anne's eyes, and though she found the caring and empathy she needed so badly at this moment, she also saw curiosity. Caitlin's loyalty to her sister, to Clay, and to this new baby she'd never met, dried her tears and refocused her thoughts.

It would be so easy to tell Anne about Clay. She needed a shoulder to cry on. But she was also not certain if that shoulder could be trusted. She had always been wise enough to be wary. She'd spent years of her life keeping her feelings for Clay to herself.

She forced a smile to her face. "I guess I was just being silly. Andrew being the first grandchild and all. It's a special time in my life to have my first nephew. Don't you think?"

Anne didn't fall for Caitlin's evasions. "Save the pabulum for the kid, okay?"

"Anne, if you're going to be my friend, you'll have to understand that these family events just get the better of me sometimes."

Anne's eyes narrowed as she scrutinized her friend. "I am your friend, and I'll prove it to you by not asking any more questions. I want you to be happy, and right now, you don't look so hot, toots."

Caitlin looked down at the telegram. "I'm okay. Really."

"Sure. So go make your call."

"Okay." Caitlin went to her desk and scrambled through the top left-hand drawer for the fistful of nickels she would need for the pay phone. At the door she hesitated. She glanced back over her shoulder to see Anne still observing her every move. "I think I'll call Matthew at his dorm first and tell him the news."

"Good idea," Anne replied, and then turned back to her studies.

Caitlin went down the hall to the telephone at the end of the corridor. She inserted a nickel and dialed Matthew's number.

It took nearly ten minutes before he came to the telephone. He was out of breath when he picked up the receiver.

"What's up?" he said.

"I just became an aunt!" she said, trying to sound excited when she was not.

"Congratulations. Boy or girl?"

"Boy. Andrew. He's awful little . . . just five pounds. I'm going to call home and get the particulars."

"Does this mean you're going back there for the weekend?"

"No, why should it?"

"I dunno. My family always made a big deal about stuff like that . . . parties, christenings."

"I'm sure my parents will plan a large baptism brunch or something, but that's six weeks from now. I'll go to that."

"Good."

"What's so special about this weekend anyway?" Caitlin asked coyly.

"It's a surprise. You said you like surprises."

"I do and I don't. Tell me now."

"Nope," Matthew teased. "You'll find out on Friday."

"Okay. I'll see you then."

"Until then, my love," he said, and hung up the phone.

Caitlin dialed her parents' Oak Park house and found no one home. She then dialed the Burkes' home number and received no answer. The same was true at Sheilagh's apartment. Caitlin assumed that everyone was at the hospital fawning over Andrew.

She checked the telegram once again and realized that her mother had not told her which hospital Sheilagh was in. She started to forget the entire matter and simply send a congratulatory card. Maybe she could catch the three-o'clock bus into South Bend and find a card at the Walgreen's. Maybe she should buy a baby gift, too. Maybe she should call Matthew back and ask him to accompany her to town.

To her surprise, she found herself smiling when she thought about him. She wondered what his surprise was. Was he planning a romantic dinner at an Italian restaurant or had he found a new place where they could be alone? Would she finally relent this time and let him go all the way? Was she ready to make love to Matthew even though she still found herself fantasizing about Clay sometimes in the middle of the day when she least expected it? Had it been less than a year ago that she and Clay had worked at Emerald together . . . ?

Suddenly she realized how she could track her family down. Caitlin pushed an Indian-head nickel into the slot on the pay phone. She telephoned the Emerald offices. Martha O'Boland answered the call.

"Hello, Martha. It's Caitlin," she said to the longtime employee whom she had known for over a decade.

"Caitlin! How wonderful to hear from you! How is school? Your studies . . . are you doing well? Are you dating anyone yet?"

"Whoa! Slow down, Martha! I called to find out about all the excitement there. I called the house, but no one was home . . ."

"Oh, didn't they call you yet to tell you?" Martha's voice dropped its earlier exuberance.

"Tell me what?" Caitlin felt fingers of dread reach out through the telephone wires.

"The baby isn't quite right, Caitlin."

She gulped hard. "What is that supposed to mean?"

"He's very small. Something about his lungs not developing properly. He's in the hospital on oxygen. Sheilagh had a rough time of it. She . . . she almost didn't make it."

Caitlin's hands clenched the receiver in a viselike grip. Her voice was raw with fear. "Sheilagh . . . almost died?"

"Now, don't you worry. It's over . . . it was just that for a moment it looked pretty bad. Sheilagh had some kind of poisoning . . . toxemia. Her labor was long . . . twenty-five hours. She got really tired. I don't know much more than that. I never had a baby, so I guess I'm not the one you should talk to."

Caitlin couldn't believe this. Women had babies every day. The idea that they still died from childbirth seemed barbaric, and Caitlin had never heard of toxemia. She knew nothing about pregnancies and labor. She remembered Sheilagh's fall at Thanksgiving. Something told her that this was the one time her sister should have listened to Mary Margaret and gone to the doctor. But could he have helped her? Would it have made a difference? Had Sheilagh unconsciously *wanted* to fall? Did she still harbor resentment toward this child? Maybe she truly did not want the baby after all.

"Do you know how I can get in touch with Sheilagh?"

"Oh, you can't call her, dear. She's still under sedation. But your mother and father left the hospital over an hour ago. They should be home by now. I'd try calling them again."

"Thank you, Martha." Caitlin started to hang up. "Oh, Martha?"

"Yes, Caitlin."

"I just wanted to say that I'm glad you were there for me to talk to." Caitlin sighed. "I don't know what this family would do without you, Martha. You've always been there to take care of all of us. Father . . . me . . . Sheilagh . . . Clay now, too. Thanks, Martha."

"You're welcome. And, Caitlin, I want you to know that I don't know what I would do if it weren't for all the Killians. You're the family I never had."

"You take care, Martha." Caitlin smiled down at the receiver.

"You, too, Caitlin." Martha hung up.

Caitlin placed the call to her parents' home, and Mary Margaret answered.

"Oh, Caitlin, thank God you got our wire."

"What's wrong, Mother?"

"Andrew is very sickly. Very sickly," Mary Margaret said through disjointed breaths that told Caitlin her mother was under a great deal of stress. She thought she could nearly hear her wringing her hands. "The doctor says he'll have to stay in the hospital for a month."

"A month?"

"Yes. Sheilagh can't bring him home. She'll have to go back each day to nurse him. Sheilagh says she won't do it. She told the nurses to give him the bottle. She said she wants her milk to dry up. She's just not thinking!" Mary Margaret's voice grew more strained with every word.

"Mother, calm down. I'm sure it's not the end of the world if Sheilagh doesn't nurse her baby."

"Don't you take her side, Caitlin Killian!"

Caitlin took a deep breath. "When was the last time you had any sleep, Mother?"

"Not since this whole ordeal began. Two days . . . two and a half . . ." Mary Margaret's sigh was audible over the telephone.

"I'm sure that little Andrew is getting the best of care in the hospital. Maybe he'll be better off with the nurses . . ."

"A baby should be with its mother!" Mary Margaret's voice sounded as if she had pitched herself off the edge of reason. "She did this to her child, you know . . . she caused this to happen to my first grandchild. She didn't care about that baby. She wanted to murder it. God is punishing her and the baby now. That's what's happening. I've seen it before."

Caitlin nearly dropped the receiver, her hand was shaking so forcefully from her own frustration and anger. "Don't say that, Mother! It's not true!"

"It is! She is wicked! She's always been wicked. Fornicating. Abortion. God heaps catastrophes on the wicked. That's how you can spot them!" Mary Margaret was nearly crying as the words rushed out of her mouth.

"Don't say things you can't take back, Mother. Sheilagh is not a bad person."

"She is most certainly that." Mary Margaret suddenly tried to grasp the edges of calm and pull them around her. "However, I will not discuss this with you any longer. Sheilagh got what she deserved."

"Good God in heaven, Mother! I can't believe you would want to see your own child dead, or any lasting physical deformity in your first grandchild. You can't be that self-righteous."

Caitlin's control abandoned her as she became enmeshed in the sea of her own emotions. "Why must you always blame Sheilagh? You ride her constantly, always trying to break her spirit as if she had done something personally to you. She didn't, you know. Sheilagh is Sheilagh. Maybe if you had let her go to New York and be her own person, none of this would have happened. Did you ever stop to think that maybe *you* brought all this down upon us? Did you ever think for a moment it was *your* fault?"

"Never! I am the one who has kept this family together. I am the one who has sacrificed . . . staying with your father when he . . . he . . ."

"When he what, Mother? Go ahead and say it! Say he hurt you."

"He has never hurt me. He isn't worthy of me." Mary Margaret's voice wavered from an alto to soprano, making her sound like the desperately unhappy woman she was.

"Leave Sheilagh to face her problems herself. You need to take care of your own life."

"Who do you think you are, telling *me* what to do? Just because you're hundreds of miles from home doesn't give you the right to order me about, missy!"

Anger, born years ago in Caitlin's childhood, could no longer be denied or restrained. Like a sleeping lion suddenly awakened by a life-threatening danger, it roared to life and clamped its teeth around its prey. "And who do you think you are? You aren't God, Mother!"

Caitlin slammed down the receiver. She was shaking from head to foot, as if an icy wind had just blasted through the halls. She clenched her hand into a fist and rammed it against the wall. "I hate you!" She hit the wall again. "I hate what you're doing to Sheilagh!" Her tears felt like molten lava on her cheeks as she thought about her sister and her baby.

Had her mother always been this cruel? Or was she just now seeing Mary Margaret for the jealous, vindictive, self-righteous woman she was? Hadn't Mary Margaret ever loved anybody? Caitlin wanted to run to Sheilagh and Clay, and hold them both. She wanted to reassure them that she would always love them no matter what. She would take them in when the rest of the world turned them out. She would always be there for them. Always.

Caitlin turned her back to the wall for support as she let herself drown in her own sobs. Her knees lost their strength and she sank slowly to the floor, her back sliding down the wall. She let her face fall into her hands and she cried for all the Killians . . . especially for Andrew, whose grandmother would use him as a pawn to control Sheilagh, and whose life was not welcomed by his mother or his father.

Chapter 28

ANDREW BURKE WAS thirty-four days old when Sheilagh was finally allowed to bring him home from the hospital. She should have been joyful that morning, but she was not. She was filled with dread.

"I don't know anything about babies," she said to Clay as they stood in their apartment staring down at the blue-and-white-eyelet-covered bassinet with shiny brass fittings that held an elaborate canopy.

"You'll learn. Besides, I think these things come naturally to women," Clay said, trying to reassure her.

"Bullshit," she said lowly and without much conviction as she plumped the down-filled baby-sized pillow. "I don't think anything comes naturally to me anymore. Not mothering, not acting . . ."

"Sheilagh . . . please don't berate yourself again," Clay replied with a tinge of exasperation. "We talked all this out last night. You were feeling so much better by the time we went to bed."

She looked at him with burning eyes. "I have truly become a major pain in the ass, haven't I, Clay?"

"I'm not complaining," he said, taking his eyes from her and searching the room for a stack of reports.

"You should. You spend most of your free time shuffling between the hospital to care for Andrew and here, where I'm always down in the dumps. I want you to know, I hate being like this, Clay."

"Then don't be like this." He harrumphed, knowing her bad moods never ended these days. They simply continued with another installment just like the soap operas she listened to on the radio.

"I don't know what's wrong with me," she said, raising a half-limp hand to her face and lifting a hunk of auburn hair off her shoulder. "I want to be happy again. I just can't seem to shake this doom-and-gloom feeling. It's like I'm running down a dark tunnel, but it only gets darker the harder I try to get out." She looked at him with earnest eyes. He could sense her genuine plea for understanding.

"Maybe once we get back to a normal routine . . ."

"What's normal about having a baby in the house for the first time in your life? What's normal about a deformed baby?" Sheilagh started to go on, but Clay interrupted her.

"Andrew is normal! Do you hear me? He's fine. The doctors said so!"

"Clay, I'm only being realistic."

"You sound like your mother, and I won't have that harpy or her sick ideas brought into my house!"

Clay was shaking. He was just as afraid as Sheilagh was that maybe they were being punished by some unseen force, though he had fought the illogical thought nearly every day since Andrew's birth. Clay loved his tiny, sickly son. Through his son, he had come to treasure life—the chance to breathe air, see a sun rise, and watch flowers grow—as he never had before. He let go of his resentment toward Sheilagh for trapping him into this marriage neither of them wanted and took upon himself his own portion of the responsibility. He was still in love with Caitlin, and there was nothing he could do about that either. This was his life. He intended to make the best of it.

Sheilagh responded to the forlorn slump of Clay's shoulders. She knew what he was thinking all too well. She wanted to rip the mantle of guilt from his shoulders, but she was just too damn tired to help him. It was all she could do to get through the day and stay sane. She went to him and placed her hand on his shoulder. "Clay . . . I'm sorry."

He took a deep breath. He needed to be strong for them both. "Me, too. Do you want me to back the car out of the garage?"

"Would you, please? The doctor said we could pick up Andrew after his ten-o'clock feeding."

"Yeah. I need to get my things for the office."

"You going there after you bring Andrew and me home from the hospital?"

"I have several meetings."

Sheilagh brushed a lock of his dark hair from his forehead. "You're a good man, Clay Burke," she said, then kissed his cheek and turned away from him. She didn't tell him that she wished with all her heart that she loved him the way he needed and deserved to be loved. They both knew that would be asking too much . . . too much of fate.

Clay stuffed a thick manila folder into his leather attaché case, a gift from Patrick along with a new promotion to director of sales and marketing. Clay wanted to take credit for all the work, but the truth was that it had taken him a year to finally put all of Caitlin's ideas into practice.

She was no longer at the office, but she was with him in spirit every day on every project. There were times when he had to leave the office to avoid the temptation to telephone her. Sometimes his eyes played tricks on him and he thought he saw her walking down the hall or in the crowd at a Cubs game or in the front pew at Ascension Church. But always it was another girl who looked like Caitlin. It was never her.

From Thanksgiving to Christmas, he had counted the days until she was to return to Chicago for the holidays. Then she had told her parents she was going to New York. Clay had never experienced such long days in all his life. He never wrote to Caitlin, never called, and tried to dull the pain of not seeing her with work, thoughts about his new son, and plans he'd made for his future; all of which he would abandon if Caitlin ever told him that she wanted him.

Clay appreciated Sheilagh's sincere efforts to be a good wife. But he was not happy, and neither was she. He wondered if he would ever be happy again.

Shannon had planned and schemed to become the mistress of a rich man. She was amazed at how easy it had been once she found the right one. That was the key to her success. This wasn't a game a woman could play with just anyone. The time and effort that she had invested in her selection of a partner had been critical to her success.

Patrick not only prepaid her rent for a year, he also paid

for the new modern furnishings she'd seen at John M. Smythe on Michigan Avenue. She wanted Biedermeier chairs in blond wood tones and a dining room table to match. She re-covered her sofa in a cream silk with a heavy slub. She painted the walls cream and hung gold rococo wall sconces next to an oversize round mirror. The drapes were cream silk double-lined to give extra weight, and she had them cut a foot and half too long so they would "puddle" on the dark-stained mahogany floor. Shannon loved French elegance dramatically combined with clean, modern lines.

From the outside of her plain little house, no one would guess at the lush interior, which was just how Shannon liked to think of her life. She loved the mystery and excitement of being a mistress. She felt a triumphant glow each time she thought of the fact that she was stealing another woman's husband. There was a place in society for women like her. Too many men were unhappy at home, she told herself, and they needed another woman to give them purpose and drive when their wives had failed.

Shannon had always liked sex, but lately she found she was liking it more with Patrick than she had thought possible. They had been together for over a year now, and she had accomplished many of her goals. The house was beautifully decorated. She had three gold bracelets in her jewel box, which had never held anything but a few costume pieces and the cheap pearls she had bought at Woolworth's. Patrick paid for art lessons, design lessons, and had coerced a friend of his, a small clothing manufacturer, into hiring Shannon to design a sportswear line.

She had completed the first line of tennis wear and swim wear, and was now working on ideas for sundresses. So far, Samuel Kilpatrick, her half-Irish, half-Jewish employer, had liked her ideas. The true test would come next spring when the lines were produced. Sales would tell all.

Shannon checked the white alabaster clock on the mantel, another gift from Patrick which he'd bought at an antique shop during one of their Tuesday afternoon strolls down Wells Street. She'd told him she wanted a frightfully expensive Russian samovar, and he'd promised to buy it for her. He'd told her they would choose a car for her very soon. An Oldsmobile, he had said.

Patrick was fifteen minutes late. Shannon nervously checked her wristwatch. No, the time was correct.

She stopped herself immediately. Something was wrong. Not with the time but within herself. Never before had she waited for a man filled with . . . what? With anxiety? Desperation? Anticipation? When had this change taken place? Today? Or last week when he had told her he was going out of town to a fancy food and confection convention and had not asked her to accompany him?

She had not thought to ask if his wife would go with him. No, she had more confidence in her skills than to think that he would even consider bringing Mary Margaret. She had told him she would be quite busy, thank you, and that he should not worry about her. Now that she thought about it, she was hard-pressed to remember exactly where the convention was to be held. Had he said Atlanta or San Francisco?

Shannon paced across the Aubusson carpet. She fidgeted with the pearl and diamond dinner ring he'd given her. Another ten minutes passed. She checked her hair again. Suddenly she didn't like the perfectly coiffed chignon she had paid the hairdresser ten dollars to create. She didn't look sultry enough. She needed more mascara. More Revlon Cherry Red lipstick.

She raced to the bathroom and scrambled in her makeup drawer to find her mascara. She dipped the tiny brush into the small puddle of water in the sink basin and ran it across the cake mascara. She stroked her long lashes three times, powdered the lash ends, and applied another coat. She carefully slicked her lips with the lipstick. But just as she started to take her hair down and begin anew, she stopped herself.

She peered at the flawless face in the mirror. "What am I doing?"

Since when have you become insecure, Shannon O'Rourke? she asked herself. Since when had Patrick Killian become so important? Since when did she *need* him in her life?

She backed away from the fear she saw in the bright eyes that looked back at her. Shannon had never seen fear in herself. She'd seen it in others, but that was different.

Just then the doorbell rang. A happy smile sprang onto her lips, but rather than give her a sense of relief, the smile frightened her more than anything she'd ever seen in her life.

Shannon O'Rourke was in big trouble. She had fallen in love.

Spring came to South Bend in a rush. Seemingly overnight, the snow melted under warm, swirling, humid winds. The sun shone brightly, forcing crocuses into view. Hyacinths, daffodils, and paper-whites spread across meadows like colorful quilts. The scrawny branches of maple and oak trees swelled with buds that finally popped open and unfurled spring-green leaves. Robins and cardinals returned from their hiatus to the South. Life had renewed itself once again, and no one felt better about it than Caitlin.

She was ready to put the past behind her and go on. Realistically she could no longer spend her time or emotional energy on dreams that were simply part of her childhood. Absence did not make the heart grow fonder, only wiser. What she had with Matthew was real. She cared about him, she had fun with him, and though she missed that inner connectedness she had felt with Clay, she tried not to think about it. She spent her time thinking about herself and Matthew.

On the night she had returned to South Bend from New York, Matthew met her at the train station. Anne took a cab back to St. Mary's while Caitlin and Matthew took another cab to Niles, Michigan, where Matthew had rented a motel room. It was a new motel, built on a ravine, and had a window that looked out onto the snow-covered trees. The full moon made the snow sparkle.

Caitlin had thought she would feel awkward or guilty or at least sinful if she lost her virginity without the sanctity of the sacrament of marriage, like the nuns always told her. She didn't.

She felt blessed to have Matthew in her life. She'd put away her childish dreams of Clay that were never meant to be. She gave her love to Matthew.

He was gentle, and fumbled a lot with their clothes and underwear, but when they lay naked next to each other, their lovemaking was instinctual, caring, and sweet.

He cried when it was over, his emotions nearly too powerful for him to control. Caitlin held him in her arms and assured him she would never leave him.

They fell asleep with their bodies intertwined, and when they awoke, they were still wrapped around each other. Caitlin decided that day that loving and being loved was as close as she would ever come to seeing God.

As the months passed, Matthew became more playful in his lovemaking. "Please, not another surprise, Matthew. The last time you had a surprise for me, you took me to the stadium."

"You didn't like making love in Notre Dame Stadium? I will have you know that I personally arranged for the entire student body to vacate the place, just for you. I know how you hate taking your clothes off in front of people," he teased.

"It's not football season until next September."

"No wonder everyone agreed so easily!" He leaned over and kissed her firmly yet playfully on the mouth. "Come now, woman, admit it. You love it."

"I love you." She kissed him back.

He slid his hand under her blouse and unhooked her bra. He moved his hand around to grasp her left breast in his hand. "Jesus, Mary, and Joseph, you are one voluptuous woman, Kit Cat." He kissed her earlobe and traced the shell of her outer ear with his tongue. "Make love to me . . ."

"Here? Now? Matthew! I do not think that this bench in the middle of the quad in front of a thousand students all headed for lunch is quite the acceptable place."

"Screw 'em," he breathed lowly, and kissed her ear again.

Caitlin kept her head down, pretending to the passersby that Matthew was simply whispering a secret into her ear. "Take your hand off my breast, Matthew," she ordered with a giggle.

"No."

"Yes."

"You're just no fun anymore, Kit Cat." He surreptitiously let his hand fall and eased it around to her back as he looked up to see a priest smiling down at them. Matthew nodded. The priest moved on. "Jeez! It's Saturday. Don't those guys know that tomorrow is their day to roam?"

Caitlin feigned impudence. "He's trying to keep you moral, which is more than I can say for myself."

Matthew tickled her back as his fingers struggled to refasten her bra. "It's a lost cause." He kissed the nape of her neck. "Now, about my surprise."

"Don't tell me. A motel?"

He shook his head. "On my allowance? You honestly think I would pay for a place for us to go when I have successfully sneaked you up to my room, made love to you at midnight in the quad, in the library, in the chapel . . ."

"Don't forget the backseat of John Healy's Buick at the White Castle."

"Right. I spare no expense for my girl."

Caitlin nodded and smiled. Matthew suddenly took her face

between his hands and let his eyes explore the depths of her eyes. His expression was serious and blindingly eager. She could see love, conviction, and desire in his eyes. She opened her mouth to speak, but he stopped her words with a passionate kiss. His lips were soft and inviting, and urged her to respond to him. She put her arms around his neck and pulled him closer.

Caitlin didn't feel his hand reach up and take her left hand from his neck. His kiss became more insistent as his tongue entered her mouth and touched the edges of her lips and tongue. She didn't feel his fingers as they fumbled to slip a ring on the third finger of her left hand.

Slowly and reluctantly, Matthew wrenched his lips from hers. He kept his face very near hers, and he was smiling at her when she opened her eyes.

"Marry me, Caitlin."

"Oh, Matthew, how many times are you going to ask me that? Of course I will . . . after I graduate."

"I'm never going to ask you again, Kit Cat. Is that your answer?"

"Yes," she replied with a smile.

He took her left hand and held it up between the two of them, with the diamond facing her. "Then I guess I'll have to be satisfied with a very long engagement, won't I?"

Caitlin was dumbstruck. "Oh, my God!" Her eyes were as round as full moons. Her smile seemed to light the sky. It was just a chip of a diamond, but to Caitlin it seemed enormous. "You shouldn't have done this," she said breathlessly, though she could not take her eyes off the ring. "It cost too much."

"It was worth it. I saved my Christmas money and I had some left over from my construction job last summer and I borrowed a little from my dad—"

"Your parents know?" Her head jerked up to stare at him.

"Of course they do, silly. I want you to meet them this summer after school lets out."

"I would be honored," she said, and looked back at the ring. The yellow gold of the setting glistened in the sunlight. "I just never thought . . ."

"So, I *did* surprise you?"

She gazed up into his dark, love-filled eyes. "Matthew, you have been the surprise of my life since the first day I met you."

"Good," he said, kissing her again. "Let's keep it that way."

* * *

Sheilagh paced the floor with two-month-old Andrew, who was screaming at the top of his lungs. At the very least, it sounded as if she were torturing her son. His scrawny body was so stiff with each intake of breath that she could literally hold him under his arms in front of her, his feet dangling down, and watch as he shook with tension from toes to bald head. He scrunched his eyes completely shut, opened his mouth until it seemed larger than a wide-mouthed Mason jar, and let loose a vibrating scream that could peel plaster off walls.

Sheilagh spent hours watching this tiny creature, weighing less than eight pounds, bellow like an off-key operatic soprano.

She was fascinated by her son. He ate every hour and a half, threw up every two hours, slept only two hours at night and an hour to an hour and a half during the day, and in between he did nothing but scream. Andrew was sick.

He had a milk allergy, which caused colic and the severe diaper rash that looked to Sheilagh like second-degree burns. He had bronchitis, nasal congestion, and ear infections. He developed one ailment or another every week, so that in the ninety days of his existence, Andrew Killian had not lived a single day without pain. Even he was frustrated with being sick.

Sheilagh took Andrew to the doctor, and though each time he prescribed a different ointment for his diaper rash, a new formula for his colic, or a new eardrop or nasal vacuum, nothing the doctor did gave either Andrew or Sheilagh relief.

She rocked him, sang to him, and made up fairy tales to tell him all night until he fell asleep for his two-hour respite. Sheilagh would remain in the living room of the small apartment while Clay slept soundly behind the closed door of their bedroom. She was exhausted when dawn came. Each day that the sun rose was another day she would have to endure Andrew's screams.

Her nerves were strung so tightly, they threatened to snap. To escape, she placed her squalling baby in a silver-gray baby buggy and trotted off to the Laundromat, where she would wash Andrew's diapers, sleepers, flannel sheets, and bedding in Ivory Snow flakes and wait patiently while they dried in the enormous driers. In order to keep him quiet during these outings, Sheilagh would plan her laundry trips to coincide with his meal and snack times so that he would have a baby bottle stuck in his mouth during most of the time away from home. She doubled up on apple juice for Andrew, even though the doctor had stated that he was "supposed" to still be on formula. It was the only thing he did not vomit up.

Sheilagh thought about her childless, unmarried pediatrician and wondered if the man had any idea what she was going through. It amazed her that there were any children at all in the world, considering what a pain in the ass they were.

She carried Andrew in the crook of her arm as she cleaned the dishes, made the bed, dusted and mopped the floor. As she passed by the mirror on the wall, she saw a bedraggled, incredibly tired woman wearing a faded pink babushka over her unwashed auburn hair and wondered fleetingly what had ever happened to the girl who was destined for Broadway. It was almost as if she had lived two lives in two different bodies in two different dimensions. She couldn't imagine putting on a pretty dress for her husband anymore, not that anything in her closet would still fit anyway. Despite her late nights and lack of meals, Sheilagh still carried eleven of the pounds she had gained during her pregnancy. Her waist was thick, her stomach protruded, and her breasts hung a good inch lower than they had last summer. She looked and felt old.

Sheilagh was depressed, and she didn't know what to do about it. Her mother called it "baby blues." Her father told her she was "bellyachin'." Her doctor called it "postpartum depression," but he didn't know exactly what it was or how to cure it or how long it would last. Mostly Sheilagh knew that no matter what happened, good or bad, at some point during the day, she would burst into tears for no good reason and cry out loud right along with Andrew.

She did not have any girlfriends with whom she could confide, since she was one of the first of her crowd to be married. Her contemporaries were still in college. Many had started careers in retailing or worked downtown as secretaries and went to lunch with handsome stockbrokers, attorneys, and bankers. Life had passed Sheilagh by in spades.

She didn't like her husband, her baby, or herself. She hated being a mother. She hated the fact that she had given up her life as an actress for this baby, and she hated Clay for not hating her for making a mess of his life, too.

The worst part was that for the first time in her life, Sheilagh didn't like waking up in the morning. Often she wished she were dead.

She would have liked to tell Clay all these things, but he was too busy. He intended to build Emerald into the largest chocolate kingdom on earth. Sheilagh wondered if he envisioned himself as king. In the morning he would roll out of bed, dress, and leave for work. In the past month he had begun to travel for the company. He was opening the New York market, which required that he take the New York Central train approximately every ten days. Sheilagh was left alone with Andrew.

As spring moved into May, Mary Margaret once again found herself back in the good graces of her society friends. To her credit, she was a good organizer and possessed a flair for cajoling reluctant matrons to sign up for the kind of tedious work that went into making a charity event a success. She was back in demand, and she reveled in it. This time she vowed she would make herself indispensable; never would she be put in a position to be ostracized again. Her absences gave Michael nearly free reign of the house. He came and went as he pleased. He dated the girls he liked and he answered to no one.

Patrick was having troubles of his own with Shannon. Since the birth of his grandson, he had begun to feel old. Shannon suddenly realized that her business, which Patrick had bankrolled, was not enough. She wanted more. She decided quite precipitously that she wanted a family of her own. She gave him an ultimatum. "Get a divorce, Patrick. I've had enough of all this. I want to be married. I want to have a baby like Sheilagh's."

Patrick sat on Shannon's sofa and glanced at the heavy drapes, which had to remain drawn so that the neighbors would not see him. He rose to pour another whiskey. "I'm sure Sheilagh would gladly hand him over," he said, chuckling to himself.

"I don't mean I want her brat. I mean I want a real life. Either you love me or you don't. Tell Mary Margaret you want out or I'm leaving you."

Full of himself and his power over Shannon, Patrick merely threw her a dark look. "You know the rules. I never lied to you. I will not break up my family . . ."

"What family?" Shannon stormed. "Your kids are practically gone. Mary Margaret doesn't love you, and you don't love her. And don't give me that bit about divorce being against the church rules. I want to be married, Patrick."

"Fine. Go get married." He poured three fingers of whiskey instead of two. He turned to her. "I remember when we met you seemed pretty happy with this arrangement. I even remember you telling me once—in bed, I might add—that you wanted a married man. There were no strings that way. That way no man could try to coerce you into something you didn't want. Do you remember that?"

"Yes, I do. But I've changed. I'm older now. I want something better for myself." She stood with her hands on her hips.

"Well, I haven't changed." He downed the whiskey, placed the glass on the credenza, and reached for his hat. "I had a great time with you, Shannon. But I won't do this. It's wrong."

"Oh, ha! I'm wrong? I'm the sinner here? What about adultery? That's okay, I suppose," she wailed as fear pressed in on her.

Patrick adjusted his hat. "As long as I'm calling the shots, it's okay," he said pompously. He laid his hand on the door latch. "You can keep the furniture."

"I intend to," she said firmly. "Patrick?"

He spun around a bit too quickly to face her. "Yes?"

"Don't let that door slam you in the ass on your way out." She kept her hands on her hips and did not move an inch toward him.

"I won't," he said, and left.

As Patrick walked down the concrete steps of the house he had bought for Shannon, not once did he dream this would be the last he would see of her. Give her a few weeks without him and his money, and she would come crawling back. Shannon loved him. He would bet his life on it. She needed him. This was simply a passing whim of hers. She would get over this baby thing in time, and then they would go back to normal.

Days passed into weeks. The weeks droned on and still Patrick did not hear from Shannon. She did not come crawling back. She did not plead with him. There were no frantic phone calls, as there had been in the past. She was not rushing to shower him with apologies.

Patrick got the sick feeling that Shannon had moved on.

It was on Sunday, two weeks after Mother's Day, that Patrick saw Shannon at the twelve-o'clock mass at Ascension Church. His heart nearly leapt out of his throat when he saw the man she was with. He was a tall, young man of about thirty-four with dark hair and a massive, virile physique. Patrick suddenly felt incredibly middle-aged, overweight, and lonely.

He watched her as she stood, knelt, and prayed. He watched the tilt of her head beneath the wide-brimmed black hat she wore when she smiled at the man next to her. He noticed that she reached out for his hand and held it firmly when they knelt for the Offertory. Patrick felt his heart sink in a quagmire of jealousy, loss, and pain. He had made a mistake. A grave mistake. Shannon was not coming back to him. She was moving on with her life, and Patrick realized for the first time that he truly loved her. Now it was too late.

He hung his head and tried to pray, but he didn't know how. He found no solace in the Gospel reading, nor in the words the priest spoke during the homily. He watched his wife as she greeted her Rosary Sodality friends and the couples they had known for twenty years in Oak Park. He noticed that they gave perfunctory glances toward him, as if he were a nonentity.

He had spent his entire life choosing not to love. He told himself he did not need love and did not need to give love. He had no real friends. His wife did not care for him, his children only tolerated him. He had believed he had emotional control over Shannon. He'd told himself their affair was a matter of lust. When had it gone wrong? When had the balance of power tipped away from him?

The congregation filed out into the sunshine. As they did, Patrick noticed that the handsome man escorted Shannon to a shiny new black Cadillac. The man must be a professional or wealthy by birth, he thought. Waves of jealousy threatened to pull Patrick into their undertow. He positioned himself on the church steps so that Shannon could not miss him when her car passed him by, but she never looked his way. She was too busy kissing her companion on the cheek. Her smiles were filled with joy.

It was Michael who nudged his father. "Come on. We'll be late for the Cubs game."

"I'm coming," Patrick said as he started down the church steps, still not taking his eyes off the retreating black Cadillac. As he followed his son, Patrick realized he had no one to blame but himself.

He'd become weak. These emotions he felt for Shannon could be easily erased. He would be tough again. He would never let another human being get close to him again. So he'd faltered this time. So what? It would never happen again. It was time for him to get back to using people before they used him.

Sheilagh stood next to Mary Margaret holding a squawling Andrew. Clay handed a quarter to the newsboy for a copy of the Sunday *Chicago Tribune*.

"Let me hold him, Sheilagh," Mary Margaret said tersely. "I don't know what you do to make him cry so much. It was quite distracting to hear him screaming . . ."

"Mother . . . stop." Sheilagh ground out the words through clenched teeth as she handed over her son. "I did not make him cry. I am *trying* to make him stop crying. And I doubt very seriously that Andrew upset the congregation when I walked out of mass with him after the first few minutes!"

"I could still hear him. So could others." Mary Margaret cooed to the baby and chucked him under his chin. To Sheilagh's disgust, Andrew quieted down to a whimper.

Sheilagh balled her fists at her sides and rolled her eyes. "Oooh! It makes me so mad when he does that." She knew that Andrew had been winding down for hours. Near noon was normally about the time of day that he would sleep for twenty to thirty minutes out of sheer exhaustion. It galled her that her mother would take full advantage of the situation and try to beat Sheilagh down again. To her credit, Mary Margaret was predictable, Sheilagh thought, but on the other hand, she had begun to believe her mother's put-downs.

Mary Margaret threw her daughter a supercilious smile. "I just don't know how it's possible that you didn't inherit any of my nurturing instincts. Sometimes, Sheilagh, I think you are either lazy or plain stupid."

Sheilagh couldn't hold back this time. Anger beat inside her like a war drum. "Don't call me stupid." Her eyes were white-hot with the anger that had been lying beneath her depression.

Believing she had won a large measure of control over Sheilagh in the past year, Mary Margaret was ready for the confrontation. Her words were a mere whisper, but they sank into Sheilagh's heart like deadly arrows. "I'll say as I please because I speak the truth, Sheilagh Burke, and you know it. You are an incompetent mother if ever I've seen one. I should have known you wouldn't be any good at this job or anything else in life. Look at you. When was the last time you washed your hair or pressed your dress? You come to church looking as if you just rolled out of bed. No wonder your husband never looks at you. Did you see how Emily Reilly and Erica Kelly just passed you by? I did. Do you know why they did that? Because they don't want to be associated with a—" Mary Margaret glanced to the left and to the right to make certain no one was listening, then she pushed her face so close to her daughter's that the rush of her hot breath made Sheilagh blink "—*whore*."

"Shut up, Mo . . . ther," Sheilagh snarled back. She tried to reach for Andrew, but Mary Margaret turned her body and the baby away from Sheilagh, though she kept her gaze locked on her daughter's.

"Not until I'm finished, missy." Mary Margaret took a deep breath. "Everyone in this parish is going to know the truth if you don't start shaping up. Take care of yourself, Sheilagh. Quit being so lazy and self-indulgent, and find your pride. Start being a mother to your son and teach him to stop his bawling."

Sheilagh felt the prick of tears in her eyes, and though it took all the self-control she could muster to beat them back, she kept her eyes dry as she made another grab for her baby. This time she was able to wrench him from her mother's firm hold. Andrew instantly burst into tears.

"Now see what you've done!" Mary Margaret chided haughtily.

"I didn't do anything but reclaim him from a harpy!" Sheilagh retorted, and spun on her heel to stomp away.

Sheilagh was looking down at her red-faced son instead of where she was going, and she bumped into Emily Reilly.

Emily was dressed in a new red and white striped linen suit. It had cost fifty-nine dollars, Sheilagh knew, because she had tried the suit on. But on Sheilagh and Clay's meager budget, it might as well have been a thousand.

"Hi," Sheilagh finally said. "I'm sorry. I guess I wasn't aware of where I was going."

Emily looked down her long, perfectly powdered nose over the edge of her brilliantly cherry red lips at Sheilagh. She touched the brim of her red straw hat. She pressed a conceited smile across her face.

Another twenty-five bucks for the hat, Sheilagh thought.

"Sheilagh? Is that you?" Emily rolled out the words over the barbed end of her tongue.

"Yes," Sheilagh replied softly, feeling sick to her stomach. She didn't like playing the role of the sinner, the downcast.

"Why, I hardly recognized you! Erica said it was you during Communion, but I said, 'No. That's not *our* Sheilagh! You've gained a little weight, haven't you, dear? And what happened to your hair? A new color for spring that we don't know about?"

Emily's titters were almost more than Sheilagh could bear. "Yeah, I call it bloodshot baby red."

Emily glanced only momentarily at Andrew, who was squirming and pitching about in Sheilagh's arms. His face was scrunching up and contorting the way it did whenever his stomach had begun agitating. Sheilagh knew the newest baby formula the doctor had ordered was not going to keep Andrew from colic any more than the previous dozen. "Would you like to hold my darling baby, Emily? He's such a joy."

"Well, I don't know much about babies," Emily replied, and lifted a gloved finger to touch Andrew's tiny hand.

"Oh, go ahead, Emily," Sheilagh urged maliciously. "He won't bite. He doesn't get teeth for another four or five months, so they tell me." Sheilagh held Andrew out for Emily to take.

Emily gingerly held him in her arms.

Andrew's face contorted. His eyes were screwed shut.

Emily chucked him under the chin with her snowy white gloved finger. "Cooocheee Cooo."

Andrew's lips parted. His body tensed.

"Cooocheee Cooo."

Andrew's projectile vomit covered Emily's gloved hand, and the sleeve and bodice of her brand-new linen suit.

"Oooohhh, my Gawd!" Sheilagh feigned shock as she slapped her hand against her cheek. "I'm sooo sorry. He just never ever does anything like that." She made no move to take back her son.

"Ugh!" Emily's nose crinkled as she turned her head away from the foul smell. "Here." She thrust the baby at Sheilagh. "Quick! A handkerchief. Do you have one, Sheilagh?"

Sheilagh took Andrew back and flung him over her shoulder so that when he vomited the second time, it would project into the bushes behind her. That was the beauty of colic and projectile vomiting, Sheilagh thought; it could be aimed like a gun. "I'm so sorry, Emily. He's never done this. I guess I didn't come prepared," Sheilagh said, and walked off as Emily rummaged through her purse searching for a handkerchief.

Sheilagh walked up to Clay, who was talking to Michael about the baseball game.

"Oh, there you are, Sheilagh. Michael wants me to take him to the Cubs game this afternoon. I said I would."

"Fine," Sheilagh snapped as she wiped Andrew's mouth with the edge of a clean diaper she pulled out of her oversize purse.

"What's the matter with you, sis?" Michael asked.

"Nothin'. Give me the keys to the car," she ordered Clay tersely.

He dug in his pants pockets. "If you don't want me to go, just say so."

"No! Believe me, I want you to go! I honestly would rather be alone today." She snatched the keys out of Clay's hand and stalked off to the church parking lot.

Sheilagh opened the back door and laid Andrew in his bassinet, then covered him with a thin receiving blanket, which he kicked off immediately, all the while continuing to cry.

She got into the front seat and started the car. The good thing about church on Sunday was the drive home, which almost always rocked Andrew to sleep, Sheilagh thought as she pulled out of the parking lot and drove past the front of the church where her family was still standing.

She saw Clay and Michael walk off together toward the corner where they could catch the bus. Clay had his arm around Michael's shoulder, and they seemed to be quite content in their camaraderie. She saw her mother, who was speaking to two other equally well-dressed women of her age whose daughters stood off to the left with their perfectly dressed children. She saw her father standing alone smoking a cigarette, gazing off to the west and looking as if he'd just lost his best friend.

They were an odd family, each orbiting around the others, making pathways of their own. Only God knew, Sheilagh thought, how long it would be until they all collided.

Chapter 29 ──────────────

$\mathcal{I}$T WAS A freak June storm. Clay was in New York. Mary Margaret and Patrick had gone to Lake Geneva to host a dinner party for the Art Guild. Michael was in his fourth day at summer camp. Andrew had only Sheilagh to care for him.

The Canadian winds blasted down through Wisconsin and into Illinois with a vengeance. They carried bitter rains and pelting hail. The mercury dropped from a balmy sixty-five degrees to a bone-chilling forty-one in less than an hour. Lightning split the dark clouds and turned the raindrops to silver pellets. As night fell, the temperature continued to drop.

Sheilagh sat in the rocking chair holding her son and listening to the thunder. With each flash of lightning she cursed aloud. "Damn storm!" Andrew had almost fallen into a blessed sleep when the storm began. With each crack of thunder, he jolted awake and began screaming again. He vomited. He belched. He wailed. She placed her hand on his forehead. He still had a fever. The baby aspirin should start to work soon. The last time he had bronchitis, the aspirin brought his temperature back to normal in less than two hours.

Sheilagh rocked and sang to herself. She felt as if she were going insane.

It had been over ninety days since she had slept all night. She often thought she would do anything, *anything*, just to be able to sleep. How she wanted to sleep! She often felt that two solid weeks of sleep would not be enough. She could never catch up. Never.

Lightning zig-zagged against the ebony sky. Sheilagh braced. Andrew wailed. The thunder boomed. Wind whistled through the cracks in the paper-thin walls of the cheap apartment. The cold sank into her back between her shoulder blades, where she was most achy from standing and walking the baby all day. She pulled a blanket around her shoulders. The wind crept through the electrical sockets and sent long tendrils of cold wafting across the floor. Sheilagh curled her toes.

"Hush, hush, Andrew," she said in singsong tones as she stared blank-faced out the window.

Andrew cried out again, choked on his phlegm, and cried some more.

He had already survived four major bouts of bronchitis. Twice, he had developed pneumonia before he'd shown any signs of fever, though the accumulation of phlegm in his stomach always caused vomiting. He was sick so often that Sheilagh kept the bottle of belladonna and paregoric, prescribed by Dr. Carter for the baby's vomiting, on top of the dresser next to the crib. She was always careful to fill the medicine dropper only halfway, because the doctor had told her that too much narcotic could kill a baby as small as Andrew.

She picked him up and put him over her shoulder. She patted and rubbed his back. He screamed into her ear, shattering her nerves.

"Hush, baby," she whispered, and rubbed his back again.

She felt like a somnambulist. There were no emotions left in Sheilagh anymore, just dull, endless body motions repeated over and over. She ran her hand up his back and onto the smooth skin at the nape of his neck. He had just the beginnings of hair on his head. It was fine and featherlike auburn fuzz, but it felt like the rarest silk. Sheilagh's eyes blinked once . . . twice. She touched the soft hair and the smooth, rounded back of his head.

"How tiny you still are, baby," she said aloud. She continued to stare at the lightning.

Andrew needed her.

That was what Sheilagh's life boiled down to . . . Her baby depended on her for everything. She bathed him, groomed him, fed him, changed him. She loved him.

The thought hit her like the lightning's flash. Sheilagh loved Andrew. He had not given her a thing. She wasn't even sure if he loved her back. But she knew that she loved him without condition.

She lifted him from her shoulder and laid him in the crook of her arm, gazing into his face. He was three months old now and had begun to look more like a human being. He had her hair color and her green eyes, now that their baby blue had begun to recede. He had a wide rib cage like Clay's, and narrow hips. But his skin and his high cheekbones were Sheilagh's. He was Sheilagh's child through and through, and for the first time, she looked at her son as the gift he truly was. For the first time, she was glad she had not aborted this child.

She picked him up and kissed him on the mouth. "I love you, Andrew."

He stopped crying. He seemed to be stunned by the sensation on his mouth. For a long moment he looked up into his mother's eyes, as if seeing her for the first time. They were not a baby's eyes with a blank stare, but the eyes of one who understands. Sheilagh saw that look for only a quarter of a second, but she knew she had not imagined it.

She kissed him again. This time he smiled at her. It was his first real smile.

Sheilagh nearly leaped for joy. "You understand me, don't you, Drew? I love you!"

Andrew cooed.

Sheilagh smiled at her son.

Andrew sneezed. Then he smiled again. Then he farted.

Sheilagh burst into laughter and clunked her head against the back of the rocker. "You are my son! That's for sure!" She laughed again.

"I guess it's time to get you to bed," she said to him.

She padded barefoot across the cold wooden floor to the bedroom. She placed him in his new open-slatted crib, a hand-me-down from one of her mother's Rosary Sodality friends at church. She covered Andrew with several blankets and tiptoed out of the room. As she shut the door, he sneezed again.

She went to the radiator under the window and opened the valve, hoping that the building superintendent had not closed down the furnace for the summer. Then she fell into bed, fully dressed.

Sheilagh awoke in the morning to an icy apartment. She was huddled beneath two blankets and a comforter, with only her face exposed. She touched her nose. It felt as if she'd been outside in a snowstorm. She rose, stuck her feet in Clay's slippers, and headed for the bathroom. The tiled floor felt twice as cold. She knew the heat had not come on at all during the night.

She gazed at herself in the mirror, leaning both hands on either side of the white porcelain basin. She yawned. She felt her empty stomach growl. She thought of cornflakes and milk for breakfast. She ran a hand through her hair. She should get a haircut and a body wave. She looked at the dark circles under her eyes and the pallid look to her skin and wondered how much rouge it would take to make her look alive again.

Then she thought of Andrew. He had slept all night! He had never slept the night through before. When she'd been in the pediatrician's office last month, she had spoken to a woman who had just had her third child, and the woman had told her that three months was a turning point for infants. She could start to expect things to improve. He would eat better, sleep better, have more personality, so the woman had said.

Sheilagh was feeling elated when suddenly she remembered that the last sound she had heard from Andrew was a sneeze. She yanked the blanket from her shoulders and hurried into his room.

He was lying on his stomach, as he usually did while sleeping. She smiled to herself, thinking how silly she had been to be alarmed.

She walked over to the crib, looked down at him, and started to touch his head but retracted her hand. It had been so long since they had both slept, she did not want to wake him. Instead, she gazed at her still son.

Andrew was not breathing.

"Andrew?" Her hand shot to his back and she turned him over. He was ice-cold. Cold as death. Chills covered her body. *"Andrew?"* He was blue. His lungs didn't move in his tiny chest.

"Andrew!" She flung him to her chest. Maybe if she held him close to her heart, her love would warm him. Her feet padded across the floor and then slid quickly back and forth in Clay's slippers. "My baby!" Tears blinded her. Sobs caught in her throat.

Panic seized her, but her body seemed to know what to do. She threw on a winter coat and pulled the heaviest blanket off her bed and wrapped it around first Andrew, then herself. Perhaps the blanket would have magical powers the way it did when she was a child hiding beneath it from the bogeyman.

She opened the apartment door. She could barely see through her tears. The car, she thought. The keys . . .

She quickly went back to the cheap coffee table where she had placed the car keys. She raced out the door and down the stairs.

This time she held Andrew next to her chest as she started the car. The motor was cold and the engine would not turn over. She pressed the starter button again. She pulled the choke.

The car would not start. She looked at the round outdoor thermometer on the outside of the white, barnlike garage. It was thirty-one degrees.

The battery must be dead.

It was eleven blocks to the pediatrician's office. She should call him, but that would take time. She had to get Andrew to the doctor as fast as possible. She got out of the car, took off Clay's slippers and left them by the side of the car, and ran.

Sheilagh ran down the wet, icy sidewalks as the morning sun rose in the east. The sun was warm on her face, promising that the sudden wintry blast would be gone by noon. She clutched Andrew to her chest and raced across an intersection, forcing a motorist to slam on the brakes. She ran faster.

Sheilagh's feet were nearly frozen. She cut the bottom of her right foot on a piece of a broken Coke bottle, but she hardly felt the pain. Her mind was racing faster than her feet.

"Don't be dead. Don't be dead. My life will be over if my baby is dead . . ." She recited the litany over and over.

She ran. She ran past old women on their way to eight-o'clock mass. She ran past a little boy in corduroy overalls riding a tricycle. She ran past a newsboy with an armful of the morning edition of the *Chicago Tribune*. She hated how life kept going on around her when her world was coming apart.

"Don't be dead. Don't be dead . . ."

She raced across three more intersections until she saw the redbrick building. She flew up the steps and nearly tripped on the blanket's edge.

She opened the door and burst into the empty reception room. The nurse had just come to her desk behind the opaque sliding glass window.

"Help me!" Sheilagh screamed as she charged up to the window.

The nurse slid the glass aside, took one look at Sheilagh, and scrambled around from behind her desk. "Come! Quickly!" She motioned to Sheilagh to come into the examining room area.

Sheilagh opened the door and followed the nurse down the hall.

"Dr. Carter!" the nurse yelled, nearly as frantic as Sheilagh.

The young doctor stepped into the hallway. He thrust his arms out to Sheilagh. "Give him to me." Sheilagh placed Andrew in his arms. "Get the respirator!" he ordered the nurse, who quickly and efficiently wheeled a respirator and the familiar oxygen tent to the side of the examining table.

The doctor laid Andrew on the table. He placed his fingers on the baby's neck, checking for a heartbeat.

Sheilagh wrung her hands. She moved from foot to foot as if she would jump out of her skin. Unchecked tears streamed down her cheeks. Her eyes shot frantically from the nurse to the doctor to Andrew and back to the doctor again.

She watched as the doctor halted the nurse in her ministrations. "What?"

The nurse dropped her hands and lowered her eyes.

Sheilagh's eyes shot back to the doctor. She felt her stomach fall from her body. "No." She shook her head slowly. "No! No! Nooo!" Her head shook violently, spilling tears to the floor. "Not my baby!"

"Sheilagh . . ." The doctor came around from his side of the examining table to hers. "Sheilagh . . ."

"Nooo!" She tried to pick up Andrew again. Her knees buckled. She sank to the floor. She knelt with her hands still on her dead baby. "Not my baby. Don't let him be dead." She looked at the doctor's shoes through her tears. "I'll do anything . . ." She raised her head and saw his black trousers, then his white lab coat, then his forlorn face. His compassionate eyes. Sheilagh lost the last shred of hope.

"Oh, God . . ." Her face fell to her hands and she cried until she could cry no more. Then she collapsed.

A narcotic veil kept Sheilagh from seeing Clay clearly. She didn't know where she was or how she had gotten there. She could hear him crying, but she didn't know what he was crying about. She drifted off to sleep and had nightmares about dead babies. When she woke up, she thought she was in her bedroom, and she was certain that Dr. Carter was with her. He injected something into her arm, and she sailed away on a boat over a sea of fairy dust where all the babies looked like Andrew. She stayed there for a very long time and played with him. He was older and could talk now. He pleaded with her never to go back home. She promised she would stay with him always.

Sheilagh thought her mother came to her in her dreams. Then she was sitting in her rocking chair, but there was no baby in her arms. The room around her seemed black, with no sunshine. Her mother was with her.

"I should have known you would do something like this."
Mary Margaret's voice came to her as if she were talking
through a megaphone underwater.

"Like what, Mother?"

"Kill your baby."

"Oh, I would never do that," Sheilagh wanted to say, but she
was so numb, she couldn't feel her own words in her throat.

"You killed him with the belladonna. Did you give him too
much on purpose? Are your own selfish needs so great that you
would resort to murder? My God! How is it possible I could
have given birth to a devil like you? You are a wicked, wicked
girl, Sheilagh. I will have nothing to do with you. You have
brought nothing but disgrace to this family. After the funeral,
I never want to see you again."

"What funeral?"

"Andrew's funeral, of course. Haven't you heard a word I've
said? That's just like you, Sheilagh. You never do anything
right. You never listen. You're lazy and disobedient. Maybe
it's a good thing Andrew is dead. At least he won't have to
go through life with you as a mother."

"What are you saying? Andrew isn't dead. He's in his crib."

"Andrew is dead, Sheilagh. You murdered him, just like
you intended. You just keep piling sin upon sin, don't you,
Sheilagh?" Mary Margaret's voice faded.

Sheilagh looked around the black room again, but this time
her mother was gone and Patrick was there.

His voice, too, seemed to gurgle at her. "Poison," he said
accusingly. "Your mother warned me that you were a vile
creature, but I never wanted to believe it. Now I must. I will
keep your secret for you, Sheilagh. I never want anyone to
know the truth. In exchange for that, I want you to disappear.
I will not have the good Killian name sullied by your scandals
anymore. I'm doing you a favor, Sheilagh. You just remember that."

Her eyes crossed as she tried to focus on her father. She
wanted to ask him why he never loved anyone but himself. She
wanted to know why they were all so unimportant to him.
What had they done . . . *she* done . . . that made him keep his
love buttoned up the way he did? "I'll keep your secret, too,"
she said.

"I have no secrets, Sheilagh."

"Yes, you do. The man you killed . . . your mistress that we
all know about . . . Your secrets are worse than mine."

"Keep your mouth shut, Sheilagh. God, but I will be glad never to have to lay eyes on you again."

She looked up at the ghostly figure that sounded like her father, but she saw no one. "I don't understand what all of you are trying to tell me. I didn't hurt Andrew. I didn't give him any medicine today. Andrew isn't dead. I just talked with him," Sheilagh said to the darkness.

Nobody was there to listen.

The funeral was wrenching for Caitlin. She had seen Andrew only once, when she had come home for his christening, then had quickly raced back to school and Matthew, trying to keep as much distance as possible between her new life and the old one in Chicago.

Caitlin talked to her mother, who shed no light on the events of the night that Andrew died, except to blame Sheilagh for incompetence. Clay was despondent but strong as he spoke with the friends, neighbors, and coworkers who came to the funeral home and then to the requiem mass. Caitlin finally talked to the doctor and nurse, and discovered that Andrew's bronchitis had turned into pneumonia. In his short life he had fought pneumonia twice before, and because his lungs had never properly developed in the first place, he was simply too weak to keep fighting. Dr. Carter told Caitlin that Andrew's chances of living a year had been poor. She knew that his death was not Sheilagh's fault, but God's choice. She only wished that Sheilagh knew it.

Matthew held Caitlin's hand as they stood at the grave site and listened to the priest who prayed the last prayers over Andrew's coffin. Caitlin slipped a glance at Clay. He looked devastated. She noticed how he pulled Sheilagh to his side, as if he was the one who needed her support. Just then, he raised his head as if he sensed Caitlin's eyes on him. His blue gaze was full of pain, but in that moment, Caitlin saw his love for her hiding in the depths. He turned away and hung his head.

The priest blessed the casket with holy water. "In the name of the Father . . ."

Sheilagh teetered on her black pumps, which Clay had bought for the funeral, a gesture of apology for being in New York when Andrew died. She grabbed Clay's arm for support and leaned into him without looking up at him. She could barely see the coffin through the black veil that hung over her face . . .

Michael stood between Mary Margaret and Patrick. He closed his eyes and promised God that he would save ten lives his first year as a doctor to make up for Andrew's death.

" . . . and the Son and the Holy Ghost. Amen."

The rite was over. Sheilagh could hear people blowing their noses. She heard muffled voices offer condolences. She could feel her head bob up and down as she looked at the mournful faces around her. Her hand was patted, caressed, and sometimes shaken as the people left the grave site. She felt Caitlin's arms go around her and hug her. She remembered meeting a pleasant boy named Matthew, who was supposed to be Caitlin's fiancé, but she wasn't sure. The clearest memory she would keep about her son's funeral was the expression of love in her sister's eyes every time she looked at Clay.

Sheilagh was not the only person to see and feel the strong chemistry between Clay and Caitlin. Matthew saw it, too.

It was three weeks after the funeral when Caitlin received her grades from St. Mary's in the mail. She used the occasion as an excuse to telephone Matthew in Michigan City, where he was spending the summer with his parents.

"I got my grades!" She blurted. "All A's!"

"You sound so surprised," Matthew said. "I knew you could do it."

"I was worried about political science. It was tough."

"Yeah."

"What's the matter, Matthew? You don't sound excited for me. Did your grades disappoint you?"

"No. I got the same. All A's."

"You should be excited."

"Yeah."

"What is it, Matthew?"

"I've got a lot on my mind."

"Like what?"

"Like us. Like how come this is the first time you've called me since you've been home? Like how come I write to you almost every day, and I've gotten only four letters from you? You haven't mentioned anything about seeing me. No plans for the Fourth of July. Why is that, Kit Cat?"

"It's been hard here, you know? Andrew's death has put a pall on everything. Sheilagh is really weird. I think the doctor still has her on some sleeping medicine. Work is a pain. I thought I would love coming back to Emerald, but it doesn't have the same old zing. I think it's because I miss you so much."

"Yeah? I think it's because you're in love with your sister's husband."

"Matthew! How can you say such a thing?"

"Simple. I've got eyes. I saw how you looked at him at the funeral. You see him every day now. Must be hell knowing you can't have him."

Caitlin felt her stomach lurch. "What a horrible thing to say, Matthew Lindsey. I'm engaged to you, aren't I?"

"True. But do I really have your heart, Kit Cat?"

Caitlin knew that Matthew was searching for reassurance. They had been apart for nearly a month, and she realized it was much too long. How could it have been so long already? She seemed swamped every day with work and seeing her old high school friends at lunch, having board meetings and sales meetings with Clay. There were weekend trips to Lake Geneva, bridal showers for Sheilagh's girlfriends, picnics with her friends, and Cubs games with Michael. Caitlin was home again. It was as if someone had slipped the calendar back to last summer, and St. Mary's had never existed. Matthew had never existed.

"Yes, you really have my heart, Matthew," she said. "Why don't you come to Oak Park this weekend and I'll show you."

"I'd like that . . . a lot. Can we be alone?" he asked playfully.

"That might be a bit difficult."

"Why?"

"Because my mother is already giving me lectures about the proper conduct for a bride-to-be."

"Does she know you're forcing me to wait three more years?"

"Yes. She thinks it's admirable."

"Good. Maybe this time when I meet her it will be under better circumstances and she can get to know me and like me."

"I know she will." Caitlin's voice trailed off. She could not imagine Mary Margaret genuinely liking anyone anymore. There was a brittle edge to her mother that had formed over the years. Caitlin guessed it probably had always been there, she just hadn't seen it before. Now that she had been away from the family for a year, she looked at everything differently.

Caitlin wasn't so sure she wanted Matthew to meet her family again. Sheilagh was still despondent over Andrew's death. Her father had spent the past month drinking far more than usual, which was a lot to begin with. He was sullen and distant. He talked to no one at work unless it was strictly business. To Caitlin he seemed sad, but she didn't know why.

She realized with a jolt that the main reason she had not previously invited Matthew to Oak Park was that she was ashamed of her family. She didn't want him to be subjected to her mother's indefatigable scrutiny, or her father's embarrassing drunkenness. Caitlin was afraid that Matthew would reject her once he learned the truth about her family. She realized that she was repeating a pattern of denying herself close relationships because she knew she must protect the family secrets. She wondered if her actions stemmed from loyalty and honor or simple shame.

"Tell me you love me."

"I love you, Matthew," Caitlin said perfunctorily.

"And that you will meet me at the train station on Friday afternoon."

"I will."

"Good. I'll see you then. And Kit Cat?"

"Yes, Matthew?"

"Try to mean it the next time you tell me you love me," he said, and hung up the phone.

Matthew arrived at four o'clock on Friday afternoon. Caitlin was at the train station waiting for him. In those few moments as she paced up and down beside track number two, she realized that she had indeed missed him. Only a handful of passengers disembarked from the train since most people went out of town on Fridays, headed for the sandy shores of Indiana. Matthew was nearly the last passenger off the train.

Caitlin ran to his open arms.

"Kit Cat!" He picked her up and whirled her around and then kissed her soundly on the lips. He held her face in his hands and looked deep into her eyes. "Are you still my girl?"

"Oh, yes, Matthew," she said, and kissed him back.

"We're going to have a glorious weekend, aren't we?"

"I hope so. I hope so," she said, and put her head on his shoulder as they walked out of the train station with their arms around each other.

In the weeks since the funeral, Sheilagh had noticed that though her mother telephoned her most mornings to inquire as to her well-being, Mary Margaret could not hide the condemnation in her voice. However, it was not Mary Margaret's disapproval of her that changed her life; Sheilagh wanted to believe that one day her mother would empathize with her.

Patrick came to her apartment, unannounced. She opened the door and invited him in.

"I sent Clay to Detroit for two days," he said abruptly, "so he won't be around while you pack."

"Am I going somewhere?"

"New York," he said flatly, as he withdrew an envelope from his breast pocket. "In here you'll find a train ticket and a letter from my attorney to Herb Klein in New York, who will handle your divorce for you. I've already paid his fees. There's enough money to pay your expenses for six months. That ought to get you started in your career."

Sheilagh watched his steel blue eyes as he spoke. There was not a spark of light in them. It was as if his soul were dead.

The scene of him in her apartment after Andrew's death came to her. In her stupor she'd confessed to him that she knew about Joseph Alvaranti's death. Patrick needed to get her out of his life. She was a liability.

An ice-cold chill blanketed her body as she thought, *He would stop at nothing to get rid of me, too. He's my father, but that means nothing to him.*

Sheilagh never believed those fairy tales in Catholic school about devils and demons, but she knew evil when she saw it.

She took the envelope from him. "What time is the train?" she asked.

Two hours later, long after Patrick had left, she propped a note on the cheap wooden coffee table next to the plant, now dead, that someone had given her when Andrew died. She could not recall the name of the sender.

She did not look around the apartment one last time when she picked up her suitcases and opened the door. She never wanted to think about this part of her life ever again. There never had been anything for her in Chicago but pain, and here, in these grim rooms, she had plummeted to the depths.

She walked quietly down the stairs so as not to arouse Mrs. Litsky, who was much too snoopy for her own good. She walked into the sunshine and up to the cab she had called. The cabbie helped her with her suitcases and then closed the door after she climbed into the backseat. He threw the lever on his meter and sped away from the corner.

"Where you goin', miss?" he asked.

"New York City," Sheilagh said confidently.

She wondered if Clay would cry when he read the letter that told him she was leaving him for good. She wondered if he would be relieved that she intended to file for divorce. She wondered how long it would take him to forget her. Could she forget him?

"It's nice there this time of year. You been there before?"

"No, I haven't. I've wanted to visit for a long time now," she said.

She wondered if Clay would turn to Caitlin. She wondered if her mother would give her departure a second thought. She wondered if her father knew any of them existed anymore. She wondered how many times she would think of them all. She wondered if she would keep on dreaming of Andrew.

"I lived in New York for three years," the cabbie said. "I loved it when I was there, but I'm glad I left."

"Really?" Sheilagh asked. "Why did you leave?"

"Bad memories," he said, then checked himself and swerved around a parked bus.

"I know what you mean," Sheilagh replied. She wondered if Clay ever thought about Andrew. If Andrew really was an angel, which is what the nuns had told her happened to babies when they died.

She had had him for only three months. Three short months. She hated the God who would take her baby from her. She hated her mother, who had blamed and rejected her. She wondered if anyone's life was worth the pain they endured.

"How long you stayin' in New York?" the cabbie asked as he looked at Sheilagh in the rearview mirror.

She whipped off the scarf she wore over her auburn hair and rolled down the window to let the wind blow in her face. She inhaled the scents of Chicago. The vision of the headstone she had ordered for Andrew's grave came to mind. It was a simple stone with a single line etched across the face: "I loved you best." She looked at the cabbie's reflection in the rearview mirror.

"Forever," she replied, and meant it.

Chapter 30 ————————————

*T*HE SHOCKS CAME in waves.

Sheilagh filed for divorce from Clay in July. She petitioned the court to·restore her maiden name.

Mary Margaret hired an attorney to file the necessary papers to officially eliminate Sheilagh from her will and as an heir to any part of the Emerald fortune.

Despondent and angry over his loss of Shannon, Patrick did nothing to thwart Mary Margaret's actions against his oldest daughter. He felt an incredible need to protect himself. He announced to the family that Sheilagh's abandonment of the family should be punished. He reminded them of his childhood, and said that he refused to share his wealth with anyone *he* did not deem worthy.

He painted a picture of Sheilagh that was as black as possible to cover up his participation in her departure. Patrick stepped into this new phase of his life weighted down with greed.

Mary Margaret forbade both Michael and Caitlin from having any communication with Sheilagh. Neither of them paid their mother any mind, though they did not hear from their sister for weeks. She left no forwarding address and no telephone number. It was as if she no longer existed.

"Sheilagh doesn't know anyone in New York," Michael said as he pitched a baseball to Caitlin.

It was a balmy summer night in Oak Park. The Killian house was lit up like a Christmas tree since Mary Margaret was entertaining her ladies' circle from the church. Caitlin had suggested she and Michael go to the backyard and play catch like they used to. They stood in puddles of golden light coming from the kitchen and dining room windows and threw the ball back and forth. It seemed odd not to have Sheilagh cheerleading them, keeping count of catches and errors.

"I bet she lives with that Abe . . . what was his name?"

"Meindel," Michael said. He caught the ball and practiced his curve ball.

Caitlin nearly missed the perfect pitch. "Got it!" she said, straightening up. "Do you think he sent her the money for the trip?"

"Yep."

"So do I," Caitlin replied, and sent the baseball sailing back to her brother. "Do you think she likes this Abe guy?"

"Naw." Michael eased out his arm and gloved the ball in a fluid motion. "She needs him, though."

"Needs him more than Clay?"

"Yep. She never stopped wanting to be an actress, Cat. All that time you were in school, I could see it. She tried to be something she wasn't, and it never worked. Sheilagh is Sheilagh. Nobody can stop her."

Caitlin nodded. She saw her mother pass across the dining room window. Mary Margaret still wore the hat she'd pinned to her head for evening mass. There was something so tight and controlled about their mother that Caitlin shook her head in dismay. "Someday Mother is going to find out that she can't play God with us."

Michael laughed derisively. "And who's going to teach her that lesson? You?"

"Maybe."

"You'll never have the guts." He threw the ball back. "Saint Caitlin isn't capable of telling the old bat off."

"And I suppose you are?"

"Naw. Personally, I think it's a waste of time and breath. I'm gonna do like Sheilagh . . . just get the hell out. And I'm never going to look back. Never."

"That's a long time, Michael. What if she needs you?"

Michael paused for a moment and studied the stitching on the ball. He looked up, and even through the darkness, Caitlin could see the resolve in his eyes. "I saved my money from my orderly job at the hospital. I've got the job for weekends all this next year. I have a master plan, one better than Sheilagh's. And I have a better idea of what to expect from dear old Mom and Dad than Sheilagh did. You see, she screwed up when she figured they would care what happened to her. Thanks to Sheilagh, you and I know how far they'll go to make us do what they want. They would write me off twice as fast." Michael hissed as he pulled back his arm and sent the ball whizzing through the air like a rocket.

Caitlin caught the ball, but it hit with such an impact that her wrist was jarred. "But you're their only son."

"Precisely. It'll be twice as rough on me when I leave."

Caitlin didn't want to hear any of this. She wanted to believe that her parents' anger against Sheilagh would be short-lived and that soon Patrick and Mary Margaret would take her back. Caitlin wanted them to be a happy family.

"You're too young to be so cynical, Michael," she said.

"And it's about time you wised up."

"Maybe it is," she answered. She knew it was time for her to stop wearing blinders. She was afraid that she didn't know how to live without her fantasies. Would she feel she needed to run away as Sheilagh had? It was one thing to go to college. It was another to give up her dream of working at Emerald.

Caitlin was afraid to delve any deeper into herself. Was she still living her life, dreaming of working at Emerald in particular, solely for the purpose of winning her father's approval? Did she believe that if she stayed in Chicago, she could win Mary Margaret's love? Was Michael right after all? Was she only kidding herself?

"Hey! Heads up!" Michael yelled as he pitched a perfect fastball.

Caitlin snapped out of her reverie and stuck her gloved hand in front of her face to nab the ball. She grinned at Michael. "Pretty good for a rookie, huh?"

"Yeah," he said, and walked out of the puddle of light like an actor leaving center stage. He joined Caitlin within her own lighted sphere. "So, Cat . . . when is Matthew coming to visit again?"

"This weekend," she replied sheepishly, looking down at the baseball.

"Does he know about Sheilagh leaving?"

"No. Why should he?"

"Because now Clay is a free man."

"What's that got to do with anything?" She did not raise her eyes for Michael's scrutiny.

"Good answer, Cat." Michael patted her shoulder. "I hope you mean it, 'cause I like Matthew. He's a swell guy."

"Yeah . . . swell." Caitlin felt a lump in her throat.

Michael looked up at the house. There was no sign of the ladies' meeting breaking up. "I'm gonna brave the interior and listen to the news report. You wanna join me in my room?"

"In a minute," she said as she took off the glove and handed it to Michael. "I think I'll just stay out here and enjoy this cool air."

"Can't say that I blame you."

As Michael walked away, she could hear the *plot, plat* sounds as he threw the ball in the air and caught it in his worn mitt. She walked over to the terrace and sat in one of the wrought-iron chairs. The new black and white striped canvas seat cushions were covered with night dew, but she didn't care. She looked up at the jet black sky. She picked out the North Star and followed it down the handle of the Little Dipper. She wondered what Matthew was doing tonight. Was he looking at the stars or was he following the latest war reports on the radio, like Michael? Was he thinking about her?

For a brief moment, Caitlin indulged in a thought about Clay, but she quickly stopped herself. Whatever there had been between them was over. Caitlin was engaged to Matthew. She had chosen to walk a new road, and it had no room for regret.

And Sheilagh? Where was she tonight? Did she have a roof over her head? Was she with Abe? Was there a show to rehearse? Was she happy?

For the first time, Caitlin realized that though she missed Sheilagh, she was also very angry with her sister. "Why did you leave me, too?" Caitlin did not understand why Sheilagh hadn't trusted her with her plans. Why had Sheilagh found it necessary to break with all of them? They had promised one another they would stick together, no matter what. But now Sheilagh had broken the sibling bond that had been so important to the three of them.

"What good are your promises, Sheilagh?" Caitlin said aloud to the stars. She continued to stare at the sky for a long time, but they never answered back.

By the summer of 1940, the war was escalating in Europe. France had fallen, and the British were left alone to fight the enemy. Edward R. Murrow's raspy voice broke across America on CBS radio stations.

"This is London . . ." his reports began, and went on to tell of blackouts in London, air raids, British school children being sent by buses and carloads to the English countryside to avoid the air attacks. The newly formed Home Guard was manned by elderly men who did not lack courage. A new invention called radar was employed by the British at eighteen points along the east and southeast coastlines. The radar ferreted out

Messerschmitts and pointed out their positions to the British Hurricanes flown by the RAF pilots.

The Royal Air Force was finally hitting back at Germany with a blitzkrieg of its own. On July 29, seventeen German planes sank in the English Channel. Only one RAF plane was lost. On August 8, eight hundred German planes blasted London. America cheered on their unofficial ally.

The new heroes of the day were the RAF pilots, the young men, some still boys, who pitted themselves against the massive German air force. They were courageous beyond measure, independent, and loyal to their comrades. They were indefatigable, often accomplishing as many as four air missions a day. Each time they went up in their Hurricanes, they knew they were tempting death. They were a rare, unconventional, and daring breed of man, and they were in short supply.

Matthew and Caitlin sat together, in between Mary Margaret and Michael, in the living room of the Oak Park home listening to Edward R. Murrow's latest report. "The city of London is beseiged. For three days and three nights, London has stood up to the bombings from the Germans . . ."

Matthew listened intently to the details of the fires, the six hundred fighters and six hundred bombers that comprised the German air fleet. He listened to the horrific description of the more than four hundred dead Londoners.

"It's hard to imagine . . . that could be Chicago . . ." Matthew said.

"What? The Germans here? Never!" Mary Margaret clacked her tongue in shock.

"Why not?" Matthew turned to her. "If they have the effrontery to take on London, why not Chicago? Or New York?"

Caitlin instantly thought of Sheilagh all alone somewhere in New York. It was September 10 now, and still none of them had heard from her. She had worried about her sister's disappearance during those first days and weeks, but now Caitlin's sixth sense told her that Sheilagh was all right. She would contact Caitlin in due time. Next week Caitlin would be returning to St. Mary's, where it would be easier and safer for Sheilagh to write or cable without subjecting herself to Mary Margaret's scrutiny. Knowing Sheilagh, she was probably waiting more anxiously for Caitlin to return to college than Caitlin was.

"I agree with you, Matthew," Caitlin announced, reveling

in the chance to support Matthew against her mother.

"Me, too," Michael said. "Boy! Wouldn't it be neat to fly one of those Hurricanes?"

"Sure would, Michael," Matthew said pensively.

Mary Margaret leaned back in her chair. "You just take those foolish ideas out of your head, Michael Killian. The United States is not going to war, and you will be old and gray before I'll let you fly an airplane."

"If I were twenty-one, you wouldn't have anything to say about it," Michael said, puffing out his chest.

"Don't you sass me," Mary Margaret bit back.

As usual, Caitlin jumped in and stopped the family fight before it got out of hand. "He was just teasing." She glared at Michael through slitted eyes. "Weren't you, Michael?"

Michael's exuberance fell off his face. "Sure."

Just then, Patrick and Clay walked through the front door. Both were loaded down with briefcases and manila files.

Clay was seldom invited to the Killian house anymore unless it was for business meetings. Initially Patrick had wanted to fire Clay, but he could not find a more capable, loyal, and talented employee; except for Caitlin, and she was away at school. Patrick decided to keep Clay on the payroll.

"What's the news?" Patrick asked in a loud voice.

Caitlin's head spun around. She saw only Clay.

"Shhh!!" Mary Margaret flapped her hand up and down at them. "Listen for yourself," she said tartly to her husband.

Clay said nothing as he put the files he was holding on the dining room table. He walked back into the room and smiled at Caitlin, who was still watching him. His eyes went to Matthew, who was watching Caitlin. Clay walked over to him and presented his hand. "How're you doin', Matt?"

"Fine," Matthew said with a bit too much honey. He reached over and took Caitlin's hand from her lap and squeezed it tightly.

Clay nodded to Michael, who smiled back at him.

He sat away from the group in a Chippendale chair near the window. He still did not feel comfortable around the Killians when the setting was anything but business. He felt guilty about Sheilagh. He felt guilty about Andrew. And no matter what he did or said, Mary Margaret would always consider him a pariah.

It had been a difficult year for Clay emotionally. With Sheilagh he had felt trapped, and without her he felt adrift. Only she knew the grief he suffered over Andrew's death. Only she could hold him in that certain way and soothe his mind and soul by telling him that she did not hold him accountable for the mess they had made of their lives. He had needed to hear it from her. He still did. He missed her.

Clay knew he could never say these things to Caitlin, because she would not understand. Or perhaps she would. It didn't make much difference now, because she was engaged to Matthew.

The hell of it was that he really liked Matthew. The three times that Matthew had come to visit over the summer, he had spent the right kind of time with Clay in which they exchanged useless chatter about the Cubs and the White Sox, the war, Matthew's new flying lessons, and Clay's determination to make Emerald Chocolates world-famous. Clay liked the bond he had made with Matthew, because Matthew knew nothing about Sheilagh and nothing about his love for Caitlin.

Clay watched Caitlin and Matthew together as they listened to the radio. Matthew was attentive to Caitlin and often teased and joked with her, making her smile again. *I've not been able to do that for Caitlin for a long time,* Clay thought. A part of him was happy for Caitlin, but another very large part of him knew that he would always love her.

" . . . high explosives and incendiaries have nearly decimated the docks, gasworks, and rail terminals. Hundreds of fires are burning all over the city. The German planes have left, and already Londoners have begun putting out fires and cleaning up," Edward R. Murrow's voice said.

Clay leaned forward in his chair. Suddenly his problems seemed insignificant compared to the life-threatening situation in London.

A few minutes later, Edward R. Murrow finished his report and signed off. Michael got up and switched off the radio.

"Caitlin, come to the kitchen and help me with the dessert," Mary Margaret said, rising from her chair. Caitlin dutifully followed her mother, her head still reverberating with the news from London.

Matthew rose and stuck his hands in his pockets. He stared intently at the radio, as if it were still transmitting. "If I were over there, I'd give those Nazis hell!"

Michael looked up at him. "Yeah. Me, too."

"I'm serious, Michael. I should have my pilot's license in a few more weeks. I can bank and roll with the best of them," Matthew said proudly.

Clay stood up and stretched. "I know what you mean about wanting to go over there. I kept thinking we would jump in there and help out France, but we didn't, and look what happened. Now Britain is being pelted. Damn! It doesn't make any sense to me. Are we just going to sit back and let the Nazis take over the whole world?"

Matthew nodded vigorously. "That's just what's going to happen if we don't take a stand. What kind of ally are we?"

Clay moved closer to Matthew, feeling the bond of like opinions. "You know, Sheilagh knew this producer in New York who was Jewish, and she told me some absolute horror stories about the torture the Jews are enduring in Germany."

Michael crooked his arms behind his head and leaned back on the sofa. "You didn't believe her, did you?"

"Yes, I did," Clay answered thoughtfully. "Though I know most Americans don't believe it. Sheilagh thought she could help save some of them by performing in that play. She thought she could change the world..."

"Sheilagh has always been like that, trying to rescue everyone," Michael said.

As Matthew listened to the two of them, he felt as if he were an outsider. As much as he tried to deny it, Clay was part of the Killians, and they were part of him. They shared a common history. Matthew shared only a year of college with Caitlin. He wondered if he would ever fit in.

Clay looked at Matthew. "You know, I tried to enlist."

"You what? When?" Michael asked.

"The week after Sheilagh left. I had thought about it before. Not seriously then, because of Sheilagh and the baby. Ever since the Germans invaded Poland, I've been convinced this country would be involved. I still am. It's only a matter of time. And really, I don't think much good is going to happen until we do. Anyway, they wouldn't take me."

"Why not?" Matthew inquired. "You look healthy to me."

"Oh, it's not that. I'm the sole surviving son. The last of the Burkes."

"So that exempts you?" Michael asked, knowing he was the last of the Killians.

"Sure does."

Matthew leaned back on his heels. "Well, I don't have that problem. I've got two brothers. I'm in perfect health, and pretty soon I'll be a regulation pilot. I'll be in demand."

Just then, Mary Margaret and Caitlin returned to the living room carrying huge hunks of chocolate silk pie for everyone. Mary Margaret served Michael and herself. Caitlin handed the first slice to Matthew. When she turned to Clay and offered him the dessert, an electric spark zinged from her hand to his.

"Static electricity," Caitlin whispered with a smile.

For the first time in a very long while, she allowed her eyes to meet his. His smile was intensely loving, and it broke her heart. She suddenly wished they could be alone to talk. Only this time she didn't want to discuss the unavailability of sugar or the lack of a good marketing program for the year. Caitlin wanted to talk about *them*. She wanted to touch him and hold him. She wanted to help him wash away the pain of Andrew's death. She wanted to love him again.

Clay was looking at her as if she were the last woman on earth. Caitlin could nearly hear her own thoughts echoing in his brain. He needed his friend back.

"This is great pie, Kit Cat. Did you make it?" Matthew's voice seemed to come to Caitlin's ears from a million miles away.

"Yes, I did," she replied, releasing the Haviland china plate into Clay's custody.

"This is Caitlin's invention," Mary Margaret said proudly, sinking her fork into the mound of whipped cream.

"Yep, Caitlin is the *best* cook, Matthew. You're gonna be real glad you married her," Michael said pointedly, still watching Clay's face.

Matthew put his arm around Caitlin's shoulder and brushed her cheek with a kiss that even Mary Margaret would accept as chaste. "I'm already glad," Matthew said tersely.

He watched Clay out of the corner of his eye. He had seen every nuance of the exchange between his fiancée and her sister's husband. He saw the gleam in their eyes that they both struggled to cloud. He saw the spark that passed between them. He sensed the tension they created by keeping their distance from each other. Tonight only confirmed it. Caitlin loved Clay. Clay loved Caitlin. And Matthew intended to enlist in the RAF.

October 1940

Caitlin met Matthew on the steps of Notre Dame Church. In a brown paper bag she carried two turkey sandwiches, two pears, and two homemade chocolate chunk oatmeal cookies. He had telephoned her at her dorm and told her he had another surprise for her. She had teased him and questioned him about it, which for Matthew was always half the fun. She was certain he had found a new place for them to be alone. Knowing Matthew, it would be something outrageous and fun. Being practical was not part of his makeup.

School had been in session for three weeks, and for Caitlin, this school term had not come soon enough. She needed some distance from Clay in order to sort out her thoughts and emotions. She knew she would always feel a bond with Clay; he had been a major part of her childhood and adolescence. She realized, too, that it was time for her to put away her illusions of Clay and instead learn more about herself.

As she peeled away her own mask, she realized she was angry with Clay for making love to Sheilagh. She may not have had any right to feel that way, but she did nevertheless. She felt betrayed by her sister. Once she faced that demon, her bitterness gradually faded.

The school term gave Caitlin the space she needed to come to terms with her own confused emotions. She was feeling whole and happy again.

She closed her eyes and lifted her face to the warm Indian summer sun. An early frost had produced brilliant copper, gold, and crimson leaves.

Caitlin was deep in thought when Matthew walked up.

"Penny for your thoughts, Kit Cat," he said, and kissed her soundly on the mouth.

Caitlin reveled in the kiss, thinking Matthew's lips were most enticing. She put her arms around his neck and pulled him closer. When she did, she felt an odd cloth strap and metal buckle hanging next to his ear scrape against her skin.

Caitlin's eyes flew open. "What in the world?" She looked at the aviator's cloth cap flogged loosely on Matthew's head. Stretched across his forehead was a pair of aviator goggles.

"This is my surprise," he said proudly, touching the cap and rubbing his hand over the smooth crown.

"You're *not* taking me up in an airplane!"

"No, I'm not," he replied solemnly. He sat down on the steps next to her. "I've been trying to think of a way to tell you this for two weeks." He took her hand and gazed at it.

A sense of dread swept over Caitlin. "Why do I feel like I'm not going to like this?"

"Kit Cat, I love you. You know that. But . . ."

"Oh, God . . ." Caitlin felt as if her blood had turned to ice. Her stomach lurched. She was afraid. "Michael told me you were thinking about enlisting. I guess I unconsciously deluded myself into not taking the idea seriously. I didn't want to think of you . . . so far away and in danger. Is that what all those flying lessons were for?" She jerked her head away from him and stared off across campus through a veil of tears.

"Not initially, no. I told you I just wanted to learn for the fun of it. But the world is changing so fast that I feel as if I can't sit on the sidelines anymore."

"Why do you feel as if you have to save the world? Why can't you just be satisfied with staying here?" *Staying with me,* she wanted to ask selfishly. *Maybe I need you, too.*

"Kit Cat." He took her hand.

Angrily she snatched it back. She didn't want to reward him for placing himself in jeopardy. "Don't call me that!"

His voice was mellow when he spoke. "You've known since the day we met that I was different. I take a lot of risks. I picked you out of that crowd on the train that day. Remember?"

She could only nod since her words were dammed up behind a painful lump in her throat.

"I took a chance on you. I'm still taking a chance on you."

"How do you figure that?"

"I'm hoping you won't run off with Clay while I'm gone. I'm hoping you'll still be my girl when I come home." Now it was Matthew's turn to choke back his emotions.

Caitlin twisted to face him. The autumn sun danced in her chestnut hair. A huge tear fell in a glistening pool onto the granite step. "Clay?"

Matthew lovingly took both her hands in his. He rubbed his thumb over each finger. He touched the ring he'd given her. "I know he loves you. I saw it. Each time I went to Chicago, he was there. You can't hide your feelings, Caitlin. You love him. Maybe you always will."

"I love *you*, Matthew."

"I know you do. I believe that. Otherwise I wouldn't have hung around all summer."

"So, why are you going away? Because of me?"

He lifted his hand to her cheek. "No. Don't ever think that. I truly do feel I have to help the Brits. Somebody has got to stop that bastard. Maybe if enough guys like me are over there, together we can make a difference."

He kissed her softly, a kiss of farewell.

Caitlin could not stop the flow of her tears. "I can't say anything to change your mind?"

"No."

"When?"

"The bus leaves in an hour."

She started to tremble. "An hour." She whispered the word as if it would be her last. "That's all?"

" 'Fraid so." He squeezed her hands.

She felt her heart breaking. "Hold me," she pleaded, and slipped into his embrace. Suddenly she felt small and weak, like a child. She accused herself of doing him a disservice with her many thoughts of Clay. Guilt beat at her. *Give me more time,* she wanted to scream. *In time I will forget about Clay. In time I will love you better.* But she did not have time.

"You will write to me, won't you?" he asked.

"Every day."

"Promise?"

"Oh, yes, Matthew. And you'll see. I'll be right here when you come home."

He lifted her chin with his forefinger. "I hope so, Kit Cat."

"I will, Matthew. I will."

Chapter 31 ————————————————

O<small>N</small> O<small>CTOBER</small> 29, 1940, a blindfolded Secretary of War Henry L. Stimson drew the first draft number under the new selective service law. Nazi U-boats cruised the North Atlantic. Wendell Willkie campaigned for president in Elwood, Indiana, but with the election less than a week away, Caitlin knew that FDR would win again.

She was surprised at how mundane her life had become that autumn with Matthew overseas. She went to classes, exchanged gossip with Anne, and listened to the World Series in Cincinnati, where the Reds beat the Detroit Tigers 2–1 and took the Series in seven games. She went to the theater and saw *The Grapes of Wrath* for the second time. Not a day went by that she didn't check the dormitory mailboxes to see if there was another thin airmail letter from Matthew.

She wrote to him every day without fail. Her letters had to be boring, she thought, though Matthew claimed in his own letters that they "meant the world" to him.

Caitlin was afraid for Matthew. He was ill prepared for warfare, but the RAF was so desperate for fliers since the Battle of Britain began that they were taking any and all volunteers. In the first battles before Matthew left, the RAF had taken heavy losses, though the German losses were double that of the British. Caitlin didn't care about the statistics; she cared about the blacked-out lines in the letters she received from Matthew where pertinent information about his flying, his ability, and the whereabouts of his next mission were censored. She did not like the fact that when he first got to England, he flew only one mission a day. Less than three weeks later, he was now flying as many as four. His chances of dying had quadrupled.

By the end of November, Caitlin listened to the news every evening after dinner before she started her homework.

She no longer had as much interest in her new math courses as she did in the war in England. She tried to piece together Matthew's letters and the reports she heard on the CBS radio station.

Matthew counted out his hits and downed Nazi planes the way she counted the strikeouts in the World Series. She was aghast at how quickly his count raced from single digits to double digits. She couldn't help but wonder about some Berlin girl who was waiting for the lover who would never return to her. Did Matthew ever think of the Nazi pilots as people? Or were they just numbers? Numbers of dead. Numbers of injured. Numbers of grieving widows and family.

Caitlin went to the chapel daily and prayed.

As the weeks pressed on toward December, she found that even she had become numb to the bloodshed. Eventually she not only forgot about the people, she pushed the numbers out of her brain. Now she thought of the war as places. Sometimes she thought she was taking a crash course in British geography. Liverpool was nearly destroyed in the flames after a Nazi bomber attack. Coventry was bombarded for two weeks in November. Birmingham and Bristol took similar beatings. London was attacked again and again. And always the RAF was in the air to defend the country.

Caitlin had been out Christmas-shopping the second week in December when she returned to her dorm room and found Anne dressed in the mink jacket her father had given her the Christmas before.

Caitlin brushed wet snow off her shoulders after tossing her shopping bags on the bed. "Why didn't you tell me you wanted to shop? We could have taken the bus together."

"Uh. Cat? This isn't about shopping."

Caitlin rifled through one of her bags. "No? Let me show you this great scarf I found for Sheilagh. Boy! Am I glad she sent me that Thanksgiving card. I think I missed her as much as I miss Matthew, if that's possible." She pulled out a tissue-wrapped bundle. "Take a look at this . . ." She looked up at Anne.

"Cat?"

Caitlin stopped midmotion, holding the pretty cobalt in blue and gold-edged silk scarf in her hand. Anne's face was filled with anguish. Her body movements were jerky and stilted. Something was terribly, terribly wrong. "What is it, Anne?"

"Something has happened . . ."

"Oh, my God." Caitlin dropped the scarf and held out her arms to Anne. "Your father. Something has happened to your father," she guessed.

Anne's eyes were pain-filled. "No, Cat. There was a telephone call for you while you were out. It was Matthew's mother. He . . ."

Caitlin's face turned ashen. Chills blanketed her body. She shook her head.

"She got the telegram yesterday. It was over Liverpool. I told her I would put you on the train so that you could go to the memorial service tomorrow."

Caitlin remembered the radio report. "But it was just another city . . . I thought it was just another English city . . . I didn't know it was where Matthew was . . . I should have known."

Anne held out her arms. "Cat, how could you know?"

"I thought I would just know somehow," she sobbed, and went to Anne's arms. "Maybe there's been some mistake. Some terrible mistake. Maybe they didn't get the right plane."

Anne smoothed Caitlin's hair. "No. It was the right plane. He painted your name on the side of it where he kept track of his hits. It said 'Kit Cat.' "

"Oh, God . . ." Caitlin's body was racked with sobs. Her shoulders heaved up and down. "I loved him."

"I know you did, honey."

"But . . . do you think I loved him enough?"

"Of course you did," Anne replied softly. "Why would you think otherwise?"

"Because . . ." Caitlin was crying so hard, Anne could barely understand her.

"You can tell me, Cat. Maybe you'll feel better."

"Just because . . ." Caitlin stopped herself. She did not want to diminish her love for Matthew by even speaking Clay's name. This was Matthew's hour. She wanted him to know that she had indeed waited for him. Matthew knew she had loved Clay, but he loved her enough for the both of them. Clay had been Caitlin's first love, but Matthew had been her first lover.

Matthew and his memory would always be a part of her. For that she thanked God.

December 11, 1940

Sheilagh waited nervously by the telephone, chewing on a hangnail. Her eyes darted to the clock. It was a quarter to three. What was taking Abe so long? He should have finished lunch at Sardi's by one-thirty, two at the latest, and been back to the office with good news.

She uncrossed her legs and rose from the couch. She paced barefooted up and down the apartment. This was a big day for Abe. If he could convince the very wealthy, very snooty, and very conservative Gerald Van Horten to invest in his newest play, they would both be on their way to fame and fortune.

Abe had written the lead for Sheilagh. It was her vehicle to stardom; he'd said no one could play Janice as well as she could.

"Damn right I can," she mumbled to herself. "I lived that part."

Janice Alive was the story of a young girl from the deep South who was forced to leave home after the birth of her illegitimate daughter. Janice swore to avenge herself against her traditionalist father, though he died of cancer before she got the chance. Janice's most dramatic moments came during the deathbed scene.

Sheilagh could hardly wait to begin rehearsals. Just then, the phone rang. She snatched the receiver off the cradle.

"Cut the salutations. Did you get it?" she said.

Abe laughed on the other end. "I love you, too, baby."

"Abe, puhleese." Sheilagh was so anxious, she felt as if she were about to jump out of her skin.

"I got it!"

"You did? You really did?"

"I really did!"

"When? Where? Oh, God, Abe. I can't believe it!"

"We open in February. Better start learning your lines. I told you I'd make you famous."

"You did, Abe," she said gratefully.

"I'll be late tonight. I've got a million details to work out. I just wanted to give you the news," he explained before he hung up.

Sheilagh replaced the receiver and spun around the room, hugging herself and squealing with delight. She stopped at the window and realized it had started snowing.

Everywhere there were signs of Christmas. Lights were being strung around the window at O'Malley's Bar across the street. The empty lot on the corner had received another shipment of Christmas trees. Abe said he'd never had a Christmas tree since he was Jewish, and Sheilagh could not imagine a December without one.

Suddenly, she felt incredibly homesick. She glanced toward the telephone. She could never go back to Chicago. She could no longer pretend her life was happy. She missed Michael. She missed Caitlin even more. Her eyes traveled to the tiny desk calendar next to the phone. It was December eleventh. Caitlin's birthday.

Her eyes brightened. She raced to the bedroom, retrieved her purse, and dumped out the contents on the bed. She found the little phone and address book. She looked up Caitlin's number at Saint Mary's.

She picked up the receiver, dialed the operator, and placed the call. Caitlin responded with a rush of excitement.

"Sheilagh, is it you?"

"It's me!"

"I can't believe it. How are you? Are you acting? Where are you living?"

"Slow down. I'll tell you everything. The reason I called is to wish you a happy birthday."

"Thanks."

"And I wanted to know if you could come to New York in February for my Broadway opening night!"

"Broadway? Are you serious? You did it, Sheilagh?"

"I haven't done it yet, but I've just been given the chance. I gotta be great, I've just got to," she said with determination. "And, Cat, I want you to be here. You and Michael. Remember how we said we'd always stick together?"

"I do."

"I'll send you two train tickets. You can stay with me. Just for the weekend, Cat. Oh, say you will."

"My leaving won't be a problem, but how do I get Michael out of Chicago without Mother and Father finding out?"

"Yeah. That's going to be tricky. Hmmm." Sheilagh paused, then she said brightly, "I know! Tell them you're having a little brothers weekend at school. Say Michael will go over to Notre Dame and look around the campus and see if he likes it. They'll let him go, because they trust you."

"Do you think it'll work?"

"Sure. I'll send Michael two tickets. One that'll get him to South Bend, and you can ride together the rest of the way. That way Mother won't have to drive him to South Bend."

"What if she finds out there is no little brothers weekend?"

"Tell her you miss Michael. She'll do it for you. Michael says she's been pretty sympathetic toward you since Matthew . . ." Sheilagh's voice fell away. "I'm sorry about him, Cat. I wish I could be there to give you a hug."

Caitlin felt her eyes flood with tears. "Yeah. Me, too."

"Say you'll come to New York."

"I'll do the best I can."

"Deal. Well, I better go. I'll write you another long letter tonight, okay? I'll give you all the specifics."

"Thanks, Sheilagh," Caitlin said. "For remembering Matthew."

"Gosh, Cat. I wish I could have known him. I barely remember him at the funeral." This time it was Sheilagh's voice that ended abruptly. She realized then that both she and her sister were barely coming out of their teens and already they had experienced sorrow and loss. She wondered if they were stronger for the experience.

"Thanks for calling, Sheilagh."

"Happy Birthday, little sister," Sheilagh said, and hung up.

February, 1941

The world seemed to have spun out of joint, Sheilagh thought as she waited for Caitlin and Michael's train to arrive at Grand Central Station. She'd never seen so many army and navy uniforms in her life. Soldiers hustled quickly to make their trains. Wartime lovers kissed good-bye and hello. The newspapers stated that since the draft, train and bus travel had risen sharply. Sheilagh could see they were right.

Lost in thought, she nearly missed the arrival of the streamliner train.

"Sheilagh!" Michael shouted as he alighted. He rushed up to her and hugged her.

"My God, Michael! You've grown a foot!"

"Nah. Only two and a half inches since summer. *And*"—he grabbed her hand and placed it against his cheek—"I'm growing a beard."

Caitlin came up just then, placed her suitcase on the ground, and embraced her sister. "You look terrific, Sheilagh! I didn't think you'd look this good." Caitlin laughed.

"I'm happy. Truly happy. It makes a difference," she said. "C'mon. I've got so much to show you!"

Caitlin and Michael found New York fascinating. Michael wanted to eat at every deli, visit the Empire State Building, and ride in a New York cab, which they did on their way to the theater. Caitlin wanted to go to Macy's, but mostly, she said, she wanted to meet Abe.

Sheilagh complied with Caitlin's last request.

They agreed to meet Abe at the Shubert Theater, where he was attending to last-minute details before opening night. Sheilagh paid the cab driver as Michael retrieved their suitcases from the trunk.

The trio stood across the street staring at the marquee.

"Gosh," Caitlin gushed. "I didn't think your name would be so big."

"I did!" Sheilagh said triumphantly.

Michael looked to Sheilagh with admiration in his eyes. "You never gave up, did you?"

"No, Michael. I never did."

"I'm gonna remember this, Sheilagh. I'm not gonna let anything or anyone stop me, either."

"I hope not. And, Michael, it could be even more difficult for you now that I've gone. They only have you and Caitlin now. They may fight you."

"I'll be strong."

Sheilagh shook her head. "I was often weak, Michael, but I was always determined."

"Determined," he repeated. "I'll remember."

Sheilagh took Michael's arm as they strolled into the theater. They passed through the empty lobby, where they deposited their luggage in the ticket office and then entered the main floor.

Abe was in a huddle with the director, but as Sheilagh, Michael, and Caitlin walked down the carpeted aisle, his head turned. A broad smile covered his face.

Sheilagh went to him and held his hand as she kissed his cheek.

Michael hung back and whispered to Caitlin. "Wow! I didn't think he'd be so short."

"Michael!" Caitlin shot her brother a chastising look.

"Well . . ." Michael shrugged his shoulders sheepishly.

Sheilagh made the introductions and everyone shook hands, but it was clear that the very impatient director did not appreciate the family reunion.

"Sheilagh," Abe said, "I'll be finished here in a moment. Why not take Caitlin and Michael backstage and show them your dressing room? I'll join you there shortly."

"Sure." Sheilagh showed them the prop room and the costume department; she introduced them to Sal, the lighting operator, and Josh Eldridge, one of the understudies.

Finally they came to a row of doors painted dark green. On the last door was a silver star with Sheilagh's name beneath it.

"Jeepers!" Michael said.

"Ditto!" Caitlin exclaimed.

Sheilagh proudly opened the door to the small room. Caitlin and Michael timidly yet reverently entered the room.

Caitlin's eyes were wide. "It's just the way you always said it would be, Sheilagh. The flowered chintz chaise, a dressing screen, beautiful costumes, more makeup than I've seen at Woolworth's, and even the opening-night roses . . ." Caitlin stretched out her hand to touch the crimson blooms.

"Roses?" Sheilagh had not seen them. "From who?" She picked up the card, which was propped next to the sterling silver vase. She opened it. "They're from Abe," she said with a rush of grateful emotion. "Isn't he wonderful?"

Michael and Caitlin exchanged a quizzical look.

"Isn't he supposed to give flowers to the star?" Caitlin asked.

Sheilagh's face was suddenly serious. "I think you should know that if it weren't for Abe, I wouldn't have this part. I haven't been in New York a year yet, but I've already learned that there are a lot of talented people who never get the chance I've got. It wasn't talent or luck that got me this job. It was Abe. I owe him my career, and I'll always be grateful to him for that." Sheilagh eyes misted with tears.

Caitlin put her arms around her sister. "I understand, Sheilagh. Abe is your best friend."

"Yes, Caitlin. Abe is my best friend."

* * *

The curtain went up that night to standing room only, thanks to Abe's advertising blitz on the radio. The first act went smoothly. The second act kept the audience off balance with laughter and tears. The third act sent them to their feet, thundering their applause. Caitlin and Michael stood next to Abe, clapping and cheering at Sheilagh's triumph.

The stage was deluged with flowers. Abe hired four photographers to take pictures of Sheilagh during her curtain calls. He wanted a record of history in the making. He spied the photographer from *Look* and gave the man a nod and a smile.

Abe put his arm around Michael's shoulder. "Can you feel it, Michael? The air is full of it."

"Feel what?"

"Great reviews. We're gonna get raves." Abe grinned.

"Yes, sir," Michael replied as he struggled to feel the air in the theater. He wanted to know what Abe meant, but he didn't feel a thing.

They sat at a back table in Sardi's until long after midnight, waiting for the reviews to come in. Abe had commissioned Josh Eldridge to gather the newspapers while he, Sheilagh, Caitlin, and Michael finished dinner.

Abe ordered champagne and poured Caitlin and Michael their first glasses of the bubbly wine. Sheilagh was as nervous as a cat. When Josh finally dashed into Sardi's with the newspapers, she thought she would have an anxiety attack.

"Look at this one," Abe said, reading aloud from the *New York Times*. "Sheilagh Killian's performance was stellar, and she has star material written all over her."

"This one is from *The Mirror*," Caitlin read. "Abe Meindel has established himself as a writer and producer to watch. He not only has an eye for talent, but he knows how to cut and hone the perfect part for his leading lady. Never has this reviewer witnessed so much talent in one so young. Sheilagh Killian . . . Broadway loves you."

Caitlin smiled the whole night through. Dawn was breaking as they walked from Sardi's to Abe's apartment on the upper East Side. It was a long walk, but none of them cared. The champagne had initially numbed them against the February cold, but it was their mutual friendship and love that warmed them all the way through.

Caitlin and Michael left early Sunday morning to return to

the Midwest and pretend to their parents they knew nothing of Sheilagh's life in New York. Their mother and father would condemn Sheilagh for living with Abe without the benefit of marriage. Mary Margaret would never understand that Sheilagh did not need children that her brother and sister were her family, and for Sheilagh, that was enough. Sheilagh was free of restrictions in New York. She could be as creative as her talent allowed her to be. They were glad for her, because she was happy.

From that day on, Caitlin would always think of Sheilagh as the dream maker.

Clay gave himself a full year to mourn the death of his son. While Caitlin was away at school, he spent his days working for his former father-in-law and spent his evenings with his parents. Once Sheilagh left for New York, Clay moved back home to help his mother care for his father, who had suffered a heart attack that fall.

Robert and Clay grew close during that year. On a leave of absence due to his illness, Robert was no longer deluged with his political duties. Together the two men listened to the war news on the radio each night. Because Clay had been an only child, he and his parents had always been close, but the days seemed to slow down for Clay. He took time to discover his father's deep sense of duty to his fellow man and his determination to remain honest in a world of crooked politicians.

They sat in overstuffed club chairs, which Aileen had recently re-covered in a cozy red plaid, in front of the fireplace in Robert's library. Aileen was conducting a symposium at the University of Chicago on "Finite Man in an Infinite Universe." Clay adored his mother for her willingness to explain the inexplicable in a changing world that often seemed cold and uncaring.

The radio was tuned to WBBM. The announcer spoke of the escalating war in Europe and of American troops being dispatched to fight the Japanese at Guadalcanal.

Clay had warmed hot spice tea that Aileen had brewed earlier that evening. He poured some, added lemon and sugar, and handed it to Robert.

The china cup and saucer teetered slightly in his hand. "I guess I got the shakes again." Robert tried to sound lighthearted, but Clay knew that his father was concerned about his deterioratiing strength.

"Maybe you'd like some of Mom's banana bread."

"Not now. I'd rather talk to you, son."

"All right," Clay said, crossing his legs. "What's on your mind?"

As Robert leaned his head back on the chair, the lamplight revealed the sallow look to his skin. Robert had lost more weight until he was almost gaunt, Clay thought. His face was lined. For weeks Clay had not wanted to admit it, but his father's heart problems were not going away, he was not improving.

"I have a great deal on my mind these days, Clay. Like your mother, I, too, sometimes wonder what my purpose was in this life. Oh, I know I helped some people out over the years. Raised you. Loved your mother. But I had no real impact. I've thought a lot about this." He paused and sipped his tea.

Clay said nothing, knowing that this discussion was important to Robert.

"During the majority of my years in public office, it seemed to me that the bad guys always won. You know what I mean?" He turned his head only slightly toward Clay before continuing. "I kept thinking that if I could convince some of those bastards that the right way was just as easy as the wrong way, then maybe I could make a difference in this world. But you know, the truth of the matter is that they were right and I was wrong."

"What?" Clay said incredulously. "You can't mean that."

"The crooks and the thieves do have the power in this world. For a while. That's the key . . . Nobody wins at everything all the time. You take Hitler, for instance. Right now he's riding pretty goddamn high. He's got everybody in the free world jumping through hoops. He's gonna get a lot more powerful before this thing is over. But you watch; he's going to trip himself up just like every politician on the take I've ever seen. That's the beauty of life, Clay. Somehow, he'll get his. They always do. Oh, he may stay in power for another few years. But eventually he'll get so full of himself that he'll forget to watch his backside. He'll trust the wrong people. He'll lose his focus and make the wrong decisions. Whether we go over there and fight him or not won't make any difference in the long run."

"If we defeat him, we lessen the damage he can do," Clay observed.

"Oh, I agree with that. But in the long run, guys like him bring about their own ruination."

Clay set his teacup down. "Why do I have the feeling this is leading up to something?"

"Because it is. Patrick Killian is a lot like Hitler. He's a self-centered crook if ever I saw one, but he's smart in some ways, too, Clay. I don't know for a fact, because it was never proven, and I never said any of this to you before, but I think you should know that I believe Patrick is a murderer."

"Jesus Christ! Where did you get that idea? I've heard stories about his gangland connections, but murder?"

"I don't know if he did or didn't. I just want you to think about the man you're working for. I didn't say anything about him when you were marrying Sheilagh because . . . well, I just always felt, like your mother, that it would never work out. I thought maybe you would leave Emerald. But you seem to love it there. I understand that. Since it looks like that place is in your blood, promise me that you'll watch your backside with him, Clay."

"Okay. I will," Clay promised.

Robert leaned over and gazed at his son. His eyes were weary, though filled with genuine concern. "Clay, I'm dying . . ."

"Dad! Don't say that! You'll be fine with some rest . . ."

"No, Clay." He shook his head. "I'm not getting better, and you know it. But I'd like to see a few things settled before I die. And that's what I wanted to talk to you about."

"Settled?"

"You and Caitlin."

"What about her?"

"You love her, don't you?"

"Yes. A great deal."

"Then marry her, son. I'd like to be alive for that wedding. I don't think I'll make it to see my grandchildren, but I'd like to know you're with someone who loves you as much as you love her. Caitlin is good people. I couldn't ask for a better daughter-in-law. And, Clay, I want it to be the grandest party Chicago has ever seen. I want you to be happy, and I want this whole town to know that you are. Promise me you'll do that . . . even if I'm not around . . ."

"Dad." Clay slipped off his chair and crouched next to his father's chair. "You're not going to die. Now, you promise me you'll stay alive for my wedding."

"I'll try."

Robert did not die that fall. He was infirm but still able to attend Clay and Caitlin's engagement party in the winter of 1942, and Caitlin's graduation from St. Mary's College one year early in the spring.

Clay and Caitlin were married in Ascension Church on June

20, 1942. Their church wedding was made possible because Clay had sought and obtained an annulment of his marriage to Sheilagh rather than a divorce. Caitlin was attended by twelve bridesmaids, most of them her girlfriends from St. Mary's. She had begged Sheilagh to be her maid of honor, but Sheilagh had declined repeatedly, stating that she was opening that Saturday night in a new play. Clay understood full well Sheilagh's reluctance to attend his wedding.

The high mass nuptials were held at eleven o'clock in the morning and were followed by a champagne brunch for three hundred at the Drake Hotel. Robert Burke sat in a wheelchair at the head table and gave the first toast to the bride and groom, an honor traditionally given to the best man.

The press covered the story with reporters and photographers. Every society doyenne and local chocolatier and confectioner was invited, along with all of Caitlin's friends from high school and college. Gene Krupa's band played all afternoon. Twice the hotel had to send out for more champagne. The party went on till sunset. Clay and Caitlin were exhausted by the time the reception broke up and they were able to retreat to their room upstairs in the hotel. Clay had planned a wedding trip to Quebec, Montreal, and Niagara Falls, but their train did not leave until the following morning.

Clay wanted Caitlin's wedding night to be a time she would never forget. He had always thought of himself as a romantic man, though his marriage to Sheilagh might have suggested otherwise. He wanted Caitlin to know that he cherished her.

Instead of the bridal suite, he selected the presidential suite because the furnishings were more expensive and traditional. He wanted the mahogany bed with rice carvings and lace hangings for Caitlin.

He'd arranged for fresh strawberries dipped in chocolate to be delivered to the room with a bottle of Piper Heidsieck.

When he unlocked the door, he carried her over the threshold. Caitlin's veil got caught on the stem of the dead bolt in the door.

"Ouch!" she wailed as she felt one of the hairpins being yanked out of her head. "My veil . . . my hair."

Clay didn't understand what was happening and continued into the room.

"Clay! Ahhh! My veil is caught in the door!" Her hand flew to her head.

Clay placed her on the floor and unfastened the veil. He kicked the door shut. "It's just as well. It's time to get you out of that thing." He came toward her with a seductive smile.

"Clay?" Caitlin smiled back at him.

He took her into his arms and kissed her. It was a long, lingering kiss that he wanted to last forever. He held her face in his hands. "I want you to know always that I love you, Caitlin."

Caitlin covered his hands with her own. "And I love you."

Clay kissed her deeply this time. His lips devoured her mouth. He had thought about this moment all day . . . all week . . . all month. Hell, he had thought about it for years.

Caitlin had insisted that she finish college before they married and that they wait until their wedding day to make love. Because his affair with Sheilagh had been so disastrous, Clay had not wanted to make any mistakes, either. But seeing Caitlin on weekends at school, or when she had come home for a vacation, had been torturous for Clay. He had thought his passion for Sheilagh could never be equaled, but he'd been wrong.

Every time he so much as looked at Caitlin, at her shimmering her blue eyes, he struggled with himself not to take her. He wanted this marriage to last. He wanted her to know she was the most important person in his life, that she would never be second best to Sheilagh. He'd told her he would keep his distance.

Clay almost failed to live up to his promise. In the past year he thought he'd go out of his mind. Now that his wedding night was here, he couldn't wait a second longer to make Caitlin truly his.

Clay began taking the pins out of Caitlin's hair. He kissed her ear playfully as he found a clump of pins above her right temple. He withdrew them gingerly, and the veil fell to the floor.

Caitlin's dress was a designer original fashioned by the best seamstress on the near North Side. The white peau de soie gown was traditionally cut tight to the waist with a full skirt, long sleeves ending in pointed cuffs at the wrists, a high collar, and covered buttons down the back. As Clay pulled Caitlin into his arms and kissed her, he slid his hands to her back to unbutton her gown.

He had thought this would be a simple matter until he realized that each of the buttons was fastened with a loop. His fingers suddenly seemed twice their size as he fumbled with the tiny fastenings.

Caitlin began laughing. "I can't help you with this one, Clay," she teased.

"But how did you get into the damn thing?"

"They used a metal hook to button them."

Clay's face fell. Gone was the smoldering seduction in his eyes. "You mean you're stuck in this dress? God, Caitlin . . . I don't think I can wait any longer."

"Oh, Clay. I'm sorry. I was just having fun at your expense." She laughed again. "You should see your face."

She kissed him quickly and turned around. "Didn't the bellman bring up my bag?"

"Sure. It's over there." Clay pointed to the folding luggage rack.

"I brought the hook," she said brightly.

"There is a God!" Clay rushed to help her find the hook.

Caitlin pulled it out of her bag and handed it to Clay, who spun her around and went to work. "Say! This thing works faster than the hand method," he said.

"I know," she agreed as he unhooked the last loop and let the dress drop. She stood wearing only a silk satin slip, white hose, and lace garter belt and panties. She turned back to him. "I wanted you to save your hands for more important things," she said breathlessly.

"Oh, God," Clay said, gazing at Caitlin's body. The setting summer sun cast a golden glow about the room. The lights in the city were just beginning to twinkle as day moved into night.

Clay placed his hand on Caitlin's shoulder. He felt the rolled satin strap of her slip as it fell down her arm. "I don't think I can ever get enough of you, Caitlin Killian," he said as his head fell to her shoulder and he kissed her soft skin.

"I'm Caitlin Burke now, Clay. Finally."

"Finally," he said, and moved his mouth to the tender spot at the base of her throat where he could feel her pulse. He moved the straps down her arms and exposed her voluptuous breasts.

Slowly his lips began their journey down the valley between her breasts. He cupped her breast with his hand as he moved his lips to her nipple. With his tongue he teased her again and again, until he heard her breathing deeper.

Her hands sank into his hair as she pressed him to her. She arched her body against him. She was telling him she wanted more of him, but this time he was in no hurry. All night would not have been long enough to savor every delectable inch of the woman he loved.

His hands slid along the curves of her waist to her hips. He tugged on her slip and pulled it down. It fell in a puddle at her feet. Then he pulled off her panties. She wore only her garter belt and white silk hose.

Clay dropped to his knees and kissed the flat plain of her abdomen before parting her legs with his hand. Caitlin's fingers were tangled in his hair. She moaned when he kissed the valley between her legs and used his tongue to bring her, gasping, to passion's edge.

"Oh, God, Clay," she said as her legs began to quiver.

Clay stood slowly, blazing a trail of hot kisses back to her breasts, before scooping her up in his arms and carrying her to the bedroom.

She kissed his eyes, ears, cheeks, and lips as he held her in his arms and carried her to the four-poster bed. He laid her gently down.

Caitlin had the oddest sensation of something smooth and cool beneath her naked back. "What?"

She tore her eyes from Clay and looked beneath her. The entire bed was covered with pink rose petals. They were the same rose petals her flower girls had strewn before her as she'd walked down the aisle that morning. Caitlin had never known Clay was so romantic. She was pleased at the thought of the many facets of his character that she had yet to discover. She turned back to him with love-filled eyes.

"Clay . . . darling, you have no idea how special you've made me feel."

"I want you to know that you'll always be the most important person in my life."

Caitlin knew what he was trying to tell her—that even though Sheilagh had been first in his life, he loved her more. She opened her arms to him. "I love you, Clay."

"I adore you," he said, and kissed her. Then he pulled away. "I think it's time to help you out of these." He slowly unhooked her hose and rolled them down her legs. He kissed each knee before peeling off the stockings completely. Then he unsnapped the garter belt. "I think I like you this way . . ." he said, letting his hands roam the length of her.

"I think it's unfair that I don't get to do the same to you," Caitlin teased as she sat up and began pulling at his bow tie. She tossed it on the floor before taking the studs from his tuxedo shirt.

Quickly Clay doffed his tuxedo jacket, suspenders, cummerbund, shoes, and slacks. He kept his eyes on Caitlin as he stripped off the rest of his clothes.

Caitlin smiled to herself. With each garment he discarded, Clay's hands moved faster and faster. His eyes were growing smoky with passion. He had wanted her for a long time, and now that wait seemed doubly torturous.

Clay stretched out next to his wife atop the rose petals. He kissed her deeply, ringing her lips with his tongue before delving into the sweet interior of her mouth. Clay groaned. He caressed her breasts and rolled the buds of her nipples between his finger and thumb until they became hard.

"Clay . . ."

He sank his hand between her legs and felt her hot moistness. Suddenly he felt himself grow even harder.

He rose onto his elbows as Caitlin put her arms around him and pulled him on top of her. She opened her legs eagerly.

Caitlin's breath was coming in fast rushes, as if she'd been running for a long time. She could feel her heart slamming against her rib cage. Clay entered her, and Caitlin thought she'd never felt anything as sweet and powerful.

Clay pressed deeper.

Caitlin called his name.

Perspiration broke out on Clay's forehead. He kissed her throat before capturing her mouth again. Her hips rose to bring him further inside. He thought he was drowning, but he knew he was entering paradise.

"Clay!" She called his name again as she rose to passion's summit. She gyrated her hips and felt him drive himself deeper. Liquid fire raced through Caitlin's body. She wanted more of him. Her fingers pressed into his back. She could feel his muscles tighten. His body felt like twisted steel beneath his satin-smooth skin. She kissed his ear and etched a hot string of kisses down his throat to the crook in his shoulder. She opened her mouth and traced tiny circles with her tongue. She felt as if she were flying to a high summit. Her muscles tightened. She felt the walls of her vagina pulsate around him. His strokes were quick and deep. She groaned. She nearly screamed.

She arched her back as she exploded into her orgasm.

Caitlin's mind seemed to leave her body as her spirit sailed into the universe. But she could feel Clay's spirit with her. She felt as if they were one soul. It was more than a sensation; it was an ancient knowing.

"Oh, God, Caitlin . . ." Clay said in a rush as he expelled himself inside her. He clung to her as a series of aftershocks coursed through him.

The heat from their bodies mingled with the rose petals and filled the air with a flowery perfume. Caitlin held Clay in her arms, cradling his head against her breast. Their breathing slowed as they seemed to fall back to earth together. Clay traced a bead of perspiration as it fell between her breasts. In the afterglow of his lovemaking he pulled Caitlin to him.

"I never want us to be any further apart in our minds or souls than we are right now," he said.

Caitlin kissed him. "We'll always be this close," she vowed.

She had waited all her life for Clay. The wait was worth it.

Chapter 32

June 11, 1971
County Clare, Ireland

LORD RICHARD BUTLER went to the post office in Ennistymon to place a transatlantic call to Carin's apartment. He counted the rings. Eight . . . nine . . . ten. He was becoming frustrated by his inability to reach Carin. He had telephoned her the day she was to arrive home, but there had been no answer at her apartment. He had even gone so far as to call her mother's house, but there had been no answer there, either. That was 3 days ago. At first he had worried that she had not made it home safely, but there was nothing in the newspapers about an airplane crash. He checked Western Union for a cable from her, but found none. It was too early to check the post office, but he checked anyway. Again he was disappointed. Again he realized that nothing in his life would be the same without Carin.

"I'm sorry, sir. There seems to be no answer. Do you wish to place another call at this time?"

"Yes. But I don't know the number. Emerald Chocolate corporate offices in Oak Park, Illinois, operator."

"One moment while I get the number for you, sir."

Richard could hear dial tones and then connections being made. The phone rang and was answered by an older woman.

"Emerald Chocolates. How may I direct your call?" Martha O'Boland answered the call just as she had for forty years.

"Carin Burke, please."

"And who may I say is calling?"

"Richard Butler."

"Oh." Martha paused for a second as if she were finishing some task. "I'm sorry, sir, Miss Burke is not receiving any calls at the moment. Do you wish to leave a message?"

Richard felt his earlier anticipation and exuberance flood out of his body, replaced by disappointment. "Tell her that I phoned. Ask her to wire me. Oh, and tell her that I will call her tonight at . . . at . . ." He checked his watch and counted off the time difference between Ennistymon and Chicago. "At nine o'clock tonight Chicago time."

"Yes, sir."

"Thank you," Richard said, and hung up.

Richard should have felt relieved to know that Carin had not come to harm, but there had been something in the secretary's voice that made him suspicious. He didn't want to admit that it nearly sounded as if Carin was avoiding him.

Richard hopped back into the Land-Rover and started the engine. He replayed the conversation in his mind. No, there was definitely something going on that was not to his liking . . . not one bit.

Mary Margaret Killian leaned over Martha O'Boland's shoulder and peeled the phone message to Carin off the memo pad. "I'll take care of this, Martha."

Martha shrugged. "Thank you," she said dutifully, and went back to her typing.

Mary Margaret walked down the hall toward her husband's office. To the right was Caitlin's office, then Clay's office, and to the left was Carin's office. She stopped at the open door and tapped on the doorjamb.

"May I come in, dear?"

Carin was just finishing a phone conversation. She waved her grandmother in. "Of course; what's up?"

"Not very much." Mary Margaret lowered herself stiffly to the French bergère chair opposite Carin's French Provincial desk.

Carin remembered that Mary Margaret had strongly protested when in redecorating the office, Carin insisted upon this overly feminine furniture. Mary Margaret pointed out to Caitlin that she was indulging Carin. That Caitlin was too soft and needed to stand up to Carin.

Caitlin had not put so much importance on the matter. Each office was to be a reflection of the individual rather than conform to a corporate image. Mary Margaret did not agree. In the end, Carin got her furniture, Caitlin forgot the incident, and Mary Margaret erased one of her own points on the mental scorecard she kept. Mary Margaret did not like losing.

She pressed a smile on her lips and patted the palm of her left hand with the wrinkled fingers of her right. "I wanted to talk to you about this young man you have met."

Carin shoulders went rigid as she braced for one of Mary Margaret's lectures. "Now?"

"Yes."

"I'm very busy, Grandma. Can't this wait till later?"

"I won't see you later. You never come to visit me anymore. You're always busy. Why, I've hardly seen you since you returned three days ago. Your mother has done all the talking about him, and that isn't much. We need to know a bit more about this man."

"Why?"

Mary Margaret's face became a mask of concern. Carin had seen this face before, usually right before her grandmother began meddling in her life. "You can't be too careful nowadays, dear. Those young men out there can be vicious where a sweet, *monied* young woman like you is concerned."

Oh, God, Carin moaned to herself. Here it comes.

"I know that look of incredulity, young lady. You're thinking, What could old Grandmother know? The truth is that I know a great deal about people; it's just that no one ever bothers to listen to me. I know I'm right about this." Mary Margaret's voice rose as she wagged her forefinger at her granddaughter. "Let's look at the facts. This man is penniless—"

"He is not!" Carin said.

"Oh? That's not what I hear from Aileen Burke."

Carin felt betrayed. "Grandma Aileen told you that?"

"Not in so many words, but she did spend a great deal of time telling me about this run-down castle that he's spent every dime on . . . and that now he is not employed, nor did his parents leave him anything but that castle. I know he was slick enough and smart enough to charm Aileen, which isn't easy. He knew he would need an ally. I find it curious that you have not heard from this man who professed to love you so much."

"I will," Carin replied, halfheartedly now that her confidence had lost its foothold.

"I'm sure you will."

Carin's eyes widened in astonishment. "But you just said—"

"He will call you, not because he loves you, but because he wants a job. He wants the Emerald money. Mark my words."

Carin suddenly felt quite world-weary. "I hope not, Grandma . . ."

"My dear child." Mary Margaret rose and put her arms around Carin's shoulders. "Don't take his dalliance with you so much to heart; that's all I'm saying. You enjoyed your trip to Ireland, but leave it at that." She patted Carin's shoulder affectionately. "I know what will cheer you up. Why don't you come over to the house tonight for dinner? I would love to make your favorite dessert, and then we could talk some more. You spend all your time at the office, and I never seem to see you anymore. One of these days I'll be gone, and then—"

"Okay, Grandmother. That's sounds lovely. What time?"

Mary Margaret pretended to study her watch. "Let's see . . . I have a short Rosary Sodality meeting, but it should be over by seven-thirty. Why not come to the house about eight. We can talk, and I promise to have that dessert in your tummy by nine, and you'll be home asleep by ten-thirty at the latest."

Mary Margaret popped a prim kiss onto Carin's forehead, then turned and left the office.

Mary Margaret's suspicions hung in the air like a toxic cloud.

Carin didn't want to believe her grandmother, but she had to admit having given it some thought during the past few days, she could no longer deny her distrust. Richard *had* asked too many questions about the chocolate business. He *had* point-blank suggested that Emerald hire him. He *had* told her that he desperately needed money. He *had* been much too impressed with the fact that she was the "chocolate heiress" he'd read about in *Gourmet* magazine.

Doubts whirled about Carin. She wanted to believe in love, just as she believed that someday she would be the writer she knew she could be. She was an adult now. It was time for her to give up fairy tales. But she was not sure she knew how.

Richard telephoned Carin at her apartment at precisely nine o'clock that evening, just as he had told the secretary he would. Since it was the middle of the night in Ireland, the village was deadly quiet. Only the street lamps stayed on to welcome him to town. The overseas operator let the telephone ring twenty times before she came back on the line to him.

"I'm sorry, sir."

"I'll try back in fifteen minutes," Richard replied, holding on to hope.

He went to the tobacconist's shop, where he found a coin-operated newspaper machine. He bought the last copy of the *London Times* and scanned the business page. He spied an article that reminded him of a former client of his. He decided that first thing in the morning, he would call his client and begin to rebuild his "book" of clients. He needed to make money again, a lot of money, if he intended to ask Carin to marry him. The last thing Richard wanted was to have the Killian clan reject him for something as silly as a lack of a proper portfolio.

Making money had always come easily to Richard. He had chosen to put his money in his castle . . . in his dream. True, the money had not lasted as long or gone as far as he had hoped. But whether he went back to the rat race in London or chose to spend his talents building Emerald Chocolates for his prospective father-in-law, Richard *would* make money.

He waited exactly sixteen minutes to make his call, thinking that the extra minute would somehow make a difference. There was no answer. He hung up.

"She had to know I would be calling," he said aloud. "Where *are* you, Carin?"

This time he waited seventeen and a half minutes before placing another call. He insisted that the operator let the phone ring twenty-five times before disconnecting.

With each ring, Richard lost faith.

Carin was not at home. It was not until he placed the sixth overseas call and did not connect that he finally crawled into his Land-Rover and drove back to his castle. He had stayed in Ennistymon for nearly one and a half hours. It was obvious that Carin was either avoiding his calls or hadn't received his message. Neither scenario boded well for Richard.

Richard could feel Carin slipping away from him. He had come close to paradise. But for Richard, close just wasn't good enough.

Chapter 33 ————————————

*T*HE STORY ABOUT the deaths of two judges poisoned by Emerald Chocolates fell from page one to page two, and then to page four in the *Chicago Tribune* on the third day after Michael arrived in town. The police investigators had painstakingly questioned every Emerald employee. They had searched the machine area for the possibility of an accidental poisoning, but no rat poison and no pesticides of any kind had been found. Inspector Gregory had even commented favorably on the sterile factory conditions.

All this frustrated Patrick. His fuse was short these days, though Michael knew his father had never been a model of patience.

In the three days since his arrival, Michael had managed to have two arguments with his father over the fact that according to Patrick, Michael was a doctor now and didn't care about Emerald. Michael never denied his father's accusations. Eventually the argument turned to Sheilagh.

Michael sensed that Patrick had wanted Sheilagh to remain in New York. There was little about his blustering that indicated he was in any way glad to have his eldest daughter home again. Michael realized his father harbored more than just a grudge against her; he was afraid of her.

At the same time, Mary Margaret oddly refused to admit to Sheilagh's existence, much less that she was back in town. Tense and anxious, she changed the subject quickly whenever Sheilagh's name was mentioned.

Michael went out to Caitlin's house for barbecued chicken and endured the appropriate cajoling and pleading with him to stay in their house instead of the Sherman House.

"I just don't understand it," Caitlin said, peeling another carrot for the salad. "Sheilagh doesn't want to stay with us either. It's a waste of money."

Michael put an arm around her shoulders. "Hey, don't get

down now. I don't mean to hurt your feelings, Cat. It's not you or your house or your hospitality I'm turning down. I just want some time alone. Sheilagh's the same way. We're thinkin' about a lot of things right now."

Catlin shoved the carrot peelings into the In-Sink-Erator and flipped the switch. "Yeah?" She sounded hurt. "I know she's having a tough time being here. I understand that. It took a lot for her to come back. And now you tell me Father's been giving you the third degree about her, too."

"Contrariness is in their blood," Michael said lightly, chomping on a carrot. "I expected it."

"So Sheilagh says, but it still hurts." Caitlin put down the peeler and leaned on the counter so that she could look into her brother's face dead on. "What's going on, Michael?"

He stopped chewing, and swallowed. God, it hurt more than he knew. "Bridget and I are having some problems."

"When did this start?"

"The day I met her." Michael tried to laugh, but the seriousness of his situation strangled the sound.

"The day you met her, Michael Killian, you fell head over heels."

"Who wouldn't? She was a vision. Top model for Patricia Stevens. Drove that bottle green MG with the tan interior and the convertible top. I loved that car . . . uh, girl, I mean." Michael rolled the carrot between his thumb and forefinger as memories washed over him. "God, I had completely forgotten about that car. Those days. We had a blast back then. Drinks on the lakefront. Dancing up at the club in Lake Geneva. We used to listen to jazz bands at the wildest honky-tonks. Then we'd drive home on the Outer Drive, Bridget kissing my ear and neck, and then she'd start playing with me. Christ, I damn near plowed into a semi truck one night when she . . ." He looked sheepishly up at Caitlin. "I shouldn't be telling you all this."

"Sure you should. You think Clay and I are any different?"

"Naw. I guess not."

"So, Michael, why isn't it still like that?"

"I dunno!" He slammed the flat of his hand down on the butcher block counter. "She's not the same anymore. She complains all the time about wanting things. Gowns, parties, jewelry . . . a bigger house . . . a bigger car . . . We *had* to move to River Oaks. It just goes on and on. I'm sick of it."

"I would think so."

Michael's eyes moved up to Caitlin's face. The setting sun

slid through the slats of the wooden louvers that covered the windows, and lit Caitlin's eyes. Her chestnut hair showed not a tinge of gray, though Michael could already boast half a head of it. She wore very little makeup, just mascara and a bit of blush on her cheeks. He could see only faint lines at the corner of her eyes, and deeper lines on the sides of her mouth. He reached out and touched her hand. "I think I figured out why you're so beautiful," he said as he watched her blush. "It's because you've always known you were loved. Clay's been a good husband to you, hasn't he?"

"The best."

"Cat?" Michael's voice was thoughtful. "Do you think it's true that I'm to blame for the problems Bridget and I are having?"

Caitlin had to work to stifle her knowing smile. "I don't know, Michael. It's possible. What do you think?"

"That's the hell of it, Cat. I don't know what I think. Bridget says I am."

"Did you ever stop to think that the reason she keeps demanding things from you is because what she's really asking for is love?"

"I never thought about it."

"Think about it, Michael." Caitlin patted his hand and went back to making a salad.

After that conversation with Caitlin, Michael was more grateful that he had chosen to stay at a hotel. Any more psychoanalysis by his sister and she would have him thinking that Bridget was not to blame for anything. Besides, what did Caitlin know about his life anyway? She had spent her whole life wrapped up in Emerald. He drove back to his hotel that night feeling relieved to escape his family.

Michael barely slept; there were too many memories to knock around. He rose, brushed his teeth, went back to bed, and remolded his pillow a dozen times, but nothing helped. At twelve forty-five, he was wide-awake. He pulled on his slacks, stuck his arms down the sleeves of his Arrow button-down shirt, and decided that what he needed was a drink and a drive.

The drink he wanted was to be found on Rush Street at Mr. Kelly's. Most of the diners were gone, and the place was winding down. There were still several couples seated at tables, and four men at the bar discussing that afternoon's Cubs game. Michael chose a solitary table in the corner where he could watch the comings and goings without being disturbed.

He ordered a Cutty and water, and sipped it slowly.

Damn Caitlin, he thought. This was all her fault. He hadn't thought about those early days with Bridget for years . . . decades. When was it exactly? Fifty? Fifty-one? He was so bad with dates. But he remembered the time of year. It was autumn and she was beautiful.

He had four season tickets to the Northwestern games, and he had been trying to sell them outside Dyke Stadium on the first day of the season. He heard her voice and felt the touch of her fingers on his shoulder before he saw her face.

"Hey! How much you want for the tickets?" asked the most melodic voice this side of Dinah Shore.

Michael had been yelling at a passerby who looked like a former defensive tight end, who Michael was certain could afford to buy his tickets.

"How much, Bubba?" She poked his shoulder.

Michael started to turn around. A breeze picked up the scent of Shalimar. The sun spiraled through her long, nearly black hair, making it glisten. Her skin was the color of cream, and her eyes were dark brown in a heart-shaped face. She wore dramatic makeup: thick, arched brows, ruby red lips, and incredibly long, thick lashes she had coated with black mascara. Her nails were long and lacquered in blood red.

Her body was long and lean, yet he could tell from the tight-waisted fit of her brown tweed suit that her breasts were ample. Short of Elizabeth Taylor, this girl was the most perfectly formed human being he had ever seen, on-screen or off. *Even Sheilagh could take lessons,* he thought.

"What did you call me?"

"Bubba, Bubba," she crooned playfully.

"You got the wrong guy." He turned his back to her.

He felt the heat of her anger on the back of his neck.

"Why, you little shit!" Bridget chortled, but Michael didn't budge. "Fine. Be that way. Don't take my money. I'll find somebody else."

She started to walk away but Michael grabbed her arm. "Testing. I was only testing."

"Testing what?" she retaliated, her eyes spitting indignation at him.

"Here," he said, handing her one of the tickets.

"I don't want your damn tickets now!" She tried to wrench her arm out of his grip.

"No, I'm serious. You take 'em. Take 'em all. You and your boyfriend can put in a cheer for me. On the house."

Her beautiful eyes scrutinized Michael's face. "Yeah?"

"Sure." He gave her the tickets.

"And what are you going to be doing?" she asked as her anger dissipated.

"Studying. This is my last year of med school. I start my internship next year."

"Really? So, what kind of doctor are you going to be?"

Michael smiled. "A good one."

Michael didn't see Bridget for another year. He graduated from Northwestern med school and pulled Cook County for his internship. They called it a hellhole, and it was. He worked over ninety hours a week and slept the rest. At Cook County Hospital, trauma was the name of the game.

He worked as an intern for three months. If he'd been a medic in South Korea, his baptism by fire could not have contained fewer flames.

The night he saw Bridget again, he had forgotten all about the beautiful girl he'd given his tickets to.

She came in on a stretcher.

"Jesus, what happened to her?" Michael asked the ambulance driver as he looked down at Bridget's bloody and bruised face.

"She musta pissed off her boyfriend."

Michael walked over to the girl. He still did not recognize her. "It's okay. I'll get you fixed up. Take it easy," he said soothingly. Michael began cleaning the blood that came from a cut lip. The blood had been smeared across her cheek, making the cut look worse than it was. Her right eye was badly bruised and nearly swollen shut, but he could tell there was no permanent damage.

"Well, sweetheart, it looks to me like he took the news about us a tad too seriously," Michael joked as he went to work suturing the lacerated lower lip. "I want you to know that I'm excellent at this kind of work, but you gotta promise me you won't go back to that turd. I only work cheap the first go-around. If you come back here like this again, I'll charge plenty."

Michael continued working, talking and joking to soothe the girl's traumatized emotions. "He didn't hurt you anywhere else, did he?"

The girl rolled her head slowly from side to side.

"If he raped you, tell me," Michael said as he leaned close to her face so that the orderly and nurse could not hear him.

She rolled her head again.

"Good." Then he gave the girl a tetanus injection. "Now, look, James here is gonna take you out in the hall so you can rest for a bit. When you feel strong enough to go home, we'll get you some transportation if you need it."

With her lower lip jutting out past her upper lip and decorated with nine fine black stitches, Bridget said the words that were to change Michael's life forever. "Thanks, Bubba."

Michael's jaw dropped. "I gave you my season passes!" He remembered how she had looked that day. She was sweet, spunky, and beautiful, and some asshole had done this to her. It made him sick.

She tried to smile, but it hurt too much. "I need a ride home."

Michael smiled for the both of them. "I'll have to charge you," he joked, and drove her home three hours later when his shift was over.

He sipped the last of his scotch and ordered a second when the waitress came around for last call. This was Bridget's favorite drink, too, he thought.

We had a wild romance, didn't we, doll?

In the mid-fifties, Bridget O'Shea was in every local publication, modeling everything from Evans furs to John M. Smythe furniture, Peacock crystal, and weekend packages at the Ambassador East Hotel. Michael Killian was envied by every single one of his intern friends. By dating Bridget O'Shea, Michael found his own name making its way into the society columns with such ease, it set Mary Margaret's teeth on edge.

When Bridget worked the style show luncheon for the American Heart Association, reporters scribbled down his name in their pads. Because she was the most beautiful and professional model in Chicago, she was the first choice of every charity style show in the city. Her face was familiar, her name a buzzword in many homes when the *Tribune* arrived.

Bridget worked hard. She took acting lessons, dancing lessons—both modern and jazz—to keep in shape. She was one of the first models to insist on getting television commercials. Her diction lessons paid off when she had to recite the copy for "Lip-lickin' good, Pappy's puppy food."

It was Bridget's money that paid for their first apartment during Michael's residency. It was Bridget's salary that paid for the European vacation she gave him for a graduation gift. It was Bridget who stayed up with him making coffee and grilling him with questions when he studied for his board exams. It was Bridget who never complained the next morning when she had to make a seven-o'clock photo shoot in a bathing suit next to the icy cold Chicago River. He'd always said Bri was a good egg.

Why didn't he say it anymore?

"Maybe you are just a turd like Caitlin said," he mumbled to himself. Then he downed his drink.

Michael had yet to telephone Houston and let Bridget know that he had arrived safely and that he had not come to blows with his father . . . yet.

Michael did not want to talk to Bridget. And she did not want to talk to him.

Is it over? he wondered. Had they come to the end of the line?

Michael remembered their last moment together, and this time he looked at it from Bridget's perspective. He dropped his face into his hands, ashamed at what he saw. Bridget had been reaching out to him, and he had turned her away. He did that a lot and never thought much of it. He gave her the cold shoulder because she was always nagging him . . . or so he thought.

Michael had withheld love and affection from Bridget to punish her. But for what? What had she done?

She's a woman . . . just like Mary Margaret. The thought blasted in an instantaneous flash across his mind. It came and went so quickly, he nearly missed it. It was the most important revelation of his life.

What was he thinking? Bridget was nothing like his mother. The only similarity was that they were both female. How could he be so simple-minded as to blame Bridget for the things his mother had done to him . . . *like withholding love* . . . The second blast of realization was louder than the first.

His childhood came whirling back to him in a kaleidoscope. He twisted his memories this way and that, distorting the colors, but eventually they all fell into a pattern. The pattern that had determined his behavior so that now, at age forty-five, his marriage was in peril. Sadly, Michael had to admit he was largely responsible for putting it there. Bridget had only been responding to his actions. She was trying to protect herself from further rejection.

"My God . . . what have I done?"

Suddenly Michael knew exactly what he had to do. He got up from the table, threw down a ten-dollar bill, and searched out the nearest pay phone. He placed a dime in the slot.

The phone in his River Oaks home rang ten times. "Try it again, operator, please."

This time the phone rang fifteen times. Michael hung up and headed for his rented car.

Where could she be? Had something happened? Was she allright?

Questions raced through Michael's head as he drove back to the hotel. By the time he reached his room and flopped down on the bed, he had answered all of the questions for himself.

Bridget had left him.

Chapter 34 ———————————

June 12

CAITLIN LAY NAKED next to Clay, her left hand resting on his chest and her face buried in his shoulder. She was crying.

Clay pulled her closer and, with his right hand, pulled her chestnut hair off her face and placed it behind her ear. "What's wrong, sweetheart? Did I disappoint you that badly?" He chuckled, hoping that humor would ease her distress.

"Never." She smiled, thinking of their impassioned love-making. But she still could not stem the tears.

Clay felt her body shake as her sobs fought for release. "Go ahead and let it out, honey. You could use a good cry." He stroked her arm. "I know you've been disappointed in me . . . leaving Emerald high and dry, and now most of my job has fallen to Carin. I wish she had the guts to leave, too. But honestly, honey, I don't want you to worry. I'm meeting Sam Morrison from General Foods. They're interested in my idea for Jewels Chocolates. We're going to be fine. I don't want you to worry about money. We may have to sell the house, but there will be other houses."

"It's not the h—house or the business."

"Tell me, please. I don't want you to be upset."

"It's . . ." Caitlin gulped back a sob as memories worked their dark subterfuge. She had always wanted Clay to think that she was strong. That she could take anything. She had liked being his rock, his helpmate. She never wanted him to think that she doubted him, but she did. For a long time she had been able to suppress her fears, but this crisis at the business had forced her to look back across the years and face her demons.

Out of the chaos of Sheilagh's mistakes with Clay and Andrew's death, Caitlin had won a more mature and loving Clay. Out of the chaos of Matthew's death, Clay had won an emotionally healthy and more independent Caitlin.

Visions of her wedding day to Clay in June of 1942 broke across Caitlin's mind like dawn. It had been a large and glorious society affair. Not a pew in Ascension Church was empty. Mary Margaret had finally won back the respect of all her society friends, and they turned out for the gala reception at the Drake Hotel in droves. On that day, Clay told Caitlin she was the most beautiful woman in the world. It was one time Caitlin actually *felt* beautiful. The years since then had been peaceful and loving, both of them consumed in their work at Emerald and in each other. If ever there were soul mates, it was Caitlin and Clay.

But even soul mates stumble, Caitlin thought. She had not paid enough attention to Clay these past five years . . . or maybe she never had. Otherwise his animosity toward Patrick would not have given rise to this schism. She should have been more attuned to his needs and frustrations. She felt as if she had failed. "I should have known you were unhappy at Emerald."

"Don't assume guilt that you don't deserve, Cat. How could you know? Perhaps even if I'd come to you with my misgivings about Patrick or stood up for myself or a million and one other things I could have done, all this would have happened anyway. Don't you see that?"

"In a way," she sniffed.

Clay arched his body back on the bed and pulled her face up to his and kissed her on her tear-soaked lips. "I love you, Caitlin. I love the fact that you take on the world in my defense. But it's time I grew up, too. I won't be the fall guy for Patrick anymore. Besides, there's something more about him that I sense ever since I've left."

"Like what?"

"I don't know, but it's not good. Something at the core of him makes my blood turn cold. Not evil, but not good either. I replay our conversations in my sleep, and all I hear is his selfish demands, his callousness. I can't believe how for so many years I just assumed he loved the company as much as you or I. To us, Emerald was nearly a living entity. To Patrick, it was a money machine, and we were necessary cogs. It wouldn't surprise me one bit to get that phone call from the police we've all been waiting to receive and find out they've booked Patrick for the poisonings." He looked at Caitlin's pensive face. "Does it upset you to hear me say these things about your father?"

"No. He *is* selfish. He *does* use people and discard them. He crushes hearts like rock candy to feed his ego. After a lifetime of that kind of thinking, what would taking a physical life matter? I've thought the same as you do nearly all my life. I always kept thinking if I were prettier or smarter or more ambitious, then maybe he would love me more. That's the lesson I've learned from this crisis . . . Bastards *should* be left behind."

Clay kissed Caitlin's forehead exuberantly. "My God! You are my kind of woman, Caitlin Burke!" He drew her up on top of him and stroked her round hips sensually. "Yes," he said, placing his right hand on the nape of her neck and drawing her lips to his, "my woman." His tongue darted between her parted lips, luring her tongue into the sensual trap he baited for her. A moan rushed up her throat, and Clay swallowed it with a kiss that nearly engulfed her.

A sense of knowing told Clay that Caitlin needed reassurance now more than she had for a very long time. He wanted her to know that he loved her intensely. He wasn't famous or fabulously rich. He was just a man. But he loved her with all his heart.

Clay slid his hand down Caitlin's smooth shoulder to her back and then around to her side where her breast was crushed against his chest. He kissed her so deeply, he could nearly feel their souls fuse. It was as if he could read her emotions off the tableau in her heart. Then he knew what had hurt Caitlin the most.

"Thank you for loving me," he whispered. "Please don't cry anymore. And don't ever, ever think for one minute that I still hold Sheilagh in my heart, because I don't."

"How . . . did you know I thought that?" she asked as she raised stunned eyes to him.

His smile was compassionate and loving. "I should have known it a very long time ago. I hope it wasn't just that I was insensitive. I hope it's because I've gained some wisdom since then.

"Sheilagh is your sister," he went on. "She and I shared a brief few years and more tragedy than I want to experience again. It can never compare with the life I've had with you . . . or the years still to come. You're the girl in my dreams, the one I want to grow old with. It's you I love. I'm the one who should be asking you—am I enough for you?"

Caitlin peered deeply into Clay's blue eyes. There she saw the young boy she'd met at the World's Fair so long ago and the courageous man she loved today. She smiled happily at him. "You're all I've ever wanted, Clay Burke. You're more than enough for me."

June 13

"Shit!" Carin spilled coffee on her paperwork. She scrambled about, trying to clean up the swiftly moving stream of dark liquid before it annihilated the weekly report she had just spent four hours compiling. She used telephone memos to try to sop up the coffee, but just made a bigger mess. "Shit!" she screamed aloud.

Martha had been walking down the hall. She peered in the office doorway. "My goodness! Let me help," she said, and rushed to the desk. She picked up a blank piece of paper and stopped the stream before it trickled down onto the white alpaca rug. "I'll go get some paper towels from the bathroom."

"Thanks, Martha, you're a love."

Just then the phone rang. Carin picked it up. "Yes?" The other end went dead. "Shit. Now I've disconnected the line!"

Carin continued to sort the non-coffee-stained paperwork from her stained paperwork. "What's taking Martha so long?" She glanced into the hall, but there was no sign of her. Carin shook her head and then went to the bathroom herself and got the necessary paper towels to clean up the spilled coffee. Over the years Martha had become a bit absentminded. Of late, she seemed more in a dither than usual, but then, most of them were about to snap under the pressure and tension this poisoning business had caused.

Carin, for one, was sick of dodging phone calls from the press. Until the past few days back in Chicago, she had had no idea the United States supported so many journalists. She was besieged with calls from the *Trib,* the *Wall Street Journal,* API, UPI, Reuters, ABC, CBS, NBC, and WGN. She'd met with free-lancers, disc jockeys, staff writers for every news magazine, and even one audacious hippie type who wrote for *Playboy* and wanted to do an article on sex, chocolate, and poison as if it were some new S and M kick.

Carin sank into her desk chair and threw her pen onto the papers. She stared at them, these slim white sheets that represented decisions. She noticed that since her father and mother had jumped ship, her grandfather had not blinked an eye, nor taken the helm. He had simply slid the lifeboats over to Carin. Patrick was nearly as batty as Martha, she finally concluded. She propped her feet up on the desk, leaned back, and closed her eyes.

She should be devising a new PR plan that would turn the tragedy of the poisoning to their advantage. But how? She didn't want to admit how close they were to admitting defeat.

Carin had already pulled every television and print ad for the next two months. Rather than use the Victorian-looking ads, she wanted a direct, blunt approach in which Emerald clearly admitted the crisis, yet pressed home their dedication to quality and purity of product. Once production was up and rolling again, she would implement the use of double cellophane wrapping around every Emerald gift box. The bar candy, she would leave as it was. She hoped the public would see this as a sign of Emerald's confidence in its product. She'd met with the advertising staff and ordered them to start from scratch.

The recalled candy was still arriving back at the warehouse every day by the truckload. The police had taken samples, tested them, and found "nothing conclusive." God! She was tired of hearing those words. The cost of shipping their stock back to the factory was staggering, but they were under FBI orders. Even though the first shock of the story had passed, Emerald Chocolate was still being mentioned on every radio and television broadcast in Chicago. It didn't help that Howard K. Smith had made it his personal duty to keep track of the story until the killer was brought to justice.

Murder. That's what she was involved with now. It was hard to imagine. Less than a month ago she had been preparing for her trip to Ireland. Life had been chugging along as it always had. Since then, not only had she fallen in love for the first time, but her family had split apart at the seams, and in some odd way was already mending along new lines.

Sheilagh had come back home. That in itself was a miracle. The greatest insight Carin had ever had into her parents had come in the last few days from watching Michael, Sheilagh, Clay, and Caitlin all together again, as it must have been when they were young.

Carin had purposefully sat on the sidelines and observed these four middle-aged people teasing one another as if they were teenagers. She had never realized how deeply their lives had come together. She also had never known to what lengths her mother and father had gone to keep Killian family secrets from her. Carin had known that her father and Sheilagh had been married at one time, but to hear her grandmother or mother talk about it, it sounded as if it were no more than going steady. For years there had been whispers about a baby, but Carin had never heard the name Andrew until yesterday afternoon when she'd accidentally come upon Michael and Sheilagh on the terrace of her parents' home.

Sheilagh, wearing a swimsuit, was stretched out, belly-down, on a chaise lounge reading a Jacqueline Susann novel, while Michael smeared Coppertone lotion on the backs of her legs.

She shut the book. "That feels wonderful. No wonder you doctors have to insure your hands."

"We do nothing of the kind."

"Oh, really?" She twisted her head and shoulders around to look up at him. "I thought it was a professional thing like a dancer and her legs."

"We have big egos, but not that big."

"Well"—she smiled brightly—"I just want you to know that I like you even though you are a doctor. I never cared for the profession myself."

"Sheilagh! How can you say that? You bought me my first toy doctor kit." He punched her shoulder playfully.

"I did? I don't remember it." A frown creased her forehead. "I can't believe I ever thought highly of a doctor."

"Why?"

Her eyes clouded. "Because of Andrew. I don't think a week goes by that I don't ask myself, What if I'd had a better doctor? What if I had paid better attention to his instructions? What could I have done?"

"Oh, God, Sheilagh . . ." Michael's tones were mournful. "I had no idea you still thought of him so much . . . after all this time. I had almost forgotten about him. I never thought how hard it must be for you to come back here . . . and remember. Did you go to the cemetery?"

"Yesterday. I wanted to ask Clay if he ever went, but I didn't want to upset Caitlin . . . I didn't want her to be reminded."

Michael smoothed a handful of lotion onto Sheilagh's shoulder, using the Coppertone as an excuse to try to soothe her pain. "I think you love us all too much, Sheilagh Killian."

"Naw. No such thing." She tried to smile.

Michael was pensive for a long moment before speaking again. "I never understood why Mother used to go out of her way to make life miserable for you."

"Part of it is because I know too much."

"Like what?"

"I know where the bodies are buried . . . secrets . . ." Sheilagh said, and even from across the terrace, Carin could see a shadow pass over her face. She tossed her gleaming hair over her shoulder as if to ward off the evil. "Mary Margaret still thinks it's her calling in life to roughen my road."

"What are you going to do about her?"

"I'm not sure. Sometimes I think she really does believe I died thirty years ago. She has always been the greatest mystery to me. What is it that makes her tick? Before I left for this trip, I promised myself I would find out."

"Holy Cow!" Michael saw the determined gleam in Sheilagh's eyes. "You intend to confront her face-to-face?"

"Yep."

"When?"

"As soon as these idiot detectives find the killer." Sheilagh stood and stretched. She picked up a terry cloth robe and stuck her arms into the sleeves. She smiled maliciously. "Then, little brother, I'm going to find the answer to my question."

"Which is?"

"What is it about me that pisses her off?"

"What about Father? What are you going to do about him?"

"That *is* a question. I'm more of a threat to him than you can imagine, Michael. I just haven't decided if destroying him would be worth it."

"Sheilagh, what do you know that's so terrible?

"Plenty, little brother. And it's my secret to tell . . . or keep." Sheilagh flicked the ends of the terry cloth belt around her narrow waist and walked triumphantly into the house.

Carin had been home from Ireland for only five days, and in that short time she had made a hundred small discoveries and one very large one . . . the Killian family was not at all the perfect family she had grown up thinking it was.

The mystery of the poisoned chocolate was only the first case to be solved. Apparently the Killian past was littered with jealousies, hatreds, and dark intrigues. What kind of people were Sheilagh, Michael, and Caitlin? What did Sheilagh know about Patrick that was so sinister, she would not share it even with Michael? How were they able to keep so much so secret for so long? Carin felt she hardly knew her own family. She felt duped, even betrayed. She shivered as she wondered if the dark side of the Killians was part of her, too.

County Clare, Ireland

Lord Richard Butler had done everything he could to reach Carin, and he had failed. He was exhausted from the effort. Never in his life had he been so obsessed with a woman. Each day that passed without hearing from her seemed to add to an ever-widening chasm. There was nothing he could put his finger on, only that he knew deep in his heart he was losing her.

He remembered the way she looked, the sound of her laughter, the warm feel of her skin next to his. He sat in the morning room and recalled every morning they'd spent together. He went to the banquet room and relived the witches' banquet. He slept in the antique bed where she had slept and he especially remembered every detail of touching her, kissing her.

Richard crossed his arms behind his head and stared at the ceiling. What was she thinking right now? Did she miss him as much as he missed her? He would give anything to talk to her on the telephone. But for some reason, she clearly had not gotten his messages.

Twice now he had gotten through to Emerald Chocolates. Once he had talked to Martha, the secretary, and once he had spoken to Mrs. Killian, who Richard assumed was Carin's grandmother.

He had sent a telegram to Carin two days before, and each day, twice a day, he had gone to Ennistymon and checked the Western Union office for a reply, but there was no word from Carin. Each day he returned to the castle more depressed than ever.

The door opened a crack and Lidia backed in, weighted down with groceries. She plopped the mesh bag of fresh vegetables on the counter, took one look at Richard, who had started to rise to help her, and said: "Don't bother. Go ahead and finish with yer mopin'."

"My what?"

"You heard what I said. Yer good fer nothin' lately."

"That's not true. I've been working with a couple of old clients, and I'm going to London soon to close a deal. I should make a nice commission."

"Good fer you! But that ain't why yer sad. I've seen yer money-weary face, and this ain't it. Yer missin' Carin." Lidia nodded vigorously as if to confirm her observation.

Richard could not refute the truth. "I am. I miss her something awful."

Lidia chuckled to herself. "You sound so surprised."

"I am. But it's more than just missing her. I have tried to call her and can't get through. I left messages, but she hasn't attempted to call me. She knows to cable. She said she would."

"I'm thinkin' she must be very busy with the police investigation an' all."

"What investigation?"

"Don't you read the newspapers?" She pointed to the *London Times* that Richard had bought at the tobacconist's shop. "Read for yerself."

He retrieved the days-old paper from the opposite end of the banquette and read the details about the chocolate poisoning. "My God! No wonder she hasn't been home."

"So you see? Yer probably makin' a big deal out of nothin'."

"Yeah? Then how come I don't feel as relieved as I should?" Richard's expression was earnest as he suddenly felt the room blanketed with an ominous chill.

"Sometimes I question the amount of brains in yer head. You fall in love wi' a beautiful woman, you don't put yer claim on her, you send her back across half the world, and you expect her to wait for you to make a move?"

"You don't think she knows that I love her?"

"How could she? What did she have here with you other than what it appears to the rest of us . . . a summer romance? That's all it was, wasn't it?"

"Hell no!" He slammed his fist on the table.

"Prove it," she challenged.

"I will," he said, and stalked out of the room.

June 14
Chicago, Illinois

Tony Vallenti stood in his wife's hotel room looking out at the city lights through a rainstorm. He did not know where Sheilagh was tonight, and he was worried.

Tony had struggled for four days over his decision to come to Chicago to be with Sheilagh. On the one hand, he trusted her to know her own mind, and she knew she could call on him for support. On the other hand, Sheilagh was stubborn and proud as hell and might not ever pick up the phone. He had carried around his plane ticket to Chicago since the day he'd seen Sheilagh off at the airport.

Every night Sheilagh had telephoned him, and though she stated that everything was fine, she was okay, and nothing earth-shattering had transpired, Tony could sense she was depressed and making every effort to conceal her emotions from him. He could hear pain in her voice.

Sheilagh was hiding something, and she didn't love him or trust him enough to confide in him.

Rain splattered against the huge wall of glass, distorting the buildings and traffic below. She was out there somewhere . . . but where?

He had telephoned Caitlin and informed her that he had arrived in the city. Fortunately for him, the concierge at the hotel recognized him from that piece in *TV Guide* about him a month ago when he did a return stint on his old soap opera, and graciously let him into Sheilagh's hotel room.

Tony checked his watch. It was nearly nine o'clock, and Caitlin had said that Sheilagh had left two hours ago. Tony went to the nightstand where the telephone was located and was about to dial Caitlin's number again when he heard a key in the door.

He hung up the phone and sprinted to the door.

Sheilagh was looking down as she depressed the little clamp to collapse her umbrella. She was wearing a multicolored pastel striped raincoat with a hood, but he could see that her silk skirt and shoes were soaked. She wore a pensive expression filled with stress and confusion. This visit had been difficult for her, and he knew instantly that he had made the right decision in coming here.

"Princess?" he said softly so as not to startle her.

She raised her head slowly, as if it were a great effort to do so. A streak of joy raced across her green eyes, leaving a wake of tears. "Tony," she breathed as if she had just been rescued. She held out her arms.

Tony scooped her up in an embrace. "Princess . . ." He kissed her face and tasted rainwater and tears. He pushed back the hood and sank his hand into her thick auburn hair. It smelled like Shalimar. He kissed her lips hungrily, giving her love but not taking from her.

She needed him, he thought. For the first time since they had met, Sheilagh needed Tony.

"You're here? You're really here!" she said with an odd mixture of delight and melancholy.

"Of course I am." He peered into her eyes, then kissed her cheeks, nose, forehead, and chin.

Her fingertips dug into his shoulders as if she were clinging to the edge of a cliff. "Thank God . . ."

He kissed her mouth ravenously, molding his lips to hers. His kiss was at once coaxing and gently sympathetic, and then infused her with strength. He opened his mouth further. *Let me take away the pain*, his lips were saying. He held her nape in one hand and used the other to press the small of her back into him. His kiss grew more ardent as his tongue traced the edge of her lips and then plunged with a need of its own into the interior of her mouth. She took his kisses and stored them up one by one. She breathed his breath and soaked up his strength.

Sheilagh pulled apart the thin veil that had kept him from being truly intimate with her and allowed him entry into her soul.

"I'm here, princess," he finally said as he dragged his mouth from hers. "It feels like an eternity since I've held you in my arms. And it's only been a few days."

"I know," she whimpered. "I . . . I . . ."

He pulled away from her and stared into her eyes. "Go ahead . . . I need to hear you say it."

"I need you so . . ." Sheilagh burst into tears.

Tony crushed her to his chest and rested her head in the crook of his neck. He stroked her head and let his fingers fall to the edge of her hair. "I know, my love. I know."

Sheilagh felt the barriers around her heart collapse. For nearly fifty years she had blocked her pains and sorrows deep within herself. She had told herself that there was nothing odd about her never taking roles that played in Chicago. She'd lied to herself long enough and hard enough until she believed that her parents truly did not matter to her anymore. Sometimes she could go for weeks pretending they had never lived. But that was acting. Now she had to face the person who frightened her most in life . . . the real Sheilagh.

"I'm glad I came, you know. Coming back here has been harder than I anticipated, but it's given me a chance to think about a lot of things."

"And what did you discover?" he asked as he unzipped her raincoat, slid it off her back, and then flung it into the corner behind them, never taking his eyes from her face or his arms from around her waist. Tony wanted her to feel secure and safe and loved.

Sheilagh's lips were still cherry red from his ardent kisses, but they trembled ever so slightly. "That I've let pride stand in the way of my happiness. All these years I was ashamed of the Sheilagh Killian from Chicago. I had come to believe that my mother was right . . . that I was a wicked girl and that I had done something dark and evil. I tried to bury that girl in New York. I became someone else, or so I thought. I never told you the truth about myself, because I was afraid if I did, you would despise me the way they had."

"Sheilagh, my darling, I could never despise you," he said. "I love you."

She placed her fingertips on his lips to lovingly hush him. "I know that now. I know it probably for the first time. Your being here is like . . . I dunno . . . a sign or something. My heart was calling out to you, and you heard me. I never realized how much you're a part of me. I would sit in Caitlin's kitchen and watch her and Clay go about their morning rituals or fix dinner and I would think, *They even move as if they are one.* Then I would think, *That's just how Tony and I are.*

"It's so odd, too, because it's not the big things, but the little things. Like how you bring my glass of water to me at night without thinking. Or I set out your reading glasses next to your book and fold your T-shirts with the arms back first so there's no crease down the front.

"Naively, I believed that we would keep going on that way . . . melding little bits of ourselves to one another. And, too, I was stupidly foolish enough to believe that I had buried the past and that it would never rise up again to hurt me."

"And it resurrected, huh?" He touched her cheek and gazed more deeply into her eyes.

"It did. I need to talk to you, Tony. For the first time I'm ready to share my past with you, but please, I need to hear once more that you love me."

"Oh, God, Sheilagh. I do love you. Nothing you could tell me is going to stop me from loving you. I told you that a thousand times, but I suppose seeing is believing."

Sheilagh smiled at him, the man she loved nearly as much as life itself. They walked with their arms around each other into the sitting room of Sheilagh's suite and seated themselves on the powder blue sofa. Tony kept his arm around her as she began her tale.

Sheilagh told him about her father, his drinking, infidelities, and bootlegging. She told him about the horrible night she discovered that he had been involved in a gangland slaying. She told him of the torrent of tears she had cried over that man's death and over the death of her faith in God. She told him of her vow never to live by Patrick's rules again.

She told him about Caitlin and Michael and their promise to one another and the love they had shared all those years and how it had kept them going.

When she came to the part about Clay, she could not look at Tony, but chose instead to stare out the rain-streaked window at the city lights. She cried when she told him about her attempted abortion. She cried even more when she spoke Andrew's name aloud.

She told him about the funeral, what she remembered and the cruel things her mother had said to her. She told him about her father's renunciation of her and her flight from Chicago.

She told him about her reunion now with Clay. She told him that she had come that very night from her baby's grave.

"I left pink roses and blue delphiniums," she finally said over a strangled sob.

"I want to go there with you, tomorrow. Would that be all right?"

"Oh, yes, Tony. I would like that very much." She wiped away her tears and looked up at her husband. "You don't look shocked at any of this," she said with surprise.

"You thought I would reject you, didn't you?"

She nodded slowly. "I did."

"My darling," he said with a loving smile, and gathered her onto his lap as if she were a small child. "We all have done and said things we're not proud of, especially by the time you get to be our age. In fact, I don't see how anybody gets to our age without accumulating a dozen or so failures. I think you did pretty damn well under the circumstances. Do not think for one minute that what your father did or didn't do is any reflection on you. You did the best you knew how. In fact, I don't see anything that you should be ashamed of."

"You don't?" she replied as renewed hope curved the edges of her mouth upward.

"No, I don't. I think this whole thing of your parents disinheriting you is bullshit. You don't give a flip about their chocolate company any more than I would. Or their money. We have our own money. What hurts is their rejection."

"Yes . . ." Suddenly she felt nineteen again as she fought a wave of tears.

He pulled her against his chest again. "I know, baby, and the best thing you can do is cry it out. Then we need to go and tell them so."

Sheilagh placed her hands on his chest, straightened up, and stared at him with determined green eyes. "I know."

"You're fifty years old, Sheilagh, and you're still afraid of your own parents. Your mother *cannot* hurt you anymore. You are talented, beautiful, world-famous, respected, and loved. Your mother is and has been jealous of you all her life. I'll bet my last dollar on that. But I tell you what, I've never met the woman, but I'd love to get inside her head."

"Tony, she's my mother, not an acting challenge," Sheilagh scoffed.

"To get through this, maybe that's how we should look at them both for now. Sound good?"

"Yes. Very good."

Tony smiled at her. "Now, I've had a long trip, I'm tired . . ."

Sheilagh's eyelids lowered slightly so that she was looking at him seductively through her long, sooty lashes. "Not too tired, I hope."

Tony's grin was sensually wicked as he lowered his gaze to her lips. He slid his hand up her knee onto her thigh and then higher still. "I thought I mentioned that when you came in the door. I'm horny as hell."

"Mmmm. This could take all night."

"At least." Tony breathed out the words just as his mouth captured hers in an explosive kiss.

Chapter 35

CARIN COULD NOT sleep. She tossed and turned so many times in bed, she felt as if she'd just finished a gymnastics class. Her body was exhausted, but her mind was keenly alert. She was haunted by the double specters of Richard's loving arms and Mary Margaret's barbs, which were meant to create fissures in Carin's trust.

She could still hear Mary Margaret's voice telling her that Richard was nothing more than a summer romance; that he was an opportunist; that he was the kind of man who preyed upon rich American women and divested them of their money before breaking their hearts.

"You're just in love with love," Mary Margaret had said that evening. "You don't honestly believe that he thinks about you any more than his other women, do you? He probably can't even remember your name. You must be careful, Carin. Careful."

When Carin had spoken to Caitlin about the fact that she had not heard from Richard, her mother had not rushed to Richard's defense.

Caitlin's eyes had been filled with caring as she looked at her daughter across the table. "I think you *should* be careful, Carin. I can't say that Richard does or doesn't love you, because I've never met the man. I know he must be special, otherwise you wouldn't have fallen so hard for him. On the other hand, we know very little about him."

"But Gran loved him, too!" Carin protested.

Caitlin's smile quieted Carin down. "Honey, Aileen believes in UFOs. I have to take her observations with a grain of salt. She is the dearest woman I've ever known and she loves us all to a fault, but she has her moments."

Carin's face slumped. "You think Gran is a crackpot just like her colleagues at the university."

"I wouldn't go that far. I think in many ways she's very wise, but she is getting on in years, and lately she's been displaying some . . . well, rather odd behavior. Did you know she told your father she saw ghosts over in Ireland?"

"She told him about that?"

"Carin! You mean you knew this and you don't question her mental state?"

"Oh, for Pete's sake, Mom. Sometimes I think you've had your head in a chocolate bar too long. Gran isn't nuts. She probably did see ghosts."

"Did you see them?"

"I was only looking at Richard." Carin grinned widely as her mother rolled her eyes. "I believe Gran, is all I'm saying . . ."

Caitlin tapped her fingers impatiently against the top of Carin's hand for emphasis. "You are as impractical as Aileen. You both believe in fantasies. And that will be your undoing."

"I love him, Mom," was all Carin could answer.

Now Carin punched her pillow angrily and fell face-first into the soft down. She hated having to defend Richard. She hated that her family was her greatest adversary.

"I do love him," she said aloud to the night. "But does he love me?"

Just then a bolt of lightning sheared the night sky, and thunder boomed so loudly, the windows rattled. Carin shot up to a sitting position. The storm was building in intensity. Then more lightning flashed. Thunder rolled and buzzed.

Buzzed?

Carin's ears pricked to attention.

Buzz.

There it was again. She yanked the sheet up to her nose. The thunder boomed outside. Then she heard the buzz for the third time.

She dropped the sheet. "Jeez! There's somebody at the door! I'm coming!" she shouted as she hauled herself out of bed and jogged down the hall. Her apartment was on the first floor of a two-story redbrick brownstone with dark forest green trim and shutters. She glanced at the clock and sourly noted that it was 2:14 in the morning.

Buzz. Knock. Knock.

"Damn it, I'm coming!" she shouted through the lace curtains that hung over the oval glass in the Victorian door. She could see a man's figure standing in the rain, but judging from the size and height, it could only be her father or her uncle Michael.

Dread caused her fingers to tremble as she pulled back the curtains. He was shrouded in darkness, and she could not see his face. She reached over to flip the light switch.

When he moved backward a slight step, the light from the coach lamps on either side of the door illuminated his face.

"Richard!" she screamed as her hands scrambled up the door to unlock the dead bolt, release the chain lock, and turn the doorknob.

She flew into his arms.

Rain pelted them as he kissed her passionately. "Carin, I love you," he breathed in short pants, as if he had run all the way from Ireland. "I missed you." He kissed her again and again, swallowing her words before they had a chance to be heard.

Carin scooped up his wet hair and gently pressed him closer. Her heart beat like a trip-hammer against her rib cage. She felt simultaneously weak and strong.

All her misgivings scurried away from her like frightened mice. Richard was here. Richard loved her. Richard held her tightly as if he intended never to let her go.

"I missed you, too," was all she could say, and it sounded so incredibly true. *I had nearly come to the place where there were no more dreams*, she thought. Once again Richard had rescued her.

"I heard you calling me," he said between kisses.

"I didn't know where to call. You have no phone."

He shook his head and grinned widely. "No. No. In my dreams, I heard you calling me. I told you to dream of me."

"I nearly forgot," she said, gazing at his sultry lips, which he parted slowly before claiming her mouth once again.

"Never forget me, Carin," he moaned as he pulled her into him.

"I won't," she promised as she lifted her face to the pelting rain. "Let's go inside," she said, and took his hand.

His clothes were soaking wet. Her pastel blue baby doll pajamas were plastered to her bare skin. He could see not only the outline of her silhouette, but her thighs and buttocks and the exact mold of her breasts with their taut nipples.

They had only crossed the threshold when Richard yanked Carin back to him and enfolded her in his arms while using his foot to kick the door shut.

"Tell me you love me, Carin," he said.

"I do, Richard."

"Thank God!" He groaned with relief as he threw his head back and then slowly rolled it forward to peer at her. In the light from the etched-glass fixture above, he read confusion in her eyes. "What is it? What's wrong?"

"Why didn't you call, Richard? You promised me you would."

"I did call!"

"You didn't!"

"I did. Didn't you get any of my messages? I called the Emerald offices twice and left messages for you."

"What messages? When?"

"Three days after you arrived home, I talked to the secretary, and she said she would tell you I called. The next time, I spoke with your grandmother . . ."

"Aha! So that's it! No wonder Mary Margaret has been trying to dissuade me so intensely."

"Dissuade you? About me?"

"Yes, Richard. She tells me that you're nothing but an opportunist. Is that true?"

"Absolutely," he said cockily. "I want all of it. Every bit. I want your body and your money. I want your energy and talent and joy for life to ring forever in the halls of my castle. I want your love to shine in the faces of our children. I want you to hold my hand and buck me up when I need it. I want you to scold me when I say the wrong things or do anything that hurts you in any way. I'm just a man, Carin. I want to love you, and I want to be loved in return. Titles aren't worth a shit in America, and worth even less in an impoverished country. I haven't got much to give you, except a good heart and a promise that I will never, ever let you go. Marry me, Carin."

Carin hung on each of his impassioned words as he spoke them, and still she was not prepared for his proposal. She was stunned, and she was even more shocked to realize that Mary Margaret had worked her witchery well. She was unsure.

Richard read her thoughts as easily as if they had been inscribed a half inch deep on clay tablets. He had to convince her that his feelings for her were true and properly motivated, but he was afraid that his battle for her had already been forfeited to a foe he had never met.

He reached down and grasped the edges of her baby doll top and yanked the thin, wet material over her head, tossing it aside.

"Richard?!"

He slid his hands sensually down her back, splaying his fingers wide and pulling them around her rib cage and then up to fill themselves with her breasts. With his thumb and forefinger he coaxed and prodded the nipples until they became firm buds.

His left hand glided down the smooth slope of Carin's hip and slipped between the wet material and cool flesh. With a single movement, he divested her of the bottom half of her baby dolls.

She was glorious, he thought as he gazed at her body. Tiny droplets of rain caught the light and seemed to wink at him as they dropped off the ends of her fingertips, the sides of her hips and slopes of her breasts. As she reached up to unbutton his shirt, he touched her breast again. She responded by pressing her flesh into his hand. She unbuckled his belt. Unzipped his pants. She blazed a trail of sultry kisses that were more tongue than lips down the flatlands of his belly to his lower abdomen and then lower still.

She sank to her knees and with both hands she yanked down his briefs until he, too, was completely naked. He was hard and long and big. Carefully she pressed her lips to the end of his penis. He clutched her hair, and as he did, she felt his fingers tremble with pent-up passion. Richard's entire body began to quake as Carin made love to him. A low, soft groan rumbled deep within Richard's throat. It raced up to nearly escape and then was swallowed back into exile. Another moan began the tremulous roller coaster ride as Carin worked her spell on him.

"God, Carin," he moaned finally, and sank to his knees beside her. He kissed her softly at first and then captured her lower lip between his lips. He touched her tongue with the tip of his tongue. As his mouth opened further, he sucked in oxygen through his nostrils and blew it out across the crest of Carin's cheek.

Never had Richard been so inflamed with sexual need. He was glad he had saved his climax for her.

Her lips still his prisoner, Richard lifted her into his arms and carried her down the hall to the bedroom where he could see the unmade bed through the open door.

Gently he laid her upon the bed, then he leaned over and turned off the lamp on the nightstand. Carin looked through the darkness into Richard's smoky eyes.

She touched his cheek and traced the edge of his jaw and the outline of his kiss-swollen lips. She slipped her hand around his neck to his nape and pulled him to her.

The kiss was an explosion inside Carin as Richard spread her legs apart with his hand and sank his fingers into her. Demanding entrance, his fingers spread her open and then retreated. They danced upon her and around her, at once insistent and then mocking her reluctance. She was teased and taunted. She was forced to admit her passion.

Her hips rose to his attention.

Richard claimed her cries as his own when his tongue plunged into her mouth.

Carin was deliciously assaulted as Richard's tongue probed and danced. He tore his mouth from hers, abandoned her lips, and sought refuge in the swell of her breasts. He used his tongue to bring her nipples to full erection. Back and forth, he gave them equal attention.

Passion knocked the wind out of Carin. She pressed her head back against the pillow and tried to breathe but couldn't. Her hands roamed across the tight muscles of Richard's shoulders, down his rib cage, and onto his flanks. She could stand the torture no more.

"Please, Richard . . ." she begged, and pulled him on top of her.

Richard positioned himself above her and slowly lowered his body between her open legs. He crooked his elbows on either side of her head and rested his weight on them. "I'll try not to hurt you, Carin," he said, remembering all too well that she was still a virgin.

"Please," was all she could say.

He entered her, and Carin had never felt anything quite so exquisite in her life. He was big, but she was very wet. She felt only a slight twinge as his penis broke through her maidenhead. Mostly she remembered thinking that he felt like satin. The smoothest, most luxurious satin skin she had ever known. She wanted him inside her always.

He was more than gentle; he was empathetic to her needs, the rises and falls of her passion. He never stopped kissing some part of her body, and no matter where he placed his lips, another part of her body screamed out for attention. As his slick strokings increased in tempo, she trembled and quaked and quivered. She felt hot, then icy cold, and then on fire again.

Richard plunged deeper and found that he had crossed some invisible boundary that divided his former life from his future life. He knew at that moment that it was not he who had claimed Carin, but she who held him. He opened the door to his own soul and let her in. Like the beacon of light that searches the seas for the lost vessel, Carin had shown him the way to safe harbor. He smiled at the light and walked across the light beams into a new realm filled with gentle love.

"I love you, Carin," he said, pushing himself deep inside her.

Carin's orgasm burst around her like a celestial storm. Stars collided. Planets exploded. Meteorites streaked through the atmosphere, leaving tails of colored lights. The heavens sang with a thousand ancient voices that told Carin she had been right to give Richard her love.

"I love you, Richard," she said, gasping for breath.

Her words came to him like light fairies and fluttered down to his heart. Playfully they etched Carin's name there.

"Carin!" Richard groaned aloud as he ejaculated.

He slipped his weary arms beneath her and rolled to his back, pulling her atop him. He opened his eyes.

She was still quivering, her eyes sultry but satisfied. She had lowered her eyes and gazed at his mouth. She kissed him with a kiss meant to intoxicate.

"I'll marry you, Richard," she said huskily.

He lifted his hand to sweep a lock of coppery hair from her forehead. His fingers were trembling, not so much from sexual exhaustion as from humble reverence for the love he had found. "That's good," he replied past the lump in his throat. He felt complete.

"It's good?" she asked as she kissed his eyelid, tasted salt, and wondered if it was perspiration or a tear.

"Yes, very good. Because I had already determined that I would not let you out of this room tonight until you said yes."

A wicked smile worked its way onto Carin's lips. "Is that so? Well, in that case, my answer is no."

She lifted her hand up and over her own hips and buttocks down the crook between his legs. She filled her hand with him. With gentle pressure she massaged him. He grew hard.

"Oh, Carin . . ." Richard moaned. "I think I've met my match . . ." He closed his eyes.

Chapter 36

June 15

CARIN AND RICHARD playfully helped each other dress. They stood in the tiny bathroom in front of the mirror, checking one another's grooming.

"Which do you think will be the worst? Your mother or your father?"

"Mother. Definitely Mother."

"Did she have bad things to say about me, too?"

"Richard, it's just that they don't know you."

"Hell, Carin, you don't even know me. I mean, put yourself in their position. If I had a daughter and she came to me and said, 'Hey, Dad. I want to marry this bloke from Ireland. He hasn't a farthing, just a rotty castle and a lot of dreams,' I'd lock her up for good!"

Carin hit him on the arm. "Oh, Richard. You make it sound so terrible."

"Carin, I was a stockbroker for a few years. I know how to read a balance sheet. My bottom line sucks."

"It'll be okay. Really," she reassured him, and ducked under his arms, leaving him to stare at himself in the mirror.

"This one could be tough, old man." He straightened his tie.

Carin picked up the Princess phone beside her bed and dialed her mother's number in Wilmette. It rang three times and was picked up by Mrs. Shaunessy, the cleaning woman who came in once a week.

"Are my parents home, Mrs. Shaunessy?" Carin asked.

"Yes, they are. Do you wish to speak with either of them?"

"Just tell them I'm on my way over and not to leave until I get there."

"Yes, ma'am."

"Thanks, Mrs. Shaunessy." Carin hung up the phone.

"All set?" Richard asked as he walked into the room.

"Let's go," Carin said brightly.

"Boy! A lot *has* happened since you've been to Ireland," Richard said.

"Does it bother you that my parents are unemployed?"

Richard laughed, leaned over, and kissed her soundly on the lips. He held her chin between his thumb and forefinger. "No. It only bothers me when *I'm* unemployed."

Carin immediately felt doubt creep in like an ugly troll. "Which you are," she said, testing him.

"Which I am not. I told you I have some clients who have remained my friends. I made a few phone calls. I begged a little." He chuckled and spread his arms wide. "And voilà! I'm back in the broker business. It's a reduced salary, for now, but I'll be putting deals together for an investment company that has millions to lend and wants to make certain that they lend the money to worthy businessmen. It may take some time, but if I did it once, I can do it again."

"I know you can," Carin said as she grabbed his hand and pulled him to the door. "Time to meet my parents."

Michael screwed up tying his tie. He yanked at his collar and started over.

Jesus! He was having a rough time lately. All he thought about was Bridget. He couldn't keep his mind on the crisis his father was going through, he barely listened when Clay talked about his plans for a new upscale gourmet chocolate company . . . and who the hell was gonna pay twenty-five bucks a pound for truffles? Who gave a shit? Not Michael, that's for sure.

He stared at his reflection in the mirror. As far as he could see, it wouldn't be long before he was divorced. Bridget was going to leave him.

He had called the house all night long, which had cost him $15.60 in room service for coffee, and a night's sleep. Now he really looked like shit.

Michael walked back to the bed and flopped down. The last thing he felt like doing was going to Emerald today, but he'd promised Clay . . . like the nice guy he was.

He laid a hand over his eyes. What was he doing here in Chicago when his life was in Houston? He had patients who needed him. He had lives to save. A marriage to save . . .

"Oh, Bri, what has become of us?"

The phone rang.

"Michael?" a voice like Bridget's said.

"Bridget?" Michael's heart pounded like a jackhammer. "Is that you?"

"Yes, Michael."

"Where have you been? I called and called. I was worried when there was no answer."

"You called me?" She sounded shocked, utterly confused by his statement.

"Yes, I did. I . . . I wanted to talk to you."

"About what?"

"About us. I wanted to tell you that I was wrong. I wanted to tell you that I love you. I know I've been a bastard lately and—"

"I haven't been there for you either, Michael," Bridget admitted.

"Hear me out. I don't want you to do anything rash . . . Give me a chance to make it up to you . . . please . . ."

"That's why I called, Michael . . ."

"Oh, God." Michael felt as if the floor had swallowed him up. He braced himself.

"I wanted to tell you the same thing. We've both made some mistakes. I want a second chance."

"*You* want? Jesus! Bri, I'm the one who's apologizing here."

"No, Michael, I am."

"Fine. Great. We're even. As soon as I get this thing over with today for Caitlin, I'm coming home."

"Michael, you don't have to do that."

"Shit, Bri. You just said we could work it out . . ."

"Shut up, Michael," Bridget interrupted. "I've been trying to tell you I'm downstairs in the lobby."

"Oh, God!" Michael emotions rode the roller coaster car back up to the summit. "Well, darlin', get on that elevator and get up here!"

"Michael?"

He could hear her smile over the wire. "Yes?"

"I love you, too."

Tony kissed Sheilagh awake. She stretched languorously and smiled at him.

"This is the *only* way to wake up." She sighed as Tony flipped the sheet off her naked body and raked her with his eyes.

In an instant his mouth was on hers again and his hand skimmed across her breast to her rib cage, waist, and onto her rounded hip. "Tell me you want me again," he demanded.

"I want you," she whispered into his ear, and then pulled on his earlobe with her teeth. She moved her hand from his shoulder down his upper arm. *Tony's been working out since I left New York,* she thought. His biceps were rock-hard, and as he moved over her, she felt them flex and relax, then flex again.

Tony made love to Sheilagh until she turned the tables and made love to him. They were mutually giving about everything in their lives, and especially in bed. Sheilagh had never felt as responsive as she did this morning. It was as if she were a totally new person. In a way, she was.

She was no longer afraid.

Tony was hers first and last; once and always. He had held her through her tears most of the night and was still gentle and loving with her in the morning. He coaxed her fears out of her one by one and shot them down like a hunter.

He told her stories about some of the shameful things he had done when he was growing up, which sounded much worse to him than they did to Sheilagh. He pointed out how her perception of her family might be very different now as an adult. She wondered if she had been wrong about her father. She wondered what misperceptions she'd built about her mother.

It was time to find out.

Tony eased himself inside Sheilagh and slowly, ever so slowly, brought her to the pinnacle of sensual excitement. He kissed her nipple, teased her tongue, and thrust inside her. Sheilagh lifted her hips to bring him closer, deeper. She held her breath and then expelled his name.

Tony climaxed inside her, though he continued to stroke for several moments to make certain of her pleasure. He rolled to her side and pulled her into his arms.

He kissed her temple where he could feel the rapid pulse beat of her heart. "I've never seen a chocolate factory, my love. What do you say? Want to give me a guided tour?"

"You mean . . . starting with my father's office?"

Tony nodded and kissed her forehead. "That would be a good place to start."

"You'll hold my hand?"

"Through the whole tour."

Sheilagh lifted her face to him and smiled confidently. "I think that with you, I can do anything." Then she snuggled into the crook of his arm. "Tony?"

"Hmmm?"

"I never thought growing up would be so hard."

Carin and Richard pulled up to the Greek Revival mansion and parked the Mustang in the wide circular drive. Carin held Richard's hand as they went up the front steps.

Caitlin was descending the staircase when Carin and Richard walked into the foyer.

"Hi, Mom." Carin smiled, moved a step closer to Richard, and waited for her mother. "I have someone I want you to meet."

Caitlin took one look at the glow in her daughter's face and knew that the man standing next to her was Richard. Though she was taken aback at his sudden arrival, she graciously walked up to him and extended her hand. "You must be Richard. Carin has told us a lot about you."

"I'm pleased to meet you, Mrs. Burke." He shook Caitlin's hand before slipping his arm around Carin.

Caitlin felt suddenly awkward. She knew Carin cared about this man, but until this moment, she'd given the concept of Richard's importance in Carin's life hardly a moment's thought. As she looked at the rapturous expressions on both their faces, she realized that their relationship was serious. "You've come a great distance, Richard. When did you arrive?"

"Last night."

Caitlin didn't want to know where he had spent last night. She didn't want to admit that her daughter was all grown-up. "It was a good flight? No problems? We've had the oddest summer storms this year—"

"Mom," Carin said, realizing this was going to be more difficult for her parents than she'd thought. "Where's Dad?"

"In his study."

"Let's go find him. Hmmm?" Carin led the way toward the study.

Caitlin was suddenly anxious. She wasn't sure she wanted to hear what Carin and Richard were about to say. She didn't know enough about this man. What if her mother was right and Richard was a fortune hunter? What if he was simply trying to weasel his way into the Emerald fortune? Of course, who knew what was going to be left of Emerald after the board meeting today? Did Richard know about all their problems? About the poisonings and their impact on the company? What did this intruder want with her daughter?

They entered the dark-paneled study with its forest green drapes and deep crimson Persian carpets. It smelled of woodsmoke, leather, and old books. It was Carin's favorite room.

"Daddy?" Carin said as they entered.

Clay sat at his desk, his reading glasses perched on the bridge of his nose, poring over a stack of papers. "Yes, Carin," he mumbled before looking up.

"I'd like you to meet Lord Richard Butler," she said proudly.

Clay's head popped up and he peered over the rim of his glasses at the young man standing before him. Quickly Clay whipped the glasses off and stood. He shook Richard's hand, but Carin noticed that Clay's smile was too broad, his eyes wary.

"How do you do, Lord Butler?"

"Please, call me Richard."

"Glad to," Clay replied, then looked to Caitlin for further direction.

Caitlin, who was standing closer to the door and behind Carin and Richard, shrugged her shoulders.

Without Caitlin to guide him, Clay was left to his own devices. "Have a seat." He motioned to the wing chair opposite him. He looked at his daughter. "I didn't know we were expecting a visit from Lord . . . Richard."

"Neither did I." She laughed lightly and gazed lovingly at Richard. "It was just as much a surprise to me as it is to you."

"I doubt that," Clay replied. He couldn't help thinking Richard resembled himself when he was that age. Was it so long ago? How was it possible that Carin could be old enough to be bringing a man here to meet them? And that was precisely what she was doing. Richard was not just another of Carin's dates whom she met for a tennis game at the club or drinks someplace, and then a month later, none of them ever saw the man again. Carin's face was filled with love. Clay had seen that look in Caitlin's face nearly every day of their life together. Richard was important to Carin. The question was: How important was she to him?

"Carin told us about your castle in Ireland. So did my mother. I understand it needs a great deal of work."

"Daddy!" Carin exclaimed, red-faced.

"Well, damn it, Carin. I don't know who this guy is, now do I?" Clay directed his question to Richard.

"No, sir. And I understand your position. Truly. Carin tells me that certain members of her family have misgivings about my intentions. That I might be a fortune hunter."

"That possibility has been raised," Caitlin admitted.

"Mr. Burke. Mrs. Burke. I know that my financial situation at the present time leaves a great deal to be desired. However, I am not penniless and I am not without prospects. As I told Carin, I have met with my previous employer and I have my old position back, though at a reduced salary for the time being. Once I get my book of clients back up to where both my employer and I would like it to be, I assure you I will have no problem supporting your daughter."

Carin heard her mother's intake of breath.

"You've proposed?" Caitlin asked.

"Yes, Mom. And I accepted."

"But you hardly know each other . . ."

"Mom." Carin held up her hand. "You've told me the story about you and Daddy a hundred times—how you knew when you first saw him that you loved him. And you were only a little kid! I'm a grown woman. I think I would know about something this important, don't you?"

"I would hope so," Caitlin agreed.

Richard patted Carin's hand. "Your parents have every right to be concerned and cautious. They don't know me from Adam." He turned to Clay. "I intend to change that. I want to get to know you, and vice versa. I'll tell you anything you want to know."

Clay looked at his daughter. She was beautiful and obviously happy. He felt his heart wrench. "I can tell she loves you . . ."

"And I love her more than anything in the world. More than my castle, even more than my life in Ireland. If she told me she wanted to live in the United States, I would do that for her," Richard said earnestly. "I love your daughter, Mr. Burke. To prove it, I insist that all of her family monies—inheritances, trust funds, or whatever she has due her, and I have no idea if she has any of these—be legally put into a fund to which I have no access. I will sign any legal document your attorney draws up stating that I am not entitled to any of her money should there be a divorce. I assure you I never want to lose her. But I will gladly do this to allay any of the family's fears about my intentions. I hope that in the future, I'll be able to make enough money to support both us and our children."

"It seems to me you've thought this out quite thoroughly," Clay said, obviously still not convinced.

"Actually, I just thought of it. I don't know what else I can do to convince you that my intentions are honorable. I guess it comes down to trust. I want to marry your daughter. She wants to marry me. I'll do the best by her that I can."

Clay looked over at Caitlin, who smiled at him. He turned back to Richard. "Frankly, Richard, I think it took a lot of guts for you to come here and face us. I don't think I could have done any better myself. I was just thinking that I have to face my father-in-law today, though for business reasons, but I hope I do as well as you did."

"Oh, Daddy! I love you!" Carin went to her father and flung her arms around his neck. Clay hugged her back.

Caitlin placed her hand on Richard's shoulder. "It's too early in the day for champagne . . ."

"Who says?" Clay retorted playfully.

"Yeah, Mom. Who says?"

"Well . . . Carin, you get the crystal. I'll see if there's a chilled bottle in the garage refrigerator."

Richard looked quizzically at Carin. "That's where we keep all the white wine, beer, and sodas. Mother likes being prepared for unexpected celebrations. Believe me, there's always some champagne around this house."

"Really?" Richard smiled. "I think I like this family more all the time."

"Good," Carin said as she went to him and kissed him. "They have their faults, but they're the only family I've got."

Chapter 37 ———————————

$\mathcal{I}$T WAS A picture-perfect June day as Clay pulled the Cadillac into his old parking space at Emerald. He shut off the ignition before turning to Caitlin. "I have the oddest sensation of having been away from here for a very long time, when in actuality it's been only a week."

"What a week." Caitlin sighed as she looked out the windshield at the brilliant blue sky, full, leafy green trees, and brightly colored flowers around the Emerald office building. Her emotions were rioting inside her. She had spent nearly her entire adult life inside this white stucco building with its green-tiled roof. Memories had piled atop one another like the pages of a book, and now she was willingly closing the cover.

She looked over to Clay and saw that his blue eyes were misted, too.

"You don't have to do this, Cat," he said sincerely as he took her hand in his. "You can walk into this board meeting today and tell them you're staying. You don't have to give it all up for me."

"I know I don't. But it's time for me to grow up, too. I've been fooling myself thinking that I was going to get some kind of approval out of my father which he is incapable of giving. I'm halfway through my life, and I'd rather spend the last half pleasing myself, building something of my own—our own—rather than continue to jump through hoops for him."

Clay leaned over the armrest and pulled her closer to him. Their noses nearly touched. He smiled seductively. "I can think of many advantages to sharing offices with you and not having to worry about your father being around."

Caitlin lovingly touched his cheek. Their lips nearly touched. "What about the secretary?"

Clay's blue eyes smoldered. "I won't hire one . . . for a while."

Clay kissed her playfully at first, but then he sensed the

415

sadness she must be feeling at leaving her childhood dreams to build a new dream with him. He had been grateful to Caitlin for so many things over the years. She had been his best friend; she always understood his faults and confusions better than he did. She was his playmate, his counsel and his lover. He could barely remember his life before her. Even when there had been Sheilagh, there was also Caitlin. She was as much a part of him as the blood that ran in his veins.

Clay was not certain if Caitlin truly wanted to leave Emerald, though she said she did. He could only hope that she was wise enough to be making this move as much for herself as she was for him.

She rested her head on the back of the seat. "It's been a long time since we necked in your car." She laughed and looked up at the office building. Her eyes immediately went to her father's window. She could see Patrick's silhouette through the venetian blinds. "Now I remember why," she said, jerking her thumb in Patrick's direction.

"Brother," Clay grumbled. "My deal with General Foods can't get finalized soon enough. It would definitely boost my confidence."

"It won't be long. In the meantime, let's get this over with."

They got out of the car, and as Clay inserted the key in the car door to lock it, a brand-new red Chevrolet pulled up behind them and honked the horn. Caitlin immediately spied the Hertz Rent a Car sign on the bumper.

"It's Michael!" She waved to her brother. There was someone in the car with him. As she walked over, she realized it was Bridget. She beamed brightly, unable to hide her happiness.

Caitlin bent down and leaned through the open passenger's window. "Bridget! What a surprise. I'm so glad to see you."

"You're not as happy about it as I am," Michael said, smiling at Bridget and holding her hand.

"I feel like a kid again," Bridget said. "It's so strange. I've always loved Michael, but somehow we lost our way. I wanted him to know, all of you to know, that I am on his side. I felt I should be with him for this board meeting. I don't think Patrick would agree with me—"

"You're right about that!" Michael interjected. "I can guarantee that all this solidarity will thoroughly piss him off."

Caitlin laughed. "Go park your car and we'll walk in with you," she said.

"Okay," Michael answered.

* * *

Patrick watched them from his office window with his hands clasped behind his back. He pursed his lips together tightly as he assessed the situation. "Here they come, Mary Margaret," he said to his wife, who was opening and sorting his mail. With both Caitlin and Clay gone, Mary Margaret felt as if she were truly helping for the first time. Patrick thought she slowed routine duties, but he was too preoccupied to argue with her.

"Who?" Mary Margaret said, opening the telephone bill from Illinois Bell.

"The traitors," he said angrily. "And they've brought Benedict Arnold with them. Good God, he's even brought Bridget. Look at 'em," he snarled as he reached into his inside breast pocket for a thick Havana cigar. "They're too lily-livered to petition for themselves. They had to drag Michael and Bridget along to help them plead for their jobs back."

Mary Margaret put the phone bill down on the desk. "Do you really think they're coming back?"

Patrick rolled his eyes. "Of course they are. Where else could they go? What else could Caitlin do? I know that girl's Achilles' heel, Mary Margaret. She can't live without this company. It's in her blood. She'll bring Clay around. You'll see."

Mary Margaret strained to catch a glimpse of the four approaching figures, but they were already at the front doors. She looked up at her husband, who seemed bloated with self-importance. How she would love to see him brought down . . . all the way down.

She remembered when they were young and the children were still at home. Patrick had shut her out of his life a long time ago. She wondered if he knew that she had prayed every day for someone to come along and cut Patrick Killian down to size.

All these years of going to mass every morning; devotions seven days a week during Lent for the past forty years; praying the rosary during the hundreds upon hundreds of nights when Patrick was gone; she had done all those things asking God to free her from Patrick Killian. But God had never listened.

For many years she had believed that God wanted her to stay with Patrick. Now for the first time she wondered if God was telling her to make the decision for herself. Maybe the church was wrong about divorce. Maybe it wasn't the best thing to stay married to a man who was mentally cruel.

Maybe the young girls were right these days to keep their financial independence so that they could walk away when a marriage became destructive. Perhaps if she had not stayed with Patrick, she might have built better relationships with her children. Because her religion told her it was a sin to divorce, she had used all her energy to maintain her sanity, a small sense of herself in an untenable situation. She felt she had needed to shut out her children in order to stay with Patrick. She had been wrong, and her decision had left her lonely and unloved.

As she thought of her grown children, she was filled with pride. All of them had pressed both Patrick and Mary Margaret to the wall and made their own decisions. Maybe that was the way it was supposed to be.

Mary Margaret watched Patrick crunch his cigar between his teeth. He passed it from one side of his mouth to the other. He was worried. Plenty worried. An obdurate smile settled on Mary Margaret's lips.

Patrick started to turn away from the window when he saw a green and white Checker cab pull to a stop on Oak Park Avenue. The back door opened and a long, shapely leg moved into the sunshine, followed by the other leg. The shoes were expensive, the skirt French silk.

"Who in the hell?" He scrunched his eyes half-closed to focus on the woman alighting from the cab. He held his breath.

The sunlight hit the crown of her auburn head and splashed reflected light over her, illuminating the very air around her.

Patrick yanked the cigar out of his mouth. "Sheilagh." He spoke her name with reverence as he stuck his hand between the venetian slats and pulled them apart for a better view. From this distance she looked as if she had not aged a day since she left Chicago. He had forgotten, God how he had forgotten her beauty, the power of her presence, the electricity of her smiles.

She stood next to the cab while the good-looking blond man who was with her leaned through the passenger's window and paid the cabbie. The man was nearly as dazzlingly magnetic as Sheilagh was. For a moment Patrick couldn't remember his new son-in-law's name. *Tony. Yes, that was it. Tony.*

They walked arm in arm toward the front door. Sheilagh smiled at Tony, and he said something that made her laugh. She paused a step, pulled him to her, and kissed him.

"On my goddamn front lawn!" Patrick bellowed, and stuck his cigar back in his mouth.

"What are you talking about?" Mary Margaret snapped.

"Sheilagh . . . up to her old tricks. Necking on my property."

"You must be seeing things, Patrick. Sheilagh would never come here."

"Oh, yeah? Come look at this!" He gestured toward the window.

Mary Margaret walked around the desk and peered through the slats. The sight of her eldest daughter after thirty years nearly made her dizzy. She felt as if something had pulled her out of time and space, as if she were in another dimension where everything moved much slower. Mary Margaret watched the summer breeze flap Sheilagh's yellow, tangerine, and beige silk skirt around her legs. Even from this distance she could see the happiness in her daughter's face. Sheilagh looked as if she were on her way to a fancy luncheon with friends. There was not a whit of anxiety about her movements, not a hint that she was about to see the family from whom she had been estranged for thirty years.

Mary Margaret's mouth went dry. What should she say to her eldest daughter? How could she appologize to her? How could she ever explain herself? How was it going to feel to lose Sheilagh once again?

Patrick placed his hand on his leather swivel chair and turned it around so that he could lower his enormous bulk into it. "I want to know what the hell she's doing here. Why now, after all this time? Do you suppose it could have anything to do with the poisonings? But then, you don't know much about that kind of thing, do you, Mary Margaret?"

Mary Margaret eyed him suspiciously. She refused to jump to his bait. She was calm as ice. "I would never put poison in a batch of candy. It's silly."

"Why is that?"

She smiled malevolently. "If I wanted to kill you, Patrick, I would have done it a long time ago."

"You say that as if you had considered it," he retorted with a nearly undetectable quiver to his voice. But Mary Margaret caught it.

It was the first time she had ever possessed power over Patrick and chosen not to wield it. The realization was as heady as brandy. Had she been an impetuous person and a decade or two younger, she would have jumped for glee. Instead, she simply looked away from him, out the window once again.

Patrick rounded the desk and went to the door to the outer office.

Martha instantly looked up.

"Martha, is the conference room ready for the board meeting?"

"Yes. I took care of everything. I'm still getting a lot of calls from the newspapers, but I've told them you'll give a statement after the board meeting."

"You *what*?" Patrick stalked over to her desk. "Are you crazy? I don't want to talk to those bastards."

Martha's hands were trembling, so she shoved them onto her lap out of Patrick's sight. "I thought that's what you wanted . . ."

"Where did you get an idea like that?"

"From you! Three days ago you told me to hold them off until after the board meeting."

"I said that?"

"You did," she answered, her lower lip quivering.

Patrick was thoughtful for a moment. He gazed at Martha, thinking she looked on the verge of tears. He didn't know what she had to cry about. He was the one who was on the line right now. She was just an employee. "Take it easy, Martha." He tried to think of words to console her. He didn't want Clay and Caitlin to come in and find Martha, normally the most calm person in the company, in hysterics. "This will all be over soon."

"I know . . ." she replied.

"Besides, you're taking this too seriously. It's not your company, you know."

Martha's eyes dried instantly as they narrowed. "Oh, yes. I'm well aware of that fact." Her voice was hard.

Patrick gave her a quizzical look and thought that he would never understand women. "I want you to take notes during the meeting. Make sure you jot down even idle conversation. If Clay so much as opens his mouth, write that down, too. I want to catch that bastard in his lies."

"What?"

"C'mon, Martha. You're a smart woman. Haven't you figured this out yet?"

"I don't understand."

"Clay poisoned my chocolate. It makes perfect sense. He's wanted to take over this company for years. And I'm going to nail his ass but good."

"How?"

"I'm going to have him indicted by a grand jury. You just wait and see. I've had my attorney going over my records, and I've got enough evidence to prove that Clay's intentions have always been to oust me. He's slowly taken over nearly every aspect of my business, from sales to purchasing."

"But you gave him those responsibilities," Martha said incredulously. "Clay would never try to destroy a company he spent his whole life building up."

"Jesus, Martha, since when did you start defending him against me?"

Martha's hands were shaking, as were her shoulders. Patrick couldn't tell if she was angry or sad, but she looked as if she was at the breaking point. Nevertheless, her voice was steady.

"I've taken his side ever since I realized he was right and you were wrong."

Patrick's eyes flew open at the attack. "Shit. I'm surrounded by mutineers. If you're tossing your hat into his ring, just fucking say so."

"I . . . I didn't say that," Martha replied, backing down.

Patrick was appeased. "All right then." He sighed, glad not to have to confront her, too.

He turned back to his office. "Mary Margaret, let's go. They should all be waiting for us in the conference room by now."

Martha walked behind Patrick and Mary Margaret as they left the executive wing and headed down the hall.

Patrick opened the heavy wood door.

They all faced him. Clay and Caitlin, Sheilagh and Tony, Michael and Bridget. He nodded as he walked around the room to his chair at the head of the table. Martha pulled up a chair on casters and sat at Patrick's right elbow, where she could hear all that was said. She steadied her pencil and opened her green steno notebook.

Mary Margaret felt as if her heart had stopped beating as she stared at Sheilagh. She wanted to run to her and hug her and beg her forgiveness, but she knew that Sheilagh would never understand. Mary Margaret was aware that they were all watching her. She tried to smile but couldn't. She bit her tongue to stop the tears that were welling in her eyes.

"M–Michael," she finally choked out. "How lovely that you've brought Bridget." She went to her son and gave him and his wife quick hugs. She was astonished at how good they both felt in her arms. She moved on to Caitlin and Clay. "Nice to see you, dear," she said to Caitlin, and kissed her on the cheek. She clasped Clay's hand in her own and squeezed it. "It'll be okay," she whispered.

She had started toward Sheilagh and Tony when Patrick's voice boomed across the table at her. "For God's sake, Mary Margaret! This is a board meeting, not a family picnic! Sit down so we can get on with this."

Like so many times in the long-ago past when she bent to Patrick's will, Mary Margaret felt her children's pity. She didn't like it any more now than she had then. She lifted her head and met his eyes. Her lips were tight with anger when she spoke. "My daughter has come home for the first time in thirty years. I have never met her husband. You may start your meeting when I'm finished." She turned back to Sheilagh and Tony, and extended her hand. "I'm pleased to meet you, Tony."

"My pleasure," Tony replied, a bit astonished.

"Mary Margaret!" Patrick blustered. "You can talk to her all you want afterward."

Mary Margaret's eyes were as cold as ice when she looked at her daughter. "Maybe that would be best," she said, and went to her chair at the far end of the table.

Sheilagh watched her mother seat herself, and then they all sat. She had been prepared for many things today, but the tension between her mother and father had never been so strong. Sheilagh had never seen her mother stand up to her father like that, and most astonishingly, Mary Margaret had been defending her. This made no sense, she thought as she heard her father begin.

"Everyone here knows this company is on the edge of ruin. Just the fact of the poisonings nearly destroyed us. Now we have the FBI demanding we shut down our factory and recall all our candy. And we have Clay's decision to leave."

"Now, wait just a minute!" Clay began to protest.

"Shut up!" Patrick shouted. "You can have your say later."

Sheilagh felt as if she'd heard this kind of tyrannical outburst from her father nearly all her life. Some things never change, she thought. Since she truly did not care what her father had to say about the company, she let her gaze roam the table.

In a way, this scene felt so familiar. It was almost like being back in the Oak Park house sitting in the dining room at dinner. Patrick was always blustering about something. He placed the blame for every problem on someone else. Mary Margaret sat at the opposite end of the table, meekly keeping her mouth shut. But, this wasn't 1935; this was 1971, and as Sheilagh's eyes traveled to her mother, she realized that there was nothing meek about the expression in her mother's eyes. In fact, they were filled with hate, and that hatred was directed at Patrick. For the first time, Sheilagh could actually envision her mother poisoning the chocolate.

And yet, she thought, it couldn't have been Mother. Her mother had changed. Her physical appearance had been a shock to Sheilagh. Mary Margaret was thin. Too thin. And when had her hair turned gray? Why didn't she color it as she used to? How old was she now? Sixty-eight? And when had her hands become knotted with arthritis? She remembered those hands that had knit mittens for them every year for Christmas. And when had she developed a slight dowager's hump? Her mother had never been a tall woman; now she looked like a shrunken child.

Mary Margaret was impeccably dressed, as always, in an Adolfo summer suit and plain black Capezio pumps. Sheilagh noticed how the lines in her mother's face had deepened; the ones around her mouth were born of bitterness . . . and sorrow. There was no light in her eyes, only an angry glimmer. Sheilagh no longer saw only the ice maiden she had once dubbed her mother.

Suddenly Sheilagh felt incredible sympathy for the old woman who had long ago intimidated her with cruelties and vile manipulations. Sheilagh felt sorrow for anyone who, like Mary Margaret, had wasted her life. Maybe there was a reason why she had been born a Killian. It was Sheilagh's anger against her parents that had forced her to move to New York. Her drive and determination had been born of her need to prove her worthiness to her parents. Now it was Sheilagh's own self-esteem that mattered to her.

Suddenly Sheilagh realized that neither her mother nor her father could ever hurt her again. In the years gone by, she had indeed grown strong, powerful in her own right, fulfilled by love. Tony loved her for herself, her audiences loved her for her talent. She was blessed.

Mary Margaret, on the other hand, had never had a chance to be anything but Patrick Killian's wife.

A tear pricked Sheilagh's eye. She scooped it up with her forefinger and looked at it. She had cried for her mother. Sheilagh guessed she had grown up more than she realized.

Her thoughts were interrupted by the sound of Patrick's fist slamming against the table. "Goddamn it, Clay! I'll have your ass in jail! I swear to God I will!"

"Father! You can't mean this!" Caitlin said, shooting to her feet.

Clay grabbed her arm. "It's all right, Caitlin. I have nothing left to say to the bastard."

"That's right! That's right! I'm the bastard. You're nothing but a murderer!" Patrick accused, jabbing his fat forefinger in Clay's direction.

Suddenly the table had become a cacophony of swear words, gesticulations, and protests. Sheilagh said nothing as she listened to the verbal brawl. Her eyes flew from her mother, who was trying to be heard over the din, shouting at Patrick to sit down. Michael was now at Clay's side, urging him to walk out. Bridget was cussing under her breath. Caitlin was near tears.

Sheilagh's eyes fell on Martha for the first time that afternoon. Her hand was flying across the steno pad. Her head hung down, but Sheilagh detected a slight jerking of Martha's shoulders. She peered more closely at Martha. A stream of tears fell into spreading puddles on the steno pad. Sheilagh's heart went out to her. Martha had worked at Emerald all her life. How painful to her it must be to see the company coming apart. Then, suddenly, Martha's pencil snapped in two. This was not normal. Sheilagh became alarmed, and more curious.

"Martha?" She said, but got no reaction.

"Martha!" she said a bit louder.

Martha looked up. Her eyes were red. She'd been crying for a while, maybe since the beginning of the meeting. Sheilagh found that odd and intriguing.

"What is it, Martha?" she asked, though her words did not stop the others from arguing.

"Nothing," Martha sobbed.

Sheilagh pressed her. "You can tell me, Martha."

"No, I can't."

"Yes, you can."

Caitlin heard Sheilagh talking to Martha, and focused her attention on the exchange. Mary Margaret followed suit. The din died. All eyes were suddenly on Martha.

Martha looked at Sheilagh. "Yes. I think you'd be the only one who would understand."

"And why is that, Martha?" Sheilagh asked, thinking the woman looked as if her mind had snapped. Her eyes were glassy now and she barely blinked. Her voice was flat and unemotional.

"You hate him, too," Martha said.

"Who?"

"Patrick."

Sheilagh was deeply shocked by what she was hearing, but she pressed on. "Tell me about it, Martha. Tell me why you hate my father."

"For what he did to me."

"Which was?"

"He didn't love me," Martha sniffed. "Of course, he didn't love any of you. Least of all her——his wife, I mean. Not Shannon. That was another matter. He told me he loved me, but it was a lie. He always lied. I know that much. He did a lot of things that were much worse than lying, but they didn't have much to do with me, so I didn't care."

She raised her eyes and glanced around the table. "You all pretended to love me, but you didn't. Maybe Caitlin did. She was always nice to me. You told me I was part of the family, but I wasn't. Not really. That's what he held over my head all those years. Kept telling me I didn't have anyone but him. I was his first mistress. He even came back to me when Shannon dumped him. A few years later, I got pregnant." Her smile was twisted when she looked at Mary Margaret.

Mary Margaret had not been surprised by anything she had heard until Martha's last statement. She felt her blood run cold.

"You didn't know that, did you?" Martha asked pointedly.

Mary Margaret could not speak. She shook her head.

"I didn't think so. Remember when I took that six-month leave of absence in forty-five? You were all so caught up in your own lives, none of you paid attention to me. I went to a Catholic home in New York City. I even went to see Sheilagh onstage, but she never knew it. I gave my son up for adoption. I told Patrick about it. He told me he'd pay for an abortion. Can you believe that? I made him pay for my expenses, though. After the war, jobs were scarce. I tried to find something in New York, but I couldn't. I didn't want to come back here. I hated Patrick for what he did to me. But I had a girlfriend here who let me live with her for free. I still needed a job. The only one I could find was here. Patrick gave me a twenty-dollar-a-week raise. He thought that was enough to buy my silence. But I knew then that what I really wanted was revenge."

"Revenge?" The shock in Caitlin's voice expressed what they were all feeling.

"Over the years I devised a hundred schemes. Then I realized I was wasting my life. I gave up my schemes. Then, last fall, my son found me. I finished work one day and walked out the back, and he was waiting by the side door. He asked if I was Martha

O'Boland. I said I was. He told me he'd been adopted by a good family and had been very happy with them. When he grew up he was curious about his real mother. They even helped him to track me down."

Suddenly Martha's sobs caught in her throat as a new wave of tears washed over her. She swallowed her pain. "He was such a handsome boy. He looked a lot like you, Sheilagh. You could have been twins; he, the auburn-haired, green-eyed god, and she, the goddess. Naturally he wanted to know who his father was. I told him about Patrick."

"And that was your revenge?" Patrick demanded.

Martha did not give Patrick so much as a glance. "Jerry—that was my boy's name—confronted Patrick with the truth. But he said he didn't believe it. He accused Jerry of being a scam artist. Of staging a hoax to get money out of him. Neither of us had talked about money from Patrick. Jerry just wanted a father. Just like you did, Michael. And you, Caitlin . . . and Sheilagh," Martha said, looking directly at Sheilagh again.

"Jerry was devastated when Patrick turned him away. He cried in my arms all that night. He told me he couldn't stay in Chicago and that he'd only come for a visit. He went back to his family in New York filled with regret and pain. He should never have come here. He knew it and I knew it. Then, six months later, I got a letter from his mother . . ." Martha choked on the word. "Jerry enlisted in the army. He went to Vietnam."

"Oh, God." Caitlin's skin became clammy as she realized where Martha's story was heading. She reached out her hand to touch Martha, but she waved her away.

She looked at Caitlin. "Do you remember when I left for three weeks this past April?"

"Yes."

"Jerry died on maneuvers in Vietnam. I went to New York for his funeral. I met his adoptive parents. And you know what was so strange? I'd never met them before in my life, but they showed me more love, more caring, in the week that I was there than this whole family has in the forty years I've known you."

Martha's red eyes were blazing with anger as she spun to face Patrick for the first time. "I poisoned your precious chocolate. I wanted those judges to die. I wanted you to suffer the way I've suffered. I wanted you to know that somebody died because of your selfishness. So you see, Patrick. I really didn't kill those men. You did."

Shock rippled around the room.

"Jesus Christ," Patrick said in a near whisper. "I . . . I didn't know."

Michael slipped out of the room to telephone Inspector Gregory. Tony grabbed Sheilagh's hand and squeezed it. Caitlin went to Martha and put her arms around her as Martha unleashed her anguish. Caitlin continued to hold her as Bridget, Tony, and Clay left the room.

"Go ahead and cry it out, Martha," Caitlin said.

"You were the only one who ever cared about me," Martha said between sobs.

"Shhh." Caitlin patted her back and continued holding her until they heard the police sirens coming from the street.

Martha's head jerked up. "Oh, God." Her eyes were filled with panic.

"Don't be afraid, Martha. I'll see to it that you get some help. You've suffered a lot of pain and anger."

"You think I'm crazy!" Martha said, her expression wild.

"I think you're very upset. I think the police will see that, too."

The door opened and four uniformed policemen stepped in. Caitlin held up her hand to stop them. "She's okay. She just needs a little help to the car, don't you, Martha?"

"You'll come with me?" Martha asked Caitlin.

"Of course I will."

Caitlin walked with Martha out to the police car.

The tall officer with dark hair turned to Patrick. "Could I have a word with you, sir? Inspector Gregory should be here in a moment."

"Certainly," Patrick said, and left with the officer.

The conference room was empty except for Sheilagh and Mary Margaret. Sheilagh looked at her mother.

"Mother? Are you . . . okay?" Sheilagh asked, thinking her mother looked unusually pale.

Mary Margaret found a strained smile to put on her face. "Fine, dear. Just fine. Of course, it is quite a shock to hear your husband's mistress tell your family that she bore his child."

Mary Margaret began to rise, but her legs were unsteady and she immediately fell back into her chair.

"Mother!" Sheilagh rushed to her side. She leaned over to touch her mother's arm. My God, she's so fragile, Sheilagh thought.

"I'll be fine. Really."

"Did you know? About Martha, I mean."

"No, I didn't. I never heard of this Shannon woman either, although I watched all your faces when Martha talked about her. You all knew, didn't you?"

"Yes. We did."

"Even Michael."

"Yes, Mother."

"Yet you all protected me?"

"Yes, I suppose we did."

Mary Margaret's eyes brimmed with tears. "I knew he had women, but never their names. I was glad for that. Maybe if I'd known, I'd have tried to . . . well, God only knows what I might have done. But none of you told me. I find that amazing. You loved me then?"

"Yes," Sheilagh confessed.

"After all I'd done to you."

Sheilagh's eyes grew wide with surprise. She couldn't believe her mother was admitting to her wrongdoing. "Are you saying that just because Martha confessed today?"

"No, dear. I've thought about a great many things over the past weeks. That's not true. I've thought about them for years." Mary Margaret looked at Sheilagh.

Sheilagh felt her heart melt. Her mother's eyes were the eyes of a child begging for love and attention. Mary Margaret's face was so tiny and bore so many lines, she looked like a doll that had been thrown into a fire. Sheilagh's mouth dried up and her tongue was stuck against the roof of her mouth. She felt humbled.

"I came here expecting anger. Lots of anger. Mostly my own, I guess, for what you did to me . . . disinheriting me the way you did . . . cutting me out of your lives."

"*We* cut *you* out? You're the one who left without a word, Sheilagh Killian." Mary Margaret blasted her with a voice hoarse with emotion. "*You left me!*"

"Mother . . ."

Rage and pain filled Mary Margaret to the brim. "I thought I would never forgive you, Sheilagh. I thought I would never find the heart to want to put my arms around you and tell you the truth . . ."

"And what is the truth?" Sheilagh demanded.

"That I loved you best of all," Mary Margaret said in a small voice.

"You . . . what?" Sheilagh choked in disbelief. "You always said I was the wicked one. I was never good enough for you. You criticized everything I did or said. You tried to control me. You tried to run my life!"

"I know. I did all those terrible things."

"Why? *Why*?" Sheilagh demanded, and dropped to her knees and sank back on her heels. "I have to know."

Mary Margaret's eyes had lost their color behind a wall of tears. "I wanted you to stay here. I thought if I broke your spirit, you would never leave me. I thought if you realized your dreams were nearly impossible . . . you would stay in Chicago and keep me company. I never had a marriage. I only had you."

"But Caitlin and Michael . . . they were your children, too."

Mary Margaret flapped her hand downward, and it fell to her lap. "Caitlin was an Emerald woman. She counted too much on your father's praise. Michael was a rebel from the day he was born. I *always* knew he would leave."

Mary Margaret laid her hand on Sheilagh's head. "You are as beautiful as you were the day you left."

"Mother, I'm nearly fifty years old."

Mary Margaret smiled. "Tony loves you . . ."

"Yes."

Mary Margaret nodded. "It shows. I never had that. Treasure it well."

"Oh, Mother." Sheilagh dropped her head into Mary Margaret's thin lap. "I've hated you for so long. I was wrong."

"Sheilagh." Mary Margaret reveled in the silky touch of her daughter's hair. "I'm so sorry for calling you wicked. Please forgive me."

Sheilagh's eyes were filled with tears when she raised her head. "I forgive you," Sheilagh said with a weak laugh. "I never, ever thought I would say that!"

"Don't be too hard on yourself, Sheilagh. After all, we're all a bit wicked now and again, aren't we?" Mary Margaret smiled impishly.

"Yes, Mother, I see what you mean." Sheilagh kissed her mother's withered cheek. "You must know something. I wasn't running away from you."

"Oh, I know, dear. You wanted your career . . ."

"Yes, but that's not the whole truth. Father gave me money to leave. He told me he wanted me out of town. I was afraid of him, Mother. I was afraid he might kill me if I stayed."

Mary Margaret held her daughter's face in her hands as she peered into her eyes. "It's true what they say, then?"

Sheilagh could only nod her head.

"Sheilagh," Mary Margaret replied in that cold, determined voice she remembered so well. "I think I should talk to your father. And I don't want you to hear what I have to say to him."

"All right." Sheilagh stood. "I'll go get him for you."

"Do that, dear. And then afterward, I want to get to know Tony."

Sheilagh nodded and left the room. In a few minutes Patrick walked into the conference room.

Mary Margaret rose slowly, smoothed the folds of her Adolfo skirt and clasped her hands primly in front of her.

"I'm leaving you, Patrick. I want the Lake Geneva house, the Buick, the silver, crystal, and china. And I want Emerald since you haven't the foggiest notion of what to do with it. You want to bankrupt the firm, and I think that is a waste of your father's dream and all these years of Killian dedication. You are your own worst enemy, Patrick. I won't divorce you. But that is only in case the Catholic church is right about divorce being a sin. I'll keep all your sins out of the press. You can have the Oak Park house, all its furnishings, and the Cadillac."

With the greatest effort, he spoke. "When did you decide all this?"

"Exactly fifty-one years and two months ago."

Patrick looked at his wife and saw the steely glint in her eyes. Suddenly he saw the entire canvas of his life wiped away as if the painter had thrown linseed oil on the picture. The images of his relationships with his daughters, his son, and his wife blurred and became illusion. The labels by which he defined himself suddenly lost their meaning. Family man? Corporate owner? Dutiful parishoner of Ascension Church? Who was Patrick Killian anymore, anyway? "Why didn't you tell me?"

"I wasn't ready," she said icily.

"And now you are?"

"Yes," she replied. She picked up her handbag and turned to exit the office.

"Where are you going?"

Mary Margaret only half faced him. "What an odd question, Patrick. You never asked me that before. Why on earth would you start now?" She turned her back on him and closed the door quietly behind her.

Epilogue ————————————

June 1991
Butler Castle near Lisdoonvarna, Ireland

*L*ADY CARIN BUTLER glared at the blinking computer cursor as a cacophony of pounding hammers, buzzing drills, and whirring electric saws echoed throughout the castle. A stereo blasted to life, sending U2 screaming through the stone- and marble-floored hallways like a wailing banshee. Carin cracked open the lead glass casement window she had painstakingly refurbished, and was greeted by the roar of a cement mixer. She slammed the window shut.

"Damn!" she cursed. She snapped off the power switch on the computer, a familiar motion of late that did not please her publisher in London. Too bad her life wasn't like one of her romance novels; she'd write herself into a vacation retreat with perfect weather and tranquil beaches, and her son would never, ever complain that he was bored.

"William! Turn that thing down!" she yelled at her thirteen-year-old son as she left her study and stomped toward his room. Carin could nearly feel the music penetrating the five-hundred-year-old oak door, then rushing at her to assault her eardrums. "Did you hear me?" she yelled, but her voice was crushed by bass tones coming from the woofers. Carin placed her hand on the vibrating brass doorknob and opened the door.

William was dressed in an old T-shirt that read "I Love New York." Carin recognized it as hers. Most mothers had daughters who raided their closets; her problem was her son. He wanted all her old American artifacts ... T-shirts, western bandannas, tacky belts from her funky seventies days, even visors, mugs, posters, college wall pennants, and especially her old record collection. William bopped to the music as he moved his equalizer to the new black lacquer shelves he and his father had built. William was outwardly expressing his emerging personality, he'd explained, which explained why his room now had gray walls and carpeting, teal accents on his desk, and black lacquer furniture. He wanted a mural of a Ferrari Testerosa executed in pink and teal neon lights, but Carin had vetoed that idea. "This is not a nightclub, William."

"Why not? I must be allowed to explore the full range of my creative possibilities."

"I should never have taken you to that seminar with me." She sighed. "No neon."

Carin's memories made her smile at her son. They always seemed to be at sixes and sevens, and yet they shared a bond, a sense of humor and mutual respect, that kept them from ever allowing anger to rule them. At times they were like crocodiles snapping at each other, but with toothless jaws. The effect was like a strong massage, rejuvenating and healthy once all the toxins and poisons were eliminated.

"William, turn that thing down! You know I'm trying to work!"

William flashed his father's bright blue eyes at her. He wore his hair short around the ears and in back and longer on top, looking like one of those Ralph Lauren models, complete with the Gandhi glasses perched across the bridge of his strong aquiline nose. William smiled at her. All at once Carin was flooded with flashes of William at birth, William at three, then five, ten, and now . . . he would soon be a man. She wanted to cry, but she hated the blaring song. She motioned with her hand for him to turn it down.

William's shoulder's slumped theatrically, but he turned off the stereo. "What were you saying, Mom?" he asked with all the innocence of an Irish saint.

"I can't work with all that racket."

William chortled. "How could you hear my music with all *that* racket?" He jerked his thumb toward the window. He smiled again and walked toward her.

When did he grow so big? Carin thought, noticing that he was already an inch taller than she was.

"Besides, you've worked too hard already, and it's nearly lunchtime. Let's find Dad, and I'll make sandwiches." He put his arm around her, and as he did, consciously straightened his spine and lifted his chin, as if checking the progress of his growth.

Lady Carin Butler accompanied her son down the Gothic linenfold oak-paneled hallway to the sixteenth-century circular staircase. She noticed pieces of plaster crumbling away from some of the exposed wood beams. She made a mental note to have the mason repair it.

"Mum? Is it all right if I go to Dublin in July with the Kimmeys?"

"And what will you do there?"

"I dunno. Shop, buy some videocassettes for the VCR that Aunt Sheilagh sent. I'd like to go to the new record shop that Darby told me about. They have two-for-one summer specials."

"And you won't go to that awful barbershop again? I don't want you coming home with pink hair and a crucifix in your ear."

"Mum! You act like I did that. Darby got blue hair, not pink, and it was a peace sign earring. You know? From *your* childhood. Hippies and all that."

Carin harrumphed as they reached the landing and started across the geometrically designed parquet floor. "I was never a hippie—you got that? And I never had peace symbol earrings."

"But I saw them in your jewelry . . ." William rolled his eyes in his head when he realized his slip.

"And what were you doing in my jewelry case?" she demanded, then shook her head. "Forget it. Aunt Sheilagh gave them to me."

"Then she was the hippie."

Sentiment lifted the right side of Carin's mouth while nostalgia lifted the left. "There are no stereotypes for Aunt Sheilagh. Suffice it to say that she not only did it all, she did it first."

"There's a difference?"

"You bet there is." Carin grinned proudly. "When you really grow up, you'll know what it is."

They walked out the front door, down the resurfaced steps, and across the lawn to the greenhouse.

The castle had changed a great deal since she and Richard had married twenty years ago. The majority had been completely restored. They had added a one-story wing to the left of the castle front, which now housed their Sweete Shoppe, which was open to tourists six days a week. It was there that they sold her father's Chocolate Jewels.

Carin was proud of Clay's new company, which he'd founded as soon as his deal with General Foods had gone through in 1971. From its inception, Carin knew Jewels was going to be different. It was Caitlin's idea to mold the chocolates in the shapes of jewels—pear-shaped bonbons were filled with fruit-flavored cream; round prism cuts contained cognac ganaches and Grand Marnier liqueurs. Beveled trillion cuts, marquise cuts, emerald and heart-shaped cuts, were dusted with cocoa as light as angel's breath. There were strings of pearls in white chocolate and deepest dark chocolate. They copied the Duchess of Windsor's rings, waterfall necklaces, and bracelets in chocolate.

But it was the packaging that Jewels was most noted for. With every two-pound purchase, the Jewels were placed in keepsake jewelry boxes. All the boxes were fashioned after antique jewelry cases. Some were satin-covered with hand-painted flowers on top. Others were made of embossed tin or crimson-velvet-covered wooden boxes with gold latches. Watered satins in every color of the spectrum was used according to holiday and occasion. Jewels Chocolates were unique and expensive, and the world ate them by the ton.

Richard had not only found the original investor for Jewels, he had also become vice president of international sales. Carin's dream of becoming a novelist had filled her days, but she had still dabbled in promotion and marketing of Jewels from time to time. She was also able to fill her need for the chocolate industry by running her Sweete Shoppe.

Carin's mind wandered back over the years to the time in 1971 when her grandmother Mary Margaret separated from her grandfather, Patrick. Mary Margaret was too Catholic ever to divorce him, but she had made a more productive life for herself once they were apart. She took over the helm of Emerald when Patrick began threatening to bankrupt the company. He gladly stepped aside and turned his shares over to his wife.

For decades, Mary Margaret had observed Emerald Chocolates from the sidelines. She realized from the start that Caitlin was her most valuable asset. She persuaded Caitlin to stay with the company for double her salary and half the profits. Clay urged her to stay now that Patrick was out of the picture. Emerald was back on top within two years. In 1978 Mary Margaret handed the company completely over to Caitlin, having long ago rewritten her will to generously include Michael and Sheilagh.

Patrick had refused to acknowledge Mary Margaret's triumph. He withdrew from the family when he stepped down from the presidency. Caitlin, Mary Margaret, and Sheilagh believed that Patrick could have spent his last years getting to know his family and grandchildren, but he didn't. Again he chose not to take a risk on love. He pushed them all away.

In 1976 he died of a massive heart attack, alone in the Oak Park house.

Mary Margaret was now spending the remaining years of her life living in Lake Geneva and flying across the country to visit Michael and Bridget and their children in Houston, and to New York to see Sheilagh and Tony.

Martha O'Boland had been found not guilty by reason of insanity. She was receiving professional help in a mental hospital and would probably never be released. The Killians never saw her again after the trial, though once, Caitlin tried to visit her; Martha refused the visit.

Martha's insanity plea had been regarded by the press as a defensive tactic. Controversy and debate had swirled around her during the trial. Journalists had hounded Martha for years, trying to pry the real story out of her, but she had refused all comment on her actions except to say, "I can keep secrets better than the Killians."

Martha's silence only fascinated a curious press all the more.

Carin looked around her and hoped that the workmen would be finished by the time Sheilagh and Tony arrived in three days. They were bringing Mary Margaret with them. Her grandmother was over ninety, and the word from home was that she was as feisty as ever.

They had all learned a lot since the infamous Emerald Chocolate poisonings. It had been a tragic time in their lives, but through the crisis they had found one another. Never had her family been so close. Never had they cherished one another so much.

Carin felt bad sometimes that her grandfather had ostracized himself from everyone, but that had been his choice. Caitlin told Carin that people change every day, but only when they decide they want to do the changing.

The sun split into shards as it shot through the old Victorian beveled-glass panes of the greenhouse. Prisms of light danced around the hothouse flowers, vegetables, and fruits like plant fairies of Celtic mythology. Carin could hear the rusty cranking of the water spigot as Richard shut it off.

"Come for me, love?" he asked, standing between the bromeliads and the tuberous begonias.

Carin remembered the first day she'd met her husband. He still wore his shirt-sleeves rolled up past his elbows, and his biceps were still tight. He was forty-nine, and his wavy, thick hair was the same chestnut brown as the day they'd met, save for the artistic sprinkling of gray at his temples. His blue gaze was sensual and intense. It was uncanny, Carin thought, how Richard always seemed to ooze sex the minute she was in sight of him. It was especially surprising, considering his apron was probably covered in dirt and manure, Carin guessed, if she knew Richard.

"Richard, you're a filthy mess," she observed, watching sweat drip from his neck and arms.

"Is that any way to address your lord and master?" he taunted her, coming toward her. Now she could smell the particular manure he'd used today. Sheep, it was. The worst of all.

"Richard . . ." She giggled and backed away. "Don't you dare . . ." She turned the corner around the rabbit fern and nearly knocked a flat of lichen to the tiled floor. Suddenly she felt William's arms around her waist.

"I've snagged her for you, Pa!" William gloated.

Carin's eyes grew large, reflecting her mock fear. "You wouldn't . . ." Richard moved closer, his voluptuous lips moving into a triumphant grin. Just as his six-two-inch frame was about to engulf her, he dropped his arms, pushed his head forward, and planted a forceful kiss on her cheek. He stood back and laughed heartily.

"None the worse for wear, you are, my love."

As Carin laughed with him, she turned to William. "Go on to lunch, and as soon as Richard is cleaned up, we'll meet you in the kitchen."

Richard peeled off his apron, went to the blue and yellow Spanish-tiled basin, and washed his hands. He splashed water on his face and the back of his neck. Then he dried off with a cotton towel. He beamed down at her. "Is this better?" he asked, and pulled her to him.

He kissed her deeply and long, a lover's kiss, the kind Richard preferred. His hands were pressed to the small of her back, and as his tongue sought the interior of her mouth, he pulled her closer still. Carin could feel the strong muscles in her thighs and the hard stomach he kept flat by swimming, biking, and tennis. Carin leaned into him, into his kiss, relishing it as if it might be her last. At moments like this she knew in the deepest recesses of her mind and soul that nothing, not castles, publishing contracts, inheritances, lands and titles, nothing was more important than this man and this life they shared.

Dear Reader

I hope you enjoyed *The Way of the Wicked*. I had a *delicious* time writing it, and I have five extra pounds to prove that I personally tasted most of the fabulous chocolates I wrote about.

The cookies described in the book are from old family recipes. To my knowledge, neither the chocolate chunk cookie recipe nor the cocoa cookie recipe has ever been printed. The chocolate chunk recipe was my maternal grandmother's favorite, and she called them "ranch cookies." The cocoa cookies are called "Christmas chocolate cookies" and were devised in the early 1950s by my next-door neighbor, Harriet Hazzard. Harriet passed away years ago, but I think of her when I bake those cookies every year.

If you would like an autographed copy of these recipes an full baking and icing instructions, please write to me at 11200 Westheimer, #946, Houston, Texas 77042.

The WONDER of WOODIWISS

continues with the publication of
her newest novel in trade paperback—

FOREVER IN YOUR EMBRACE
☐ #89818-7
$12.50 U.S. ($15.00 Canada)

**THE FLAME AND
THE FLOWER**
☐ #00525-5
$5.99 U.S. ($6.99 Canada)

**THE WOLF AND
THE DOVE**
☐ #00778-9
$5.99 U.S. ($6.99 Canada)

SHANNA
☐ #38588-0
$5.99 U.S. ($6.99 Canada)

ASHES IN THE WIND
☐ #76984-0
$5.99 U.S. ($6.99 Canada)

A ROSE IN WINTER
☐ #84400-1
$5.99 U.S. ($6.99 Canada)

**COME LOVE A
STRANGER**
☐ #89936-1
$5.99 U.S. ($6.99 Canada)

SO WORTHY MY LOVE
☐ #76148-3
$5.95 U.S. ($6.95 Canada)